FEMME FERAL

FEMME FERAL

SAM BECKBESSINGER

BLOOMSBURY ★ ARCHER

LONDON · OXFORD · NEW YORK · NEW DELHI · SYDNEY

BLOOMSBURY ARCHER
Bloomsbury Publishing Plc
50 Bedford Square, London, WC1B 3DP, UK
Bloomsbury Publishing Ireland Limited,
29 Earlsfort Terrace, Dublin 2, D02 AY28, Ireland

BLOOMSBURY, BLOOMSBURY ARCHER and the Archer logo
are trademarks of Bloomsbury Publishing Plc

First published in Great Britain 2026

Copyright © Sam Beckbessinger, 2026

Sam Beckbessinger has asserted their right under the Copyright,
Designs and Patents Act, 1988, to be identified as Author of this work

Epigraph extract of the essay 'Man Child' in *Sister Outsider* by Audre Lorde reproduced
with kind permission from Charlotte Sheedy Literary Agency

Extract of the poem 'Housewife' by Anne Sexton reproduced with kind permission
from SLL/Sterling Lord Literistic, Inc. Copyright by Linda Gray Sexton

This is a work of fiction. Names and characters are the product of the author's imagination
and any resemblance to actual persons, living or dead, is entirely coincidental

All rights reserved. No part of this publication may be: i) reproduced or transmitted in
any form, electronic or mechanical, including photocopying, recording or by means of
any information storage or retrieval system without prior permission in writing from the
publishers; or ii) used or reproduced in any way for the training, development or operation
of artificial intelligence (AI) technologies, including generative AI technologies. The rights
holders expressly reserve this publication from the text and data mining exception
as per Article 4(3) of the Digital Single Market Directive (EU) 2019/790

A catalogue record for this book is available from the British Library

ISBN: HB: 978-1-5266-8787-6; EXPORT EXCLUSIVE: 978-1-0372-0867-6;
TPB: 978-1-5266-8788-3; EBOOK: 978-1-5266-8786-9

4 6 8 10 9 7 5 3

Typeset by Six Red Marbles India
Printed and bound in Great Britain by Clays Ltd, Elcograf S.p.A

To find out more about our authors and books visit www.bloomsbury.com
and sign up for our newsletters
For product safety related questions contact productsafety@bloomsbury.com

*For my mum, who rages, rages against
the dying of the light*

If they cannot love and resist at the same time, they probably will not survive ...
This is what mothers teach – love, survival.
Audre Lorde

My devil had long been caged. He came out roaring.
Robert Louis Stevenson

Fruit Moon

Hot Flushes

Ellie

On the day the change begins, I find myself sprawled on asphalt, blood on my hands, blood in my mouth, clothing ripped, knees shredded, no idea how I got there.

'Sorry! Hey, sorry, are you okay?' A young man kneels beside me in a hi-vis vest and neon-pink helmet. His bike lies on the verge beside us, front wheel still spinning lazily in the air. Tikatikatikatikatik.

A small crowd has gathered. That's Londoners for you – most stand-offish people in the world until someone needs help – and now too many are trying to help me at once, asking if I need a doctor, offering their hands to help me stand, sweeping my things back into my bag. All I really want, though, is—

'Can anyone see my phone?' Pain as my swollen tongue brushes a tooth.

I barely notice her, the tiny old woman who hands it to me, a scruffy Maltese tucked into her armpit. I'm too busy jabbing at the screen, trying to coax it awake without slicing my fingertip on the jagged lightning-bolt crack. I'm mentally adding another item onto the infinite to-do list in my brain: *Replace phone screen*. I'm checking the time, twitching the phone around to see through shattered glass, because today of all days, I cannot afford to be late.

'You stepped right into the bike lane,' the cyclist whines. 'Texting.'

I nod away his non-apology, exploring the wetness on the side of my face with trembling fingers. A chip of asphalt drops to the ground, bright with my blood. I find the flap of skin on my left temple and pull my fingers away, hissing.

'That needs stitches. Let me take you to A&E,' insists the old woman with the dog. Her skin is crumpled as a sandwich wrapper, nose soft and bulbous across her face. Poor thing, growing up before we understood the importance of factor 50. The Maltese snuffles at me, probably smelling my cat.

I spit out a bright glob of blood, calculating that I've only got half an hour to get to Mayfair. 'I have to get to work.'

'You might have concussion, dearie.'

'I don't have time to have a concussion,' I grumble, hauling myself up. The pavement tilts, but I manage to grab the cyclist's grass-stained jacket just in time. He's scrawny, business casual under the hi-vis, and thankfully, free of visible bruises. 'I didn't hurt you, did I?'

He shakes his head.

After a breath waiting for the world to stop shifting, I try a tentative step forward and – thank fuck – my foot finds the earth where I expect it to.

Dog-grandma is standing too close, watching me too intently. 'Let me take you to the hospital, luvvie. You're injured.'

'I'm fine. Thank you.' I gesture at the cyclist's grass stain. 'Vinegar and washing-up liquid will get that out. Soak for fifteen minutes then give it a good scrub.'

'Sure.' The cyclist blinks at me. It's the *yes, yes, Mum* look I know too well from Paige.

'Just trust me. You can't let it set in.' One of the onlookers hands over my bag. I fish out a packet of wet wipes, flinching as my fingers brush the skin flap. Three wipes come away soaked in red.

'You're bleeding quite a lot, dear,' the old woman tries again. The Maltese concurs with a little yip. Grotty small dog: probably included in the starter kit you get on the day you suddenly turn old, along with a plastic rain hood, a shopping trolley and a suspicion of immigrants.

I riffle through my bag for a plaster, wishing gravity would decide which way it's pulling. 'I don't need help, thank you.'

The old woman is still staring, small chips of blue through hooded eyelids. 'But you do,' she says. Her hair is white-wild, the contours of skull visible beneath thin skin.

Eyes fixed on me, she sticks her thumb into her mouth and sucks it wetly. Then she pulls it free with a slurp and raises it before my face, glistening.

Before I can flinch, she leans close and drags the frigid digit right across my forehead to my temple, scrubbing at the open wound like you'd clean a grubby child.

Ew. Eww eww eww.

I recoil, pain cracking through my skull. My stomach lurches as I wipe away the slobber, smiling weakly to defuse the weirdness. She's old. I don't want to be rude. But all I can picture is her germs squirming their way into my bloodstream as I finally locate a plaster from my bag and press it on, like a shield, so she can't saliva me again.

'Thank you,' I manage, stepping firmly back, fretting that my thirty minutes has dwindled to twenty-eight.

The corners of the old woman's mouth twitch, sending a cascade of ripples through the cracked landscapes of her cheeks. 'Good luck, luvvie.' Then she's gone, lost among the onlookers.

The cyclist is still muttering about getting me an ambulance when I free myself, bag tucked firmly under arm, happy to melt into the crowd around the Highbury & Islington turnstiles. Heat creeps up my neck, my cheeks prickling with embarrassment.

Pressed flat to a grubby wall, I take a moment to inspect the damage. There's a blotch of blood on my white shirt, but a cardigan from my bag will cover that up. Nothing I can do about the rips across the knees of my jeans, but I can probably get away with calling that a fashion statement. The jeans were already a risk, cartoonishly baggy, but anything too skinny would mark me as out of touch. They were labelled as 'mom jeans' and – of course – it's always risky to wear mom jeans if you are in fact a 'mom' and not a size 6 teenager. But I need my best armour today, so the look is carefully calibrated: approachable but cool, groomed but effortless, professional but never matronly. The impossible tightrope of the working woman's wardrobe.

The plaster's absorption pad is already swollen with blood, a huge, nude-coloured tick. No problem, I have many more in my bag.

I also have snack bars, a battery pack, USB cables, a reusable shopping bag, an emergency sewing kit, earbuds, a sachet of mayonnaise, tampons, a face mask, Tic Tacs, seventeen hair ties, a make-up bag, a reusable mug still ringed with two-month-old dried coffee, hand sanitiser, antiviral throat spray, a tiny torch shaped like the Duracell bunny my husband gave me as a joke, hand lotion, a red Sharpie, a black Sharpie, floss, a location tracker, a space blanket, ibuprofen, self-defence spray, an EpiPen (I have no known allergies, but you never know if someone else might need it), and £200 in cash sewn into the lining. Paige teases me for being a doomsday prepper, but on a handbag scale.

My cracked phone buzzes in my hand. Mo: *Dad's gone AWOL again*. I quickly text back reminding him we put a tracker in his shoes, and to check the family location-sharing app. *But he's probably at the off-licence buying contraband*, I add. 'Contraband' being the Werther's toffees he's obsessed with despite his raging type 2 diabetes. *Frisk him when he gets back.*

I scan the other notifications as I hurtle down the escalator, nudging past the inevitable idiots standing on the left. Twenty Slack messages from Lanying, my doom-monger lieutenant – those can wait. My dentist telling me I'm overdue for a check-up. My boss Don wanting to know where I am. My brother asking if I've had a chance to call the estate agent about selling our mother's house. I update my mental to-do list: *Reassure Lanying. Book dentist appointment. Follow up with bloody estate agent, even though it would be so much easier for Byron to do seeing he doesn't actually have a bloody job right now. Set up meeting with Don*. And then, finally, among the hundred fish-hooks of need, a message requiring nothing from me except a smile: Paige wishing me luck for today.

Dazzle them, Mum. I'm so proud of you.

It's been another record-breaking hot August, and it must be fifty degrees Celsius on the Victoria Line. Finding myself sandwiched between an over-perfumed banker and a tourist who hasn't noticed that her backpack is trying to fuse with my sternum, I regret the cardigan. But there's no space to pull it off now without dislocating my shoulder. The stink of the carriage is so thick that breathing feels like sipping rancid soup. Droplets of sweat stream between my bra and my belt, and I can only hope that the wetness I feel racing down the side of my face is sweat, too. I'm light-headed, definitely. But I just need to get through the morning, then my brain can go ahead and have all the concussion it likes.

Twisting to evade the backpack, I manoeuvre my phone out my pocket, tap into Tranquillity and request a random meditation. Got to eat your own dog food, as I keep telling my team. But then my own voice is in my ears, made more resonant by some magic of sound engineering, overlaid with a gentle piano track. 'Picture a deep blue sky, clouds rolling softly across it, the sun warm on your skin. Feel your stress melting off and dripping onto soft grass...'

Cringe. I tap the exit button and make a mental note to delete that one from the archives. Before we could afford celebrity voice artists, back when I was employee number four and the only one with half-decent enunciation, I recorded some of the meditations myself. Those scripts strike me as unbearably cheesy now.

Instead, I close my eyes and mentally go through more of the List to calm myself. *Pick up pastries before Town Hall. Remind Paige about her therapy appointment. Post the minutes of the product strategy meeting. Email the council about our overdue refund. Check if the press release about Don's retirement is ready to go. Go for a swim at Hampstead Heath.* That one's been on there for a while. *Order more of the special cat food for Artio.*

The to-do list in my head is replicated in several places in what I think of as The System, as in, The-System-That-Keeps-My-Entire-Life-Functioning. There's a digital master list managed by an app so advanced that NASA could probably use it to plan spaceship launches. Every morning, as a centring ritual, I copy a focused subset of the List onto a fresh page in my bullet journal, a Japanese brand sold only by a specialist shop in Wimbledon: the Midori MD non-bleed 176 gsm with thread-stitch binding. There's a stack of blank ones piled in my attic and I live in dread fear they'll one day be discontinued. I'm not neurotic; you're neurotic.

I open my eyes to see that a young man in lime-coloured tracksuit pants is staring at me, wide-eyed. He gestures, *do you want my seat?*

I frown. I'm forty-four, dammit, not eighty-four. Then I feel something tickle my throat, and I touch it, and my fingers come away bloody.

Lanying pounces the moment I walk into the office, my arms now loaded with four precarious boxes of savoury pastry cups from the corner bakery, and still three minutes to spare before Town Hall. The worry crease on Lanying's forehead that acts as a reliable barometer of how bad my day's going to be is already deep-etched. Her eyes flick up to the plaster, where I can feel a slow trickle of blood has started seeping around the edges again, despite my best efforts in the loo a few minutes ago.

'What happened?'

'I'm fine. Tried to tango with a Brompton.'

Truth is, I'm woozy, the ground heaving like I'm on a ship, my flesh still simmering from the train – but there's no time for any of that.

'Sure? You look pale.' She pulls a small pack of wet wipes from the pocket of her wide-leg jeans. Lanying believes in dressing for the job you want, so I suspect she sneaks into my house at night to snap photos of my garment tags.

'I'm fine,' I repeat, sidestepping an intern zipping by on an electric skateboard. 'What's up?'

'We've got a problem.' She glances around like a woman about to confess to a murder, then ushers me towards the Mindfulness Zone where there are no eavesdroppers except the plastic ferns, which smell faintly of detergent. 'The engineers found a critical vulnerability in the payment gateway.'

I shift the pastries to my hip. 'Critical like—'

'Critical like customer credit card numbers might be exposed. Maybe already are.'

The pastries turn to lead in my arms. 'Well. Shit.'

'Zayn wants to pull two teams to completely re-architect it.'

'Two teams?' My voice sharpens, but I keep it low. 'We're two months out from Demo Day. We can't just hit pause on the corporate module.'

I glance past the ferns at the steady stream of people filtering into the auditorium for the morning's Town Hall, chatty, cheerful, clutching their refillable coffee cups and team-branded water bottles.

They have no idea how close we are to losing all of it.

Demo Day isn't just another MedTech conference. It's *the* MedTech conference, where companies parade prototypes of shiny next-gen features they haven't built yet and never will, in hopes of raising money to build completely unrelated ones. And here we are, limping towards it with an app held together with zip-ties and caffeine fumes. We *cannot* fuck it up.

Because even if we have the fastest-growing mental health app in the world, there's one tiny problem: growth costs money. And we're almost out of it. We've got two months until Demo Day and enough cash to pay salaries for four. If we don't raise, we're done.

We haven't told the staff, obviously. Only the execs know. And Lanying, who can sniff out peril like sharks sniff blood.

We could have done what our competitors do, which is sell out early on the strength of bullshit buzzwords and cheap dopamine hacks, but we've taken the unfashionable approach of slow, rigorous science and endless ethical reviews, which has landed us an NHS endorsement but little investor interest. Frankly, the only reason we've even made it this far is sheer bloody-mindedness and my military-grade spreadsheets. Plus eighty-hour work weeks. When my mum died three years ago, I took a single afternoon off. Poor Lanying, who joined us as a bright-eyed graduate, has aged worse than second-term Obama. But we just have to hold it together for a few months more. Demo Day's our shot.

'Just patch it,' I say, wiping my sweaty face. 'Tell Arun and Trilbi to push through this weekend. They owe me a favour.'

'They won't do it.'

'They will. It was a big favour.' That's how I keep this place running: a system of social credit as byzantine as the mob.

Lanying mutters about houses and cards as she follows me to the auditorium. 'We can't just keep duct-taping things, Ellie. The analytics pipeline is a shitshow, and Werner Herzog's just asked to re-record his meditation *again*...'

'Lan, can we do this after Town Hall, please?'

She stops short, blinking. Then her face splits into a grin. 'Oh crap, is it today?'

Even with everything else I've gone through this morning, I can't suppress a smile. Of course, nothing's been confirmed yet, but rumours spread.

The worry line vanishes as she squeezes my elbow. 'Nobody deserves it more, you know.'

Ninety twenty- and thirty-somethings in graphic tees crowd the auditorium, swarming me as I hand out pastries: gluten-free for Carlos, vegan for Thandeka, no raisins for Kayla. Some of them have heard the gossip, too, and flash me thumbs ups.

'Cor, Ellie, been in a fight?'

'Gotta be tough to survive the mean streets of Islington,' I quip, hoping no one notices I'm leaning on the edge of the table for support.

The auditorium is set up with bright-coloured beanbags and a huge fake tree, like an overfunded nursery school. It essentially *is* a nursery school. In my mid-forties, I'm almost the oldest person in the room by a decade.

The actual oldest person in the room, our CEO Don, turns to me as I flop into my usual beanbag behind his. 'I tried to find you earlier,' he says. He's in a bright orange polo neck, blue blazer and jeans, his round tortoiseshell glasses betraying his roots as an academic – a time before he decided his research on meditation and pain relief could be more helpful in the form of a startup than in stuffy research papers no one read. He's only fifty-seven, so still not that old in any ordinary context, but tech years are like dog years.

'Crazy day.'

'I just wish we could have talked before,' he says in his thick Scots brogue. His bushy eyebrows are bunched tight. Understandable that he'd be anxious today.

I give him an encouraging pat. Don's a big thinker, loves to philosophise, never actually makes a decision, which is equal parts lovable and infuriating. He'll keep equivocating until the sun explodes, if you let him. I do what I do and reassure him, guide him.

'It's okay, Don. It's time.'

Don pauses a moment, like he wants to say more, but the office manager is done testing the microphone and calls him up.

His eyes return to me as he opens the meeting, getting the normal nonsense out of the way. Birthdays, shout-outs, special mentions.

My face is burning hotter and hotter but I keep my expression flat, willing him to hurry up. To get to the meat.

The big announcement.

The very-long-fucking-overdue announcement.

They're making me CEO.

Earned piece by piece over the past five brutal years, the hundred late nights, the million fires put out. Figuring out how to build an app with no money to hire experts, doing everything that needed doing. Teaching myself about positive psychology, UX design, software frameworks, engagement metrics, agile development. Dragging myself to work after late nights holding my sobbing, puking daughter and making myself care about the precise wording of the sign-up button.

It was all for *this*. For something being *mine*. At last. Bought by my persistence. Paid for in grit.

CEO.

I take a deep breath. The room seems to be warping around the edges, like I'm watching everything through 3D glasses. The air conditioning must be broken, because I'm dying of heat. I tell myself, just a little longer, then I can go and lie down – preferably in an ice bath. But this is my moment. I can't miss it.

It's only then that I notice the man sitting next to Don's empty beanbag. A stranger. Similar age to me. An auditor, maybe? But he's ungroomed in the way that only self-assured white men can get away with. His shirt is linen, crumpled. His hair is twice as big as his head, an Art Garfunkel fuzz helmet with the volume of an award-winning cabbage. Arty type. Maybe someone from the PR agency, here to handle the messaging around Don's retirement.

Onstage, in a symphony of nervous throat-clearing, Don's finally getting to the real purpose of the meeting. 'Well. Yes. I'm sure some of you have noticed, or, ah, *possibly* noticed, one's always at risk of spotlight syndrome, I suppose… But I've, well, I'm sure some of you may have noticed I've been reducing my involvement in day-to-day operations. Or maybe you haven't – Ellie basically runs everything around here already.'

Affectionate laughter from the crowd. I keep my face neutral. But God, I'm sweating so much under my cardigan. I can feel a drop of it sliding down my neck, joining up with the rivers pouring down my back.

'Anyway. I wanted to say clearly. And officially. I'll be stepping fully out of my executive role. Stepping aside, mind you, not vanishing. I'll still be involved strategically, as chairman. But the ship, as it were, is getting a new captain.'

Don smiles at me. Brief. Solemn. 'First, I'm very pleased to announce that Ellie's getting a long-overdue promotion. To Chief Product Officer.'

I blink, sure I've misheard. But Don says it again. 'CPO.'

The room breaks out in uneven applause, most of the team clapping for me joyfully, only some hesitation from those who've been around long enough to understand what's *not* being said.

I do not clap. I do not move. I just keep staring at Don, disbelieving. Those two traitorous syllables echoing through my mind: *Product*.

Don clears his throat. Finally breaks eye contact. 'And it's my great pleasure to introduce you to Andreas Nicoll, who will be your new CEO.'

The rumpled man stands, turns and waves to everyone. The applause this time is tepid, faces craning over to take a proper look at him.

Don's voice fades to a distant hum, talking about Andreas's background, about how the company's vision remains unchanged, how excited he is for the future. I can't follow any of it.

All I can see is the back of Andreas's head, a whorl of curls, scraggly enough to expose glimpses of pink skin underneath. His scalp seems to be breathing, in and out, in a way that skulls definitely should not do. I remove my cardigan. Fuck the bloodstain. Fuck looking professional. It's too hot in here, unbearably hot. My skin prickles from sweat-salt. But they're not going to see me cry, dammit. That was the first piece of advice I got from the only woman boss I ever had, half a lifetime ago: keep your tears in the toilets, or you'll be forever branded a sensitive girl.

The room's silent. I've missed something. Everyone is staring at me.

'Ellie, want to discuss our results for the month?' Don repeats.

I nod, swallowing, trying to get some moisture back in my mouth. But all the moisture in my body currently seems to be streaming down my back. I peel myself off the beanbag. Force myself onto feet that feel like stilts. Familiar engagement figures are projected up on the wall, DAU/MAU and Average Session Lengths and One-day Retention Ratios. They might as well be cuneiform carvings on the walls of an ancient temple right now.

Something is wrong with my mouth. It doesn't seem to be able to communicate with my brain. I turn to face them, and the room just keeps spinning. One hundred and eighty swirling eyes stare at me. A nervous laugh from somewhere near the back.

Don clears his throat, grabs my cardigan from the beanbag and hands it to me.

I look down. My entire white shirt is drenched through, clinging to my skin, my lace bra fully on show, the skin of my chest a deep red flush.

'I'm sorry,' I manage, 'I'm not feeling—'

My vision closes like the end of a Looney Tunes cartoon as I fall flat on my face in front of them, fade to black.

Dry Eyes
○
Ellie

Dr Ncube has a goatee so sharp he must trim it with a ruler and scalpel, probably trying to create some definition on a face still softened with boy fat. He holds his index fingers on either side of my face.

'Look back and forth between my two fingers. Dizzy?'

'No.'

'Who brought you into the hospital today?' He moves behind me and kneads the muscles at the base of my neck. Good luck to him. The last time I tried going for a massage, the masseuse described it as prodding bricks.

'My boss Don.' Judas.

'What day is it?'

'Thursday.'

He flicks a torch into my eyes. 'And what were those words I asked you to remember earlier?'

'Yellow. City. Brother.'

'Well, I don't think you have concussion. But you *are* dehydrated. And that,' he gestures at my leaking forehead, 'needs stitches.'

My mind is already on my phone, which hasn't stopped vibrating in my pocket since I arrived. Bit rude to check one's emails in the middle of an A&E exam, probably.

'You say you didn't see the bicycle?'

I shake my head. 'I haven't been sleeping well.'

'Since when?'

'Insomnia? Oh, since Tamagotchis. Since Britney and Justin. Since belly chains.' The doctor isn't impressed with my answer, so I consider the question properly. 'I guess… a few months ago is when it got really bad.'

'Notice any other changes?'

I raise my arms to show him how I've already sweated through the Tranquillity-branded T-shirt I excavated from the company storeroom. They only had extra smalls left, so the logo is stretched tight across my tits, three inches of my softening belly exposed to the air.

'Boiling alive in my own skin.'

'Anything else? Headaches? Changes in mood?'

I think back over the past few weeks. Tranquillity's looming bankruptcy. Paige moving out. Don's retirement. My father-in-law switching to a new medication regime that's making him even more scatty. It's all been mayhem; hard to say if it's been any worse than usual. Once chaos reaches a certain level of chaoticness, degrees of it no longer matter, and I reached that level sometime in my mid-twenties.

'Not sure.'

'Mmm.' He skims my chart. 'When was your last menstrual period?'

I blink at him.

Fuck.

My brain whirrs with frantic arithmetic, trying to remember the last time Mo and I mustered enough energy between the housework and our jobs and arguing over whose turn it is to clean up the cat vomit to have sex. But I don't need the maths, because suddenly it's so obvious. Trouble sleeping. Bouts of dizziness. That feeling that there's some alien force working away in my cells, some powerful new imperative that's hijacked my body. And my brain is running parallel simulations, one where we reset the clock and do it all older and wiser this time and take out a second mortgage to pay for childcare, and one where I track down the infinitely kind doctor who did my abortion when I was nineteen to find out if he's still practising… when Dr Ncube taps his pen on the clipboard and brings me back to where I am.

Fuck. 'You think I'm pregnant.'

The doctor frowns. 'We should test to rule it out of course,' he says carefully. 'But, given your age, I think it's more likely that you've entered perimenopause.'

You can basically hear the record-scratch.

My mouth gapes. Through the curtain, one of the nurses is singing along to Elton John by way of Dua Lipa. Dr Ncube smiles at me placidly, waiting for me to absorb the information.

'But I'm forty-four,' I manage at last.

He shrugs. 'Average age of menopause is fifty-one.'

'But that's—'

'Average. You're within the range we'd consider normal.'

I mull this over. 'Okay, so – what – no more periods? Farewell birth control? That sounds great, actually.'

The doctor takes off his glasses and polishes them with the corner of his shirt. 'Menopause itself is the end of ovulation, yes. Once it's been twelve months from your last period, we'll officially say you've entered menopause. But most women experience some years of hormonal disruption before then.'

'Some *years*?'

'Most women report five to six. But of course—'

'Average. Right. So, fuck. The full shebang, huh?' I cast my mind around for some helpful facts about menopause, but all I can come up with are what I suspect are jokes from male stand-up comedians in the nineties. 'Hot flushes. Wanting to stab people. Cobwebs in your minge. What else can I expect?'

'Fatigue is common.'

'Check.'

'Forgetfulness.'

I think of my notebook. What if the System has just been a way to cope for the fact that I can't remember anything unless I write it down?

'Honestly, there are dozens of potential symptoms. It's different for everyone. Some barely notice; others find it very disruptive. The best way to predict how yours will go is to ask your mother about her experience.'

'You got a Ouija board?'

'I'm sorry?'

'Never mind.'

He clears his throat. 'I must advise you that it's still possible to fall pregnant during this time. Many women start releasing multiple eggs in each ovulation, so you'd have an increased chance of twins—'

'A going-out-of-business sale.'

'At your age, it would be considered a geriatric pregnancy. But of course, if having another baby is important to you, we can discuss—'

'I don't want another baby,' I say, suddenly very sure about this.

'Then keep using birth control.'

'Got it.' The word 'geriatric' makes me feel so repulsive, I can't at this moment imagine ending up in bed with anyone ever again. 'Okay, so how do we fix me?'

'You're not broken. You're going through a very ordinary life change.' He dabs the dried blood off my forehead with an alcohol wipe. 'You might need to take it easy for a while.'

'Sure! Guess I'll just quit my job, buy some muumuus and go on a pottery retreat in Yorkshire, shall I?'

His face is impassive. 'You could schedule an appointment with your GP to discuss hormone therapy, or the contraceptive pill. Some people find that helps them manage the worst of the symptoms.'

'I'll do that, then.'

Dr Ncube shrugs, like sure, if I feel I really must. Like a stronger, more enlightened woman would just get on with it.

I might be projecting.

I squeeze my eyes as he stitches my head together, trying to tune out the painful tugs of the needle, silently adding another item to the infinite List: *Figure out menopause.*

Don's in reception, leisurely paging through a book on graphic design. He leaps to his feet when he sees me. 'Everything okay?'

'Apparently I've just come down with a mild case of the menopause.'

'Ah.' He takes my handbag and leads the way to his car. 'Inez's was a scoosh. One day she realised she hadn't had a period for six months, and that was that. Barely noticed.'

'Bully for Inez.'

'I'm sorry. That was, ah, insensitive.'

I pat one of his elbow patches. Bloody elbow patches. A stereotype to the end, our Don.

'I was just about to call Mo. Tell him to meet you at home?'

'Don, I can't. I have back-to-back meetings, and there's some crisis with the billing system—'

'Don't even try to argue with me about this.'

I grumble, but allow him to open the door of his tan Mercedes for me. I've always loved this absurd thing, its sleek caramel lines, its interior smelling of beeswax and cologne. A throwback, just like Don, solid and dependable... or so I assumed until today. The Mercedes hasn't humiliated me in front of everyone I work with.

He keeps glancing at me as we pull out of the parking garage and into the lunchtime traffic. Driving through Zone One, why does Don bother? Faster to walk. Faster to hitch yourself to a sledge pulled by slugs.

'I tried to find you this morning,' Don says. 'I wish we'd had a chance to talk first. But there was some urgency.'

I keep my eyes fixed on the road. Inhale for four. Hold for four. Exhale for six. Studies say this activates the vagus nerve and calms you down. I elongate the exhale as much as I can, hoping it settles the hot simmer under my ribs.

'I'm just confused,' I say finally. 'In all our conversations...'

'It wasn't up to me, El.' The car hums along, hot air blasting out of the A/C-less fan.

'The board?'

'They feel we need new blood. Fresh ideas.'

'Like this Andreas guy?' My voice is sharper than I intend, so I force a small smile to soften the words.

'They don't want to replace you. It's just...' He shrugs helplessly.

'I understand,' I say, though I don't. 'They don't think I'm ready?'

'They think you're very, very good at your job.'

My hands tighten in my lap, but I keep my expression neutral. Inhale. Hold. Exhale. I purse my lips against the whiny diatribe rising up inside, like *so my job is to be a helpmeet but never a leader*; like *you know if I were a man...* no. No point in that. Anger is a hideous, pointless emotion. Better to focus on what you can control. I push the ugliness down, down, down.

We're silent for the next few miles. I tip my head back slightly so that my suddenly watery eyes don't start running down my cheeks. Another trick from that first job, all those years ago. And it's so unfair; I only cry when I'm *furious*. Exactly the last way to get all the tech bros I work with to take my fury seriously.

Inhale. Hold. Exhale.

'They found a new tumour,' Don says eventually, his knuckles whitening against the wheel. 'Pancreas. We're restarting chemo on Friday.'

'Oh God. Don.' My anger deflates. From Don's lack of focus over the past few months, I knew it was bad, but I didn't realise it was stage-three bad. Inhale, redirect, how can I help? Add to List: *Send Inez a care package*. I remember from last time what she likes: unscented moisturising creams, ginger tea, fluffy socks, a bag of weed filched from Mo, for the nausea. There is a whole subsection of the System devoted to thoughtful gifts for every person in my life.

'Andreas already had an offer from another startup. I had to move quickly.' He grimaces. 'I need to leave knowing it's going to be okay. We can't let it fall apart, not after everything.'

I nod, because I don't trust myself to speak, despite the sting of his words. I know what this means to him. Inez was Tranquillity's first customer, five years ago. Don used to record guided meditations for her to listen to while she was lying on chemo beds, visualising her cancer cells as blobs of living poison, imagining herself powerful, tearing them apart one by one. Cheesy, but backed up by mountains of positive psychology research. We've diversified since then to guided meditation programmes for post-surgical rehabilitation, arthritis, heart disease, chronic pain, depression. But there's nothing like the earliest meditations Don recorded. They were love letters.

But that was a long time ago. Now, Tranquillity is a business. It's a hundred jobs. It's a set of shares that represents almost all my life savings. It's three million active users across twenty countries sending us thankful emails, every day, telling us how much we've helped them. It's a complicated machine that requires a million decisions every day to keep running. And me: the conductor keeping the orchestra in time, albeit doomed to do so from the background, it seems. It's the only job I've ever really cared about. So what am I supposed to do now? Walk away? Just when the business needs me the most?

We finally pull up in front of my house. He tries a playful smile, but it's like his face has forgotten how. 'I don't want to see you online for the rest of the day.'

'Promise,' I lie, already composing five emails in my mind that I intend to type out as soon as I get to my laptop. I lean into the driver's window and give his shoulder a squeeze. 'Don, I'm so sorry.'

'So am I.' He sighs. He places his hand gently on mine, as his forced smile relaxes into a realer, sadder one. 'Get some rest, please.'

I'd fucking love to, I think, as my phone buzzes again in my pocket.

Trouble Sleeping

○

Ellie

My afternoon of 'rest' includes:

- Talking our senior UX designer out of quitting over the new font choices in the iOS app.
- Catching two spelling mistakes in the press release about Don's retirement (add to List: *Hire new copywriter*).
- Risking my life on our ancient stepladder to rescue Artie from the roof (add to List: *Buy less-deadly stepladder*).
- Rewriting the introduction to the investor pitch document we'll circulate before Demo Day (underlined twice: *Hire new copywriter*).
- Cancelling the 'Congratulations on becoming CEO!' surprise party that Mo had thoughtfully organised for me, and then not-so-thoughtfully had been too mortified to cancel on my behalf.
- Settling several tiny meltdowns within my team (add to List: *Insist Lanying takes a holiday*).
- Drafting a thank-you email to the board for my promotion, a tight upbeat message that doesn't betray an ounce of bitterness.
- Helping the day nurse change the net jockstrap that holds Yusuf's balls in place, swollen as they are from congestive heart failure (something Mo refuses to do

because 'it's my dad, it would be weird', as though me doing it is not).
- Apologising to the still-furious cat who apparently wanted to live on the roof forever.
- Mediating an argument between two engineers about the best fix for the credit card issue (add to List: *Revise backlog*).
- Cleaning the stitches on my forehead (add to List: *Buy antibiotic ointment*).
- Bribing Artie for forgiveness with inexplicably fish-shaped beef treats.

Ultimately, I end the day with six more things on the List than I scratched off. But I do most of this in bed while wearing my Steve Buscemi–face pyjamas, which counts for something.

The smell of Paige's tea tree shampoo wafts up the stairs sometime around dusk. Wordlessly, she tucks herself around me, burying her head into the back of my neck. The heat in my belly dissipates as the bone-deep familiarity of her downy arms snakes over my torso.

'Dad said you didn't want anyone to come round. So I figured it was really bad.'

I don't respond, just pull her arms tighter around my waist. I can't help but check the width of her arm, touching thumb to forefinger, leaving a gap of air around her porcelain bones. The neurotic habit of years is not going to vanish in a couple of weeks, sue me. Caring carves its grooves into you.

She doesn't notice, murmuring into my shoulder, 'Screw them, Mum. They don't deserve you.'

It's only with her here now that I realise how badly I've missed her, my sweet serious sad girl. She moved into student housing a month ago, ostensibly for a couple of summer courses, but really so she has extra time to settle in before starting her second year at LSE. She spent her first year living at home because I didn't trust her to navigate a cafeteria on her own.

I'll be blaming myself for her eating disorder until I die, but Paige deserves at least some of the credit for hiding it so well, for so long. She committed herself to anorexia with a sly zeal I wish she'd applied to literally any other goal in her life, disguising it as ethical veganism, disguising it as an exercise regime to try to get onto the athletics team, disguising it as constipation requiring copious volumes of over-the-counter laxatives, disguising it as an increasingly restrictive set of food intolerances. She tracked a non-existent period, diligently wrapping and throwing out clean tampons five days a month so I wouldn't notice she'd stopped menstruating. For months, I told Mo she looked thin, and he teased me for worrying. Anyway, *anorexia*? How old-fashioned, I told myself. How unimaginable. How unfeminist. And then, two days before her fifteenth birthday, she passed out in the middle of Oxford Street, and we learned that her body was so hungry it couldn't even power her heartbeat.

She could have died. She nearly did. My brilliant, perfect girl – who I failed so utterly.

But after years of therapy and in-patient clinics and recovery programmes and a solemn promise that she'll tell me if it starts again, we admitted it was finally time to see if she can manage in the world by herself.

Okay, fine: if *I* can manage with her in the world, by herself.

But she really does seem okay. Cheek-flushed and cheerful as she pulls away to dust crisp crumbs off the duvet (thanks, Mo), her curls bouncing with life. Paige got my boobs, lucky girl, and my facial structure, but otherwise she's a carbon copy of her father, the exact shade of warm-brown skin and impossibly thick hair.

'How are we going to get back at Don?' she says. 'Want to fart into a box and post it to his house?'

I snort. 'We could throw a bedbug-infested sock through the window of his Mercedes.'

As she stretches, I notice there's a distinct whiff of boy about her, which twists my guts. Not because she's having sex – I'm no prude: when she told me she wanted to have sex with her sixth-form boyfriend, I got her on the pill, booked them a hotel room and took her out for celebration waffles the next morning. No, what doesn't thrill me is that she's currently having sex with a smug narcissist named Theo with a superiority complex in place of a personality, who once accused me of 'supporting fascism' because I read the *Guardian*.

'Don't look at me like that.' She pokes me with her toe.

'Like what?'

'Like you're worried. You don't have to be on hyper-alert 24/7 Mum Mode any more. You did your job. And I'm doing great.'

I scoop her into a hug. 'It's almost like I love you or something.'

'Gross.' She wrestles away, tucking her wild hair behind an ear the exact same shape as mine. I sometimes wonder, was it me? Did I make womanhood look so unappealing that she chose to destroy herself rather than grow into a woman's body?

Midnight finds me in a halo of light under the bedsheet as I read page after page of depressing essays on my phone with titles like 'Nobody Told Me Menopause Would Make Me Insane' and 'The Hair! The Hair Everywhere!' and 'Me and My Menopausal Vagina'. I click through a horrible Subreddit called 'Menopause Support for MEN', where the top posts are 'Who turned my wife into the SheHulk?' and 'Dr Jekyll and Mrs Menopause'. I briefly consider posting gifs of the world's tiniest violin, but I figure I don't have time to deal with getting doxxed on top of everything else.

Mo snores contentedly beside me. The sheets cling to my skin, stippled in sweat. The menopause blogs say that this is because my decreased oestrogen levels have caused my hypothalamus to become oversensitive to slight changes in body temperature, triggering a cascade of effects throughout every system in my body, so it's convinced I'm freezing to death in a tundra and is doing its best to warm me up. Idly, I wonder if anyone's run double-blind tests about whether guided meditation could convince a dysfunctional thermal regulation system that it's fine, actually, and sitting in a triple-glazed terraced house in Barnsbury with the heating eternally stuck on 22 (item 732 on the List – *Get someone in to fix the heating* – has been on there for months).

I rip off my pyjamas, puddling a dozen Steve Buscemis onto the floor. It helps a little. I consider pressing my naked body against Mo and sliding my hand into his pants, his favourite way to wake up when we were both much younger and sleep was much less precious. But he's out cold, and anyway, I'm too hot to move, let alone muster the energy for a spousal hand job.

I plug in my phone and lie in the dark, willing myself to sleep. My skin prickles with heat. My stomach aches, as if something restless were curled there, twisting and squirming and impatient to be born.

The blankets cling to my legs and I kick them off, staring out the bedroom window, to the sliver of moon I can see through my neighbour's chestnut tree.

My bedside clock says one o'clock.

One thirty.

Two.

The heat only gets worse. Lava bubbling in my abdomen.

I slip from bed and throw on a robe, thinking I'll just go to the kitchen to gulp some iced water, but when I get downstairs the cool draught creeping around the Victorian front door is so delicious that I follow it outside, finding myself standing on the pavement in front of my house at three in the morning, breeze brushing my naked legs, a glimpse of silver winking through the trees.

I should go back in. But the moon pulls me into the night, as irresistibly as a tide.

The pavement is cool on my bare feet, smooth and worn from two hundred years of footsteps. Most of Barnsbury's a conservation area, a peaceful pocket of north London tucked between Camden and Islington, built for the Victorian bourgeoisie and now claimed by the liberal intelligentsia. Handsome terraces line the street in stately symmetry, doors painted in polite pastels and framed by statues of sphinxes. Ah, but look carefully, and you'll spot signs of the constant work of upkeep: scaffolding, skips, bursting bags of garden waste. Don't be fooled, none of this is in service of beauty, but of fear. The old money's in Chelsea and Kensington. Around here, we're all mortgaged up to the eyeballs, haunted by rumours of slipping house values, trembling at the thought of what will happen when our fixed-rate mortgages expire or our startups fail. Terrified little strivers. Sure, we're all good champagne socialists in public, pontificating about how a house price crash might be the best thing for the country, give first-time buyers a chance. It's only in dark hours like these that the small honest voice inside of me says, *but it's not fair*. I didn't grow up middle class – I grew up in an ex-council in Chingford. I fucking clawed my way here, tooth and nail. I did everything right, and where am I?

CPO.

The neighbourhood is silent now, or as silent as London can ever be even in its leafiest boroughs, which still includes the soft rumble of cars up the high street a few blocks away, the screech of a fox, the distant wail of an ambulance siren. I march towards the glow of Islington, a ten-minute walk. The asphalt glitters in the light of a moon which is just visible through glowing cirrus clouds.

I find myself rambling along Upper Street. This was all squats and anarchist cafes in the eighties. Now it's small-plates restaurants and estate agents, long-shuttered at this hour. Likewise the Ottolenghi. The Oliver Bonas, where you can buy everything you could possibly need, assuming that what you need is pillow mist, embroidered toiletry bags and affirmation cards. There's no one else on the street, just me and my bare feet, the heavy rhythm of my breathing. And finally, *finally*, my anger dissolves, like rain touching skin after a too hot summer's day.

It's delicious, being a night walker. I haven't done this in years. But tonight, I could be nineteen again, wandering the streets alone after a rave at Bagley's, brain still softened by Ecstasy, too wired for bed, nerve endings on fire, invulnerable, sure I was the baddest bitch in London, ready to lick up the whole world.

But that was many years ago now. Before the accumulation of a lifetime's unpleasant experiences taught me the contours of fear. Now, I am a *perimenopausal* woman wandering the streets in a bathrobe, who must look unhinged.

Upper Street becomes Holloway Road. Up ahead, security lights glow through a glass-plated office building, a greenhouse growing nothing but laptops. I turn off the high street and saunter down a darker side road, lost in memories of living in a warehouse in Bethnal Green with six other twenty-somethings, working as a stagehand at a fringe theatre in Spitalfields, sweating my arse off to try to get my own pretentious plays produced. It was less glamorous than it sounds. There was just one bathroom, and I was the only one who believed in cleaning, the cockroaches so big and so bold we could recognise them by their shell markings and started giving them names. Before Tranquillity. Before Paige. Before all my artist friends were priced out of London. Before my father died and my mother spun out into the abyss of her depression. Before I was confronted by the costs of childcare and realised I had to either get a real job or become a housewife and go insane.

Before I got so fucking old.

I'm so bound up wondering about the path between that person and me that I don't notice the boys until I almost crash into them.

Four of them, sixteen or seventeen, lounging in the plaza in front of the Emirates Stadium. One of them straddles a memorial cannon like he's about to ride it into battle. Bottles litter the ground around them. They stink of booze, pot, testosterone. Red-faced and merry.

I've seen boys like these before, loitering around the neighbourhood, catcalling, wolf-whistling. Exuding menace, wrapping it in jest. Harmless kids. Probably.

They freeze at the sight of me, likely more confused by my get-up than anything else – my bathrobe, my filthy bare feet. None of them move. They are sizing up the moment, sizing up each other. I could be a source of trouble, or a source of fun. I could be a madwoman. I could be their mother yelling at them to go home.

Or, I could be prey.

The possibilities stand poised on a knife edge.

I decide the best thing to do is to act like nothing's wrong. I swerve past them, head up, eyes straight ahead, hoping that if I don't acknowledge them, they might just leave me alone. I quicken my pace just enough that it won't look like I'm running. Something sharp pierces my foot, a bottle cap or a stone, but I keep moving, aware I must act like I am not afraid, so I do not trigger anything to be afraid of. A dance every woman who has ever attempted to walk in the world is intimately familiar with.

I have almost reached the safety of the shadows, and then…

'Walk of shame, love?' one of them calls after me.

Their hyena cackles crack the night. They dissolve into an unintelligible shouting hubbub. I catch snatches of their banter.

'Eww…'

'… my nan…'

'… dare you.'

My hand instinctively reaches for my phone. But it's not in my pocket, of course. It's on my bedside table, back at home, where I should be. So foolish. Of all the ways to run into trouble, going wandering around the city at night near-naked has to be the stupidest.

'Hey! Don't be rude!' one calls. Cackle cackle cackle.

I keep walking. Keep my eyes fixed in front of me. Resist the urge to look back. Remind myself that I am a middle-class white woman in one of the wealthiest cities in the world, and they are literal children. I have all the power here. They haven't really done anything. I have no reason to be afraid.

But I am.

I'm afraid on a cellular level. Afraid in my skin, which is prickling with gooseflesh. Afraid in my muscles, which are tensing so tightly that it feels they are stretching my bones. Afraid in my pores, which are opening a hundred streams of sweat all over my body. Afraid in my stomach, which roils and boils and twists inside of me.

But amid the fear, there's something else. A flash of *rage*. Because I was minding my own fucking business. I was walking around my own fucking city. And these goddamn kids, these teenagers, are making me feel scared, *for sport*.

I'm not sure whether they're following me. I can't look back. Looking back will tell them I'm afraid. I am Lot's wife. I must not turn. I must keep walking. I must stay calm. Inhale. Hold. Exhale.

My pulse pounds in my throat. Horribly, I feel another hot flush come on. *Not now*, I beg my body. The heat that has been simmering inside of me all day comes to a boil. My face burns. Sweat runs down my neck. My head swells empty like a balloon, ready to float away.

The air grows heavy behind me. Something rushing up behind.

I break into a run.

I veer up the stairs towards the stadium like a prey animal seeking high ground, soles slapping concrete. The building looms ahead, an oversized UFO crash-landed among the biscuit brick. I throw myself into its shadow.

I still have not looked back. I don't need to. I can *feel* them after me, teeth glinting in the night. My brain flips through a violent flipbook, a highlights reel of every true-crime show I've ever watched.

An air-conditioning vent blasts a gust of hot air straight into my face. CCTV cameras hang over every entrance. Good, I think, surely they won't try anything if cameras are watching?

One of the heavy glass doors is propped ajar with a frayed length of blue rope. I don't hesitate. I shove it open and slip inside.

Darkness. My ears throb in the sudden silence. The screed floor is slick. Recently washed – the door must have been left open to help it dry. That means someone's nearby. A cleaner. A person. Help.

I squeeze through the turnstiles. A sharp edge catches at my waist and something rips off, clothing or skin, I can't tell. I don't stop.

The concourse opens up, impossibly vast, an endless track wrapped around the empty stadium, stinking of stale beer and sweat. Tall as the seating tiers, lined with shuttered shops and locked gates. Meagre moonlight filters through windows far above, too faint to illuminate the cavernous space.

I run blindly. My feet pounding the wet floor, the sound echoing in every direction. Are they echoes? Or footsteps? How many footsteps? Mine? Theirs?

The fear is driving me now. I run and skid, turn and run and turn, until I realise my panic has led me somewhere I shouldn't be, through an unmarked service door, somewhere deep in the bowels of the back offices. No more wayfinding signs or fan posters here, just flashes of storage cupboards, offices, industrial shelving.

I skid around a final corner and see a portal of light at the end of a tunnel, glowing like salvation.

I sprint for it.

Light means people. People means safety.

I burst through.

And suddenly, I'm outside again. Lush grass. Open sky. The seats rise around me in great sweeping arcs, tier upon tier.

I'm in the centre of the pitch, entirely exposed.

I spin. Stare back at the tunnel I just came through.

Nothing follows.

Where are they? I heard them behind me.

Where are they?

Adrenaline burns through my limbs. My muscles bunch with power. I feel like I could spring up, high as the stands. The stadium seems to be contracting in size around me, or I am expanding. Physics becoming unstable as fear twists my brain. The seats are full of shapes. Squirming shadows that might be bin bags, boys, beasts.

Reality swims as I begin to hyperventilate. Sucking in air but no oxygen. Things growing bigger and smaller, Alice eating her cake. The prickling of my skin becomes needle-pain. The heat roiling inside of me starts to melt my bones.

My mind grasps for calm. I close my eyes. Inhale. Hold. Picture a deep blue sky. But what flashes inside me has the shape of *teeth*. What bubbles up in my throat is a *snarl*.

My legs collapse and I fall, clutching onto wet grass.

The sky dances for me, clouds drifting past, silver-tipped, curtains unveiling the full moon.

Bloat

o

Brenda

I have to be at the DVLA in an hour, so of course this is the day the sodding cat has gone missing.

My knees complain as I crouch under the bramble bush which separates my garden from my neighbours', rattling a packet of Dreamies at the darkness. Trouble is, the bloody menace could be sitting three feet in front of my face and I'd never see him. I'm eighty-two. My eyesight's not so good these days.

'Melek!' I call, trying to keep the irritation out my voice – something I've never been very good at. It's three buses to get to the DVLA offices. No way I'm going to make it.

He's not even my cat. Belonged to my neighbour, who was dragged here from Syria with her kids, only for them to abandon her here when they went on to Germany. Rayya was in her nineties by the end, still barely spoke English, had no idea how to access social care. I popped over when I could, brought her food when I had extra, helped her open jars. *I'm* the one who found her lying neatly on top of her bed a few months back, wearing her best clothes, her favourite bright blue headscarf, like she'd dressed for her own funeral. The blood had already pooled at the bottom of her body, one thick dark bruise on the bottom half of her, like a layer cake.

So, now her bloomin' cat's my problem. Melek's the fattest moggy I've ever seen, twenty-five pounds last weighed. We're still wary of each other, Melek and me. He misses Rayya. The closest we've managed to affection is that he'll occasionally sleep on the corner of my bed, as far from me as physically possible, arsehole aimed at my face. I've never been a cat person, and Melek's as stupid as a throw cushion. But I can't deny that it's been nice to have another living creature around.

Though, not around, currently. I pspspspspsps, turning my face askew, trying to peer around the void in the centre of my vision. The world swirls around the edges, but right in the middle, there's nothing – the black hole I carry with me everywhere now. Gaze too long into the abyss, and the abyss gazes back. Ha bloody ha.

A doctor with a public-school accent told me it's called Macular Degeneration, the wet kind. He scolded me for not coming in sooner to get it treated, like it's my fault you need to book an appointment eighteen months in advance these days. Posh wankers love making you feel like everything's your fault, when they're the ones gutting the NHS to sell it for scraps. He didn't like it when I told him that.

I can see fine around the edges, in my peripheral vision, but it takes a moment for my eyes to adjust, especially when the light shifts. And always the void, smack in the middle, swallowing the centre of anything I look at.

Getting old: what a laugh.

No movement from the bushes. My joints crack and squeal like a rusted engine as I stand. The mud's soaked into my knees, but luckily, when I smooth down my skirt, it covers up the worst of it. It's a pencil skirt I picked up at the Salvation Army for a fiver, bright pink to match my court shoes. I have to make a good impression. My life depends on this appointment. Sodding bloody arsehole stupid bloody cat.

Fifty-five minutes left. No choice but to talk to the blasted neighbours. Melek keeps trying to break back into Rayya's house. There's a new family living there now, a young couple with two small kids. They do something in media, like half the people who live in Walthamstow these days. They won't let him in, scared he'll smother their baby or some such nonsense. Try explaining to a cat that he's not allowed in his own home any more.

Buggers called the RSPCA on me once, saying I'm negligent for letting my cat roam. Called the police, too, after I told them exactly what I thought of them.

The pocket of my blazer starts playing a high-pitched jangly song I haven't figured out how to change. I answer the call in case it's the woman from the DVLA, still rattling the cat treats at the darkness with my other hand.

'Auntie B? I was hoping to talk about Christmas.' My niece's voice sounds strained. I can hear shouts in the background, her kids fighting over something by the sounds of it.

'Not a good time, Jen,' I say, making my way through the house to the front door. 'Also, it's August.'

'I know, it's just... I want to give you plenty of notice.' She takes a deep breath. 'We've decided it's going to be just us this year. Just the family.'

I pause, hand on my front door. 'And I'm not family?' Truth is, Jen's the last blood relative who's speaking to me. Some people can't handle honesty, is the problem. Including Jen's pillock husband, who I got into a bit of a tiff with last year. I ask her if that's what this is about.

'Well... you really lost it with him.'

'I said he's a lazy numpty who contributes nothing to your life except dirty dishes and flatulence. I stand by it.'

'See, that. And you brought drugs into my home, Auntie B.'

I did not, in fact, do that. But I *did* claim that a small bag of weed was mine to save my great-nephew's hide. Should have known that good deeds get you squat.

'So I'm not welcome, that's what you're saying.' I keep my voice steady. I don't want her to hear how it cuts me.

'I don't... Maybe if you stay at a bed and breakfast nearby, you could come for lunch. I don't want you to be alone...'

'Forget it. I don't need your pity.'

'I know you mean well, Auntie B. But your temper—'

I let her keep yammering into my ear, squirming excuses. I can feel my pulse beating in my tongue, let the fury power my footsteps across to the neighbours'. Nothing for it but to ring the doorbell and see if Melek's there.

I smell it before I see it: the sweet reek which hits me as I approach the neighbours' front door. Although it's not yet eight, the sun is baking the paving stones up to their terraced house, warming the mess that's spilled across their front step.

I crouch down, ignoring my shrieking knees, Jen's voice droning through the phone speakers. I pull on the wrap-around skiing sunglasses which help to cut out the worst of the glare.

It takes me a moment to understand what I'm seeing, moving my head side to side, catching it in glimpses around my void. Chunks of meat and fur. The bright splash across the concrete, pooled in the ragged gaps between paving stones.

I stare at it for many long seconds. Uncomprehending. There is nothing but me, my void, and the orbiting mess of meat which used to be Melek.

Jen is still wheedling in my ear. I press the 'end call' button on her, mid-sentence, and stuff the phone deep into my pocket.

The curtain twitches. A jangle at the front door, and then my neighbour is there, battle-face ready. 'Excuse me, you cannot keep—' She screams, jumping back at the sight of the gory mess on her pavement.

'Harriet?' I hear her husband call from somewhere inside the house, alarmed.

'What the fuck, Brenda?' Harriet hisses, horrified.

'You think *I'd do this* to him?' I spit.

Her husband appears, the toddler clinging to his side like a koala in Disney pyjamas. Harriet tries to push them back before they see, but the girl has spotted it and breaks into a high-pitched wail. It's the older child, the three-year-old. Are they old enough to form memories yet? I hope not. This is the kind of image which sticks with you. It certainly feels like it's burned into what's left of my retinas.

The two halves of Melek appear to have been pulled clean apart, a magic trick gone horribly wrong.

Harriet shoves the door closed on her family behind her, blocking the gruesome scene from their view. The wailing continues through the door. The toddler has triggered the baby, whose echoing screams peal out from the upper floor, tragedy call-and-response.

'What happened?' Harriet asks finally.

I shake my head. What *did* happen? This wasn't a car injury. Or any other way I've ever heard of a cat dying.

'Should I… should I call the police?' Harriet shifts her weight from side to side.

'I'll do it.' *Think, you silly bint*, I berate myself. *Proof. You need proof.* I lift my phone with shaking hands and make myself take photos. Up close, and at a distance, trying to get it all in. The blood splatter. The flapping edge of skin around his ribs. I can't bear to look too closely at his face, so familiar, the one white whisker among the black. The last living creature on this earth who'd have noticed if I was gone.

'Get me a shopping bag,' I say.

'Shouldn't you… I don't know. Wait until help gets here?'

'No one helps,' I snap. It comes out louder than I intended. I take a deep, shaking breath.

Harriet reappears, thrusting a fabric tote at me. It's emblazoned with the logo of some overpriced bookshop.

I collect the parts of him with my bare hands, trying to keep him in the centre of my vision, grateful in this moment for the void acting as my personal censorship bar. Harriet yelps but doesn't move.

The right shoulder ends in a stump. I can't see that leg among the other… parts. It must have been eaten.

Eaten. The word makes the eddy in my head swirl faster.

Finally, he's all in the bag, save a dark pool across the steps; Harriet's problem. She is watching me, eyes huge, face pale. She hasn't moved a muscle to help.

'What are you going to do?' she asks.

I grip the handles of the bag so tight that my fingers tingle. The question reverberates inside me. *What are you going to do?*

I raise my chin. 'Harriet, I'm going to find out who killed my damn cat.'

Harvest Moon

Forgetfulness
O
Ellie

Something is licking my face. Wet. Dog breath. I open my eyes to find an enormous teddy bear looming over me. It gives a happy bark to see me awake.

'Ebenezer! Off!' The dog runs back to a woman holding a lead and a latte. It's some kind of poodle-cross thing, one of those trendy Frankenbreeds that's probably called a Chowpei-Maltipoo.

I blink in the harsh daylight, peeling my face off the mud to find I'm lying in a soggy patch of grass near some bushes, a few feet from a pathway winding through an unfamiliar park. There's a rich smell, mouldy and sickly-sweet, which I realise is coming from an old greatcoat someone has thrown over me. My robe is nowhere to be seen.

I lift the coat cautiously. As suspected, I am completely naked underneath, but for the mud and grime caked onto my body. My hands are bloody. Gone sticky now, red-brown caked into the lines across my palms.

What the *fuck*?

My mind grasps for details. The boys in the stadium. Did they find me? Did they drag me somewhere, undress me, *violate me*?

But there are no wounds on my skin. No pain at all. If anything, I feel like I've just completed a juice cleanse and a three-day yoga retreat. My body hums with purity. My muscles are less tense than they've been in years. My stomach pain has vanished. In fact, apart from the rising panic, I feel bloody fantastic.

Automatically, I reach for my phone… then remember it's still plugged in next to my bed.

I check the pockets of the coat. They're empty.

There aren't many people around. A couple of joggers, taking a detour from the path I'm lying next to. A pair of young mums pushing matching pushchairs. A man in a Carhartt jacket walking a whippet. None of them make eye contact with me.

I slip into the coat behind the privacy screen of a bush. There's no belt, but enough buttons left on it to hold it mostly shut over my naked body. The fabric is stiff with dirt, the smell betraying the fact that whoever it formerly belonged to has been sleeping rough for a long time. Somebody who will miss it. I rub the sleeve in silent gratitude.

A map on the side of a bus stop shelter tells me I'm in Leyton. I can't get on a bus without a purse or phone. And it would take ages to walk home, barefoot.

How the hell did I end up all the way in east London?

I need to call Mo. But – shit – I don't remember his number. Who memorises phone numbers any more? I could find a police officer, but what would I even tell them? No need to overreact. This is a totally manageable situation and I am a grown woman. I just need to stay calm. Inhale, hold, exhale. I put my hands into the pockets of the coat and try to rub off some of the blood on the lining.

Lights glow inside a coffee shop across the road, so bland it might have been generated by an algorithm. Scandi-industrial, pothos plants draping like chandeliers, identical to every other £4 coffee shop between Sydney and San Francisco. People who look like they have 'Creative' on their business cards are already crowded around a large central table typing away on laptops. It's exactly the kind of place I'd normally pick for a quick investor meeting.

I head for the hostess, apron tied around her bare waist between a crop top and billowing parachute pants.

'Nope, no,' she's already saying before I reach her, crowding me back to the door. 'We can't help you, no.'

'Could I just use your phone—'

The door slams in my face. The young woman stands guard at the door, arms crossed, scowling at me through the glass. None of the patrons have even bothered to look up from Canva.

My face burns in embarrassment. It must be the coat. The mud on my face. My smell.

I get the beady eye from the trendy Paraguayan smoothie place next door and don't even bother to try to go inside. Instead, I head for the shabby-looking Asian grocery store on the corner.

My own smells are immediately drowned in a thousand more pleasant ones: spices, jars of pickles, fresh seafood, dried mushrooms. A shelf near the entrance offers shrink-wrapped organs and sensuous vegetables. A Vietnamese soap opera blares from an ancient CRT television mounted facing the counter.

I ask the young man working the counter if I can use his phone. His eyes, too, scan my coat, my bruised shins. But he hands his phone out to me without hesitation. It's a battered Samsung, covered in stickers of a blue cartoon cat.

I dial the number I hope is Mo's and wait while it rings.

'You need police?' The young man asks quietly, picking up the receiver on his landline ready to dial for me. He's staring at my hand, which I realise too late is still covered in blood.

I shake my head. The mobile goes to voicemail, a strange woman's voice. Wrong number. Add to List: *Make sure Paige knows my phone number by heart.* 'Can I use your toilet?'

He leads me through an overstuffed storeroom to a tiny staff cubicle. Multiple handwritten signs on the wall admonish me in a language I can't read, below an ancient magazine cut-out of Snoopy holding a tennis racket. I wash the worst of the gore off my hands, wipe the mud from my face with a paper towel, and spritz myself with the can of anti-odour spray next to the loo. This does little to improve the appearance of the deranged woman in the mirror, whose normally blonde hair is a nest of twigs and grime and whose eyes seem to have sunk an inch deeper into her skull, in sharp contrast to how fresh I feel on the inside.

The stitches on my forehead are intact, so not the source of the blood. I inspect my cheekbones with my fingers, remembering the hallucinatory feeling before I passed out last night, making sure they are still the same shape I remember.

'Get a grip,' I tell the haggard crone in the mirror, willing my heart rate to return to normal. I'm fine. I'm fine! I definitely don't feel like I've been attacked. I just need to stay calm, and figure out how to get home.

The shopkeeper presses a paper bag on me when I come out. 'I don't have any money,' I say. He shakes his head, insists. I thank him and wander outside, thinking I might try to find a library and get online, as I reach into the bag. Inside is a packet of crisps and a five-pound note.

I whisper another silent thank you to the shopkeeper and head back to the bus stop. The driver shakes his head at my proffered cash but waves me in anyway. Other passengers give me a wide berth as I make my way to the back of the bus. I run my hands down my bare calves, trying to ground myself, only to find another shock at how they prickle my hands. My legs are usually smooth as rubber.

The blogs spoke about how perimenopause changes your hair texture. Some women start going bald; others find their body hair grows coarser. Oh, all the new joys to discover.

The hair on my legs is growing back in, thick as a man's. Dark. Soft as fur.

I make it home just before eight. There's movement in the kitchen window. My poor husband is probably pacing back and forth, phoning everyone from the police to the United Nations peacekeeping force. Maybe the Avengers, just in case. I smooth down my hair, hoping I don't look too mangled, wondering what I'm going to say.

Don't panic, I think, *it's fine. I just lost some time and then woke up on the other side of the city with blood on my hands, no big deal!* But I'm ambushed before I make it up the steps to my front door.

'Just a minute, Eleanor.' Ugh. My neighbour Julia peers out her front door. Her awful dog, a badly trained Pomeranian with attachment issues, shivers at her legs, a low growl vibrating his whole tiny body. Horror of horrors, I notice that she's dyed the creature's tail pink. *Your ancestors were wolves*, I sneer telepathically.

'I really hate to bring this up,' she simpers, looking not sorry at all, 'but your father-in-law was nosing around my front garden again yesterday.'

The woman's obsessed with Yusuf. She's lived on this street since she was born – a fact she has repeated to me at least twenty times – and has decided my half-brown family represents the downfall not only of the neighbourhood, but of civilisation itself. Mo she can just about tolerate, since he's relatively fair-skinned and speaks perfect RP. Yusuf's another story.

'Look, now's not a good time.' I make a move towards my door.

'Maybe you just want to explain to him that in *our* culture, we respect private property.'

I wonder if you can roll your eyes so hard they get stuck in your throat. I swallow the urge to remind her that Yusuf has been here since the 1970s. 'I'm very sorry he violated the sanctity of your azaleas, Julia, but I've got to get in.' I start up the steps.

The dog's growls explode into a series of shrill barks. Julia nudges it back into the doorway with her leg, finally noticing my coat, my bare feet. Her eyes boggle. 'Big night?'

I pretend I don't hear this, making a show of fishing a non-existent front-door key from the depths of my pocket.

'I also noticed that the bins...' she starts up again.

I angle my body to hide my bloody hand from her beady eyes and try the door. It's unlocked, thank God.

I ease into the entrance hall, bracing myself for a relieved hug. Instead, I'm greeted by the smell of freshly baked bread and merry clanging from the kitchen. Mo calls out cheerfully, 'How was your run, love?'

I hesitate. I'm still bloody. Muddy. Confused.

I try five different versions of 'Okay, don't panic, but I just woke up in Leyton in the buff' in my head, but then think… maybe I don't have to worry him at all.

'Great, thanks!' I say, injecting as much post-running *joie de vivre* into my voice as I can. I just need a minute to take a proper look at myself. Figure out how bad things actually are.

'T-minus ten minutes in here.'

'Just enough time for a shower,' I call, hurrying up the stairs before he spots me.

My phone is still on my bedside table, plugged in right where I left it. I scan the barrage of messages that came in overnight. My brother asking me to call him about Mum's house. Lanying sending me an update on the credit card crisis. Our CFO saying something ominous about an overdue corporate tax payment. HR wanting to discuss some details about my sort-of-promotion. Much as I'm dreading showing my face in the office after yesterday's Town Hall fiasco, it would be really, really convenient to not have to spend another morning in A&E.

I stuff the coat deep into the laundry basket while googling 'blackout + sleepwalking + menopause'. The results are reassuring. I scan the link snippets while waiting for the shower to warm up. One of them is a long list of perimenopause symptoms. My eyes scan the list. *Sleep disruption. Memory loss. Paranoia.*

Even the mystery of my gory hands is answered as soon as I step into the shower and a fresh stream of blood runs down my thighs. I laugh in relief, and also because the whole thing feels like some kind of cosmic joke. After being absent for months, my period is back for a last hurrah.

'Not going to miss *you*,' I grumble, letting the water wash over my crotch. I lather the mud out my hair, shave my legs and scrub the filth off my feet until I feel like myself again. Afterwards, I turn the temperature dial to its coldest setting, my skin shivering with pleasure. I feel more in my body than usual. The shampoo smells more shampooey. The floor tiles more slick against my soles. This tiny en suite is my favourite place in the house. I am slightly abashed by how many hours I spent picking the perfect paint colour (Wimborne White, Farrow & Ball), the tiles (Claybrook), the bath sheets (White Company). Mo teased me for trying to Instagramise our bathroom, but it was something I was determined to get right. As a woman in a relationship with a man, you have two choices: accept lower standards, or do all the work yourself. There is no third option, and wishing for one will only make you resentful and furious.

It is impossible to believe, standing in this carefully considered bathroom, that anything is wrong.

I think back to the plaza last night, the young men who were there and then weren't there, the way the buildings seemed to twist, how I couldn't breathe.

Paranoia. Sleep disruption. Memory loss.

It's so clear, suddenly, what happened. So stupidly mundane I can't believe how worked up I've let myself get.

I had a panic attack.

A sneaky voice starts to mount an argument from the recesses of my mind. *You had a panic attack, and then you blacked out and stripped, and then you somehow walked from Islington to Leyton without a single person stopping you?*

I shake my head. I've had panic attacks before. It happened a lot in my twenties. It's the reason I started practising meditation, the thing that brought me to Don. Panic plus perimenopause… yes, it seems plausible that I forgot half the night. Still bizarre, for sure. But explicable.

By the time I've dried my hair and put on my face, I've convinced myself there's no need to rush to the hospital. Add to List: *Make a GP appointment.*

Mo's got two loaves cooling on the dining table when I come down, freshly plucked, buffed and moisturised back to my usual self. I sit and rip open the smaller loaf, a ball barely bigger than my fist, and cram half of it into my mouth. Mo got big into baking sourdough back in 2020 with everyone else, when there were such flour shortages he eventually started buying it in bulk from a commercial supplier who only sold bags by the pallet. He gave so much bread to the local soup kitchen they eventually asked him to cut back. I can never resist slicing into a loaf before it's cooled (which supposedly ruins the texture) so Mo started making me a separate, tiny loaf I can eat straight out of the oven. Mo calls them 'Ellie's decoy loaves'.

'You sleep okay?' I ask him, amazed he didn't notice me gone. But then, I suppose I do often go to bed long after him, wake up many hours before he does.

'Like the dead,' he says, leaning over to pour olive oil into a dipping bowl for me. 'Are you still feeling... menopausy?' He brushes a floury thumb against my forehead, as though to check whether I have a fever. I'm not sure how Mo thinks the menopause works.

Instead of responding, I nuzzle my face into his belly. I love how squishy he's become. When I first met him, he was an indie games developer who used to stay up all night coding, surviving on energy drinks, etiolated like the stems of a sprouting potato discovered in a dark cupboard. Now he's a lecturer, playing dad to a hundred bright-eyed first-year students every year. Wonderfully chubby, more potato than potato stem now, Mo is exactly who you want around on an anxious day.

He's changed remarkably little in the twenty-five years we've been together. He still loves techno because it's what he loved in his teens. He can still lose a hundred hours to a video game, only now it legitimately counts as work. He is still kind, his optimism untouched by a lifetime's disappointments. He still smokes pot every Sunday afternoon and it still doesn't affect him. He still hides it from his dad. He has never felt the need to be any different than he is, and happiness settles around him like dust.

Also, let's be honest, he's still a devastatingly beautiful man. Boyish stubble. Eyelashes so long they tangle around his warm brown eyes. His luxurious black hair is more salt than pepper these days – and bloody hell if it doesn't suit him.

Yusuf shuffles in, already dressed, but in yesterday's shirt, I notice. Mo's doing, since we only have the day nurse from nine until six. He does mornings, I do evenings. And also mornings, on the two or three days a week Mo oversleeps. Lovable, my husband, but also maddening. I can already see from Yusuf's slow, stiff walk that it's going to be a bad day. One more thing to worry about later.

Mo sets him up with today's cryptic crossword while I log my mysterious new symptoms in the surprisingly expensive menopause app I subscribed to last night, chewing my way through the bread, which is sticking to my teeth despite the olive oil.

Yusuf points his pencil at me. 'Tailless parrot and one cuckoo returning with a nut, nine.' Another person might be alarmed; I've learned by now how to tell when his gibberish is cryptic crosswords and when it's the dementia.

'Don't mock me.' I give a theatrical sigh. Yusuf's been trying to teach me how to do cryptic crosswords for years and I've yet to crack a single clue.

'Macadamia. Parrot, a macaw, without the tail, as in final letter. M, A, C, A. "Cuckoo" is mad, but "returning" means backwards. So D, A, M. Maca-dam, a nut. Macadamia, get it?'

'Oh, I am an expert on nuts, thanks,' I say, throwing a pointed look at his trousers. Can't remember who I am half the time but he can still torment me with crossword clues. Before they left Pakistan, Yusuf was a schoolteacher, but the UK education licensing office kept 'losing' the application to convert his qualifications. He eventually gave up and opened a small dry cleaner's, kept afloat by the tailoring empire Mo's mother ran from the back room. The crosswords kept his brain sharp, he used to say. He's stopped saying that now. He's still himself in the daytime, clever and kind. But there's a quick unravelling after sunset, his kindness flaking off like a sunburn to reveal raw red panic underneath. He becomes a different person then, someone harder to love.

'You get too distracted,' he says. 'The last word in the clue is the key. Always too distracted.' He taps the side of his head for emphasis.

I notice Mo watching me across the table. 'You sure you're okay?'

I finish typing *blackout* into my phone, nodding, barely paying attention. I'm just thinking that I could sort out the credit card thing today, then see the GP tomorrow, maybe, when there's less on the List.

'Maybe it's a blessing in disguise,' Mo says, forever Captain Optimism. 'The CEO thing. Might be good for you to take your foot off the pedal a bit. And, who knows – this new boss might be brilliant. Look how close you got with Don.'

I frown. The very thought of Andreas makes me feel like I could start boiling again. 'I'm not thinking about work.'

'Is it Paige?'

'Sure,' I say, to get him to stop prodding.

He nods, smug about his own insightfulness. 'I get it. It's like being suddenly ghosted by someone you've been with for nineteen years.' Mo picks up the Gen Z speak from his students.

'I just know that when Theo inevitably breaks her heart with his radical-honesty arsehole bullshit, it's going to trigger the ED again,' I say. And the pang of worry which accompanies this thought is sincere, even among the five hundred other things I have to be worried about right now.

'We should take a holiday,' he muses. 'Didn't you want to go wine tasting in Portugal?'

'Great idea, love, let's plan something,' I say, to put an end to that idea. I don't have time to go wine tasting in Portugal. Please! But I've long ago learned that *let's plan something* means *Ellie will plan something*, and if I don't, then nothing will happen.

Once I've entered the last of my symptoms into the menopause app, a cheerful message pops up, accompanied by a cartoon sun doing yoga: *It seems like you're having a tricky day!* The app encourages me to read an article about how menopause impacts memory, to join the *thousands of empowered women sharing their stories* on the forum, and then invites me to give the app five stars on the App Store.

Mo clears the plates, having to reach over the huge cardboard box that's been occupying half the dining table for three months since his new synthesiser arrived in it. He'd happily recycle the box if I asked him to, but I'm playing a game with myself where I see how long it will take him to notice it on his own. This box might outlast the polar ice caps.

He stops to plant a smooch on the top of my head as he passes. 'You love that kid too much, you know.'

'Pot. Kettle.'

But Mo doesn't move. He remains hovered over me, frowning. 'You've got...' He combs his fingers through my hair. 'Yeeugh.' He shows me what he's pulled from my head: a long string of bloody tendon, draped across his fingers like a ragged electrical pylon.

Swollen Joints

Brenda

Never had a friend in my life. It's just not a thing that ever came naturally to me. Even when I was a child, other children seemed like shrieking demons, all sticky with snot and sick and sherbet. Friendship always felt like a game I wasn't taught the rules to, and which I was constantly losing. I had to learn it by rote like maths tables. Smile back when someone smiles at you. Make eye contact when you talk to someone (trickier when there's a void in the middle of your vision). Don't tell someone when they're doing something wrong; people don't like it. Still haven't nailed *that* lesson.

So my vet Paul isn't a friend, but he is one of the few people I consider decent. I used to drive Rayya here before she passed. Paul always took the time to speak slower so she could understand, no matter how busy he was.

His reception's crammed, as usual. A tradie with cement-splashed overalls and a bright pink cat carrier covered in glitter stickers. An old biddy with a half-bald parrot on her lap. And Prince Harry, as he calls himself, the red-haired bloke who sleeps rough behind the Ladbrokes, gently stroking his ancient mastiff Trent, who's curled around his legs. Paul's the cheapest vet in north London, and even then, doesn't charge half his customers.

I've been here all morning. Only realised many hours too late that I entirely forgot about the DVLA.

Finally, the receptionist waves me through. I pause to stroke Dodo in his little basket by the reception desk. Dodo's a mostly hairless gnome-like creature with milky cataracts, a wiry tuft on his head, and a permanently protruding freckled tongue. Quite possibly the ugliest dog in the world. Paul tried for ages to get someone to adopt the hideous thing, before resigning himself to the fact that Dodo's permanent home is under the reception desk. Paul never puts down an animal unless he must.

I find him in the back, checking on the drowsy post-ops in their wall of cages, a nurse taking diligent notes on a clipboard. He waves me into the consulting room, no chit-chat, another thing I appreciate.

'There's some funniness about it, you're right,' he says, scrolling through notes on his computer. He keeps the screen angled away from me, so I can't see. I don't bother to tell him there's no need; until my eyes adjust to the darker room, I can see sod all anyway. 'I found round puncture wounds, probably teeth marks. Big ones. But I've never seen a cat bitten clean in half like this.'

'It seemed... neat.'

Paul grunts an agreement. 'My first thought was a dog – these holes are far too big for a fox. Canine jaws close like scissors, so it wouldn't be unheard of to get a clean cut like this if it was, say, a leg. But right through the body...' He adjusts his weight on the seat. 'I'm trying to picture a dog which would be big enough. Melek... I mean, he wasn't a small cat.'

'So, what killed him?'

Paul shifts again, the chair legs squeaking against the linoleum. 'A Great Dane, maybe. Wolfhound. Or one of those XL Bully dogs. Ever seen one?'

I nod. Walthamstow's full of them. Muscled miniature bulls pulling skinny lads around by their leads. There was a whole hoo-ha about banning them, but you still see plenty around here.

'We've seen a few cats killed by them this year, I'm afraid. I always say it's the owner not the breed, but they're strong enough to do real damage when they get hold of something. But they tend to grab a cat by the neck and rag them around. I've never seen one severed like this.'

I swallow the spit which has filled my mouth. 'What are you saying?'

'Well, it might have been opportunistic. Foxes get blamed for a lot of cats killed by cars, you know. They come across a dead body and… well, they're scavengers. So, what I'm thinking is, if these are dog bites, maybe when it found Melek, he was already dead.' Paul sits back, his head moving into my void.

I stare at him, Mr Abyss-Head in a white coat. 'You're saying some sicko cut my cat in half?'

The void sighs. 'I'm saying I don't know what happened, Brenda. I'm sorry.'

'Can't you test it? DNA whatsit?' They're always talking about DNA evidence on the telly.

The void lifts his hands, indicating the shabby consulting room. The peeling wallpaper. The yellowing posters about canine obesity and deworming schedules. Not the kind of place that has a secret high-tech forensics lab in the basement.

'I'm sorry, Brenda. Look. Rayya was a good lady. You've done right by her. I'll handle the cremation, no charge. You can come pick up the ashes tomorrow, okay?'

'What would I do with ashes?' But I can't argue with him about the waived bill. I've no idea how much money I owe Paul, but thankfully he never hassles me about it.

The nurse pops in, telling Paul he's needed in room 2.

'Be right there.' Paul lingers at the doorway. 'When you're ready, we get cats looking for new homes all the time. Just give me a call.'

'I'm done with pets,' I say.

'Well. Take care of yourself, Brenda.'

I wait until the door shuts behind him before sliding into the chair he's just vacated, leaning in close to the screen.

There he is: Melek, both halves spreadeagled on a steel operating table. Paul has circled the deep black holes in him, six I can see. According to the rulers at the top of the screen, the largest ones are two inches wide.

* * *

I drive home, numb, in my ancient blue 1994 Vauxhall Corsa. Illegally now, according to the email from the fussy DVLA bitch that landed in my inbox while I was at Paul's.

As you failed to show up for your appointment today, I'm afraid we're going to have to proceed with revoking your driving licence. As reported by your GP, your eyesight has deteriorated below the minimum requirements... Category G blah blah blah... Please note that if you are found to be driving, you could be fined up to £1,000 and may face criminal prosecution... blah blah blah... You are entitled to free bus travel...

Like I'm going to start taking the bus. The problem with public transport is that it's too full of the bloody public.

Nanny-state nonsense. I can drive fine as long as I go slowly – I'm not an invalid. The car's not long for this world anyway. Only has two working gears, second and third, which is fine as long as you never need to do an incline start. It's not remotely ULEZ-compliant, but they can prise the keys out of my cold, dead arthritic hands. They'll take everything from you, if you let them.

This car and I have clocked many miles together. Back in the days of my shithead husband, I'd sometimes just get in the car and go. Usually up to Blackpool, where my brothers lived. They'd tease me for not moving to the cheaper north. 'I've got as much right to London as anyone else,' I'd snap back. Sometimes I still drive up and walk the promenade, imagining them nattering beside me, just me and my ghosts.

I park behind the Sainsbury's and traipse the couple of blocks up Walthamstow High Street to my flat. It changes more every time I walk it. The old pie and mash shop built in the 1920s – one of the last places in London you could buy stewed eel – that's now a chain restaurant with only two tables inside and a constant throng of food delivery drivers loitering out front. The Lamb Brothers office where I worked back in the eighties is now a mobile phone repair shop. Back then, entertainment meant watching the dogs or seeing rock bands at the Standard, and most people worked at the factories near Blackhorse Road. Those factories are all posh breweries now, selling IPA at ten quid a pint, and half of the warehouses are towering new builds for the white-collar types who whizz down to the City every morning, and don't even bother to get to know the people who actually live here.

The market's still a grimy run-down place, only now it's cheap imported clothes and plastic houseware rather than the overripe fruit and fly-crusted meat I remember from the old days. But the side streets are unrecognisable. Butchers turned into coffee shops. Bakeries turned into coffee shops. Tailors turned into coffee shops. Who's drinking all this coffee? I often wonder.

I'd be happier if I owned my flat, and I'd see some benefit from what they're doing to the property values. I briefly owned a tidy house in Wanstead thanks to that cow Maggie Thatcher. Lost it in the early 2000s, along with the Shithead and very nearly my left hand after he shoved me onto an open dishwasher. Gained back my dignity, though, so fair trade.

My current flat's a ground-floor Warner, rented, almost 150 years old. Plumbing's not much younger. The pipes rattle and creak in greeting as I slam the door shut, pausing a minute until my eyes adjust to the darkness.

There are just a few pellets left in Melek's bowl. Automatically, I reach for the scoop to top it up, before remembering. I throw the whole lot in the bin, which is probably – I realise – where Melek's ashes will end up. Mine too, some day.

What now?

The constable I called this morning was about as much help as I expected. She took my statement over the phone, said, no, there was no need to send someone over in person. 'Not much we can do about a dead cat,' she said, voice high-pitched and nasal. Sure, I could send them the photos I took, if I wanted to. But she insisted I upload them through some website and refused to give me her email address. She read me a docket number. Promised she'd be in touch if there are any developments. Don't call us, we'll call you. Meaning, I'll never hear from them again.

Then she started asking pointed questions about the history of complaints between me and the various neighbours, like that's got anything to do with this, until I told her to shove the docket up her puckered cunt and hung up.

I could call back. Tell them about the necropsy (autopsies are for humans, Paul explained to me). But what would be the point? What's the point of any of it, any more? Melek's gone. Rayya's gone. Both my brothers are gone. Neighbourhood's unrecognisable. I'm late on my rent. The DVLA wants me stuck in my house all day. Jen's cut me off. Might be time to cash in my chips. There are extra-strength oven bags in the kitchen, and Sellotape in the wardrobe – it wouldn't take much. Eighty-two years, it's been a good run. Well, it's been a run.

Instead, I light a fag, open our neighbourhood group on Facebook and type up a post. INFORMATION WANTED. MUTILATED CAT. My Jurassic laptop computer whirrs like a jumbo jet trying to take off in a hurricane. Everything on the screen is magnified, colours inverted so it's white on black, text as big as I can make it, so I have to keep scrolling left and right to find the buttons.

I upload photos I took of Melek's poor, segmented body. In photographic negative, it's abstract, almost artistic. *Looking for information on any suspicious activity between 11 p.m. and 7 a.m., Copperwood Rd. I saw him just before I went to bed, I'm sure of it.*

Responses start almost immediately.
What the hell's wrong with you, lady?
FFS put a CW on this please.
Sick!

The post vanishes, replaced with a formal-looking notification saying it violates Facebook's community guidelines and has been removed.

My hands shake with anger. Yes, I didn't want to see it either. *My community guidelines have been violated.* And nobody cares. No one wants to help. See – there's no point in trying.

I almost miss the blinking icon over my message inbox, turned to greyscale. I catch it just in time, as my mouse moves towards the X.

A message request, from someone I don't know. I click accept, and the words appear almost immediately; the sender has been sitting there waiting to start typing.

Me too

Our cat Mr Bojangles was killed last night. I'm just a few streets away from there

And our neighbours two houses up, they had guinea pigs

Hutch opened and there's a trail of fur all through the garden

My knuckles ache as I hold my fingers above the keyboard, watching the messages come in.

We're in pieces

Police say there's nothing they can do

Can you help?

Please, can you help?

Parosmia

◯

Ellie

I make it to the office by nine, hair freshly rewashed of mysterious gristle, industrial-strength roll-on slathered over my torso, spare shirt in my bag. I cannot possibly have had a high quality of sleep last night, what with all the naked nocturnal strolling, but somehow I feel more relaxed than I've felt in months. Maybe Mo's right; maybe Andreas will be okay. I should give him a chance.

Tranquillity's reception area is decorated like a lido, on Don's insistence that they're the place with the happiest associations for most British people. In the early days of the business, Don dealt with the stress of being pulled out of academia to run a multimillion-pound tech company by obsessing about office design. There's a plug-in dispenser that pumps a mild chlorine smell into the room. I've never had the heart to tell Don that the ammonia smell of lidos is pee.

A girl is perched on one of the deckchairs. Slime-green hair in space buns, oversized band tee, voluminous cargo pants. Can't be here for a meeting, then. The front-desk manager is AWOL. This isn't my problem.

But the girl looks up at me hopefully as I walk in.

'Can I help you?' I ask, cursing myself.

'Yes, hi, thank you. I'm supposed to be starting today? They said ten, but I thought it would be good to be early?' Add to List: *Send this girl on an assertive communication workshop to get rid of that upspeak.*

'Who are you supposed to be meeting?'

'Uh, Zayn Ismail?' The head of engineering, of course. In the tech world, the more in-demand your skillset, the grubbier your get-up. If you spot someone in this building wearing stained sweatpants, chances are they're paid more than me. Has it ever happened before, and will it ever be repeated, this strange economic quirk where a group of twenty-somethings who happen to be fluent in a new technology are the only ones seeing wage growth, in any industry? The thing is, when you're dealing with code, you're dealing with the potential of infinite productivity. Infinity sucks in everything eventually, like all black holes.

I lean over the mermaid-mosaic reception desk and dial Zayn's extension by heart. The chlorine smell is particularly pungent today. Almost unbearable. They must have just replaced the dispenser. Or, who knows, maybe there's an actual puddle of pee somewhere.

No answer from Zayn, so I wave the girl to follow me. 'I'm heading to engineering anyway.'

She tells me her name is Millie and she's a new junior DevOps engineer. She stares wide-eyed at everything. The old Ferris wheel cars rescued from a bankrupt travelling funfair that now serve as phone booths. The shelves crammed with books by Martin Seligman and Mihaly Csikszentmihalyi and Epicurus. The model train tracks that wind their way through the desk area – currently empty, because after a few disastrous HR incidents, I put my foot down and the Beer Train now only makes its rounds every Friday at 4 p.m.

It's hard, in this context, to bring up the girl's wardrobe. She can't be much older than Paige, twenty-two, twenty-three. I can feel a familiar lecture rising in my throat about being thoughtful about the image you present to the world, but I swallow it. I'll bring it up once we've established rapport. On paper, Zayn will be her line manager, but he long ago decided that he's more interested in the big-picture technical architecture part of leading the engineering team and that trivialities like managing people were beneath him, so I've somehow ended up picking up the one-on-ones and performance reviews for most of his team on top of my own. At last count I had forty-three direct reports.

Sit Zayn down and tell him this can't go on is somewhere on the List, but I somehow never seem to find time to get to it.

'Where were you before?' I ask the girl over my shoulder.

'Amazon Web Services.' She shrugs. So, she's a high achiever; AWS is Mecca for DevOps nerds. 'But I wanted to do something more meaningful. Something that actually helps people.'

'Sure.' They all start here high on the idealism. It keeps them going for a while. They join the company because of the mission, but in the end, they leave it for the same reasons people always leave jobs: they hate their manager, or they get a better-paid offer, or something gets complicated with a co-worker (see above re: Beer Train). Still, it's a charade all tech companies have to play, trumpeting how they're saving the world harder than their competitors are saving the world, to reduce hiring costs. Morality theatre as cost-cutting strategy.

But am I any different? Didn't I, too, join Tranquillity out of a fantasy of helping people?

'It's just so powerful, a mental health guide in the palm of your hand? *Health through happiness.*' Millie chants the slogan I wrote a long time ago. 'It's really meaningful to me personally, you know? My older brother died when I was a teenager, and it nearly destroyed my family. Mental health professionals saved my life? But not everyone can afford that privilege. So it just seems like, democratising mental health really matters?'

I nod vaguely. It never ceases to amaze me, this generation, how quickly they announce their traumas, how much they make them a part of their personal brands. As if they're half a step away from announcing them in their email signatures, below their pronouns. *Eleanor Fourie, she/her, raised by a mentally ill parent.*

I'm fully aware that I sound like an old grouch, complaining about the destigmatisation of mental health, especially here, but I just cannot believe it's healthy to make the worst things that ever happened to you the bedrock of your personality. *Beware of your mind's ability to create its own reality* – that's a line from one of my favourite meditations. Dwell on something, and you just reinforce its significance to you. Focus instead on the good things, the things you're grateful for, and they become more real. You can learn optimism, just like you can learn anything else. You can choose to be happy.

Zayn's not in his office, which is designed like an old hunting lodge, down to the leather armchair and oak captain's desk, the air thick with potpourri. I settle Millie at a spare spot in the engineering pit and leave her with the Wi-Fi password and instructions for how to get hold of IT.

There are only a couple of others around at this hour. I pretend not to notice their attempts to hail me, no doubt with questions I've already answered on the company wiki if they'd only bother to look. After yesterday's Town Hall meltdown, I try to project confidence with my posture, holding an imaginary orange under my chin to push my shoulders back, a trick I once learned from a Power Poses workshop.

I find Andreas chatting to the head of HR (I refuse to call her the 'Positivity Officer'). Andreas makes a show of being delighted to see me. Up close, I notice the layer of dog fur matted through the loose weave of his creased linen shirt. Birkenstocks and socks poke out from his rumbled beige chinos, and I immediately detect that whatever he had for breakfast included raw onion. Add to List: *Log on to the HR portal and check his salary.*

'Ellie! I'm sorry we didn't have a chance to chat yesterday. I've heard so much about you.'

I nod politely. Wish I could say the same.

'I'm perched in one of the meeting rooms. Tea?'

I lean as far away from his breath as I can without being obvious. 'Thanks, I'm a coffee person. My blood's 90 per cent caffeine at this point.'

'Oh, but this is special. It's silver needle – I picked it up in Colombo.' He's already leading me to one of the meeting rooms. It's my old office, I note. All the execs' offices have themes: Zayn's hunting lodge, the CFO's music room. Don's office – ex-office now, I guess – is a treehouse you used to only be able to access via a rope ladder, until the Diversity Champion insisted we add a ramp from the smoothie bar. Don spent ages wheedling me to choose a 'fun' theme. Every time he asked what I wanted, I'd reply 'nothing', until eventually, he designed me a white cube with nothing in it but a transparent Perspex desk and clear acrylic chair. I never used it. I prefer camping at the desk of whoever's sick that day – that's how you really learn what's going on in your team. Eventually, Don gave in and turned the Nothing Office into a meeting room.

Now, a shiny top-of-the-range MacBook Pro sits on the Perspex table, still in its plastic protective cover. Mine's four years old, A-key broken, so I spend half my day rewriting my sentences into A-less contortions. I feel too bad to ask for a new one, given the cash flow situation.

Andreas is still going on about the tea as he settles behind it. '... the unopened buds of the Pai Hao plant and hand-twist them... thirty thousand buds just to make a kilo of the stuff...' He lifts the lid on an ornate metal teapot that's been steeping on the tabletop. Quite a choice, bringing in your own teapot on your first day at a new job.

Sad twists of loose-leaf float in the water. The smell slaps me in the face, like if you left a mackerel to rot, doused it in bog spray and then warmed it up in the microwave.

'Mmm, flowery,' I say, because I have to say something.

'It really opens up the senses,' he says, pouring a few centimetres into a thimble-sized teacup for me. I usually drink my coffee out of a 500ml flask.

He leans back in his chair, sipping at his own reeking microcup with thin lips. 'So, Ellie. If you were me, what would be your first priority?'

Uh, make sure we still exist in six months, I think, but say, 'I presume Don's filled you in on the financial situation?'

'Of course. And I know how critical it is we put on a good show at Demo Day.'

The knots in my shoulders loosen. I brave the smallest slurp of the tea. Doesn't taste half as bad as it smells, honestly. Maybe the same will be true for Andreas.

'We've got to keep our focus on the corporate module,' I say. 'Companies are losing billions in lost productivity to stress and burnout, and this would let them roll out Tranquillity as an employee perk. Bulk sales mean steady cash flow, and that'll keep the investors happy. It's our best shot.'

He nods, face impassive. 'Don's plan?'

I shake my head. I love Don, but historically that man was only interested in ideas that might win him a Nobel Prize, and over the past few months, his interests have understandably narrowed to even more immediate concerns. 'Don's been preoccupied lately.'

'Right, his wife. Very sad,' Andreas says. There's a pause that's either respectful or awkward – I can't tell which. 'But do *you* think the corporate module is sexy enough?'

'Is... *sexy* the goal? The corporate module gets the app into people's hands, where it can help them.'

Andreas pushes up his linen sleeves, revealing skinny arms. 'Okay, but what would you do with Tranquillity if there were no limits?'

I squint. 'Limits like the need to keep paying our staff?'

'Come on, just ideate with me. Blue sky.'

I lean back. 'Why are you asking me?' The one the board thinks has no *fresh ideas*, apparently.

'Come now. Don speaks very highly of you.'

My eyes drift out of the window, to the London-grey sky through the trees. I could just run outside. I could literally just grab my bag and leave. Get on a train to Bruges. Go and have some stereotype menopausal *Eat Pray Love* experience across the Continent. Pick up pottery and an Italian lover. Never come back.

'Personalised meditations,' I say finally. 'Today, Tranquillity is essentially an audio library. Our only edge is having better meditations than our competitors.' *Because I insisted we hire actual meditation experts to write them*, I don't add. 'There's never been anything particularly innovative about the tech itself. But what if we used natural language models to create exactly the meditation you need, in that moment? Imagine opening the app to a prompt – "Tell me what's on your mind?" The user records some audio. Our system analyses the text for key themes and suggests something from our library. Christ, with what you can do with large language models these days, we could generate a custom script on the fly, just for you, exactly what you need to hear right now. A meditation app that actually listens to you.'

Andreas leans forward. 'That's brilliant.'

'It's really not,' I sigh, plummeting back to earth. 'It's entirely impractical. The safety risks are mind-boggling. It would get us into a whole new regulation category with the CQC. We'd lose our NHS endorsement. We'd need to hire AI experts, clinical advisers, MLOps engineers. We'd have to commission a new effectiveness trial, which would take years, by which time whatever AI models we'd used would already be obsolete. We'd need to run the models locally to protect user data, which means building infrastructure that none of our current team has the faintest clue how to manage. We'd basically have to refocus the entire company on building something that might never work.'

'It's a moonshot,' Andreas says, his eyes shining.

'It's a fancy,' I shoot back. Maybe my problem is that I know too much to be visionary. Or I'm missing the specific form of arrogance which presumes that the reason something's never been done before is that no one else has ever thought of it; when, mostly, the reason something hasn't been done before is that if you really think about it, it's a stupid thing to do.

Andreas contemplates me over his tiny stinking teacup. 'Don says you've been here a long time.'

'From the beginning.'

'And you're the Chief Product Officer, right?'

'As of yesterday.'

'And what is that, exactly?'

Huh? I can't figure out if this is a veiled insult. 'The normal... I... define the roadmap, manage the product managers...'

'Oh, I see, like a *project* manager.'

'No, that's...' And it dawns on me. 'You haven't worked at a tech company before.'

He grins. 'Guilty. I ran a creative consultancy. Branding, experience design, trend forecasting. Spent a few years studying mime in

Étampes in my twenties. I think they wanted a real outsider. Fresh ideas, you know.'

Can you actually crush your own teeth with just your jaw muscles? So this is what the board wanted instead of me. A literal clown.

But hope bobs like a dumpling in my simmering fury. The engineers don't suffer fools. It's taken me years to earn their respect. Accumulate favours, understand the intricacies of the tech stack, plot each staff member's individual motivations. This poor man won't last a month.

All I need to do is wait for him to fail. Bring my A-game, keep holding this place together. Easy... as long as I have no more weird wardrobe malfunctions, no more public hot flushes, no more uncharacteristic bouts of rage. I'll show them how ready I am. I'll show them my *fresh ideas*, if that's what it takes. I'll work harder than anyone, harder than I have before. It's not over yet.

Standing, I murmur something about needing to reply to some emails.

'Oh, by the way. You brought the pastries yesterday, right?' Andreas asks casually, just as my hand is on the doorknob.

'Yes, but—' I start to explain that it was a once-off thing for Don's retirement. The pastries are his favourite.

'Next week, let's try a fruit platter. Avoid that mid-morning sugar crash.'

Great. *Great*. So now I'm a project manager and the fucking errand girl too.

I force a smile at him.

It's just me baring my teeth.

Shortness of Breath

◐

Brenda

The bloke who opens the door is red-eyed. The smell of cooking oil clings to him, someone who's spent many long hours over a fryer. He introduces himself as Jin, squeezes my hand tight, says he's so grateful I've come.

Two others are waiting on mismatched settees in the cramped lounge, cradling tea in chipped mugs. A man and a woman. All three are late thirties, early forties – too old for flatshares, but that's how it is these days, isn't it?

Jin bustles off to make tea, and the room slowly fades into focus as I remove my skiing sunglasses and my eyes adjust to the light. It's a proper patchwork of a place – shabby, but they've made an effort. House plants, bookshelves that look like they were rescued from the pavement. Someone's a painter, because there are cheeky oil portraits everywhere, stuck up with Command strips, nothing to threaten a renter's deposit. A Deliveroo jacket hangs by the door next to a knock-off fur coat. There are signs, everywhere, of the elaborate household mythology they've built up around the cat. His name is on the chore chart, his duties listed as 'make biscuits' and 'lick own bum'. A framed photograph above the radiator proclaims him Housemate of the Week for being a 'fancy boy'. Half the lounge is claimed by a ceiling-high cat tree. Useless now.

'You're the investigator?' the other man asks. The skin around his nose is red and inflamed.

I hesitate, casting my mind back over the Facebook messages and realise nothing I said actually indicated that Melek was my cat. The tone of the replies, *Can you help? Please, can you help?* Finally, I nod. These poor sods just want to believe that someone cares. And it's not a lie, exactly. I am, after all, *investigating*. They're just a couple of streets away from me. Whatever killed their cat might have killed Melek, too.

'Are you with the council?' the woman asks, eyes scanning my clothing. I'm wearing my DVLA interview skirt again, thank heavens, rather than the ratty housedress I usually live in these days.

'Private,' I mumble. They glance at each other, but don't ask any more questions.

'We found him by the bins outside,' the woman tells me, once Jin's returned with my tea.

'Who found him?' I ask, pulling out the notebook I keep my shopping lists in, trying to look more official. Cheery text on the cover admonishes me to BE A BOSSBITCH, godawful, but it was the only option at WH Smith. I hold it over the skirt hem so they don't see the mud stains from yesterday.

They talk me through the details. Mr Bojangles was mutilated, some of him is missing. Yes, they're sure it couldn't have been a car. It happened the same night Melek was killed, 31 August. It must have been after 2 a.m. because Jin fed the cat when he got home from his shift. The woman, Marta, found the body just after six. Narrows the window. They posted on their street's WhatsApp group asking if anyone saw anything, which is how they heard the neighbour's guinea pigs had also been killed. Same night.

I ask if I can see the cat, expecting someone to pull out their phone to show me a photo. But Marta waves me through to the kitchen and pulls a sad lump from the salad drawer of the fridge. 'We didn't know what else to do with him.'

The parcel is a supermarket plastic bag containing something wrapped in a bedsheet, floral once, now tie-dyed in red-brown. 'We thought somebody would... would take him, or the police...' Her eyes meet mine, pleading. Some people haven't seen enough of the world to know how little to expect, yet.

'That's why I'm here,' I say, hoping I sound more bolshy than I feel.

She lays the body gently on the kitchen table before excusing herself, mopping tears from her cheeks. 'Sorry. I can't see him again.' She vanishes back to the sitting room, leaving me with the lump of cold meat on the table.

I tug the fabric at one end, revealing a delicate face. He's small, half Melek's size, playing the dandy in a neat tuxedo coat. His eyes are closed, peaceful. He might be asleep, but for the way his head seems like it's been pulled into the chest, like a turtle retracting into a shell.

Working slowly, I unwrap the rest of him. A huge chunk has been taken out of his back, scooped clean away.

I have to swallow the bile rising in my throat, and allow my void to blur it out for a moment, before leaning closer. What would Paul look for? I probe the edges of the hole, careful of the jutting rib shards. Yes, there: a puncture wound, just like on Melek. Similarly huge. Too big to be the canine tooth of any animal left on this soggy island. Maybe someone went through him with a wooden stake? But Paul seemed so sure they were tooth marks.

I take some photographs before wrapping him up again and sliding the bundle into the plastic shopping bag, fury flaring hot in my knuckles.

'I want my vet to look at him,' I say, returning to the sitting room.

'Will we get him back?' the man asks, alarmed.

'Of course,' I say, resisting rolling my eyes. What are they going to do, embalm him and build a bloody tomb in their postage-stamp-sized concreted garden? Dead is dead.

They give me the address of the guinea pig owner, a few doors down. Jin sees me out, thanking me, eyes fixed on the shopping bag the whole time. He hesitates around the doorway. 'You haven't mentioned a fee,' he says finally.

'Oh,' I say, taken aback. 'No, it's not like that.'

He thanks me again, but he seems confused, and suddenly a little wary. Everything's money money money these days. I promise to give him a ring once Paul's done with the cat.

The guinea pig owners aren't home, but their uninterested cleaner waves me through a side alley to the back garden, if that's what you can term this jumble of broken children's toys lost in long grass. I must look a sight – a crumpled old bat lugging around a cat corpse in a Sainsbury's bag – but she doesn't seem bothered.

The wooden door separating the garden from the alley is undamaged. No bolt on it. I can't see any obvious holes in the fence, but I'll have to whack through the undergrowth to be sure. There's a clear route from here to Mr Bojangles's garden, assuming this dog can leap over six-foot-high fencing. A wooden hutch towers over a long run made from chicken wire, extending along the side fence.

'Where did they find the bodies?' I turn to ask the cleaner, but she's already gone back into the house.

I peer through the chicken wire, putting on my ski glasses and looking askew to get it in my better peripheral vision. The bodies are gone, but there are two clumps of fur and blood which clearly mark where they were.

Something isn't right about the scene, though. I sidle slowly up the wire, running my hands methodically up and down the run, searching for a hole. I check the corners for gaps. Nothing – it's solid, intact. No holes in the fence behind it either, as far as I can see.

I slide the latch back and forth. It's fiddly, delicate. How would an animal get in there without damaging anything? It requires human dexterity, human fingers. No way some dog did this. Not by itself, anyway.

I try to marshal my thoughts. I've seen enough police procedurals on the telly. If I *was* a private investigator, I'd go door to door, talk to neighbours, ask if anyone saw anything. I'd report each killing to the police – they won't bloody do anything, but we need the paper trail. I'd go down to the high street and ask the local vagrants if anyone's seen someone with a huge dog walking around. I'd put up posters, ask for witnesses on Facebook.

Hours and hours of tedious work.

But it just so happens that I'm retired, I can't bloody drive anywhere, and *Coronation Street* isn't on until eight.

I pick up the plastic bag from the grass, feeling the weight of poor Mr Bojangles shift in my grip. I think of Jin's message: *Please, can you help?* Maybe I can.

Yes, you sicko, I think, *I'm coming for you.*

Insatiable Hunger

●

Ellie

Here is what Andreas has accomplished in his first two weeks as Tranquillity's CEO:

- Forced the whole company to endure a three-hour-long 'Inspiration Jam' which consisted of him free-associating in front of meaningless Venn diagrams about Kurdish dance, machine learning and John Lennon.
- Asked Trilbi, a senior back-end engineer, to take minutes in a meeting.
- Consistently called Lanying 'Lauren' despite several corrections.
- Showed up in random meetings uninvited to spout nonsense phrases like 'We need to create the Uber of happiness' and 'Let's take a human-centred approach to this'.
- Complimented our Black British CFO's English.
- Asked the engineering team if we could move the entire app onto the blockchain.
- Decided that the top priority six weeks before Demo Day, with the company on the edge of bankruptcy, is to launch a major TV advertising campaign.

What I've done, in Andreas's first two weeks as CEO, is the same thing I've always done: run the fucking company.

I'm hiding in Don's treehouse, putting together a presentation for this afternoon's board meeting. The rest of the office stinks of sweat and cleaning materials in a way I cannot bear today – add to List: *Ask the cleaning team why they changed products.* But this room still smells of Don, like leather and camphor, like his Mercedes.

He hasn't removed his personal things yet. There's the photo of the two of us at the MedTech Innovation Awards four years ago. It's shocking how much younger I look – three stone lighter, in a halter dress showing off a delicate neck. These days, it's more like something a tropical bird would inflate to woo a mate, a loose wattle of skin that wobbles when I talk.

In the frame, Don's arm loops around my shoulders, pulling our foreheads close in a conspiratorial pose. In his thank-you speech, he called me his Golden Girl. It would have rankled from anyone else, but from Don it just felt sweetly old-fashioned.

Don's 'Science of Happiness' module was the most oversubscribed course at the University of East Anglia. I was a jaded third-year drama student with the insufferable habit of pontificating about how happiness is a bourgeois concept, but I was also ready to try anything to stop my persistent panic attacks. Don – then in his early thirties – already seemed ancient to us, the rangy, freckled, Scottish-accented professor every undergrad had a massive crush on. I, of course, joined their ranks, partly because (unlike some other professors who'd been warned not to shut their doors if a student was in the office) Don was so clearly devoted to Inez. He mentioned her name at least four times in every class (we kept count), so the crushes were safe. It felt like part of our education, getting to practise adoring a worthy full-grown man in total safety, in contrast to the messy flings we were having with people our own age.

These days, everyone and their corporate HR department is completely sold on the benefits of meditation, but back then it was still considered woo-woo hippie nonsense barely tolerated in a university lecture hall. Don was involved in some of the earliest lab studies, back in the mid-nineties, where they put test subjects in fMRI machines and watched their brains as they were exposed to negative stimuli in the form of electric shocks to their bare feet sticking out the bottom, as Don liked to recount with mischief in his eyes. The test subjects who'd been given meditation training reported less pain. The really spooky thing, though, was that their fMRIs told a different story: the pain centres of meditating brains light up more strongly than the non-meditating brains. The difference, Don explained, seems to be that the *narrative* parts of the brain don't get as involved. You feel the pain more, but it bothers you less. 'You can learn to endure distress,' Don said to a room of rapt undergrads. 'You can learn to feel indifferent to your own suffering.'

And to me, whose whole life up until that point had been defined by the weight of my mother's depression, and increasingly my own, this seemed nothing short of the promise of salvation.

I bought him a pair of goldfish at the end of that term, a nod to his metaphor about how you can't see the water you swim in. One ate the other then promptly died of food poisoning, but the gift made me memorable enough that Don hired me over that summer to help him transcribe a dozen interviews with terminally sick patients, which I later turned into a one-woman show for the Edinburgh Fringe, and afterwards we stayed friends for – fuck – I guess a quarter century now.

I realise I'm missing him. Add to List: *Ask if he and Inez are up for a visit.* I could suggest meeting up on the Heath for a swim: Inez is evangelical about how the pond water can transform you. I've never made the time.

I brush crumbs off my broken keyboard. My irritation with Andreas has transformed into a hole at the pit of my stomach that no quantity of crisps seems able to plug. I'm ravenous. Probably perimenopause? *Probably Perimenopause* could be the title of my memoir at this point.

For once, my phone is on silent and stuffed deep in the bottom of my bag, and I'm on a roll. I can see the shape of the business with a clarity that's eluded me for ages. I list every major achievement from the past six months – the six months when I've essentially been in charge. Yes, we're low on cash, but the rest? Every graph, trending upwards. User feedback, gushing. The corporate module, two sprints ahead of schedule. Nothing *visionary*, sure, but bloody effective. I don't hold back or imply any false modesty. I've been killing it. It's all here, in black and white and Tranquillity-brand green.

It can't undo hiring Andreas, but it must be enough to make the board understand how badly they've erred.

Climbing down the ladder, laptop tucked under my arm, I'm so engrossed in a fantasy that I'll take the board through this deck, wait until they give me a standing ovation, and then quit in a blaze of –

Falling.

One moment I'm stretching my foot down to the next rung. The next, my leg doesn't quite reach. My hand misses the rail. Like my brain has suddenly forgotten what shape my body is.

Thump. Right on the coccyx. I haven't tumbled far, just a metre or two. Pain blinds me, hot and white.

Changes in depth perception, altered spatial awareness – more symptoms? The blogs say many perimenopausal women start finding mysterious bumps and scratches on their body, but it's nothing to worry about. I palpate my lower back, feeling the beginning of a few new bruises to join the ones on my ego.

I'm still limping when I bump into Andreas as we go into the aggressively bland boardroom for the meeting. 'The Bored Room' as the sign on the door announces it, designed to be a parody version of a corporate meeting room, from the popcorn ceilings to the maroon carpets to the cheesy motivational posters on the walls. Only, as Tranquillity's expanded, the boundaries between parody and reality have blurred. Now the whiteboard holds some attempts at defining a new vision statement from the morning's ad campaign meeting ('To democratise holistic well-being') which isn't radically different to the deliberately meaningless fake vision statement poster Don had made as ironic decor ('unleash your potential'). Live long enough, and we all become the stereotype of ourselves.

I'm texting Lanying about three baby emergencies in the engineering team when Andreas loops onto my elbow in an overfamiliar greeting. 'I've been reflecting on our conversation,' he says.

I'm taken aback, wondering if he's actually come round on the corporate module, but the rest of the board starts filing in before he can continue. That would be just like him, I seethe, ruining my perfectly enjoyable sulk with an apology.

The board members greet Andreas with some coolness. I wonder at this. Didn't they fight Don hard to appoint him as CEO? Maybe they're as unimpressed with his first two weeks as I am. They greet me like nothing's wrong, and before I know it, I've slipped into easy conversation asking after their kids and wives and girlfriends and polycule partners. All the while wondering which of them spoke out against me, which of them made the case that I'm not good enough for the job.

There are no other women here. And I'm not even on the board, I just get invited to the meetings because I'm the only one who can talk about the minutiae of the business. It's not from lack of trying: we've had female board members before, it's just that none of them stick around. It's a problem the whole tech industry faces. There was a brief reform push in those more innocent pre-2016 years when Sheryl Sandberg was telling everyone the solution was just to *Lean In!*, and tech companies all hired diversity officers and sponsored Girls in STEM boot camps. The mask fell off sometime around 2018. These days the big tech companies increasingly embrace their true identities: cults to petulant billionaires who have amassed more power than ancient kings.

The statistics say that over half of women in data and tech leave the industry by the mid-point of our career, and I refuse to be another casualty. What's happening in these rooms is too important to leave to people obsessed with Andrew Huberman, long-termism and Brazilian jiu-jitsu.

Our deputy chair, Uri, the human incarnation of a Patagonia gilet, opens the meeting with an apology from Don. 'They've got a doctor's appointment,' he says. 'Between us, I don't think it will be long now.'

We all leave a respectful few seconds before we dive into the business update. My spine is throbbing as I start the presentation, but my mind feels clear. Confident. I adjust my imaginary orange, roll my shoulders back and flash my best smile, then dive into my deck, the tour through how hard I've worked, how successful I've guided us to be. I make eye contact with each of them in turn. *See, you bastards*, I try to beam the subtext into each of their brains. *It should have been me.*

Andreas barely says a word, just watches my performance, his curls growing increasingly wild every time he runs his hand through them. He's got a food stain on the sleeve of his jumper and he's inexplicably wearing a hi-vis vest. I almost pity him.

Almost.

They applaud when I'm done, and it's *nearly* the standing ovation of my fantasies. I catch a few of them casting meaningful looks at each other.

Finally, Uri clears his throat and turns the conversation to Andreas. 'Tell us about your first few weeks. Any insights?'

Andreas leans forward. Simpering smile on his face. 'I've been listening, observing. It's a hell of a business you've built. Everyone is very full of passion. Ellie's been a real help talking me through the intricacies of the product. I see why Don said he couldn't run the business without her.'

'Are we feeling confident about Demo Day?' James asks.

'Fairly. I think we could go bigger.' He winks at me.

Here it comes, I think. He's going to say something spectacularly uninformed and they'll realise their new emperor's in the buff. It's hard work to keep the smile off my face.

Andreas leans back with a languid ease. 'Well, as good as the content library is, right now we're not making use of cutting-edge innovations. If we're honest, the app's not much more than a set of glorified Spotify playlists. If we want to really disrupt mental health, we need to be thinking about personalisation.'

My mouth falls open. Surely not.

He holds up his iPad, where he's loaded a mock-up of our interface, everything stripped away except for a microphone icon and a prompt, *What's on your mind?* 'I had one of the designers whip this up. We can't fall behind on artificial intelligence. You should see what can be done these days, chatbots generating voices which sound completely human. Imagine our customers telling us what's bothering them, and we could use an AI voice to tell them exactly what to do about it. Real-time adaptive emotional intelligence. A guru in the palm of your hands; an app that actually listens to you.' Andreas meets my eyes as he says this. I'm gobsmacked. He's taken it basically word for word out of my mouth.

The board is rapt. 'I was reading in *Fast Company* that celebrities are licensing their voices to AI companies now,' says Tom, the legal guy. 'You could discuss your deepest problems with Harrison Ford.'

'We could make it interactive, offer full digital therapy,' adds Uri. I start to tell him that we already looked into that months ago, that the models are still janky and the CQC will never green-light it, but they've already moved on to riffing about recreating your dead relatives' voices so that you can resolve your issues with them, which I'm pretty sure is literally the plot of a *Black Mirror* episode.

'It's brilliant,' James says finally.

'I actually can't take the credit,' Andreas says. 'All these ideas come from the team you built, I was just listening. And they have more. Ellie, why don't you tell them about the... the corporate thing?'

My mouth is dry. The room is distorting at the edges. There's a ringing in my ears, and... *not fucking now*... a fire building in my torso.

'We've been building a new corporate module,' I say at last. Blank stares from around the table.

Andreas gestures at me to go on.

I start talking about how mental health issues are estimated to cost the economy £45 billion annually in lost productivity, but all my carefully researched stats have suddenly vanished from my brain. The board's eyes glaze over as I ramble. James holds his phone out to Uri under the table, and Uri gives a silent chuckle at whatever he sees there. Tom opens his laptop and starts typing something. I talk myself into silence, my cheeks hot. Livid.

I have no idea what happens in the rest of the meeting. I sit frozen, a silent pillar of fury with a slow flush creeping up my body, inch by inch.

Andreas comes up to me as the others file out, giving my elbow another friendly squeeze. 'That went so well!' he whispers.

I could smash his stupid tortoiseshell glasses into his smug stupid face. 'That was my idea.'

'I said it was?' He looks honestly confused. And he did, sort of. But it's him they were cheering on. Him they'll remember as having come up with it. 'Ellie, I was trying to help! See, if we work together, we can get it done, everything you want.'

I'm shaking as I pack away my laptop. My phone buzzes wildly. I glance at it to see that the three baby emergencies I was texting Lanying about have since reached puberty, joined a gang and received their first ASBOs. And Mo's telling me something about the cat having vomited on the bed again.

The others are lingering by the stairs. 'We're heading to the pub,' says Tom, slapping his arm around Andreas's shoulder. 'Join us.'

'Oh, twist my rubber arm,' Andreas grins.

'I can't,' I say, trying to figure out how I'm going to solve the work disasters, get the cat sick out of the mattress, feed Yusuf his dinner, and manage to be in Andreas's presence for one more second without twisting his obnoxious vest into a noose.

'Sorry to hear it, Ellie!' But they're already halfway down the stairs. Uri cracks a loud innuendo about AI porn.

As they walk off, a tiny voice whispers from the depths of me:
You could just rip their throats out, all of them.

The exchange with Andreas replays in my mind over and over throughout the evening. I come up with a thousand retorts I wish I'd thrown at him. In my head, I tell him how manipulative it was to frame my idea as his, how audacious it is to believe that his ignorance about our field is a strength, how the very least he could do barging into our business would be to show a little fucking humility. I continue this imaginary fight with him through my commute home, through dinner and my post-dinner CrossFit class (where at least I am able to punctuate some of my imagined wittier retorts with some actual punches to his imaginary face), through putting Yusuf and finally myself to bed.

It's like an ache in my stomach, a chomping, gnawing mouth eating me up from the inside.

I find myself sitting on the kitchen floor sometime after midnight, steadily working my way through the contents of the fridge.

The family therapist gave us a number of rules. Never make comments about other people's body weight, positive or negative. Never discuss portion sizes or calories. No low-calorie or diet foods allowed in the house. Do a family activity after the meal to try to distract her from purging or exercising. Never restrict or moralise foods. Model healthy, intuitive eating for Paige.

And of course, the minute Paige moved out, I went on a kitchen blitz and threw out anything remotely resembling junk food. I'm sorry, I know this may make me a failure of a feminist, but it's just a fact that thin women are paid more money, are treated with more respect, receive better health care. It's also true that I've gone up three dress sizes since I turned forty, and any carbohydrate I so much as make eyes at immediately rents a van and moves into my belly. You're supposed to pretend you care about being healthy, but let's be real, health looks like size 10 and a tight arse. I've worked hard convincing myself that I honestly just prefer kale to crisps, that a cheeky spoonful of hummus drizzled on top is a real indulgence.

But tonight, none of those carefully nurtured delusions are holding up. Tonight, I'm fucking ravenous.

I've already smashed through Mo's dinner leftovers, and there's nothing else vaguely snack-shaped in the cupboards. Instead, I find:

- A large tub of Greek yogurt, which I scoop directly into my mouth with my fingers.
- A punnet of sweet Rosa tomatoes, plucked off the vine, each one bursting between my teeth like eyeballs.
- The remnants of various condiments and relishes, some long past their best-before date: heaped spoonfuls of

tahini and tamarind relish and Dijon mustard and harissa paste and fig jam and miso, jars scraped dry.
- A bunch of asparagus I eat raw, gnawing through the thick stems until I swallow the whole fibrous masticated mass in a single chunk that almost chokes me.
- A litre of almond milk, slugged straight from the carton.
- Two lemons eaten whole, with the skin.
- A pack of wild-caught Scottish salmon, which slips buttery down my throat and coats my fingers in oil.

I barely pause to draw breath. It feels like there is some deficiency in my blood, some craving that nothing in this kitchen will satisfy. I try everything. I slug triple-pressed olive oil. I get into the spice drawer, sprinkle paprika directly on my tongue, crunch tiny mustard and coriander seeds between my molars, numb my tongue with cloves. It's not enough. Still, my body screams at me, *more, more*.

My stomach twists and distends, burning bile creeping up my oesophagus. Finally, all I can shove in is two zopiclones and half a bottle of Malbec, which is enough to send me into a restless sleep on the sofa.

Burning Tongue

●

Brenda

Thursday mid-morning shouldn't be prime time to see the vet, but Paul's waiting room is crammed as always. Few of Paul's patients have nine-to-fives to worry about, I suppose. On top of the usual poorly cats and dogs, there's a bloke seated next to me with a chicken on his shoulder. Deeper in the building, a dog howls. Dodo's ears are perked in concern, his scraggle of fur entirely flat against one side of his head in a canine bedhead, making him look even more lopsided than usual.

Paul's already examined eight bodies for me. Melek, Mr Bojangles, the guinea pigs and two other neighbourhood cats – all attacked on the same night, all with the same impossibly huge puncture marks on them. Then two others since: a dead Jack Russell who turned out to have eaten insecticide, and a tabby crushed by a lorry. Unrelated.

A ninth body lies in the carpet bag at my feet. A fat ginger tomcat who was found this morning in South Woodford. The owners saw my number on a poster I put up in their vet's window. The cat's got a broken neck and a long gash up his side, no puncture wounds on him that I could see, but the gash might be something; a knife, a machete. They found the body on the side of the road, so there's every chance he was also hit by a car. But he was found just a few miles away from here, so I've got to be sure.

Over the past two weeks, I've learned more than I ever wanted to know about animal serial killers. Country's rife with them, apparently, each one named after their hunting grounds. The Brighton Cat Killer stabbed sixteen cats before he was caught on video. The Northampton Cat Killer strangled and dismembered them, left them on the owners' doorsteps – he got seven before he was arrested for arson. The Norwich Cat Killer liked to mutilate them – cut off ears, slash their abdomens – went through dozens before he was finally caught, after he bludgeoned an old man to death with a hammer. That one liked to track the owners afterwards: he collected their Facebook posts, their missing cat posters. 'Zoosadism', they call it. It's one of the best signs someone's going to graduate to hurting people. I could tell you all about that, actually. I had a dog once, a sweet little dachshund named Sausage Roll, until my shithead ex… well. Less said about him, the better.

So you'd think the police would take it more seriously. But no, here I am, trying to catch the Walthamstow Cat-and-Guinea-Pig Killer with nothing but a pile of posters, rotten eyesight and a bag full of dead cat.

Seven people have been called into Paul's office since I arrived, each dog stopping to give the carpet bag a curious sniff as it passed. After days spent marching up and down the high street with my posters, my body is a tangle of pain. Exasperated, I wave at the receptionist.

'Oi, I've been here for two hours.'

'Sorry, Brenda. It's mad today. He'll see you when he's got a gap.'

But when a man with an overweight husky is called ahead of me, I decide I've had enough, and follow him into the consulting room, playing deaf to the receptionist's protests.

Paul starts shaking his head before I've even had a chance to say anything. 'Brenda, I'm sorry. Living patients have to come first.' He shepherds me back into reception, where every other occupant is suddenly staring at the floor.

I push the carpet bag at him. 'Just tell me if this one has bite marks.'

He doesn't accept the corpse. His voice is gentle but firm. 'I can't examine every dead animal in London,' he says, before returning to the husky, the door clicking closed behind him.

'Don't you even care?' I scream at the door, which does not reply.

I ask the receptionist if I can leave the body with her, if maybe she can ask Paul to take a look when he's finished his appointments for the day. Her nose wrinkles in disgust, eyes fixed on the bag. 'Try the council,' is all the advice she can offer.

'The council,' I spit back at her. 'I'd have more luck asking Dodo to do an autopsy.'

Someone in the waiting room mutters, 'Mad old bat.'

Defeated, I haul the bag home. The two bloody steps up to my flat feel like scaling Everest.

I stuff the carpet bag into my freezer and collapse into my bed, knees propped up on a hot-water bottle. But this is no time for loafing. I open my laptop on a laminate bed tray and head to the neighbourhood Facebook group, ready to post a photo of the ginger moggy and ask if anyone's seen anything. The comments on my other posts have grown increasingly anxious. *Another one. Should we be worried?*

But the group's gone. Unsearchable.

Blocked.

After ten minutes refreshing the page and swearing at the screen, I discover a message from an admin. *Hi Brenda. We've had to remove you from the group. Our inbox is full of frightened pet owners. Please take this somewhere else.*

Take it where? Doesn't matter. Away. *Where it's not our problem*, always the subtext.

Somewhere else.

Somewhere else.

Fine.

I take a swig of cod liver oil straight from the bottle. Click *Create Group*.

Catch the Walthamstow Cat-and-Guinea-Pig Killer? Too blunt.

The Feline Revenge Society? *Cat Legion Around Walthamstow*?

Citizens Against Tabby Slaughter?

Perfect.

Stuff them. I've always had this fury burning in me, with nowhere to go. Maybe this is the war I've been waiting for my whole life.

But a war needs an army. And this carpet-bag body of mine isn't going to be enough.

Within twelve hours, CATS has twenty members. Within twenty-four, there are 120. Dead pets, it seems, garner more sympathy than suffering humans. The notifications become a relentless pinging metronome on my phone.

Feeling hopeful despite myself, I schedule the first meeting for Monday 6 p.m. Fifteen people RSVP. I blow a tenner at Lidl on pastry platters and extra milk for tea, arranging them on every inch of flat surface in my lounge. The flat hasn't had visitors in years, so I spend the whole day scrubbing. Dust bunnies the size of llamas are evicted. Towers of fag ends are demolished. A layer of grime as thick as my thumb is scraped off the window.

With so many volunteers, I think, we'll blanket the borough in posters, knock on every door. Somewhere, somehow, we'll shake out a clue.

But six o'clock comes and goes. So does six ten. Six fifteen. By half past there are only two volunteers sitting in my living room. And isn't that just people for you?

Reggie. Retired security guard. Broad shoulders hunching over a wasted frame like a tortoise shell. Looks like he's got lost on the way to the pub.

Deborah. Slim. Fifties. Grey bob. Voice as posh and flat as the BBC Shipping Forecast. Seems to be involved in every single bleeding-heart animal charity in Greater London.

Teach me to get my hopes up.

Deborah perches primly on the edge of the settee like she's worried she might catch some disease. Are they judging the flat? The patched settee?

'Didn't expect the Ritz, I hope,' I snap, handing her a mug. Chipped.

'It's very homely,' Deborah says.

Homely, bloody cheek. I clamp my jaw shut. No sense chasing off the only two recruits who've shown up.

'Well, we'd best crack on,' I announce at six forty-five. I pass each of them a map of the borough, showing every suspected murder as a round dot. I'd optimistically printed fifty, just in case, in full colour. Cost a fortune.

'When were they killed?' Deborah asks, perusing the map like it's a menu.

'These five were all 31st of August,' I say. 'The ginger tomcat was earlier this week.'

'But we're not sure the ginger was the same person?' Deborah asks.

'We can't be sure.' I'm not going to admit to them that Paul can't be bothered to take a look.

'Forget the ginger, then,' Reggie grunts, flipping his map over as though checking for answers on the back.

I bite my tongue. They wouldn't be so glib if they'd met the poor ginger's owners, an Albanian family whose little boy had sobbed so hard he could barely breathe when I went to see them. But Reggie's right, the ginger's an outlier.

'That's quite the murder spree for a single night,' Deborah muses, tracing a manicured nail across the dots. 'Are you're sure it wasn't foxes?'

'It's not foxes.' I slap a photo onto the table. Melek. Blood pooling on Harriet's doorstep. 'They've been ripped up, not eaten. This is… cruelty.'

Deborah looks at the photo, then at me. 'Why are you doing this?'

Pain lances up my spine. My mouth moves before my brain can catch up. 'You don't want to be here, there's the bloody door.'

I can't see her expression, but I hear her scandalised shifting on the settee.

'I don't mean to offend you,' she says. 'I'm just trying to understand your connection to this.'

The cramp eases. I breathe out, slow.

'That was my cat,' I say. I rub the thin scar that twists between my forefinger and my thumb. The metal screw jabs into my knuckle. 'And because shitheads think they can get away with anything.'

She seems satisfied with this. I hand them each a stack of pamphlets and instructions to give them to anyone who's out late at night. Street cleaners, shift workers, taxi drivers, insomniacs. 'Talk to anyone you can, ask if they know of any animal deaths, get them to join the Facebook group. Otherwise, just keep an eye out, ring me if you see anything odd.'

'Odd like what?' Reggie asks.

'People skulking about,' I say. 'Carrying strange tools. Someone with a big dog. But don't engage. This bloke might be a nutter. Just observe. Record. Report.'

Deborah frowns, tapping her nail on the map. 'I'm surprised there's no CCTV footage.'

I blink. 'CCTV?'

'Well, of course,' she says. 'This is London. Every inch of it's on camera. Smart doorbells, street cameras, buses. Surely someone's got footage?'

I scowl, passing out pastries to cover my awkwardness. Here I've been so busy pinning posters to lamp posts like it's 1987. A whole city of eyes, better eyes than mine, and I haven't thought to check a single one.

'People might feel more inclined to help you if you were nicer to them, you know,' Deborah says, picking the crust off a cheese puff.

I don't bother to dignify that with a response.

Thinning Hair
●
Ellie

I am diligent about logging my symptoms into the menopause app. So far:

- My nails have become so thick that regular nail clippers are now useless to me; I've had to buy something that looks like a pair of pliers and is designed to cut the nails of large dogs.
- My vagina is going through an avant-garde Jackson Pollock phase, producing a never-ending exhibition of red splatter on the canvas of my clothing, and even managing to find its way onto surprising places, like the hems of my trousers.
- I'm constantly hungry, but any food I eat turns to paint stripper in my stomach and spends the next hour sloughing around my oesophagus. The only exception to this is red meat, so I've broken twenty years of guilty attempted pescatarianism and am now subsisting on a diet of plain minute steaks. I have so far managed to conceal this from Paige, although Mo is thrilled by the simpler dinner duties.
- Smells and sounds have been dialled up to eleven, which is unfortunate, since I live in a city famous for car fumes, shrieking trains and rotting garbage overflowing from bins.
- I'm covered in mystery bruises.

- My legs ache.
- My spine aches.
- My belly aches.
- My cunt aches. I can feel my clitoris retract into my body when Mo so much as looks at me, like an anxious snail.
- And the obvious: everything makes me angry. Especially the clitoris thing.

Ah, but there are over two hundred potential symptoms of perimenopause, nothing to worry about, according to the unhelpfully cheerful menopause app on my phone, which I have thrown against the wall several times.

But the strangest symptom is the hair.

I thought I was done with hair removal for the rest of my life. Lasered it off every part of my body below my eyelashes in my early thirties. Twelve sessions with a severe Polish beautician, £200 a pop, bright flashes of pain along my crotch and underarms and legs until it was all gone – my final solution to maintaining the little-girl smoothness I've carefully cultivated since I was sixteen. That was the mortifying year I went swimming with my cousins in Norfolk when one of them pointed at the hairs escaping my bikini and said it looked like I was smuggling a giant tarantula down there.

Now, it's sprung back. Long dark hairs, creeping their way into the hollow of my groin. Hairs marching down my thighs, one or two brave scouts beginning an encampment around my knees. Hairs peeking from the trenches of my armpits. Hairs marching in a line down from my belly button. Hairs jeering boldly from my chin. Unruly.

I buy an at-home laser wand. It becomes a nightly ritual, scouring my body for errant shafts, gunning them off, pew pew.

By morning, they've grown back. Thickened. Brought friends.

I email the manufacturer complaining that the machine is faulty and doesn't seem to be properly killing the root. They apologise and send me a replacement, which I return again, insisting on a refund because their £600 product is still failing me. The customer care agent accidentally copies me on an internal email to another girl at the support desk. Subject: *Karen of the month?*

I make a list of potential solutions:

- Epilation
- IPL
- Nair
- Dermaplaning
- Razors
- Wax
- Trimmers
- Bleach
- Self-induced radiation poisoning

Instead, I take to plucking them out with tweezers after every shower, one by one. There is something pleasurable in the pain, the self-punishment, the taming. The hairs are dark, but softer and straighter than pubic hair usually is. I pinch one between my thumb and forefinger and hold it up to the bare globe in my bathroom. Light glows through the shaft, striped in rich autumn browns and greys.

One person who is decisively thrilled by my new hirsutism? Mo.

He catches a glimpse of it as I'm changing into pyjamas, just a brief flash between yanking off my work skirt and pulling up my Buscemis. A raw hunger comes over his face which I haven't seen in years, and before I can say a word, he's wrestling me onto the bed, octopusing me with insistent limbs, his curious hands questing across my hips and thighs.

When his fingers brush my bush, it elicits a sharp rattling exhale. He combs through my new pelt, wrapping his fingers in, tugging gently. 'You've been keeping secrets,' he murmurs, kissing a pathway down to the edge of my knickers.

I make a token protest, thinking of my poor aching cunt, reminding him it's not our date night, and there are too many things on my

List, the door's not even locked, and Artie needs his dinner... then allow myself to melt back onto the pillows as his strong baker's hands begin to knead and roll the dough of me to life.

Mo loves to go down on me. He can gladly burrow down there for half an hour in a well-practised choreography. He resists my suggestions that he should get up and fuck me already. Mo's real kink is feeling like a good person.

I still feel *pleasure* when I have sex with Mo, but it's been a long time since I've felt *desire*. That's just biology: on a neurochemical level, pleasure is obtaining; desire is wanting, and you cannot desire what you already have. These days, when I fuck Mo, I think about the property market.

Once, in the cab home after a particularly boozy dinner party at Don and Inez's house in our thirties, I asked Mo if he'd ever consider an open marriage. My bisexual explorations were cut off so young, I'd said, I never really got to meet that part of myself. But the apps would be brutal for me now, a tired perimenopausal mum, while time has somehow transformed Mo from a scrawny dork into that most desirable of creatures: a healthy man in his forties with a stable job and no obvious issues and an expensive wardrobe (thanks, me).

Ageing happens on different timelines for men and women, and it's not fair.

The solution arrives fully formed in my mind the next morning, sharp as though my sleeping self had been hard at work all night welding it into shape. If Andreas is going to get the credit for the AI idea... let's make sure it's the credit he *deserves*.

I email him suggesting I put a team together to start working on the prototype for 'his' AI feature, carefully avoiding the broken letter A on my keyboard. *We'll keep it tight, skunkworks,* I say. *We need to be nimble, sidestep the processes & protocols we've developed for the wider product – they'll only slow us down.*

Andreas responds within minutes. He is enthused. He is glad he and I are on the same page.

We hold a kick-off meeting in the Jungle Room, one of the more bizarre relics of Don's office decor phase. A resin tiger snarls from the corner, beneath a wall of plastic ferns. My hand-picked team crowds the conference table: our three most troublesome devs, our sloppiest designer, my dimmest product manager, and Millie, the brand-new DevOps girl who doesn't know a single thing about our systems. I may as well have recruited a rugby team of penguins.

Andreas starts things off by describing his vision for the feature, overlapping circle diagrams in tow, channelling all the messiah energy of a TED Talk. The engineers exchange mutinous looks when he says we need a fully functioning app ready for Demo Day. Five weeks. But no one's brave enough to speak up and tell the new boss how insane this is. Usually, that person would be me, but now I sit unperturbed, letting Andreas's nonsense wash over the room, texting the family WhatsApp group under the table.

Me
Paige, why did I just get a fee-adjustment email from LSE?

Paige
I'm taking my econ course online for the rest of the term

Me
Why?

Paige
Because I can't put the lecturer on 2x speed irl
Lowk she talks like a sedated sloth

Me
Do you feel like that's going to give you enough structure?

Paige
It's fine mum after I flunk out I'll just sell my organs on the dark web or hoard bottled water for the post-apocalypse

Paige follows this with a wind chime emoji, which I don't bother trying to decode. Her emojis make as much sense as when Artie sits on my laptop. Paige says she likes to use the underused ones so they don't feel neglected.

Mo

Love that for you, kid. Entrepreneur queen.

Me

But everything's okay?

Paige

Paige's Premium Post-Apocalypse Puddle-Water, Now 99% Parasite-Free

Me

Let's talk about it at dinner on Wed.

Yusuf

Do you think Whitney will realise she is too good for any of the young men in that villa?

I smile at Yusuf's *Love Island* obsession before tucking my phone back into my pocket. There's no need to add *Worry about Paige* to the List; that's a perpetual item.

Andreas's wrapping up now, saying something about multi-sensory media experiences.

I observe the squad, arranged around the table with anxious expressions. The designer whose trademark skill is to *slightly* misalign things in a way that makes your brain itch. The engineer who once brought down our central database for twenty-four hours with a single typo. My dream nightmare team.

I clear my throat. 'Speed is our priority, yeah? Don't get bogged down in the process overhead. Versioning, test coverage, logging—'

i.e. the things that make the product actually work – 'we can fix that later.'

Andreas smiles, oblivious. 'Let's make history.'

I grin back. 'Can't wait, boss.'

I weigh the risks. Demo Day is our best chance to impress potential investors, but it's not our *only* chance. We've still got three months of runway left. If Andreas crashes hard enough on Demo Day to get fired, that still leaves me almost two months to swoop in and raise funding. Until then, keeping him distracted by the dangly cat toy of the AI project lets the better engineers stay focused on the corporate module.

Sabotage is how I'll save us. This is not my ego acting rash; this is me rescuing everything we've built from the idiot who will ruin it.

Still… imagine how humiliated he will be, standing on that stage, that new ugly voice inside me whispers. *Imagine how sweet that will taste.*

A brand-new instinct for revenge? Probably perimenopause.

I stroke my hand under my chin, discovering a clutch of new hairs already growing through since this morning, thick and sharp as pins.

Loss of Muscle Mass

◐

Ellie

One of the conditions of Paige moving into student housing was the promise of a weekly Wednesday-night dinner at home, which we call Mash & Trash. Ostensibly, it's so that we can continue our family tradition of watching *Love Island* together (the Trash) over dinner (the Mash), but it's no accident that I've insisted on a mealtime. It feels important to check in, especially today.

All week, I've felt a steady pressure building, the premonition of some non-specific peril circling closer. It's had me triple-checking the locks before I go to bed, doubling back to make sure the gas is off at the hob, obsessively refreshing our app analytics, combing the List for the crucial thing I'm certain I've forgotten to do. Anxiety, yes, that's on the list of symptoms.

'Just one more bite.' I dangle the fork in front of Yusuf's face.

He stares at me, wild-eyed, like I'm trying to poison him. He's still handsome in his way. Luxurious grey hair. Thick eyebrows. Square jaw. The same nose as Mo, only bigger, like seeing into Mo's future. But the panic in the eyes gives it away, betrays the protein plaques strangling the once brilliant mind behind them. That, and the bright-green dribble of spinach down his chin.

'You can't live on toffees alone, my lad. Come on, just one more.'

'Noor!' he calls loudly, as though his wife is somewhere in the next room. I remind myself that this is the man who used to slip £50 bank-notes into my handbag when Paige was small and we were too broke to buy formula and too proud to ask for help. The man who walked me down the aisle at our wedding in place of my dead father.

The shriek of the doorbell makes both of us jump. I ignore it, nudging chicken against his lips. He turns his head away. 'Not until Noor gets here.' He's particularly bad tonight. I never know the exact cause: the diabetes and the heart failure and the dementia and the medications all interact in a dance too complex to predict. This is the way we end; not with a bang, but with a series of cascading organ system failures.

Another worry.

'Try in a minute, love,' says Mo, leaning over the synthesiser box and topping us up. He's already three glasses in, cheeks flushed under the dining-room lights... two of which are dead, I notice. Add to List. 'Paige, how's debating?'

Paige has been unusually withdrawn tonight. Uninterested, she's watching a muted video on her phone under the table. Her hair's pulled back in a too-tight ponytail, and there's a suspicious mass underneath her vegan cutlets that might be her mashed potatoes. Worry squirms in my chest.

Paige doesn't look up. 'Ugh. "This house believes Britain should pay reparations to its former colonies", but they put me on the Con team,' she deadpans.

'Let me guess, and you're the only brown girl?'

'Mum in one,' she says. The corners of her mouth barely twitch.

I'm momentarily distracted by a surprising message on my phone: an update from the product manager on the AI team saying they're almost ready to show me a prototype, which can't be right; it's only been a week.

'Are you ever going to let us come and watch you?' Mo asks.

'Can you and Mum promise not to embarrass me by cheering after every single sentence I say?' Paige invited us to a school debating tournament once, and – yes – I might have gone a little overboard making supporter T-shirts with her face on. We've not been invited to any since.

Yusuf struggles to his feet, shuffling towards the doorway. 'Noor?'

I steer him back to the table. There's a pong on him which tells me that Mo missed his turn to wash him. Again. 'We can't help it if you're so brilliant and wise and charismatic,' I say to Paige.

'Then no, you may not come to watch me.'

I sigh theatrically. 'Some people would love it if their parents showed interest in their life, you know.'

Paige rolls her eyes and continues shuffling food around her plate. 'It's not like any of it matters anyway,' she mumbles. Sometimes I think Paige was born as the nihilism yin to her father's Pollyanna yang. Like the universe needed the scales to balance.

I force a smile, but there's an emptiness in the pit of my stomach, like an answering echo of my daughter's. My eyes scan her body. Is her sundress hanging off her collarbones more loosely than it should? Are her eyes looking more sunken than usual?

'Is everything going okay with uni?' I attempt, keeping my tone light.

'I got a first on my philosophy essay.' Paige shrugs.

'Flex, girl!' Mo toasts her with his nearly empty glass. I fan myself with the collar of my shirt, wishing I'd fixed the goddamn thermostat months ago. Yusuf cranes around the doorway.

'And the other classes?' I venture. I know all of Paige's tricks. Answering one question when asked another. She was here a week ago, and she ate her dinner then, didn't she? Or did I just miss it, like I missed it for so long when it happened the first time? Paige is much smarter than me, is the problem.

'It's all fine, Mum, jeez.' Paige and Mo catch each other's eyes. Mo makes a tiny eye-roll gesture. Overanxious Mummy being anxious again.

The doorbell buzzes again. A short, sharp wail, followed by a long continuing *SHRRRRRRRRRRRRRRRRRRRR*.

'For fuck's sake.' I grimace. I wave Mo to take over feeding Yusuf, wondering what fresh hellish visitation is disturbing us at this time of night.

I trip over the Please Take Me Upstairs pile at the bottom of the stairs, and sprawl hard on the floor. Another bruise to add to the collection. From my vantage point three inches from floor level, I spot Artie under the dresser, watching me with glowing eyes, among dust bunnies almost as big as he is. Add to List: *Hoover hallway.*

The shrieking doorbell pauses, then restarts.

SHRRRRRRRRRRRRRRRR.

It's awful Julia the neighbour again, all her weight leaning against the doorbell. 'Your recycling is out.' Her lips purse. The Pomeranian at her feet is staring at me, eyes bulging, pink tail draped across his body like candyfloss. His lips peel back from small teeth in a silent growl. Artie responds with a hiss in my defence.

'I'm aware that my recycling is out, Julia, because I put it there. Thank you *so much* for the update.' I move to shut the door.

'The foxes get into the bins, you know. It's better to put them out first thing in the morning.'

'Julia, the bin men come at 5 a.m.'

The Pomeranian takes a step towards me with a single sharp bark. I have to resist the urge to bark back. Julia pulls at the lead, starts muttering something about what a nice neighbourhood this used to be, reminds me that she's lived here since she was born, in case I'd forgotten.

Yusuf's shouting something from the dining room. I take a deep inhale, count silently to four, exhale, try to marshal the last dregs of my politeness. 'I'll bring them in later. So sorry, got to be going.' Polite polite polite.

I slam the door in her face... but in careful slow motion. So, really, I politely close the door.

Back at the table, Mo has given up on feeding Yusuf, and he and Paige are now laughing together at something on the wine label, their heads close, their dark curls tangling together.

I finally start my own dinner, which is now ice-cold. I attempt a softer approach. 'Paige, you know I can book an appointment with Dr Thomas for you if you need it.'

'Mum, Jesus. I'll call Dr Thomas if I need her. But I don't.'

I turn to Mo. 'What do you think, love?' Subtext: *Help me.*

Mo looks at Paige, not me. 'I think if she says she's fine, we should believe her.' *Coward.*

I stab my fork into the congealed mass on my plate. Fine. I'll be the bad guy, as usual. 'Paige, I'm sorry, it's not up to you. I'm going to call her tomorrow.'

'You're going to drag me there by my hair?'

'If I have to.'

Paige throws her napkin across the table and leaves the room.

Yusuf mimics her, shoving his half-eaten plate away. 'I won't eat without Noor,' he declares.

'*Noor's dead!*' I snap. '*She's been dead for years!*'

I clamp my lips together, horrified. Mo and Yusuf stare at me with matching round eyes. Silence, then the boom-boom-boom of Paige's boots down the passage. 'Fuck you, Mum' in Morse.

'Come on, Abba,' Mo says, his voice a parody of calm, helping his father to his feet. 'Let's get you to bed.' Not looking at me.

Alone, I reach across the table and flip over Paige's soya steak, certain I'll find a squished nest of spinach and potato underneath.

There's… nothing. A clean, bare plate.

I slump my head onto the table. I try to imagine my breath as a calm blue colour seeping into the hot-white regret in my chest.

But Mo always claims good cop so you get to be the arsehole. When Paige was little, Mo claimed make-believe so you were left with homework. Claimed the toys so you were left with the chores. Claimed the clown so you were left the nag. Claimed Chill Dad so you got the worrying, all of the worrying. And if you divvy up the hours, sure, Mo did almost half, which was a hell of a lot more than your own father ever did. But he did the fun half.

I can hear the distant rumble of Mo's voice, soothing Paige or his father, I'm not sure. Fuck his soothing. I need air. I need to buy some fucking *bulbs* for these fucking *pendant lights*.

I call out to them that I'm going to the shops. No one bothers to reply.

The street lights are glowing orbs of amber, a haze of static against the black. Far away, the gibbous moon floats above the Shard like the eye of Sauron. Halfway down the garden path something squelches under my foot. Soft. A ripe, animal smell. A little parting gift from the Pomeranian.

A growl rumbles out of the deepest part of me. I grab the recycling and toss it towards Julia's azaleas. But I've misjudged, and it somehow soars all the way across her garden, into Mrs Donovan's next door.

Someone is staring at me from across the road. She seems vaguely familiar. Stooped shoulders. Body shaped like a pepper. Another small dog at her feet. The moonlight turning her white hair into a halo. An ominous sentinel.

'Hello?' I call out to her, wondering if she needs help. Yusuf gets lost roaming the neighbourhood all the time, and we rely on kind neighbours to get him back home.

The figure doesn't reply.

I scrub my dog-shit shoe onto the grass, and when I look up, the woman is gone. Nothing there but shadows.

The corner shop smells of dust and fabric softener. The shop assistant has a newspaper spread out across the counter. He's circled some capital letters and converted each one to a number, which he's scrawled at the top of the page, decoding messages from God or the government. The headline, partially obscured by his scribbles: DOG ATTACKS ON THE RISE – ARE PANDEMIC PETS TO BLAME? I pay for the bulbs and a tub of apology ice cream, and – for the first time in a decade – find myself asking the guy if they sell loose cigarettes and matches.

He closes the paper, revealing a stack of half-filled lottery tickets. 'You should try vaping,' he says to me, rummaging below the counter. 'Healthier for you.'

'I don't smoke any more,' I tell him, snatching the slightly crushed Dunhill Light from his palm.

The nicotine hits my system like the embrace of an ex-lover. I smoke it almost down to the filter in three long drags, then dig in my bag for a breath mint, half hoping Mo won't smell the Dunhill on me. Half hoping that he will.

I hear him in the living room as I unlatch the door, loops of robotic sounds which tell me he's composing a new dubstep track. I've told him before I wish he'd picked up literally any other mid-life crisis hobby than dubstep. Chainsaw juggling, cheating on me, minor acts of genocide, anything.

I hold up the apology ice cream. 'Where's everybody?'

'Paige went home. And Dad's asleep,' Mo says. 'It's not okay for you to lose your temper with him.' He doesn't turn down the track. It sounds like our Samsung fridge is trying to communicate with dolphins.

The sound jangles through me. I inhale, deep and slow, feeling the air squashing the anger down. 'I'm sorry.' I've been saying that a lot lately. 'I feel awful.'

'He can't help it.'

'I know that.'

'He needs you to be patient.'

I nod, my body thrumming in time to the dubstep, like it's magnetised. 'Did you check his feet?' We have to do this morning and night. Yusuf's feet are entirely numb from his diabetes, so small injuries could turn into festering wounds that never heal. Mo remembers to do this about one in every four times he's supposed to.

Mo sighs, returning to fiddle on his laptop, but doesn't actually answer, so I add to List: *Check Yusuf's feet before I go to bed.*

I know I should leave it there. Apologise. Go to bed. Maybe after some actual sleep, everything will feel okay. But something has charged up the electrons in me. Something about the stranger's stare, the dog shit, the worry, the nicotine, the worry, the fucking dubstep.

'Why is it always me?' The words fall out between my teeth, hot and serrated. 'Looking after your father?'

The moment I say it, I wish I could take it back. The words of every book I've ever read about healthy communication styles flash in my mind: *Don't start a fight when you're tired. Use 'I feel' statements. Don't say 'always', stick to specifics.* Then I think, *Why the fuck am I the only one who bothers to read all these relationship manuals?*

Mo frowns. 'You're the one who said he should move in here, remember?'

'Where else could he go?'

'There are homes.'

'He's the last parent either of us has left. I wasn't going to leave him to rot in a home.'

Mo closes his laptop carefully, mercifully cutting the music. 'But you don't get to take on responsibilities and then be a cow to everyone because you've got too many responsibilities. You do see that, right?'

'I have to take responsibility, because you don't. Like with Paige.'

He's standing now. 'Paige says she's fine.'

'She barely said a word all night. You always leave me to be the bad guy—'

'Whoa, whoa, whoa…' He steps towards me, and suddenly a smile breaks over his face like a sunrise. 'You know what this is, right?' He places gentle hands on my shoulders. 'This is the menopause talking.'

The echoes of the dubstep crawl through me, carving jittery soundwaves through my nerves. '*What?*' I spit, through the sand in my mouth.

'It's like you always say: anxiety distorts your perceptions. See? This isn't you. Sweet girl.' And he kisses me on the forehead, so gentle, so maddeningly understanding. 'I'm going to bed.'

He vanishes up the stairs, walking right past the Please Take Me Upstairs pile.

I watch him go, jaw clenched so hard I might bite through.

The worst part is, he's probably fucking right. This is probably perimenopause.

I can't bear going up with him. And in any case, I'm many hours away from sleep. Years, decades away from sleep. So I storm out the kitchen door into the back garden. Every fruit fly and midge in Barnsbury swarms around my face, drawn to the smell of my sweat. I bat them away. The air is hot. Hot. Everything's too fucking hot (*Make a GP appointment*). A light wind stirs the bushes into a restless dance. The garden is another accumulation of to-dos. *Cut back the* overgrown hedge. List Paige's old trampoline on Facebook Marketplace. Repaint the shed. Fertilise the climbing beans. Skim the leaf debris off the fish pond, which is glistening in the light of the fattening moon. No one else will do this. No one but me.

I clench my hands into balls, tight like hyena paws. Step on a twig which snaps like a shin bone.

Cut back the hedge, fine, that's something useful I can do in the dark.

The shed is a jumble of shadows. The garden shears are buried somewhere deep under a pile of recycling (*Go to the recycling centre*). There's no light in here (*Buy batteries for the torch*). I stretch my hand into the darkness.

The midges have followed me inside. 'Bugger off,' I hiss at them, ineffectively.

There's a crash behind me.

I leap round to see the shadow of Artie dodging a spade he's just knocked over. He strolls over and headbutts my calf affectionately. We named him Meowriarty as a mischievous kitten, but he's turned out to be not so much a Napoleon of Crime as an adorable idiot.

The cat winds through my legs, insistent on my attention. I ignore him, squat and reach back into the darkness under the workbench. I'm sure the clippers are in here somewhere (*Reorganise the shed*). My hand pads across thick layers of dust. There's a distinct whiff of rot and decay. A bitterness in the air, tingling on my tongue. Something's died in here.

My hands grope deeper, touch something sticky, stringy across my fingertips.

A rustle. Then something runs across my hands. Warm and small and many-legged.

I shriek and pull back, knocking my head on the underside of the bench.

'Fuck!' I yelp, staggering back upright. 'Fuck. Fuck. Fuck.'

I asked Mo to put down mousetraps. Months ago. And then we'd had a whole argument about whether the humane traps were actually more inhumane, because mice are territorial and are usually killed if you relocate them. *Kinder just to kill them quick*, I'd said. And he'd promised he'd take care of it. He'd promised.

Warmth tickles my cheek: I've reopened the cut on my forehead. I kick the table leg in frustration, forgetting I'm wearing open-toed sandals. The rough edge catches the corner of my toenail, sending a hot spike of pain through my foot.

I pick up the workbench. It's so light. So much lighter than it should be. Rusting tools and cracked flowerpots crash to my feet. I push my hands together and fold the table in half, cracking it down the middle. I throw it onto the pile of rubbish. My breath is ragged huffs. I could keep going. (*Smash the shed.*) (*Tear down the house.*) (*Rip up the sky.*)

My arms shake. I look down at my hands. But these are not my hands. Too big. The muscles of my forearms too roped, bunched tight. And the hair is coarse, caught in the moonlight, casting shadows against my skin.

And I just snapped the workbench in two.

Probably perimenopause?

I breathe in deep. Hold. Exhale. Pull it together, Ellie.

The wood was old, I tell myself.

Maybe it's been hollowed out by termites.

(*Fuck.*)

It will all feel better in the morning.

Irritability

O

Brenda

Constable Gardner's lips twitch at the sight of me approaching the police station front desk. 'Brenda! Back again.' Her face is friendly enough, but I know the glint in her eye. They've started calling me Cat Lady around here. Everything I say will be re-enacted later among the squad to guffaws and hilarity. I know this, because sometimes they don't even wait for me to leave before the laughter begins. But bugger them – I don't need them to like me.

I slide my phone across the counter, photo up of the latest potential victim. A small calico with a caramel-brown face, which was split in two, right down the middle. Her family called yesterday, but she died three weeks ago, same night as Melek. They've already cremated the body, but took good photos before they did. The family found me through one of the posters Deborah put up in Chingford.

The calico is the seventeenth entry in the spreadsheet taking up more and more of my life. Victims arranged in neat colour-coded rows: time, date, address, investigation status. A trail of violence across the borough.

These are only the ones I'm sure of. Once word started spreading in the neighbourhood that there's a pet serial killer on the loose, the CATS group went mad. Most of the cats, I'm sure, were run over by cars, or caught in barbed-wire fencing, or ate something they shouldn't have. Animals aren't built for cities, is the thing. Maybe none of us are.

Nevertheless, I've called every person who contacted me. Tried my best for them. But there are so many lonely people in the world, I'm learning. Lonely, sad, anxious, desperate people. *My cat died four years ago, they said it was a car but... I saw a video on the internet of a guy who put kittens in the microwave... A boy tried to call my cat to him in the street yesterday, I screamed and took a photo of him but the police don't want to hear anything... If that sicko is hurting animals, I'd like to cut off his toes one by one and feed them to him... Please help me... Please help me... Please help me...*

If it sounded plausible, I've visited. I've sat in their front rooms, their elegant town houses, their council flats. I've drunk their tea, their instant coffee, their limescale-filled water, their organic elderflower cordial, their whisky at 9 a.m. I've looked at the photos, the awful photos, of Lady Whiskers and Luna and Frieda Cahtlo and Buttons and Dog and Oscar and Chairman Meow and Loki and Mew Paul and Tomcat Wambsgans and Duchess and Gizmo and Katy Purry and Kittgenstein. I've passed them tissues. I've promised them I won't let this go.

And each morning, my inbox is full again. CATS is up to seven hundred members. Paul remains adamant that he cannot do any more necropsies, so I'm just going on gut feeling now. And my gut says that most of these deaths aren't related. The ones on 31 August were *different*. Deliberate. Angry.

But guts only get you so far, so right now I'm standing at the front counter of Walthamstow Police Station, begging them to help me access CCTV footage.

'It's the launderette on Forest Road,' I explain. 'Their camera takes in some of the road, and I've got cats killed on either side of it. He must have walked right past.'

Another copper sidles over to enjoy the fun. Sergeant Orten, I think this one's name is. He's got a real pen and ink around him, as my ma used to say.

Constable Gardner narrows her eyes at me. Shrewd. She's showered recently, her hair hanging in limp dark rat-tails around her face. 'Have you tried just asking them?'

'Yes.'

Sergeant Orten chuckles. 'I bet you asked real polite, didn't you?'

I try to ignore him, keeping my gaze fixed on the place in the abyss where Constable Gardner's face is, hoping that I'm making convincing eye contact. 'I just need the footage.'

Constable Gardner isn't impressed. 'You know what I've been dealing with all morning? An eleven-year-old who got stabbed outside his school gates. But sure, why don't I just call up a whole special ops team to help you find missing cats?'

'The K9 unit.' Sergeant Orten shakes with silent laughter.

'Oh, oh... they can start the fur-ensics.' They both crack up at that one.

I am just barely managing to contain myself. 'If you gave me a letter or something, a warrant—'

'Tell you what, Brenda. I'll do one better. Oi, Pencil!'

The young man who must be Pencil sidles out from the back. He can't be more than twenty-two, twenty-three, police uniform hanging off a lanky skeleton he hasn't quite grown into yet. 'Ready for your first solo mission?' Sergeant Orten asks him.

The youngster flashes a bright overbite. I don't have the heart to tell him they're playing a prank on him. And I'm the prank.

I don't care – his uniform's all I'm interested in.

Doesn't feel like a *brilliant* idea to drive a cop across the borough illegally, so I pretend I took the bus in. We head out to the launderette on foot. Pencil's hands seem to be making an inventory of his gear. They move to his back trouser pocket, the right breast of his hi-vis vest, his belt.

'You're muttering,' I tell him. 'It's extremely annoying.'

'Real? My bad, miss.' His accent is south London, warm.

'Why do they call you Pencil?'

Heat radiates from his cheeks. 'Oh, that's just jokes.'

I doubt it. I only hope they're mocking his overall body shape, rather than any particular part of his anatomy. I steal a sidelong glance at him. 'How long have you been a copper?'

'Well, I'm not one yet. Twelve weeks' apprenticeship at this BCU, basic command unit, then I have to pass some exams. They'll make me do two or three years as a street constable, but I want to get into the financial crime unit. Get the tax evaders and fraudsters and rich bastards skimming money. They're the real thugs, innit?'

I shrug. There are infinite ways people can hurt each other, in my experience.

Pencil's stride is twice the length of mine, an easy sloping pace that I have to trot at double-speed to keep up with. It's an unusually warm day, even for late September. I can soon feel sweat dripping down the back of my neck. Bloomin' heels aren't helping, but without them, I'm barely five foot. Seven quid from Primark, bought two months ago, already falling apart. Don't make things like they used to.

I'm starting to relax around him, until I almost walk straight into a lamp post, which inconveniently materialises out of my void. Pencil throws his arm out to stop me, just in time. I catch him giving me a puzzled look I don't like.

'I can walk!' I snap at him.

The public-school doctor wanted me to get a white stick. Over my dead body. You cannot show weakness in this world. Anyway, I'm not *blind*, for heaven's sake. I just have a small black hole I carry around with me, which I am dealing with, thank you very much.

We turn onto Forest Road. The camera's a dark glass eye above the door of the launderette, gazing boldly across the street to deter the low-level drug dealers who used to meet outside and keep customers away. From Reggie's reconnaissance, I know that the camera captures footage across both sides of the street, which is technically illegal, but no one around here cares. Local dealers are young. Still kids really. No one likes to see it. No one does anything about it, either, except get them to move to a different street corner.

Inside is hot, humid. As my eyes adjust to the darkness, I spot a group of bored teenagers drinking 500 ml Cokes that I doubt have only Coke in them. They slink out the door at the sight of Pencil's uniform. A man sitting in the corner is reading a newspaper warning of an impending global recession. I thought we were still in the last one, to be honest.

Jakub, the manager, rushes up the minute he sees me, waving us back out the door. 'No. No way. I don't want any more of your nonsense around here.'

'All I did was put up some posters,' I say to Pencil.

'Photos of dead cats, all over my walls! Scaring all my customers!'

'I'm looking for witnesses.' The photo wasn't even that bad. It was Loki, the chubby tortoiseshell, number 15 on the spreadsheet. It's mostly showing the front of the driveway where it happened. The body is obscured by bushes. It's not the worst of them, not by a mile.

'Crazy psycho *bitch*,' Jakub spits.

My hands ball at my sides. I'm ready to go off at him.

Until, with extreme calm, Pencil pulls a notepad and namesake from his pocket. 'Sorry, was that psycho *bitch*, or psycho *witch*?' he asks, pencil poised.

Jakub's face goes purple, deep lines appearing on his forehead. His eyes flick between the notepad and the police logo on Pencil's helmet.

'We were hoping you'll give us copies of your CCTV footage,' Pencil says, all friendliness. 'August 31st – what time we saying?' he checks with me.

'Between midnight and 5 a.m. That's when the kid found the body.' My hands unclench, knuckles throbbing.

Pencil nods, pulling a small hard drive from his vest pocket. 'Better just copy the whole lot over. Cheers.'

Jakub takes the hard drive and disappears into the back room, muttering furiously.

'Clever trick, that.' I nod at his pencil.

'Best weapon we carry. It's all recorded on the bodycam, but there's just something about a well-sharpened HB graphite, innit?'

Jakub comes back holding out the hard drive, lips pursed, working hard to stop himself from saying anything else.

'Did you see us? Iconic.' Pencil winks as we head back out into the piercing sun. He holds his hand up to high-five me. I frown at his palm until he gives up.

But I'm grateful. 'That's the most helpful anyone's been from that police station,' I admit, pulling on my skiing sunglasses, waiting for my eyes to adjust, pretending that I'm looking for something else in my handbag to buy us time before we start walking.

'Helping's my job, miss!'

God, he's like a Labrador. His face, coming into focus now as my pupils finally dilate, is so eager and unlined. 'You know the sergeant was having a laugh, sending you with me?'

He shrugs. 'It's nice to get out for a bit. Between you and me, someone needs to introduce Sergeant Orten to deodorant.'

Let's not mention the fact that the lad himself smells like he's taken a shower in Lynx Gold.

'What are you going to do now? Run faces against a database?' he asks.

I laugh. 'This isn't *Inspector Morse*, flower. I don't have access to any criminal databases, do I?'

'Oh. So what's the plan?'

'I'm going to take this back to my flat, put on *The Archers*, and log the times of any cars going past and any people walking up the street alone and hope I can use this to narrow down the window when it might have happened.'

'Ah.'

I give him a wave, and start walking home. I'll have to go fetch my car from the station later, when he's off shift, so he doesn't see.

But he falls into step beside me. 'It's a whole night's footage on there. Going to take you hours, still.'

'Correct.'

'If I help, you'll be done twice as fast.'

'Don't you need to get back to Sergeant Orten?'

'They can cope without me. Besides, I've never seen a vigilante's home before.'

Vigilante. First time I've heard that word applied to me. I like it. It implies vigilant, watchful.

'Well, my boy,' I say, 'it's no bat cave.'

Generalised Anxiety

Ellie

A partial list of gloops I rub into my face every day:

- Micellar water.
- Face cleanser.
- A different, oil-based face cleanser because some teenager on Instagram said it cleans out your pores, but didn't clarify if one is meant to use this instead of the regular cleanser or in addition to it.
- Extra-rich anti-ageing moisturising cream, to undo all the cleansing.
- Additional moisturising cream for eyes, neck and hands, the places which give away your age.
- AHA serum (anti-ageing).
- Retinoid 1%, which you cannot legally buy from a chemist without a prescription, so I buy it off a dodgy Greek website (anti-ageing).
- Copper peptide serum (no idea what this does, probably anti-ageing).
- Sunscreen, which smells vaguely of oranges.
- Vitamin C serum, which smells vaguely of sunscreen (anti-ageing).

A complete list of gloops Mo rubs into his face every day:

- Body wash.

If the body wash is finished, Mo will use shampoo.

The Personalised Meditations team have co-opted the Jungle Room for their workspace. External monitors crowd the conference table and the walls are papered with rough sketches and sticky notes. The fake plants and David Livingstone prints have been piled haphazardly in a corner. The table is a graveyard of takeaway coffee cups and Monster cans. There are no windows in the room, and the place smells like the worst days of Paige's depression when you could practically chew on the sweat stink in the air.

'You said you've got a prototype ready to show me?' I say, fanning myself with a sheaf of paper, hoping no one notices my hairy forearms or the fact that my fingernails look like something out of a David Attenborough documentary.

I'm certain I misunderstood their message last night. They've only been at it for a week. The whole point of this team was that they were the people I assumed would take months to build an IKEA side table, let alone a complex new feature. I've made a point of referring to it as 'Andreas's AI feature' often and loudly, and it's caught on. Demo Day is a month away.

But they hand me one of the test phones and there it is: a green icon with the Tranquillity logo, overlaid with a robot icon. I see they've called the prototype 'Tranquillity SMART', which is perfectly terrible.

'Audio recognition doesn't work yet, so we're using text input for now,' explains the product manager. Under the prompt *What's on your mind?* is a large input box. Six faces hover over my shoulder, expectant.

I type something vague: *I've been feeling a little anxious.*

A button pulses softly into existence beneath the text box: *Listen now.* I hit play, and a soothing woman's voice purrs through the headphones.

'Close your eyes and find comfort in your breath. Inhale calm, exhale restlessness. Your heartbeat is a lullaby for your soul. Every breath is a soft caress, easing you into tranquillity. Notice your body, Ellie. Surrender to your body's knowledge…'

I slip off the headphones. Gibberish, of course, but plausible-sounding gibberish. The voice is warm. There's nothing robotic or artificial about it. Using my name was a nice touch – they must have injected it into the prompt somehow.

I haven't bothered to discuss the mechanics of the feature with the team. What database of meditations is the AI actually trained on: Instagram platitudes? Has any licensed therapist or experienced meditation practitioner reviewed this at any point? I don't have to ask to know that the answer is no. As far as I can tell, all these algorithms can produce is a lowest-common-denominator soup of blanditudes, the average of 'what people say', an approach which rests on the erroneous assumption that the average person has useful things to say about human suffering. Tech bros believe too much in the thinking abilities of large language models because they have such a shallow concept of the thinking abilities of people.

'That was… fast,' I say, to cover my awkwardness.

'Well, we barely had to build anything except the UI, to be honest,' the tallest dev tells me. He's pale and skinny with an oversized bald head, like a closed cup mushroom. 'It's all down to Millie,' he says, smiling fondly at the new girl. 'She got us a research licence from OpenMind. Full local install of their next-gen model – it's miles ahead of what's publicly available.'

My eyes narrow. 'How?'

'An old friend from AWS joined their partnerships team? She was super excited to hear about what we're building? They gave us access to run a sandboxed model locally and they'd like to co-publish a paper with us once we get some test results?'

My blood chills. 'You agreed to a partnership with OpenMind?' Shit. This project is supposed to be a nice quiet failure, a little poison in Andreas's well, enough to convince the board he's an idiot but not enough to damage Tranquillity's brand. But if OpenMind knows about it, they'll blab to the whole industry. 'Who signed off on this?'

Millie looks honestly confused. 'I didn't know anyone had to?'

There's a small furious animal climbing up my spinal cord, clawing my calm to shreds. It reaches my mouth; it twists my lips into a snarl. '*You should not have spoken to external partners without consulting me.*'

Mushroom Head comes to Millie's defence. 'Andreas told us this was the company's biggest priority right now.'

'*Andreas isn't responsible for those relationships. I am,*' the animal snaps, using my mouth. I turn back to Millie. 'You don't do this kind of thing without permission.'

Millie rolls her eyes. 'Yes, Mum.'

The animal inside me freezes. There is utter silence in the room as the word ricochets and reverberates. *Mum*. Everything that word means. That this girl thinks it's an insult. That her only model for an older woman with authority over her is the figure she can abuse, the one who is supposed to love her unconditionally, the bogeyman she defines herself in opposition to, the safe place she can project every bit of victimisation she feels.

Mum.

The animal shakes itself inside me, holding the word in its teeth.

Finally, I splutter, 'What did you just say to me?'

She stares at me, defiant, not taking it back.

'I am not your mother. *I. Am. Your. Boss.*' The animal spits out each word, slowly, individually. And for once, my fury is dry-eyed.

The girl shrugs. Her face is bright red now, clashing with her hair. 'Actually, Zayn is my boss.'

And – the little shit – she's right. I'm not the CEO. I'm fucking nobody.

'Go and clear out your desk.' The words come out of me before I can think about them.

Finally, a crack in her expression. 'What?'

'You're fired.'

'You can't do that?'

She's probably right... legally, formally, ethically. But not – crucially – practically. I open up my laptop with a flourish, and angle the screen so we can both see it clearly. As she watches, I load the HR portal on my laptop, bring up her name, and hit the big red TERMINATE button. This will remove her access to the codebase, to her laptop, to the building. Only the HR team is supposed to be able to do this. But I have admin permissions in the HR portal because before we were big enough to have a HR team, I'm the one who set it up.

The rest of the team are watching me, eyes like bushbabies.

Millie pushes to her feet. 'I'm going to find Zayn.'

'Please do.'

It's a mess, but I don't care. I'm done being everyone's punching bag. Everyone's mum.

It should probably be more difficult to smooth over than it is.

Zayn is mildly ticked off, but not interested in fighting me. 'Look, Ellie, it's you. If you fired her, I'm sure there was a good reason,' he says eventually, after asking me to explain it twice over.

There was, wasn't there?

'Insubordination,' I grunt. *Bruised ego*, whispers the animal in my spine.

'I don't love junior developers crying in my office. But I'll back you up. Of course.' He waves me off, happy to return to his bubble of code, free of management responsibilities.

HR is trickier. I'm quizzed by what seems to be half the team, and they say there really should have been a formal disciplinary process, but they'll figure it out, pay her off if needs be. 'NDA violation' is the line they decide to stick to. 'Insubordination' isn't a thing, apparently, since we are not the military. But she's still in her probation period. It's simple.

I'm already regretful. But it's best for her to be gone. And, hell, she's a software engineer with AWS on her CV, it's not like she's going to end up on the streets.

I get away with all of this because I have never lost my temper before. Because that's not even a thing people think I am able to do.

I've been doing a lot of apologising today. Paige responded to my grovelling message this morning with an emoji of a snowman, fuck knows what that means. Mo, though, shrugged off last night's argument like nothing happened, and has been sending me cheery cat memes all day, bless that man.

My brother Byron calls as I'm making my way back to my desk. It's a number I don't recognise, so I answer it. I've been letting his calls go to voicemail recently, and not reading his messages.

'Ellie, Jesus,' he says. 'I was starting to wonder if you'd gone into witness protection.'

'I've been busy,' I say, declining to add the unspoken *unlike some people*.

'We need to talk about Mum's house.'

I chew on a hangnail, toughened to leather. 'It's just not a seller's market right now.'

'So let's get a tenant in.'

I suppress a laugh. Mum was a hoarder. I'm not saying that in the cute way people describe boomers who've held on to sentimental Christmas ornaments their kids made in primary. I'm saying that in the way you describe someone who spent the last ten years of her life sleeping on the floor because her bed was piled to the ceiling with broken furniture and rotting carpets she'd picked up at the city dump.

Mum was a trusted hospice nurse in her public life; a 26 on the Hoarding Rating Scale in private. *Find a specialist cleaning service* has been on the List since she died, three years ago now. But someone needs to go through her things, find the letters, the family photographs, the heirlooms of our actual family. Tricky, because one of Mum's many 'collections' were other families' photos. She'd take them home when people died in her ward, if family members didn't collect them, which happens more often than you think. Along with teddy bears, flower vases, candles, slippers, the small offerings people bring to the dying. Mum said she just couldn't handle personal things being thrown out, forgotten. They piled up in her shed, then her living room, then her bathtub, so she had to start washing herself at the kitchen sink. It's all still sitting there, in the little house in Chingford where we grew up, that Byron and I both escaped from as soon as we could.

'Are you going to go and clean it up?'

Byron huffs. 'You know I can't leave the kids for that long.' He's a fibre splicer by trade, but he hasn't worked in months because of a chemical injury. Something else that's probably going to become my problem some day. 'Can't we just hire someone?'

'By "we" you mean "me", though.'

'Ellie, come on. I need the money.' A pause. I can hear what sounds like a pub in the background. 'Nora's pregnant again.'

'That's… that's great. Congratulations.'

'And we're pretty crammed as it is.' Byron and Nora and their three boys share a tiny two-bedroom in Sheffield.

'I get it,' I say. I have to swallow my judgement, asking why they've decided to have another kid if they don't have space. I know that's none of my business. Except that, dammit, he is making it my business. 'I'll take care of it.' God, what it is to be the eldest daughter. Family emergency fund. Family mediator. Family role model. Family therapist. Backup *mum*-from-birth.

'Thanks, Ellie. You're an angel.'

I hang up. I think of Mum, the sad graveyard of her life grown dust-covered and mildewy now, the house I've avoided stepping inside of since I was twenty-two.

I open my phone and add to List, *Call the estate agent*.

Then I delete it.

Mum is never unkind. *Mum* is never capricious.

I can't help but wonder what else I could get away with.

I head back to the Customer Support Pit, where I've set up my desk for the day. Normally, I like it here. The constant hum of voices – soothing angry customers or upselling premium plans – usually blends into a comforting white noise. But is there an edge to the chatter today? Are conversations halted abruptly as I pass, heads whipping back to their screens? Or is that just the perimenopause talking?

When I reach my desk, Lanying is already there, hovering over my laptop. Her face is alarm-bell grim. 'Ellie, we have a problem.' She leans in so close I can smell her face cream as she whispers, 'Word's got out we're almost out of cash.'

Increased Blood Pressure

○

Brenda

It's past dinner time. I'm almost through the first four hours of CCTV footage, my laptop groaning with the effort. Pencil – who's told me his name is actually Daniel – is fast asleep on the settee, snoring richly, bare feet dangling off the armrest. One sock has a hole in it which someone has darned in a cheery turquoise thread. His nan, probably, who he says he lives with in Deptford. I consider waking the boy up, offering him a sandwich. But he seems like he needs the sleep.

The footage is awful. Black and white, blurry, like staring through fog. Good thing I've got some experience comprehending shitty visuals.

I've got the spreadsheet open, too, on a new tab. It's well organised: I used to be a bookkeeper, a long time ago. I note the timestamp of every person and car that passes by. It's taking ages; I have to frequently pause, go back a little, watch a segment slowed down to try to spot more detail. Most of my notes are unhelpfully vague. *10.32 p.m. East to west. Sedan. Dark-coloured – red or blue? Number plate ends with a C or G. Two passengers.*

10.57 p.m. Pedestrian. West to east. Walking alone. Adult. Maybe male? Large.

Progress crawls. I pause. Rewind. Squint. Guess. Repeat. Mostly useless details pile up like landfill. I'm not convinced there's much point to any of this.

There's an insistent rapping on my front door. Five hard knocks, then silence. Pencil doesn't so much as twitch. Ah, to sleep like a twenty-something boy.

I check that the curtains are drawn tight and settle back into my chair. No one knocking on my front door unannounced at this hour is somebody I want to talk to.

The knocking resumes. Harder now.

My mobile vibrates loudly on the desk next to me. My landlord's name flashes onto the screen. I lunge at it and decline the call, but I'm too slow.

'I can hear your phone!' Merv's voice shouts from outside.

He can't just barge in, I know my rights. I lean back in my chair, shut my eyes.

The hammering doesn't stop. It settles into a rhythm. 'I'll stay here all night if I have to!'

Wanker. I limp through to the front hall, my body seizing from too long in the chair. I pull the living-room door behind me so I don't wake the kid. Not that there seems to be any real risk of that.

One of my landlord's brown eyes peers through the letter box, propped open by one of his gnarled fingers.

'What do you want?' I hiss through the door.

'Three months late, Brenda! I've got a family to feed.'

'You own four houses, Merv. Bugger off.'

Mervyn proceeds to make a series of guttural noises in his throat which might be him gagging on a fly or swearing at me in Welsh, I'm never sure.

'I'm sorry about this.' His eye vanishes. Something slips through the letter box and sails to the floor. 'It's a Section 21.'

'You wouldn't.'

'Look at it.'

I pick up the envelope. There it is: a notice of eviction. *Your landlord requires possession of 93A Hitchen Road within two months of receipt of this notice. If you do not leave your home by the date given, your landlord may apply to the court...* Black and white. After years of threatening, he finally did it, the bastard.

'And where am I supposed to go?'

'Call the council. Go to your family, I don't know.'

Family, that's a laugh. Jen doesn't even want me in her house over Christmas. My sister-in-law hasn't spoken to me in years. Everybody else is dead. About as much chance of them helping me as getting a council house. Last I checked, the waiting list was years long round here.

'How about I pay my rent when you fix the broken gutter?' I shoot back.

'I fixed the gutter!'

'Duct tape isn't fixed!'

'Brenda, I'm serious. You're not leaving me a choice here.'

My void expands as my blood pressure spikes. I've got pills somewhere I can never remember to take. What's the point? Something's got to kill me in the end.

'I've lived here ten years.' I have to say it slowly, my voice shaking from fury.

'I know. They've been the longest ten bloody years of my life,' Mervyn says. He lets the letter box clang closed.

'I'll get you the money,' my voice croaks. 'Just give me a week. Please.'

A long silence.

'Three months' back pay,' he says at last.

'Fine.'

He sighs. Mutters something to himself. 'Last chance. I mean it.'

I wait until I'm sure he's out of earshot before I allow myself to start cursing him.

I know the flat's nothing fancy. The fag ends have piled up again, and it's increasingly full of cat clutter. Pencil laughed at the amount of cat paraphernalia when he came in, the two new oil paintings of cats in the hallway, the blue ceramic sugar bowl shaped like a cat head, the embroidered throw pillow that says THERE'S PROBABLY CAT HAIR ON THIS. Gifts from the other victims; these things have a way of gathering their own momentum. It's Merv's investment, but my *home*.

I'm still raging when I flop back at my desk. It's a tiny, cramped thing, an old dressing table I found on the side of the road and lugged back on a shopping trolley, with just enough space for my computer. Well, it will be back on the streets soon enough, I suppose. Just like me, ha.

There's a new message on Facebook from someone with a missing cat in Ealing, on the other side of town entirely. After a moment's hesitation, I respond, *Happy to help. Our usual donation fee is £1,000.*

There's a pause. Then a response. *Of course! Pls send bank details.*

My heart's hammering. Doesn't feel right, really. But I can't exactly keep doing this if I'm sleeping outside the Sainsbury's, can I?

I glance over at Pencil, guilty. He's still fast asleep.

I move to shut the laptop, when my eyes catch on the video. A shadow has just crossed the screen, huge and black, a slinking void.

Sure it's a trick of my faulty eyes, I rewind the video and play that segment again. It's definitely there, no matter how I look at it. A dark shadow as large as a hatchback, moving strangely, like something crawling, limbs and angles. Creeping down the street at 3.14 in the morning, according to the timestamp in the corner.

I skip back, play it again. I can't make out texture or detail. Just this dark thing, like something that slipped through a hole in time from a thousand years ago.

'Hey! Wake up,' I yell at the kid.

He splutters up and shlumphs over to my side. 'W'dya'ind?' he says around a yawn.

I replay the clip. 'What the sodding hell is that?'

He pulls up a stool and leans over me to take a better look. We watch together in silence, then he takes the mouse from me and queues it up again.

'Can't say, Auntie,' he says finally. 'Really hard to see anything on this,' he says, gesturing at the grainy black-and-white pixels.

'Is it an animal?' I try.

'Can't be, right? Unless the zoo's missing a bear.' He replays the video, and we watch the dark shape hulk across the screen once again. 'Can I take the hard drive? I've got to show Sergeant Orten.'

I repress the urge to tell him to leave it, it's mine. Isn't this what I wanted, someone to help? I settle with asking him to post it on Facebook first.

'Sure thing,' he says, taking over the computer, clacking at the keys too fast for me to understand what he's doing. He frowns. 'What's wrong with your computer?'

I feel a blush creep up my neck. He means the inverted black and white, the extreme zoom, the extra-large text. 'Nothing.'

But something comes across his face, something infuriatingly like a sympathetic expression.

'Stop dawdling,' I snipe at him. 'I've got things to do, you know.'

He manages to make a short version of the video with just the few frames of the shadow playing over and over on a loop. 'Where's your browser?'

I open Internet Explorer for him. The CATS page is already loaded, fourteen new followers since I last checked.

'Rah, so many people. All this for one dead cat?'

'Seventeen.' I bring up the spreadsheet. His eyebrows climb higher and higher towards his hairline as he scrolls down the rows. Mutilations meticulously catalogued in columns and rows, my ledger of heartbreak.

'Does Sergeant Orten know about this?' he asks finally.

'Yes.'

His attention is drawn to the 'date' column. 'Lots of them on the same night.'

'Most of them,' I clarify. 'Maybe all of them, in fact. I'm less sure about these recent ones,' I say, indicating the entries scattered over the past three weeks. 'They might have been cars.'

'Same night as… whatever was on the video?'

'Same night.'

He chews his lip, looking thoughtful. 'If it's okay with you, can we hold off posting this video online? I think I have to check in with Constable Gardner. Sorry, Auntie.'

He doesn't wait for me to reply. He's already up, gathering his things, heading for the door. 'I'll call you tomorrow, yeah?' He hesitates in the doorway. 'Don't worry. Maybe the cats were a one-off thing. Something passing through. Let's hope, yeah?'

My phone pings. I glance at it, and see that £1,000 has just been deposited into my bank account. 'Here's hoping,' I mumble, as he melts into the night.

Formication

Ellie

The woman at the ticket counter of the Ladies Pond warns me that they're about to close. 'I just need a quick dip,' I beg, and she waves me through. The pressure has been coiling in me tighter and tighter all day. If cold water doesn't sap some of it out of my body, I may actually implode.

The 15 x 7 cm cracked-screen source of this anxiety hasn't stopped dinging. This morning, around the time I was firing Millie, a junior designer overheard Andreas and our CFO discussing the cash flow crisis, and rumours have spread through the business faster than nits in a playground. I've had four separate staff members come up to me this afternoon to ask if it's true everyone's about to lose their jobs. Uri thinks we need to get ahead of it and tell the team something to settle the panic. And Mo's texting to ask when I'm due home, subtext: *Yusuf's having a bad evening and I need you to take over.* I lied and told him I was stuck in a meeting.

At the lockers, I stuff the phone down to the bottom of the bag, cramming the stress in with my dress and shoes and useless tweezers. Having come straight from work, I don't have a swimsuit, but the women at the Hampstead Heath Ladies Pond have seen worse than my natty bra and knickers, my hairy legs, my talon toenails.

Go for a swim at Hampstead Heath has been on my List for months. Studies show cold-water immersion can regulate mood, calm inflammation, sap out anxiety. It's been building and building all day, like the moment before a hot flush starts, but it hasn't started.

Mostly, if I'm honest, I just couldn't bear to go home.

The evening sun shimmers on the water like hot fury. There are still five or six stragglers in the water. White-haired swimmers, the women who come every day to do laps, even through winter. Wim Hof has nothing on London's octogenarian grannies. The lifeguard has a pocket mirror and make-up set propped on her lap, preparing for a night out. A couple of moorhens swim up to me as I stand on the wooden pier, curious, their faces lifeguard-red.

The water squeezes a gasp from me as I slip in, despite the heat of the day. No amount of climate-changed September heat can penetrate this body of water; it's like a portal to the netherworld. I wonder how many generations of women have swum here for exactly this reason, what chemicals must have leached from us over the decades. If you tested the pond, what quantities of oestrogen and adrenaline and anti-ageing eye cream and radium make-up and hysteria cures would you find in each droplet?

I swat a dragonfly that's trying to land on my cheek. The surface ripples in the same subtle wind that rattles the trees. The pond floor is too deep to touch, so I froggy over to one of the floating rings dotted across the surface and hang my arms over it long enough to get my breath back. The last of the day's sunlight flickers off the leaves, like wind ruffling the fur of some enormous green creature curled around the lake.

I had such intentions, when we moved to Barnsbury, of becoming one of those fit outdoorsy types who's here four times a week. *Sign up for proper swimming classes* is still on the List. As is *Visit Inez*, come to think of it. Inez is the one who introduced me to this place, when we first moved to the area. She was shocked I'd never been here before. 'It's a slice of Eden on earth,' she'd told me. She dragged me out here a few times at dawn, leaving me paddling after her as she cut military laps through the lake. In her and Don's marriage, she was always the ambitious one. A senior manager at one of the big banks, long before that was the kind of thing women did. She quit after the last bout of cancer, and now spends her time applying the same ruthless efficiency she used to apply to the Debt Capital Markets Team: Middle East and Africa to her mah-jong club and her and Don's social life. I should have made more of an effort to spend time with her. Maybe if I'd made more space for friendship, there'd be someone I could talk to about all this. I lost touch with most of my friends when Paige was born – Mo and I were the youngest of our social circle to spawn by a decade, and none of my cool early-twenties theatre buddies were interested in hanging out with a baby.

Even the pond feels ill today. Off. Like there's something malignant and unclean, growing unseen beneath the inky water. Maybe it's thinking about Inez, of the slow death colonising her lymphatic system.

Also, I'm fairly sure that one of the white-haired women keeps looking at me.

The one at the far side of the pond, who was swimming a slow lap around the edge, but is now hanging from another of the floatation rings, is staring openly. She's wearing a bright yellow swimming costume, thick grey locs knotted in a neat bun on top of her head.

When I was a kid, the local supermarket used to display fish on ice with their eyes glassy and staring, like cracked marbles. I couldn't stand to be near them. I'd scream and grab my mother's hand and try to drag her away. She never seemed particularly moved by my distress, like her feelings were so big there was only ever room for them, never mine.

Byron once hid a fish head under my pillow. When I climbed into bed that night my fingers touched the cold clammy skin and I ripped back the pillow to see the eyes glowing there in the dark, staring up at me. I remember running to find Mum but she was gone. Vanished into the night and left my brother and me alone in the house. She used to do that sometimes, when things got too hard for her. Where did she go? Did she come somewhere like the Ladies Pond?

The woman in the yellow costume is still staring at me.

I watch her out the corner of my eye, trying to figure out if I've ever seen her before. Something about her feels familiar.

I decide I don't like it, the strange woman, the coldness of the lake, the buzzing insects that keep batting my face. I start making my way back to shore. But I'm far out. My flesh goose-pimples around my arms. I swim, but the dock doesn't seem to get any closer, like a nightmare.

The sun has properly set now. The sky is gloaming. The moon has grown fat and full, a white tick suckling on the sky.

Under the water, something brushes against my shin.

I panic, drawing my knees up high into my chest. Water rushes into my mouth. I come back up, spitting and gasping for air, two actions one cannot do simultaneously.

I tell myself I'm being a baby, startling at a fish.

But I really don't want to be here any more. I strike out again.

Another brush – this time against my thigh. And another, against the small of my back. That one is long. The touch goes on and on and on, like a ribbon being dragged along my skin. Some kind of eel, or snake.

I let out a small shriek, looking for the lifeguard, but I can't see her.

The white-haired women are all staring at me, though. The one in the yellow swimming costume swims closer.

More things are brushing against me under the water. A flash of silver breaks the water inches from my face, a shining fin. Behind me, a splash.

'Help!' I manage to gasp out. 'Help!'

The water is churning now. The murky shapes of creatures stir in the water around me. Coming at me from three dimensions. A dragonfly crashes into my forehead. A fish nudges right up into my chin, mouth open, eyes unblinking. Tiny bodies bump against me, soft and slippery and impossibly many, until the pond is alive with thousands of mouths, testing the edges of me, probing, tasting.

Something heavy hooks onto my foot, and I'm pulled under, the water closing around my face, the sane world lost in a chaos of brown murk and bubbles. My mind is a hot swirl of panic. I claw pointlessly at the water, open my mouth and inhale pond scum.

A sharp nip at my leg, a flash of pain.

Hot bites along the edges of my knickers.

A sting on my left shoulder blade.

Then someone is hauling me to the surface.

'Just float!' a strict voice commands. I gasp as I do what I'm told, letting my legs rise to the surface, allowing her to drag me back to the pier, trying to keep as much of my body out of the vicious water as I can. Still, I can feel them nudge at my back, nose at the gaps between fabric and skin, the occasional inquisitive nip. But the woman's arm around my neck is strong and firm, and she drags me through the water, not stopping until we reach the wooden dock. More hands reach down and pull me out.

They roll me face down onto the decking. Strong hands, running along my skin.

The backs of my arms and legs are covered in leeches. Each one small and squirming.

The lifeguard has reappeared. I shiver as she stretches my skin tight between her fingers, scraping them off with a credit card. Someone calls for hand sanitiser. Someone else runs from the changing room with a thick globule of it cupped in her hands. It burns where the leeches have bitten into me. The remaining few curl up and drop off, one by one. I am bleeding from a dozen tiny cuts all over my body. The blood runs over my skin in rivers, catching in the water dripping from my underwear. Some of the bites on me are larger, from fish mouths.

The pond is mirror-smooth now. Taunting.

The woman who saved me crouches close. Her mouth is set in a harsh line. 'They could smell you,' she says. 'It's coming.'

I don't know what she means. I'm shivering. Hyperventilating. Terrified. My skin prickles in the cold. I push away and stagger to the changing room, pulling my dress on straight over my wet underwear, desperate to get away as fast as I can.

The woman has followed me inside. 'You've got to deal with it, love. Look it in the face. It doesn't go away.' She says this softly, so only I will hear.

I shudder away from her, dropping my shoes against the wet tiles. I decide to leave them there. I need to be gone. *Now.*

'Let me take you home!' the woman yells after me as I wheel past her out the door.

The path crunches beneath my feet. A new List jogs through my mind. *Phone the council. Log a complaint to management, whoever that might be. Photograph the wounds in case I need the evidence for...* something. *Call my GP and line up shots for tetanus, rabies, whatever lives in leeches. Call my MP. Call animal control. Call whoever you call when you're attacked by a dozen distinct pond creatures at once.*

All the while, an answering echo in my mind, a loop of *what the fuck, what the fuck, what the fuck...*

My wet hair drips icy down the back of my neck. My fingers are numb with the cold. I stride as fast as I can across the Heath, shining under the full moon, a blank coin in the indigo sky.

The fields are almost deserted. The only other people out at this time are small gangs of teenagers, Bluetooth speakers blaring tinny sounds from their picnic blankets. They smell of beer and sex and pot and mischief. A lone runner passes, headlamp beam sweeping along the paths, stinking of sweat. My heart hammers one of Mo's dubstep compositions in my chest.

The station I need is all the way across the Heath. I want to teleport. I want Mo to wrap his arms around me and make everything okay. I want Paige to be there to crack jokes until I feel less insane. I want my mum.

I realise I've forgotten my bag in the locker room, but I can't go back for it now. I can't shake the feeling that the fish are following me, somehow, like if I dared to look back I'd see their blank eyes as they flopped up the path behind me, if I stopped to listen I'd hear their cold bodies slapping on the ground.

Bushes shiver as I walk past, smelling of autumn. Moths and beetles keep flying into my face, like I'm a light source. A tiny bat skims my hair in a frenzied flapping. The whole night is alive. Hungry for me.

I speed up, not daring to run, too scared to walk at a normal pace. I turn off the main path and take a shortcut directly across the grass.

It grows longer here. Now my mind imagines snakes twisting themselves around my ankles, dragging me – this time – into the earth.

I think of the thing that followed me through the streets, the night of the catcallers. The night before I woke up inexplicably in east London. It's the same feeling. The biological certainty of fear.

'It's a panic attack. It's only a panic attack,' I chant to myself. Probably perimenopause. Try to inhale, hold, but I've forgotten how. The air's lost its oxygen.

I dash between two plane trees. I can smell it now, and there is definitely something following me. Some animal smell. Musk. Fur. Danger.

I can't help it: I break into a run. The most full-on sprint of my life.

My breath burns in my lungs, but I'm not fast enough. I hear two extra feet pounding heavy on the ground behind me. I cannot outrun them.

Ollie

On a hill to the west of the dog pond, a boy named Ollie is hoping this will be the night of his first kiss.

Mary Kachuba and Laura Miller had invited them so lazily after school, 'Hey, want to come hang out on the Heath?', like it was nothing, like this wasn't the sudden transformation from another afternoon of manga and homework and boredom to a day he will remember for the rest of his life. He's told his mum that he's over at his mate Badger's place, Badger said the same, oldest trick in the book.

Now it's the four of them still out on the grass, hours later. He's slightly allergic, wishing he'd thought to sit on his hoodie, but there's no power on earth that would get him to move now.

It's fully twilight: moon up, sun long gone, and he's seen dark fluttering shapes at the edge of the lake he's sure are bats. He's deadly frightened of them, has been ever since one got stuck in his room as a kid, flapping terror in his face. But Mary Kachuba is wearing pink gloss on her lovely lips and she makes eye contact with him every time she reapplies it, which seems to be every five to seven minutes as far as he can tell, and he's sure *this is it*. He has no idea what sequence of events has led to these two girls inviting him and Badger out on this warm early-autumn night, but he's not going to question his good luck. He suspects it has more to do with Badger than him, how he somehow shot up five inches over the summer and how Laura's eyes keep lingering over his biceps, grown thicker since he picked up basketball, and maybe *he* should pick up basketball, Ollie thinks. But it doesn't seem to have mattered. In the past year, something has happened to all of the girls in his class where they suddenly feel ten years older than the boys. Sure of themselves. Laura and Mary keep throwing looks at each other and giggling like they have a secret plan they haven't let them in on. Whatever their plan is, all that seems to be required of Ollie is to go along with it and (crucially) *not mess this up* – and that's just fine by him.

They've been chatting about nothing, just banter about teachers and school, pretending not to notice they're a number divisible by two sitting here on a lawn, each body ripe with puberty, a ritual a million million other teenagers have participated in since there have been humans. Waiting to cross a threshold that can never be uncrossed.

It's getting cold. No one has mentioned anything about going home. Laura leans back onto Badger's chest, and his eyes meet Ollie's like *man, are you SEEING this?* and Mary is suggesting that maybe they should go for a little walk, just the two of them, and she slips her hand into Ollie's and she might as well have slipped it straight onto his groin, the way things are responding down there, and he's glad that it's dark and Mary is staring into his eyes not at his waistband. The only thing he can see is her glossy lips catching the shine of the full moon.

She pulls him into the shadows beneath an ancient oak tree, her wet lips blooming into a smile, and then she steps up to him; she's inches taller, but she whispers, 'I like your glasses,' and then his mouth is full of the taste of her, strawberry lip gloss and summer grass.

She drags him deeper into the bushes, still kissing him, tongue probing his lips. He doesn't want to be the creep with a stiffy, so he leans his crotch away from her, tries to simultaneously appreciate that *Mary Kachuba is putting her tongue in his mouth right now* and think of the most non-sexual things he can muster. Climate change. Trigonometry. Bats.

Then Mary Kachuba grabs his hand and places it on her waist, bare beneath her cropped T-shirt. Her skin is soft and smooth and impossibly warm.

The situation in his trousers has become urgent. He tries to bring his attention to a different part of his body than any of the obvious ones. The toe of his left foot, crunched in the new Vans he's already outgrown. His elbow. His grass-itchy skin. The backs of his knees, the night wind tickling them, bare beneath his school shorts.

No, not the wind.

Something is brushing up against his legs. Soft like leaves, gentle like tall grass, tender as Mary Kachuba's fingertips, which are now exploring the underside of his jaw, the two millimetres of hopeful soft stubble he has cultivated there.

He steps forward, away from the annoying brushing whatever-it-is, which conveniently is also closer to Mary Kachuba. A moment later, it follows him. This time, harder. A *nudge*.

Reluctantly, he pulls away from Mary Kachuba's strawberry tongue and turns to see what's behind him.

The night shatters open and something mad steps through the crack.

A great hulking shadow blots out the hillside. Bigger and blacker than the night. A shivering starveling body. Bulging shoulders hunched over thick front legs like a man torn apart and stitched back wrong. But it can't be a man. It's too big. Too twisted. The angles are obscene. There is no natural creature shaped like this.

Yellow eyes catch the moonlight, slick and shining like Mary's lips.

The snout is long. Wet. Meat-sweet breath hot and barely an inch from his bare shin. It's already touched him. *Nudged* him.

And now it smiles.

Rows of teeth, teeth and teeth and teeth.

Look: one quick slash, and bright blood blossoms from the boy's chest, fun fun splishsplash on the grass.

The beast recoils from the smell, thick stew of lust and lifefulness. In this half-second of distraction, girl grabs boy, clever sly little thing, and drags him to his feet. Let them run, the boy falling behind the long legs of the girl. Let them fly down the path, screaming screaming little lambs. Humans are too slow-limbed to bother chasing. It is a fine night and there are many better things to play with.

The rabbits, for instance. The Heath is thick with them, half a dozen quivering in the hedge shadow.

Nose into the brambles. Scent trail of piss and panic. Feign interest in a bare tree... slow snuffle slow along the shivering hedge... then dive!

Scattershot they dash across the open field and the beast bounds after, following the flashes of their white tails as they race for the safety of the gorse. It leaps a perfect arc into the air. Savage precision. Long limbs like a dancer. Snatching a warm small body in its jaws, just for the joy of the hot blood spurt.

A chase! A taste!

Some make it to the holes on the far side of the field. Smell them, bucks and does cowering in their honeycomb city beneath the dirt. Trivial work to scoop them out.

Nothing in its mind but instinct. No instinct but to rip, to tear, to eat, to follow its own pleasures.

It heads back to the pond, empty now of people, shadows writhing beneath black glass.

Called by its smell, the eels unbury themselves from their mud homes and slither to the surface. Dance beneath the surface of the murk, setting the surface trembling for an audience of one. Sexless until the year of their deaths. Eels know love is weakness; empathy is a trap.

The puddle of blood on the deck has dried into a sticky black mess. The beast laps at it, hungry, iron on tongue. Then it bounds across the open hills, revelling in the strength of itself, the clear logic of its muscles and claws, howling laughter to the wind.

The beast is growing stronger. The beast is plotting violence.

Hunter's Moon

Nausea

◐

Ellie

Bathroom tiles radiate warmth against my bare skin.

I recognise their texture: fine vitrified porcelain with a warm stone finish. I chose them two years ago when we redid the downstairs bathroom, teaching myself 3D modelling software so I could mock up the final effect before committing, the only way I make any decision – careful, considered, informed. They've soaked up the sunlight and are baking me gently, like a loaf of Mo's bread. Heaven.

I stretch, keeping my eyes closed, enjoying the firmness of the tiles beneath me. Must be great for your spine, this. I can't remember the last time I felt so refreshed.

The remnants of the dream slip back into the recesses of my unconscious mind. Such a lovely dream. I can't remember what it was now, but I know it was satisfying. Like plucking a hair that comes out with its root.

Why am I on the bathroom floor?

The question flashes in my mind like neon. I bat it away. Let me enjoy this relaxation for a moment, dammit. I get little enough.

There's a slow drip, drip, drip sound from somewhere.

Add to List: *Fix the tap.*

I peel apart my eyelids and take in the ceiling, which is crisscrossed with fine cobwebs glowing in the morning sunlight. Ugh, haven't dusted in here for weeks, add that to the List.

Why am I in the downstairs *bathroom?*

This time the question snags at my mind and tugs me upright like a puppet.

Around me: carnage.

The floor is covered in broken glass, ceramic shards. The mirror is smashed to bits. The towel rail has been torn off the wall. Expensive hand creams have been smashed into the tiles, little paste smears among the mirror shards. Amid this mess, I am naked, clean as a river-slick carp.

A thin whimper bubbles in my throat.

I turn to the right of me and see the bathtub.

The tap isn't leaking. It's been wrenched to an angle and water is dribbling from a crack in the base. And the tub is full almost to the brim, a lake of swirling browns and pinks. A soup of mud and gore.

Floating on the surface is a morbid crouton. A hunk of wet fur bobbing in the muck.

The air has gone suddenly thin. Not enough to fill the alveoli of my lungs.

I approach the tub, my body moving slow and clumsy, like it belongs to someone else, and I realise that the thing bobbing in the water is fat, like the haunches of a small dog.

The white fur floating in the water swirls into a fluffy cascade, like the tail of a small dog.

I reach into the water and lift it out.

It is the back half of a small dog.

As my brain tries to comprehend what I'm holding, the intestines unspool into the water with a heavy plop-plop-plop-plop.

The hind legs dangle loose beneath a cascading tail, mostly white, but with unmistakable streaks of neon pink. The bare flesh has been leached white by the tepid water. I cannot see the front half.

My brain will not work. All it can produce is an attempt at a cryptic crossword clue. *Englishman hesitates before Tehranian when describing man's best friend (10)*. Pom-er-(Ir)anian.

There are no proper towels in this bathroom, so I enshroud the sad bundle in one of the hand towels. I wrap the other around my waist, where it does little to preserve my modesty. Gritting my teeth, I reach into the vile bathtub and pull out the plug. It gurgles as it begins to drain, then stops, clogged. I dig my hand back in again and again, gagging as my fingers close around spongey clumps. Meat and hair and organs. I dump them into the small metal bin next to the toilet, for now.

Fuck. *Fuck.*

Still no sign of the other half of Julia's dog.

Dashing into the kitchen to grab the dustpan, I discover that the trail of destruction continues all the way up the passage. *Fuck. Fuck. Fuck.* Muddy footprints, shortened like I was standing on my tiptoes. *Fuck. Fuck. Fuck.*

Sweat prickles my scalp. My grandmother's swirled-glass vase is smashed across the dining-room table. There's another muddy smear along the kitchen floor. I follow it all the way to the kitchen door, which is swinging wide open, the handle loose, dangling like a tooth from a root, smeared with red.

Quickly, I wipe it all down with paper towels. I reposition the kitchen door, poke the handle back in place, grab the dustpan and brush and begin to sweep up the bits of vase, trying to keep as quiet as I can.

Mo's footsteps creak on the stairs.

There's nothing I can do about the ruin of the bathroom, visible through the open door like a crime scene. I just have time to pull the door shut when Mo appears in the other doorway, his brows furrowed in confusion, concern.

'What…' He eyes my naked torso, my newly lush pubic hair jutting out of the bottom of the insufficient hand towel.

'I knocked over a vase!' I say, overly chipper.

'Where were you? I waited up till midnight.'

I move back to the kitchen, drawing him away from the mess. 'Sorry, love. It was late so I slept on the sofa. Didn't want to wake you.'

He blinks at me. 'Where are your clothes?'

My mind scrambles for an explanation. 'We had a bit to drink, if I'm honest. Got some sick on them. They're in the washing machine.' I'm not sure where any of this is coming from. I've never been a fabulist.

All I know is that I don't want him to worry about me, and telling him this new thrilling progression of my sleepwalking into – from the evidence – sleep-rolling-in-mud and then sleep-murdering-the-neighbour's-dog then sleep-destroying-the-bathroom isn't something I know how to do.

He is looking at me with utter bafflement.

Then, of course, I finally spot the top half of the dog.

It's lying on the floor, just a few inches behind his feet. Right by the Please Take Me Upstairs pile. The black button eyes gaze at me in silent accusation from between my husband's legs.

'Dad was bad last night,' he says, voice thick with hurt.

'I'm sorry, love. It was work.' I inch to the right, hoping to encourage him to walk away from the half-a-dog.

'It's always work,' he sighs, before turning to go back upstairs, mercifully oblivious to the sad pile of fur at his feet.

And the Please Take Me Upstairs pile, for that matter.

'I'll bring you tea,' I shout after him, to no response.

Fuck.

Add to List: *Apologise to Mo.*

Empty the bin in the bathroom.

Buy a new tap, mirror, drain cleaner, vase, towel rail, hand creams.

Repair the back door.

Unclog the drain.

Put the bathroom back together without Mo noticing.

Fetch my bag and shoes from the Ladies Pond changing room.

Find a replacement dog?

Fuck.

Call the doctor.

It's not even that busy for a Saturday morning, all told.

It takes me until mid-morning to clean up the mess before I'm able to slip out the house to dispose of the evidence. The bits of Pomeranian are packed in a Fortnum & Mason basket filched from my emergency gift supply. It's the only container I could find that was big enough, and I hate myself for noticing that the rich meaty smell wafting from it is making my mouth water.

I feel wretched, obviously. Wretched, and confused, and scared, and now… goddamn it, hungry. But what am I supposed to do? Tell Julia? Or Mo? They'll think I'm going mad. Maybe I *am* going mad.

I haven't counted on the two police constables standing on Julia's porch, wearing deep scowls beneath their black helmets. Their fluorescent jackets cut sharp lines in the dreary daylight. Julia is standing in the doorway in a faded pink bathrobe that's seen too many washes. Her front door hangs off its top hinge.

'That's my neighbour.' Julia's head lifts at the sight of me. 'She must have heard something.' Her cheeks are blotchy and tear-streaked, her greying hair sticking up at odd angles.

'I'm afraid there was a burglary last night,' says the shorter of the two officers, a chubby-faced woman with an impatient air.

'Someone took Harold,' Julia wails. Her voice shakes as fresh tears spill over her cheeks. 'They tore my door off and they just… just took him! Right out of his bed!'

My stomach churns as I look past her into the cluttered living room. The dog basket is empty, a well-chewed teddy bear abandoned on the cushion. The doilies and Royal Doulton figurines crowded on Julia's end tables are untouched. I certainly have no memory of breaking in and taking the dog. But leading a trail across my neighbour's plush carpet are undeniably familiar footprints.

Did I really come back from the Heath last night, pull off the door, tiptoe past Julia's fiddle-leaf and commit doggy murder? Anyway, *how*? There was no sign in my house of a weapon, anything I might have used to rip a dog in two. I can't think about it too much without the image of the bleached wet flesh flashing into my mind, twisting my stomach.

The taller constable clears his throat, his pen poised above a notebook. 'Did you hear anything last night? See anyone unfamiliar wandering around?' The morning light glints off the handcuffs hanging from his belt.

'No,' I manage, my voice bleached. 'I was asleep.'

They ask me whether I have a video doorbell, security cameras anywhere. 'Sorry, no,' I say, mentally adding to List: *Install cameras to catch my own night-time activities.* Julia is sobbing openly now, scrubbing at her eyes with a tissue dissolving into threads.

The taller PC hands me a card. 'Think of anything, give us a ring. It's not the first break-in this month, I'm afraid. Mostly kids, you know.'

'Some pets were killed last month in Walthamstow,' adds the shorter one. 'Might be a gang thing.'

'Julia, I'm so… so sorry,' I stammer. Her trembling hands twist the threads of tissue. She seems smaller, shrunken.

She barely hears me, having already broken into a rant about how this is just what she should expect in Sadiq Khan's London, how if the cops weren't so busy arresting anyone who called pregnant people *women* they'd have time to stop the country's slide into the crime-ridden mess it is now, how she's lived in this neighbourhood since she was born, by the way…

I take this as my opportunity to leave, and walk a full twenty minutes to King's Cross before I find a quiet commercial waste bin behind an M&S, where I bury Harold's body beneath smooshed Colin the Caterpillars and day-old packaged sushi with trembling hands.

The cops are still there when I return to my own door. A third officer has now joined them and is carefully lifting dusted fingerprints off the handle with sticky tape. What if they find mine on it? That wouldn't mean anything, I tell myself, I've been over to Julia's house before.

Too late, I realise that the basket is probably covered in my DNA and fingerprints, but there's no chance I'm going back for it now.

Instead, I slink back to my own living room, now silent and reeking of Dettol. Mo's at an Ultimate Frisbee tournament, and Yusuf's taking a nap, like it might be any other Saturday.

I pull up Google Maps on my laptop, and plot a route between Hampstead Heath and my house. An hour's walk, assuming I made no other grisly detours. When did I lose my clothes? They weren't in the bathroom. Why can't I remember a single step of that journey?

The menopause app said to anticipate memory loss. Behaviour changes. Sudden and blinding rage. All normal, the posts insist. Normal, normal, normal. But this is too much.

I'm finally ready to admit to myself that I need help.

Misophonia

◐

Ellie

The GP's waiting room has seen better days. The nicotine-yellow paint is bubbled up in the corner from damp. Thick wads of public health brochures are jammed into the huge stand by the reception desk, because brochures are cheaper than time with a medical professional, I guess. A dog-eared poster on the wall admonishes me to get my five-a-day, partly covered by one asking me to PLEASE MAINTAIN SOCIAL DISTANCING which no one's bothered to take down since 2021, despite the fact that the chairs are now jammed so close together that I have to hold my elbows to prevent them from jabbing into the ribs of either of my neighbours: the teenager trying to break the world record for eating an apple as noisily as possible on my left, and on my right, the man I've dubbed the Sniffer.

It's taken me four days to get this appointment. I thought it would just take phoning the receptionist – fool! No, it took phoning the receptionist, being informed huffily that I could only make bookings through their app, installing the app, creating an account, waiting hours for it to be linked to my NHS login, completing a ten-page form about every medical malady I've suffered since birth, finally accessing the bookings form only to be told that all slots are booked out and new ones only become available at 7 a.m. each morning, trying again the next day at 7.30 a.m. because I had to help with an Yusuf-related emergency clean-up only to find that all the day's slots are already gone, trying again the next day at 7.01 to find that the appointments you can book on the app are only telephone appointments, and if you want an actual human person to check your blood pressure – greedy! – you have to... get this... phone the fucking receptionist.

I could afford private health insurance, but it's against company policy since the NHS is our largest customer. Plus, that's just playing their game, isn't it? The plan of libertarians everywhere: convincing people that public infrastructure doesn't work by systematically destroying public infrastructure. I love the NHS. I believe in the NHS. Right now, I think we should cancel the whole NHS and return to putting leeches on everything.

Almost every chair in the waiting room is occupied, and every single person here seems intent on being as noisy as possible.

I try to distract myself by updating Jira tickets on my phone, but I keep losing track of what I'm writing. The apple the teenager is eating is half the size of her head, and each bite involves a deep slurp of the juice, then *crunch-crunch-gulp* with her mouth open. I swear I can hear the muscles in her throat move with each swallow, the bolus moving peristaltically down her dry gullet. The receptionist is playing some kind of jingly gambling game on her phone. A woman on the other side of the room is watching YouTube without any headphones, subjecting us all to non-consensual Ed Sheeran, which must surely be a violation of the Geneva Convention. Each individual sound in the whole coughing, sniffing, wheezing, slurping, bleeping, throat-clearing chorus claws at my brain.

The Sniffer is the worst, that sharp inhale at the top of each breath, like he's hungry to get that last bit of air into his lungs. Each slow breath in – SNIFF – breath out, breath in – SNIFF – makes me want to lean over and stuff his tie into his nostrils.

My back itches, the ointment I smothered over the fish bites stinking of galvanic grapefruit.

The door to the doctor's room opens and a haggard woman steps out, toddler burrowed into her side. The woman slumps into the chair next to the Apple Eater, bouncing the child on her knee. The boy is fractious, clutching his ear. Tears stream down the mother's face, silent. She is the only person in the room who makes no sound, while the toddler whines and writhes.

The mother's about my age. Christ, imagine going through perimenopause *and* having a toddler. Add to List: *Buy a gratitude journal.*

I keep my eyes fixed on my phone, trying to tune it all out. There's another sound, I realise: a single long high-pitched whine. Tinnitus? Another perimenopause symptom to check off, oh fun.

Breath, SNIFF, breath.

'Oh shut it, would you?'

I jolt. The speaker is a man on the other side of the room, standing, staring in our direction. I'm ready to add my voice in approval, assuming his target is the Sniffer or the Apple Eater. But he's staring at the mother, whose face has gone a plum red. She hushes the child and pulls him into her chest, where his cries only grow louder.

Before I know what I'm doing, I'm on my feet, marching up to him, matching his height. 'Hey. What's your problem?'

'She needs to control her kid.' A gravelly smoker's voice. His head is shaved, face flushed with anger, set like an old footballer gone to seed.

'That's a *child*, what's your excuse?' It comes out more loudly than I intend. Almost shouting.

'We're in public,' he says.

'Exactly. We're in public, where the public are. Fuck off home if you can't handle it.'

Somehow we are chin to chin now, and I'm not sure if he stepped towards me or I stepped towards him. He is only a little taller. The blood thumps in my ears.

For a moment... *I wish he would push me.* So that I could push him back.

We stand there, close enough that I can see the black pores pitted across his nose, smell the mayonnaise tang of his lunch. I keep my eyes locked with his. Daring.

He disengages, flumphs back into his chair and vanishes behind *Country Living*, muttering darkly under his breath.

Where the hell did that come from? I have never yelled at a stranger before. Not even righteously. It's the noises. The bloody noises which have wound me up like this. And the exhaustion. I haven't slept properly since Julia's dog, scared of what I might do if I did.

Breath. SNIFF.

'And you!' I grab the pack of tissues from my bag and hand them to my neighbour. 'Here.'

I return to my seat. Everyone in the room is dead silent now, all eyes carefully downcast. Except for the mother's, which meet mine over a grateful little smile.

'Eleanor Fourie?' The doctor hovers in the doorway, wondering at the scene he's walked in on. He pronounces it 'Fury'. Add to List: *Legally change surname to Fury.*

The doctor is a clean-shaven man in his forties, friendly, distracted. He glances at my name and age on his computer, and asks why I've come to see him today.

In response, I pull out the stapled sheaf of papers I've prepared. All the symptoms I've logged in my menopause app, exported and neatly graphed. I've arranged it as a simple timeline with bullet-point summaries of the main issues, four colour pages printed front and back. I had to resist the urge to put together a PowerPoint.

It's been a struggle to decide what to include. The problem is, once you start looking for them, almost anything might be another symptom. Hungry? Could be menopause. Tingly toes? Menopause! Sad? Angry? Could be real feelings, could also be… you fucking guessed it, menopause. You have to walk around treating all of your emotions as Schrödinger's emotions: simultaneously real and untrustworthy, which is maddening. But the feeling of being maddened may, itself, be menopause.

The doctor's face tugs into a smile. He scans my pages for fewer than ten seconds, then tosses them on his desk. 'Very thorough!' he says, like a parent commenting on a child's drawing. 'Why don't you just tell me the highlights?'

My skin feels tight across my face. I clear my throat, wondering if I should mention the fish attack or canine dismemberment. Better start with the less bizarre, non-criminal offences. 'I'm losing time. Sleepwalking. My periods are heavier than normal. I'm always too hot and too cold. I've got acne on my chin. I'm angry all the time. The texture of my body hair has changed.'

I pull up my trouser leg to show him the new thick hair that's grown since just this morning. 'I feel… I don't know. I feel like I'm losing my fucking mind. I saw a doctor in A&E who thinks it's peri-menopause, but—'

'Why were you in A&E?' He frowns at his notes.

'I felt light-headed and passed out after a hot flush.'

He grabs on to the mention of 'hot flush', nodding before I've even finished saying the words. 'Oh yes, that does sound like menopause.' He roots around in the papers on his desk. Passes me a neon-pink leaflet that says YOUR GUIDE TO THE CHANGE! The exclamation point seems unnecessarily cruel. And the subtitle, WHAT TO EXPECT WHEN YOU'RE EXPECTING THE MENOPAUSE. 'We can check your hormone levels to be sure.'

'You mean an FSH test? I've read online that those aren't definitive since your hormones fluctuate throughout the month anyway.'

He shrugs. 'Well, it's up to you. There are a lot of lifestyle changes that can help. Do you smoke?'

'No. Which it says on the papers I gave you, actually.'

'A lot of women find that exercise helps.' His eyes flick over my body. Linger on my thickening middle, which no amount of CrossFit has been able to shake. 'I can also suggest some weight-loss programmes.'

Blood rushes into my cheeks as a slow, hot tide. I dig my nails into the palms of my hands. Inhale. Hold. Exhale. It's taking everything to keep my voice steady. 'I want to go on HRT.' The forums are all clear about the fact that HRT is a miracle. 'Apparently oral contraceptives are a good start.'

'Well, there are pros and cons. There are some studies that link HRT to an increase in cancers…'

That whine in my ears is louder. 'Those studies were debunked years ago,' I tell him. 'The cancer risks aren't an issue unless you're over sixty. There's a lot of information about this online.' Why am I the one telling him this?

'There is a hormone gel we can try.'

'The patches are better, I believe. I've included a list.' I gesture again at the sheaf of papers lying uselessly on his desk.

The doctor puts his pen down. 'I see you've done your homework.' There's a furrow now, between his brows.

'Yes.'

'Well, what the internet might not have mentioned is that there's a national shortage. Partly Brexit, partly Covid. Mostly, if I'm honest, it's because of the *increased demand*.' He smiles, and there's no humour in it. 'People going online and looking for one-size-fits-all solutions. You know, I've had four people in my surgery this week who diagnosed themselves with ADHD over the internet. Two kids who convinced themselves they have OCD. God, and all the sudden autistics…'

I take a controlled breath, hoping he doesn't notice how my nostrils flare. 'I'm sorry.' I don't know what I'm apologising for. It's reflex. 'I just need to not feel like this any more.'

'I know there's a lot of hysteria online. But the truth is that most women manage perimenopause completely fine.'

I grab the printout from him and point down the row of text. 'Look at this. Please. I've slept a total of six hours over the past three days. Last week I bled so much I found a clot in my pants the size of a mouse. I'm having panic attacks. I can't laugh without peeing. On Friday night I passed out in Hampstead Heath and somehow sleep-walked back to Barnsbury. That's *four miles*.'

He starts writing on a prescription pad. 'Let's start you on Estragel, ten patches. We can reassess in a few months.'

'Those are low dose.' God, my eyes are prickling with tears again, the rage threatening to boil out of me. I try to keep my voice steady, but even I can hear the whine in it. It's a catch-22: I need him to take me seriously, and also need him to see how not okay I am – and it is impossible to do both. All I manage is, 'I need something stronger.'

He thrusts the note at me. 'Ms Fourie, with respect, I think what you're looking for is a cure for ageing. Do let me know if you find it.'

I accept the prescription, hand shaking. 'But what about the memory loss?' I try. 'The anxiety?'

'I'm afraid if you want to discuss a second issue, you'll need to book a second appointment.'

I picture the app. The NHS login. The booking form which is only available between 7.00 and 7.05. 'I guess I'll try the Estragel.'

The doctor's already turned his back to me and is typing something into his computer. My neat sheaf of papers sits on his desk, untouched. I'm dismissed.

I swallow all the words I'd like to yell at him and storm out. I check the time on my phone, angling the screen to see round the crack. I've been in his room for less than ten minutes.

Angry Man scowls at me in the waiting room. The cacophony choir is back in session, the thousand human sounds banging on my skull, amplified by tinnitus.

I'm due back at work. Who knows how far the cash flow crisis rumours have spread by now. Instead, I find my feet carrying me up the canal to London Fields, then onto the Overground, heading entirely the wrong direction to Chingford. I travel all the way to the end of the line. I've still not calmed down, so I keep walking. I follow the road past an MOT centre, a Masonic hall, a golf course. The grass starts to break up into a muddy marsh. With no plan, I've brought myself to the edge of Epping Forest.

I used to come here a lot. I refused to step into my mother's house for the last two decades of her life because I couldn't deal with how depressing it was, so we'd meet here with Thermos flasks and trudge through the mud while she'd whinge to me about every one of her most recent problems. She was a virtuosic complainer, Mum. Every single thing was another proof point of the terrible conspiracy the universe had mounted against her. Her back ached. She wasn't sleeping. The head nurse had a vendetta against her and kept assigning her the worst shifts. Her neighbour had been robbed. An old school friend she hadn't seen in thirty years had died. It looked like they weren't going to get a pay rise and she could barely afford her bills as it was. There was war in Europe, and did I think she should build a bomb shelter? Did I think this mole looked irregular? Had I called my brother recently, and did I think he sounded stressed? Was Paige okay? Was I okay? Was she okay? It infuriated me. I used to send her endless links to Tranquillity meditations. She never listened to them, or saw a therapist, or went on the medications she so obviously needed to be on. You never met a woman more committed to her own misery than my mother.

I spent my whole life determined to be as different from her as possible. Dedicated myself to stability, to contentment, to sanity. But did I ever ask myself: was Mum always so bad? *Or did she get worse when she hit the menopause?* One of the podcasts said that among women, the most likely time for suicide is between the ages of forty-five and fifty-four.

I haven't been back to the forest since my mother died.

But now I hike through a familiar field, past the dog walkers and runners, deep into the treeline. I think of Angela Carter's Little Red Riding Hood entering the woods 'unwisely late'. I walk until there are no other people, just me and the trees and the sky and the small woodland things. They, too, clatter and bang. Birds click-clacking along branches. Small mammals scrabbling in holes. Worms and bugs pushing the soil around. Leaves brushing along leaves.

The high-pitch whine that's been following me all day is gone here. And with a chill I realise: it wasn't tinnitus. I've been hearing the hum of the electricity in the walls.

Shoulder Stiffness

Brenda

It's late afternoon. My feet ache. My calves ache. My lungs ache. My shoulder aches. Another day wasted tramping up and down the borough, stuffing flyers through letter boxes, scanning for CCTV cameras, knocking on doors, talking to anyone who answered. Had they heard about any dead animals? Seen anything, maybe a huge stray dog?

All I have to show for it is damp socks and nothing. Nothing, nothing, and more nothing.

Every opened door turns into another dead end. I spoke to a woman whose cat went missing but waltzed back a few days later. A man who went off on a long rant about the huge vicious dog tethered to the homeless man who lives behind the Ladbrokes, until I realised he was talking about Trent, Prince Harry's geriatric mastiff, who's as aggressive as a biscuit.

I've walked all the way up to Chingford today, until the city yielded to the green belt, the sky opening wide and white over Epping Forest. I can't shake the thought that I'm wasting everyone's time. The CATS volunteers' time. The police's time. My time, what little it's worth. And my dwindling funds – between printing two hundred flyers, buying snacks for the weekly meetings, and making a goodwill payment to Mervyn to get him off my case, most of that thousand-quid donation has already evaporated. Don't have it in me to put out a begging bowl.

And all for what? Some animal that went on a rampage through Walthamstow over a single night, over a month ago, and hasn't been seen since?

A huge animal, I argue with myself. *An impossibly huge animal. An impossibly huge animal that somehow unlatched a fiddly guinea pig hutch. An impossibly huge animal I see every time I close my eyes, like a piece of my personal void has detached itself and gone tearing through the world.*

It's been over a week, and still no word from Daniel. Just a curt message yesterday saying, *soz for the wait. C Gardner says nada leads & no one free to dig deeper rn. don't post vid.* I had to read the whole thing out loud, twice, before I understood what it said.

I decide to pack it in and head back south to Walthamstow. It's been drizzling, and the few kids walking home from school are dressed in macs and wellies. I stop at the Co-op to pick up a copy of the *Metro*. They ran a tiny piece on the cats a few days ago after my persistent phone calls to their office, just a few lines saying that several cats have gone missing, please contact CATS if you have any information. I lean on the counter and flip through, scanning headlines for anything about dead pets. There's nothing new.

I'll need to make tea for the CATS members who are coming over later, so I load £5 worth of gas onto my top-up key while I'm here. I've avoided putting the heat on so far, and I'm dreading the winter. It's going to be thick socks and hot-water bottles this year, just like the last.

On a whim, I also buy a pack of bacon from the bargain bin, steeply discounted and greying slightly, but I know someone who will appreciate it.

Prince Harry and Trent live in a threadbare tent buttressed from the wind with cardboard boxes, in a recessed window of the sports betting shop. Trent smells me coming and greets me with a wagging tail.

Thanking me, Harry carefully peels off a strip of the bacon. 'Now, we're going to ration this,' he says to the dog. A losing battle. Trent gobbles the first strip in one bite then fixes his eye on the rest, a long thread of drool unspooling from his lip. Harry relents and lets Trent have at the pack.

'Still looking for your fella?' he says.

I plonk onto a bollard and let my throbbing feet dangle. 'Feels like the trail's gone cold,' I admit, for the first time, lighting both of us a cigarette. 'All I've got is one bad video from a month ago. I must've missed something.'

Harry accepts his fag and pats the dog's head, looking thoughtful. 'Someone like that, they don't stop at hurting animals.'

I nod, rubbing the arch of my foot. I haven't told Harry what's in the video: that our culprit seems to be an animal, after all. Haven't told the Facebook group, either. They'll think I'm cracked.

'You're a stubborn ox, B. You'll find him.'

I scoff. That might be the nicest thing anyone's ever said about me.

'Keep him close.' I indicate the mutt, now cheerfully licking bacon grease from the pack.

'Trent knows how to look after himself.'

I'm not convinced. He didn't see the size of that shadow. It was bigger than Trent. Much bigger than Trent.

Or, as Reggie keeps repeating incredulously a few hours later, 'But it's bloomin' huge!' He scowls at my phone, where, after several hours of yelling at my computer and one humbling phone call with Jen's middle son, I've managed to load the CCTV video.

Reggie's squished on my sagging settee next to Posh Deborah and recent joiner Farah, who has three kids and insomnia and desperation for an excuse to get out the house. Squatting awkwardly on the floor is our newest recruit: Mr Bojangles's owner Jin. Jin hasn't said a word yet, not about the video, not about the beast, and certainly not about how I've turned out to be no one official at all.

'Could it be a person? Like dressed in a gorilla costume?' suggests Farah, snatching the phone back from Reggie.

'But it's bloomin' huge,' Reggie repeats, louder this time. I suppose he's mad because this scuppers his fantasies of tracking a cat killer and strangling him personally. The things some blokes will do to avoid their own problems.

'And this is the best footage you've found?' Deborah asks, with her clipped vowels.

'So far,' I say, hoping I sound more optimistic than I feel. 'But now we know what we're looking for, we can narrow our search. I want you going into any place that might have cameras. Ask if they've still got footage from the 31st of August. Tell them we're looking for a big stray dog.'

Farah hands my phone back. 'I don't think that's a dog.'

'Clearly,' I snap. 'But you try going around telling people we're looking for an indeterminate animal of unusual size, see how far that gets you.'

'We could try the animal charities,' Deborah says. 'London Wildlife Trust. RSPCA. Friends of the Earth...' She prattles off a whole list, which I scratch down in my BE A BOSSBITCH notebook. 'Well,' she shrugs in response to the stares, 'I do a lot of volunteering.'

'Could try the council,' Reggie adds, a suggestion I'm not going to dignify with a response.

'I can patrol the neighbourhood in the evenings, if that helps,' Farah says. 'I'll be awake anyway.'

'But it's probably not still *in* the neighbourhood,' Deborah points out, all reasonable practicality. 'If there's been no sign of it since August.'

Jin finally pipes up from the floor. 'My housemate's a Deliveroo driver. He's on this big WhatsApp group, like a thousand people. All across London. I can get him to post the video there, ask them to look out for it?'

I rub my shoulder, contemplating this. A thousand pairs of eyes across London? That's exactly what we need. But Daniel was crystal clear that he didn't want me to post the video. It's the only bloody instruction he's given me. 'I'll give you a photo,' I say, finding a loophole.

They file out, Reggie still muttering darkly about the size of the thing.

Jin pauses at the doorway, the last to leave, his eyes big and sad. 'You aren't who I thought you were,' he says softly.

I'm about to defend myself – *I didn't exactly say I was someone official, don't blame me if you want to go making assumptions* – but then a gentle expression unfolds across his face. 'It's just nice to meet someone who cares.'

He pulls out his wallet, offering a donation. And I'm in no position to decline.

I turn off the lights when they're gone, no point wasting the electricity. For a moment, I imagine I see movement in the shadows and crouch down to rub Melek in greeting, before remembering. No, it's just my void, eating another millimetre of my vision.

My computer wakes, whirring and grumbling like a pneumatic drill.

There's nothing new on the CATS Facebook group. Applications have slowed since it's been so long since the last bit of news. That's fine; these online warriors are far less helpful to me than the four flesh-and-blood troops who've just vacated my living room.

Deborah's right. This thing's probably not still in Walthamstow. If it was, it would have killed again by now. Either it's evaporated back into the ether, or it's somewhere else.

I spend the next hour signing up for neighbourhood groups all across north London, and going through their posts from the past few months. It's a tedious affair, picking through the crap they talk about, parkruns and Bump Clubs and squabbles over bins, advertisements from bored housewives who've managed to convince themselves their earring-making hobby is a business. There are a few missing-pet posts which I add to the spreadsheet for follow-up. I note one from a woman in Barnsbury saying her dog was stolen out of her front room four days ago; I record that one as a maybe – so far, our beast hasn't broken into any houses.

I send a photo of the animal to Jin, but refrain from sharing it more widely. Bloody Daniel. *Why* doesn't he want me to post the video? Surely something like that would drum up interest, shake something out of the tree.

I pull down my cardigan and rub arnica oil into my aching shoulder, thinking about what Prince Harry said. *You're a stubborn ox, B.*

You'll find him. But stubbornness only gets you so far. You also need luck, and that's not a currency I've ever been particularly wealthy in. There's no currency I've ever been wealthy in.

Then the other thing he said comes back to me with a jolt. 'Someone like that, they don't stop at hurting animals.' I consider this, the sharp tang of pine and cloves clawing at my nose. He was talking about animal serial killers, not impossible, shaggy shadows, but maybe the principle applies. A killer won't stop killing. There's a trail somewhere. There has to be.

I click on the table lamp and unfurl the newspaper. This time, I flick through more slowly, scanning for attacks against people.

And there it is, on page 3: BOY SAVAGED BY OUT-OF-CONTROL DOG ON HAMPSTEAD HEATH. My pulse skips as I read. A teenager named Oliver Ferrel was admitted to hospital with deep wounds across his abdomen. He and the friend he was with claim they were attacked by a large dog, shortly after 8 p.m. on Friday 29 September. The youngster's injuries are fortunately not thought to be life-threatening. No arrests have been made, and the Met urge anyone with information to contact them.

The rest of the article is a commentary on whether the list of banned dog breeds should be expanded, and an interview with someone from a related advocacy group. Journalist speak for *we don't know a damn thing.*

I type 'Hampstead Heath dog attack' into Google. There's a short piece in the *Mirror* with even fewer details than in the *Metro*. Bitter comments underneath.

This country's going to the dogs, ha ha.

I load the Hampstead Heath website, hoping there might be some kind of official statement with contact information. I search for dog attacks. Nothing comes up.

Then I try the more generic word 'death'. An article appears saying that a number of rabbit carcasses were recently found near Kenwood House, sparking fears of a new outbreak of myxomatosis, and urging the public to vaccinate their pets. I check the date. It was published last week.

Finally, after all that nothing, this feels like *something*.

My pulse hammers as I text both articles to Daniel. *Do you believe this could be the same creature? Regards, Brenda,* I type, modelling proper grammar.

He starts typing something in response. Then, the dots vanish.

on patrol will look tonight

I huff. More of this. Sit on your hands. Leave the experts to handle it. You know what? No. I don't think I will.

Body Odour

Ellie

The whole of Tranquillity knows we're almost out of cash. Interns whisper in the canteen. Devs circulate dark memes on Slack. On Thursday afternoon, I gather with the other execs in the box-fort huddle room to draft a company-wide email. Under the table, I'm tapping through Google Street View images of the roads between Hampstead Heath and my house, hoping something jogs a memory. A tension headache pulses behind my eyes. I haven't slept properly all week.

Andreas, of course, looks as unbothered as ever, lounging in one of his kaleidoscopic dashiki shirts, the picture of Disruption Chic. 'Tell them there's really nothing to worry about,' he breezes. 'Demo Day's at the end of the month, and I hear the AI project's proceeding apace. Sometimes you've just got to pivot into the headwinds.' He gestures expansively. '*Il n'y a pas de quoi fouetter un chat.*' Even not speaking a word of French, I'm sure that he's mangled the pronunciation.

'The staff are scared,' says Lanying, her voice tight. 'People have mortgages. Nursery-school fees.' Lanying – who has both, and also sends money every month to family in Gansu – adjusts her glasses with trembling fingers.

'Uri's already making overtures to potential investors,' I say, reassuring myself as much as her. 'Even if Demo Day's a complete disaster, we've got a strong story.' *And the corporate module will be ready by then*, I add silently. 'There's time. We've still got two months of cash reserves.'

'One month,' Meredith the CFO says quietly.

I almost drop my phone. 'One? No, we had *two*.' I've *counted* on two: one for Demo Day and getting Andreas fired, one for me to sign on a new investor and emerge victorious from the ashes. 'Are you including our emergency fund?'

Meredith glances at Andreas, who's now fiddling with his collar like it's the most pressing issue of the morning. She shifts uncomfortably. 'That money's already been spent.'

My jaw clenches. 'On what?' I fire up my laptop and bring up the financial dashboard.

'The marketing campaign,' Meredith says, keeping a deliberately neutral expression on her face.

The boiling begins in my stomach. The marketing campaign is Andreas's pet project, some rebranding nonsense involving flashy TV ads mostly featuring Andreas, I've gathered. I've been happy to ignore all mentions of it. Marketing is one of the very few parts of the business that's not my problem. Marketing is the girl-ghetto of the tech world, and worse, it's a ghetto that I spent the first few years of my career trapped in. Because what do you do with a degree in Theatre Studies? You end up in an ad agency, is what you do, and then your father dies and your mother throws herself onto the Hammersmith & City Line trying to follow him, and she survives, but you'll never have the courage to ask whether she tried to kill herself on purpose or just fell because of the antidepressants she was on, the plausible-deniability version of trying to kill herself, so you can't even relish in your own anger about it. So you have a baby and pour yourself into work only to one day hear some mediocre sales executive refer to you as the 'boobs and balloons brigade' so you quit that afternoon. Start over in your thirties retraining as a product manager, and because you're not really earning that much anyway, doesn't it just make more sense for you to be the one who's also dealing with every home issue and sick day while your husband gets to keep focusing on his career? And so you find yourself in your *forties*, surrounded by smug twenty-somethings who all know so much more than you, because you started too late, because you let yourself skid far too close to the black well that seems to be your genetic inheritance. Because you only just escaped it. Because you forced yourself, through sheer fucking will, to be happy. Because you learned to be happy. And you packaged that into this business, which you put everything into, and now they're sitting here around a meeting table in an absurd faux box-fort, staring at you blankly.

I clear my throat and scroll further down the dashboard. 'Let me get this straight. We've overspent a whole month's worth of operating costs?'

Andreas inspects his fingernails. 'It was the song rights. I mean, you've seen the ad.' I have not. 'You know the song is the heart of the whole campaign. And, well, it's John Lennon. Those rights don't come cheap.'

'How *not-cheap*?' The heat climbs into my chest.

Meredith shifts in her seat. '£450,000.'

My eyes bulge. 'And did it work? Did it get us new users?' I open the product analytics and scroll back through the past few weeks. There's maybe a tiny uptick. Barely a blip.

Andreas's face is bright red, almost the same colour as his awful shirt. 'Ah. We hadn't budgeted enough for the TV space, so in the end, we could only run the ad a few times.'

'How many times, exactly?'

Andreas hesitates. 'Three.'

'Three times?' I spit. 'We paid £450,000 to run the ad three times?'

'Well, no, the ad spots cost £4,000 each, so...'

'So we paid *over* £450,000 to play a Beatles song on TV for a grand total of one and a half minutes?'

Andreas sits up straighter, his tone edging towards sanctimonious. 'That's how brand awareness works, Ellie.'

'*Does* it work? Because I'm not seeing any impact of that *brand awareness* on my user figures, or any other number that an investor might care about. Or are we just planning to *vibe* our way through a Series B?'

Meredith avoids my eyes. Zayn squirms. Lanying looks like she'd rather be anywhere else. Andreas purses his thin pink lips. 'You're missing the bigger picture. We're taking a bold swing. That's what game changers do.'

My eyes prickle as the heat reaches my face. 'So you're gambling everyone's jobs on your idiotic vanity project.'

They're all staring at me.

I'm so angry. *So angry.* And, to my horror, I feel a single tear slip from my left eye and carve a slow path down my face.

'Maybe you want to take a minute to compose yourself.' Andreas says it so kindly. Hands me a tissue from his pocket. Chivalrous. Managing me. Because now I'm emotional.

And that's it. My authority gone. I stand, shaking with fury, knowing that whatever I say now, I've lost the argument.

I hide in the canteen, gobbling Peperami sticks and bug-testing the corporate module to settle my nerves. By the end of the day, I've managed to convince myself that my Demo Day sabotage plan is still an acceptable risk.

Paige hasn't been responding to my messages all week, so after work I decide to try the classic 'oh hey I happened to be in the neighbourhood and thought I'd pop in for a casual visit' move, which turns out to involve an extremely non-casual ordeal on the Central Line at rush hour, with signal failures and an internal temperature that I'm sure exceeds the legal limit for transporting livestock.

The man working the front desk at Paige's residence hall has to ask me to repeat her name three times over the sounds of the party raging in the common room. He finally nods, and tries to hail her on the intercom.

Nicole Kidman's toned biceps goad me from a magazine on the front desk. MENOPAUSAL AND *FABULOUS*, the headline blares. I flip through furiously while I wait, reading about how she's 'fifty-five and fighting fit'. I'm a decade younger than her and I'm not feeling particularly fabulous at the moment. I'm feeling confused, weepy, unattractive and hot. Isn't this what women of the world said we wanted, more older women on the covers of magazines? But why must they all look like Halle Berry, Jennifer Aniston, Salma Hayek? Where is the line between giving women tools to feel less anxious and expecting women to be eternally agreeable and placating? What fucking exercise regime do I need to follow to get Nicole Kidman's biceps?

No sign of Paige after several minutes, though the family location sharing app shows she's definitely in the building. 'I'm her mother,' I shout over the dulcet sounds of Doja Cat pounding through the floor. 'Can I just try her room?'

The receptionist shakes his head and says that's against the rules.

I resist the urge to say, 'Come on, look at me, I'm a middle-aged blonde woman in a Max Mara camel coat, I'm not going to be any trouble.' Instead, I try Paige's phone again. It goes straight to voicemail.

The doors to the common room slam open, revealing all the debauchery that a £10,000-a-year tuition fee can buy (a lot). Students of one of the top universities in the world reduced to sloppily dancing, gyrating, shrieking children. Incredible, the amount of parental capital invested in that room. The thousands of pounds collectively spent on private tutoring to ensure GCSE and A-level results. The property investments that allowed the kids to get into the finest state schools, if they didn't simply drop the money directly on private-school fees. Sure, this might look like just a room full of drunk teenagers, but it is in fact the reproduction of capital through one generation to the next. Literal reproduction, I'm certain, going by the rhythmic movements of the three pairs of legs poking out the bottom of the photo booth in the corner of the room.

Why exactly did Mo and I work so hard for Paige to have this? Because the alternative seemed worse, I guess. Because the world's been so hollowed out that the only way to ensure your children survive is to build them as thick a carapace of money as you can.

'Could I just pop my head in? See if she's in there?' I gesture to the bacchanalia. The receptionist shakes his head doggedly. Total waste of a trip.

The sour smell of vomit and booze wafts out the doors along with two girls wearing Y2K revival dresses that are the exact replicas of ones I was wearing in 2001. Just as awful the second time around. Mercifully, one of these girls is a friend of Paige's I've met before, Emma or Sophie or Mia, one of those names so bland you forget it as soon as you hear it. She's chewing gum like a lawnmower engine, the muscles in her jaw clenching visibly through her skin, probably on cocaine. Nice to know some things never change.

'Mrs Khalid!' She flops onto me into an overenthusiastic hug, enveloping us in the scent of Marc Jacobs and sambuca.

'Ellie, please.' I don't bother to tell her I didn't take Mo's surname. 'Is Paige in there?'

A concerned look crosses the girl's face. 'She's upstairs. I'll take you.' She flashes the receptionist a thumbs up and leads me to the relative quiet of the upper floors.

'I'm really glad you came,' says Mia/Megan/Ava, clacking gum. 'We've all been so worried.'

My stomach twists at the sound of this. I'm about to push for more details, but Katie/Charlotte/Lauren continues jabbering as fast as a machine gun, spewing mint-flavoured spittle into the air. It's some story I can't follow, about an incident at McDonald's, and something about Prof. Renkin's Politics II class, and about how they told Paige to speak to the Student Advice Service but she was concerned about this impacting her graduation, or somebody's graduation, and Paige saying she wants to deal with it on her own.

'Anyway, I hope you can talk some sense into her because we don't know what else to do, she's so stubborn you know, and at this rate she's going to fail the year and her life will be ruined over that creep and I don't know what she thinks she's trying to prove.' Amelia/Erin/Caitlin finishes this bewildering story as we reach Paige's door. 'Good luck!' She heads back down to the party, presumably to find more cocaine.

I take a breath and knock on Paige's door.

My worst fears are confirmed when she opens it. Paige's eyes are hollow; her normally glossy dark hair is a frizzy tangle against the ashy skin of her face. The room smells rank, windows unopened for days or weeks, unwashed sweat and sour milk. She plasters a fake smile on her face and waves me in. Dirty dishes crowd every surface, evidence that she's eating, at least, but why isn't she doing it in the cafeteria? Why isn't she at the party downstairs?

I have to move a pile of laundry off the desk chair to sit down. She flops onto the unmade bed. 'If I knew you were coming, I'd have cleaned up.' She jumps at a noise from the corridor, before it resolves into the sounds of some girls stumbling back from the party, belting out that song from *Moana*.

Confronted with her obvious anxiety, I don't even bother with my *so I was just in the neighbourhood* excuse. 'What's wrong, love?'

'Nothing.'

'Why've you been eating in your room?'

The fake smile doesn't budge. 'I've just been a bit under the weather. Figured I'd keep my germs to myself.' She ends the sentence with a little laugh which comes out of her throat rather than her chest.

'You aren't answering messages.'

'Oh, I changed my number. Sorry, forgot to tell you. Mum, really, I'm fine.'

She rakes her hair into a messy bun, and my eyes automatically audit her collarbones, taking a measure of her subcutaneous fat. When Paige was a baby, the absolute responsibility of it nearly shattered me. I couldn't understand how Mo and I, two well-educated people with resources, found parenting an infant so difficult. It felt like every minute was a brush with Paige's death, despite my elaborate spreadsheets tracking every bowel movement and crying fit, the many sub-lists within my List. 'How do other people do this?' I kept asking Mo. 'How do all the babies in the world not just die?' He was no help. I remember him shrugging, once, after a week neither of us had slept for longer than two hours at a time, and saying, 'Well, historically, most of them did.' Which was really not what I needed to hear at precisely that moment.

'Everything okay with your classes?' I try, my chest tight.

'Yeah, all good. I'm really enjoying macroeconomics.'

'And Theo?'

I've hit something. The fake smile twitches off her face, just for a moment, before being hoisted back. 'We're actually taking a break right now.'

Relief floods my body. So it's *heartbreak*. That most common of young adult hurts, so painful in the moment, so ultimately un-scarring. Her first experience of withdrawal off the drug of oxytocin. She's nineteen; she'll get over it. And, honestly, if it means she's finally shaken off that plonker, good riddance.

I'm so relieved I could cry. Instead, I arrange my face into a sympathetic expression, which probably looks about as convincing as her customer-service smile. 'I'm sorry to hear that.'

I resist the urge to spout platitudes at Paige as she makes me tea from the small transparent kettle in the corner. I silently take an inventory of the room. Her bedside table is crowded with anti-ageing face creams pilfered from my supply, below a cheery *My Neighbor Totoro* poster. There's a notepad stuck on the side of the bookshelf, with tasks in Paige's neat handwriting. *Buy sugar. Fix boots.* The beginning of the List Paige is going to carry around for the rest of her life.

Paige hands me a mug of tea, from which I surreptitiously wipe away an old coffee splodge on the rim. The forced smile on her face has finally retired for the evening, leaving her face looking heavy. I wish I could just wrap her in a hug and love her back to life, but I know that would just make her retreat further into herself.

'How's Dadu?' she asks, sagging back onto the bed with her own mug.

'His sugar readings were through the roof yesterday. I think your father's sneaking him eclairs.' I reach over to squeeze her hand. 'He misses you,' I add, meaning, of course, *I miss you.*

Brain Fog

●

Ellie

The Mumsnet forums say that Estragel can take a few weeks to start working. I try to be patient. Dutifully, I log each symptom in the app. The anxiety has abated, for now, but my body feels more like a strange wild country to me every day. Hair and stink and secretions that refuse to be tamed.

People keep asking me if I'm feeling okay. I tell them I'm not sleeping well. This is a fantastic understatement: since that excellent night's sleep when I apparently murdered Julia's pet, sleep has entirely eluded me. I lie awake all night in sticky sheets, listening to the rhythmic whines of Mo's breathing and Artie's snuffles at my feet. The hours refuse to tick away. They pile up on my chest, heavy.

The upside to insomnia is that I have time to read the entire internet every night. I hide my phone under the sheets to shield the light from Mo, tapping from solution to solution, a vast assemblage of solutions. I subscribe to email newsletters and menopause podcasts. I learn that the medical community knows more about erectile dysfunction (which affects less than 20 per cent of men) than the menopause (which affects 100 per cent of cis women if we live long enough) because we're considered too complicated for clinical trials. I read forums. I google perimenopause. I google burnout. I google ADHD. I google 'can you die of insomnia?' I google 'symptoms of spending too much time on the internet', and spend three hours clicking through the results.

Tired of disturbing poor Mo with my tossing and damp sheets, I tell him I'm going to sleep in Paige's room for a while. He seems hurt by this. Add to List, *Muster energy to care about Mo's feelings.*

I push her bed under the window and open it wide, unbothered that it's the ground floor and any pervert could climb in. Lying naked in the night breeze, I snatch brief moments of sleep between one breath and the next. Strange, violent micro-dreams, where my body breaks into a new shape. Screaming my fury through snapping fangs, screaming it into soft bodies. I wake sweating, sheets clinging to my body, heart dancing.

Everywhere that is not bed, I only want to sleep. I fall asleep on the bus. At my desk. On the sofa. In the bath. In a meeting with a potential investor. It's like that first terrible year of Paige's life all over again, when Mo once found me asleep on the toilet, breast plugged into the pump, Paige screaming infant murder from the next room.

I come home from work each day to find deliveries piled on my doorstep. A box of unmarked pills ordered off the dark web. A set of essential oils. A plant-based diet ingredient box. Red clover lozenges. Chinese herbs for slowing memory loss. An 'electronic massage wand' designed to reawaken my dry vagina. A crate of green tea. Extra-absorbent period pants. Marijuana-infused lube. Faecal transplant capsules. Oestrogen cream. Testosterone cream. High-tech Kegel balls. I don't remember ordering any of these things. I pile them in the hallway cupboard, a shameful menopause stash, promising myself I'll return them the next time I get a chance (never). Only to repeat the cycle again the next night, with new solutions.

Memory loss. Brain fog. The #6 and #8 most common symptoms reported by users of the menopause app, respectively.

The exhaustion is a drug, distorting the edges of what feels real. It becomes hard to keep track of time.

Julia's Pomeranian glares from missing-dog posters all over the neighbourhood. Each one sends a knife of guilt through me. But – thank God – there have been no police at my door... yet.

Did I kill the dog two weeks ago, or three?

When did I last properly *sleep*?

The Personalised Meditations team have managed to get the voice recognition working, sans Millie, and replaced the OpenMind integration with some dodgy open-source generative text model. I play the latest meditation the app has created for me: *Let your thoughts be the guide and the path to destiny is and you are not afraid of the guide and let your thoughts wander and let the wonder let the labyrinth your thoughts are the labyrinth into the heart of night the path the path the path the skin is your skin is the grit of soil and whisper into the night guiding night labyrinth...*

Perfect. I give the team the green light to release it to the beta testers. I tell Andreas over Slack that it's going great. He replies with a gif of Elon Musk giving a thumbs up under the text TO MARS. He asks if it will be ready for him to present at Demo Day.

Definitely. Demo it live! I respond, a grin creeping onto the 'guiding night labyrinth' of my face.

The model is meant to improve over time, storing what users say so it can tailor responses to them in future. But the system's a mess; user inputs and the meditations it generates are getting dumped back in with the training data. No one's keeping track of what it's learning from. There's no version control, no filtering the garbage. The model's just chewing up everything it's ever been fed and regurgitating word salad. Like Rupi Kaur with concussion.

But Andreas's not going to ask how any of this works. He just wants something shiny.

I diligently open Tranquillity SMART a few times a day and record some thoughts. I do this only half-conscious, like a dolphin, one brain hemisphere asleep. Some mornings there are tabs on my browser I don't remember opening. Messages sent from new accounts I don't remember setting up, tirades I would never type. Thankfully, my night-self only seems to be harassing strangers, not people I actually know. I find a new Google account used exclusively to leave terrible reviews of my GP.

I scold myself that this is not the time to be losing my mind. I need to be on top of my game, showing the board I'm ready to pick up the pieces when they inevitably realise Andreas is a clod. But if my performance at work is suffering, nobody else seems to notice. If I'm driving on instinct, they are well-honed instincts. I don't remember half the decisions I make, but I'm still making decisions, and they seem to be the right ones.

I find myself in a meeting discussing a new mentorship programme for young women in MedTech. 'Maybe we should mentor the men, teach them how to do more of the childcare,' I snark, eliciting cheers. Lanying asks me for an update on something we agreed on in the previous meeting, and I realise I have no memory of that meeting happening at all. I blag that I've taken care of it, and hope that *it* was nothing essential. I flick through my notebook looking for minutes. All I find are lines of dialogue, half remembered, from *Medea*, a play I directed when I was nineteen. 'Mortal fate is hard. You'd best get used to it.'

My team seems happy. People are still coming to me with their problems and trusting me to solve them. I'm getting away with it. Maybe what feels like snappy irritability reads to other people as decisiveness.

Maybe I'm just the best at menopause, I allow myself to think. *Maybe this is easy. Maybe other women just don't have enough grit to get on with it.*

The last time I was in a church was my mother's funeral three years ago. I was all hysterical humour then, joking about how I was going to burst into flames the moment I stepped inside, making non-stop quips about how Mum would have hated the flower arrangements ('hydrangeas, honestly, nobody actually *likes* hydrangeas'). It was during Covid, so there were only six of us, the rest of Mum's friends watching from a tiny webcam rigged up in the aisle.

This church looks exactly like that one did, in the way that all C of E churches look like each other. An embroidered wall-hanging of John 3:16 sways over old brickwork. I wonder if they buy them out of a catalogue, like an Anglican Argos. Ratty hymnals are tucked into pockets at the back of each pew. Cheery pamphlets on the noticeboard announce bake sales and choir rehearsals, and the one that drew me here when I spotted it outside M&S, desperate for answers about what's happening to me: AGEING WITH GRACE: A SUPPORT CIRCLE FOR WOMEN ENCOUNTERING THE CHANGE.

'They make it sound like we're about to grow tusks out of our arses.' This is spoken in a Geordie lilt by the woman standing next to me over the stale biscuits, bright red curls streaked through with silver, luxuriantly fat, wearing battered Doc Martens with an asymmetrical tartan skirt and a Blondie T-shirt.

'Or like we're about to be taken over by a race of alien bodysnatchers,' I reply.

The woman cackles and holds out her hand. 'I'm Carol,' she says.

'Ellie. I'm here to talk about my arse tusks. And the fact that my brain's forgotten how to sleep. You?'

'Doctor's orders, pet. Well, more like a doctor's hostage situation, really. He's withholding my anti-anxiety meds unless I go for therapy. And every actual therapist's booked up till March.'

'It might help, I guess. Talking it through in a group.'

'Ah, but we already have a group, you and me.' Carol winks, like we're both in on some secret. I have no idea what it might be, though.

The group leader, a purple-haired woman in a fuchsia kaftan, introduces herself as Ileana. 'This is a safe space for us to discuss our changing bodies. While the symptoms can be challenging, many people find that this can be a joyful time, that moving into a new phase of life can bring new wisdom.'

'And night sweats,' a woman to my left mutters.

'I see a couple of new faces,' Ileana continues, pretending she hasn't heard. 'Why don't you introduce yourselves, and tell us why you're here?'

The woman next to me stands up. Her hair is thinning. She introduces herself as Ashvini. 'Six months ago I was talking to someone and couldn't remember my husband's name. My GP put me on antidepressants. But I wasn't depressed, I was angry, all the time, and I couldn't focus, and I kept forgetting words, and I basically thought I was losing my mind. So last week, right, I'm in at the shops and suddenly it feels like I'm boiling alive in my own skin, and I thought it was a fever, so I went back to my GP, who now tells me I'm perimenopausal. And I asked for more information, but it's Tottenham, so he had to usher me out because they only book you for these ten-minute slots, you know?' We all nod. We know. 'And he said I should come here. So I'm here. Hoping one of you can tell me what the hell is happening to me.'

'Thank you for sharing, Ashvini. We'll come back to discussing these experiences in a moment.' Ileana gestures at me.

'Ellie, hi. I'm forty-four. Also just… diagnosed, I guess.'

'We try to avoid that word around here,' Ileana says gently. 'Diagnosis implies a disease. And we aim not to medicalise this very natural life transition.'

I want to say *sure, but this 'natural life transition' is also producing some very real symptoms that could be eased with medical support that the NHS seems weirdly ill-prepared to offer me.* But I'm far too British for that, so instead I bite my tongue, nod politely, boil inside.

'Carol, would you like a turn?'

The ageing punk shakes her head, not hiding the smirk on her face.

'Okay… Neil, why don't you go next.'

A well-built man shuffles to his feet on the other side of the circle, rubbing his beard nervously. 'Yeah, hi. I'm Neil. So I just turned fifty-one and I've been on the waiting list at a gender identity clinic for seven years now. That's just normal, by the way. And then a few months ago, my periods start getting insanely heavy. Like biblical floods. Agony. It caught me in the gym the other day, fun times. So I went to see my GP, who said it's perimenopause, but when I asked about HRT, she started grilling me about my transition and then flat-out refused. Something about "eligibility", but let's be real, she thinks I'm scamming for T. Which I'm getting privately, no thanks to the NHS. I just want a medical professional to tell me how to not be completely disabled every month. And now I'm panicking about finally getting seen at the gender clinic, because what if they also won't help me now, because I guess menopause is already kind of a transition, and no one will tell me what to do, and fuck, I'm just so tired.'

Nobody knows what to say to this. Eventually Neil sits, rubbing his beard angrily.

We continue around the circle. Most of them have it worse than me. Annie, an Uber driver in her fifties, admits that she keeps coming home from long shifts and then screaming at her unemployed husband for not having done any of the housework. Helen, a sixty-something teacher from Australia, was doing fine until the only HRT regimen that was working for her became impossible to source, then the incontinence got so bad she quit her job, now she's four months behind on her bills and not sure if she'll ever get another job at her age. A twenty-three-year-old law grad named Orla had her ovaries removed to cure crippling endometriosis and is now coping with the menopause and figuring out her first job at the same time.

Ileana starts talking about how many cultures have rituals that help women embrace this new stage of their 'majestic womanhood'. Carol catches my eye and mimes a gagging face. I have to suppress a laugh.

At the end, Ileana leads a prayer. 'Lord, grant us the serenity to accept the things we cannot change. Lord, grant us joy in the new wisdom of our years. Lord, help us to find peace with how we are altered—'

'You missed a bit,' Carol pipes up. 'The courage to change what you can. Pretty important part, I think.'

Ileana looks up, scandalised, hands still linked to the women on either side of her.

Carol's standing up now. 'Sorry to say it, but your problem isn't menopause, Annie, it's that your husband's a lazy shite and you should divorce him. Ashvini, that's what two decades of Tories gutting the NHS gets you. My mate Neil here's the only one who seems to understand that not everything's his bloody fault, which should honestly be all the proof he needs to show the government that he's a bloke.'

'Carol, thank you for sharing, but we were just closing our session...' Ileana begins.

'Look, I'm sure you mean well. But these lot are dealing with some proper honest-to-God shite and banging on about our *majestic bloody womanhood* isn't going to help that. Sorry.' And she flounces out the door, not bothering to look back. The others eye each other, shifting uncomfortably.

Then, to my own surprise more than anyone else's, I'm on my feet, following her out. I'm the only one.

I find Carol in the car park, puffing cherry clouds out of an enormous vape which looks like it was assembled by a mechanic. 'I should probably go back and apologise to Ileana. I was rude.'

'You were *majestic*.' I pull a cigarette from the fresh pack in my bag. I swear, your honour, it jumped in there of its own accord.

Carol's nostrils flare. I wonder if the smell of my cigarette offends her. Maybe I should admit defeat and buy a vape kit. But she's biting the corner of her lip, considering me. 'Look, you're new to this.'

'To the menopause? Or smoking?'

She shakes her head. Starts to say something, then stops herself. 'Take my number.' She keys it into my phone. 'I have this group of friends. We go on a full-moon retreat once a month. Sort of a rage room in the forest, like. You should come.'

'Thanks. But I have...' *a sweet but helpless husband, a dying father-in-law, an anxious daughter, a needy job, a brother who won't stop calling me about Mum's house* '... responsibilities.'

Carol purses her bright orange lips around the spout of her absurdly large vape. I so want to like her, but her energy is kind of manic. She might be a con artist, or just unhinged.

'Believe me,' she says, blowing a steady stream of cherry smoke out of her nose, which licks at the wild curls piled carelessly on her head. 'Sometimes you just need to let all the anger out.'

I nod politely, stubbing out my cigarette. Besides the aberration of the past few weeks, I have never been an angry person. Whatever weird moon cult this madwoman is trying to rope me into isn't for me.

Fatigue

Brenda

I watch the video again. And again. Over and over, the shadow slinks across the screen, hunched and shaggy, shoulders rolling like some half-formed nightmare. The gait's all wrong – uneven, jagged. Limbs jut at angles no creature should move at. Between the low-quality video and my low-quality eyesight, I can't make out much detail. But something in the way it moves tugs at me. I rewatch and rewatch and rewatch, and cannot shake one impossible idea: that he's walking on two legs.

The thought keeps creeping in, no matter how much I try to stuff it back down. The *it* in my head keeps slipping back into *he*. Every time I think about the mangled cats left uneaten, the rabbit corpses strewn across the Heath, the guinea pig hutch opened so carefully. Most animals don't kill for fun.

Farah had suggested some twisted bastard running around in a costume. Could that be it? Names run through my head. Paul Rogers, who microwaved his pet rabbit. Robert Thompson and Jon Venables, who used to tie rabbits onto railway tracks and watch them get run over. Dahmer cut up dead dogs and put their heads on sticks. Nasty hobbies of sick sad little men. Hurting animals, bedwetting, arson – the early warning signs someone will graduate to killing people.

But someone dressing up like an animal to do their killing, that's something else. A person channelling something wild in themselves. Telling themselves they're feral. Denying the human in them and excusing heinous acts. The irony, of course, is that humans are capable of cruelty that no wild animal is. If there's one thing I've learned in my time on this planet, it's that human beings are basically cunts.

I force myself back to the task at hand: finding a normal, flesh-and-fur, real-life animal. Something that actually makes bloody sense.

Since no one will give us the number of the boy who was attacked, my team's been asking about animal sightings all round Hampstead. A bin man told Farah that strays are the responsibility of someone called the Dog Warden, who is an employee of – you guessed it – the poxy council. It takes me three hours of rowing with an automated phone menu before I'm connected with the Camden Dog Enforcement Team.

I perk up a bit when they tell me there has, in fact, been a recent uptick in abandoned dogs, thanks to the XL Bully ban. A woman named Maya, whose face held more metal than a pincushion, takes me to the kennels to see if any of them are 'my lost dog Ruffles'. We walk past a death row of piteous creatures, barking, whimpering, turning tight anxious circles, tail-wagging, begging me to save them. The largest one, a stocky grey Bully with ears clipped into sharp triangles, has front teeth as long as arrowheads. But they are still nowhere near as wide as the puncture wounds on the cats. Not even close.

So, something else.

Deborah was right: for a city so iconically urban as London, you'd be amazed how many wildlife charities it houses. Pigeons, pollinators, pike and pipistrelles – if it's got scales or feathers or fur, it's got a local fan club. I spend several hours on the internet doggedly searching for contact information for as many of them as I can.

It takes me almost a week to work my way through the list, dialling them to ask the impossible question: is there a large mammal skulking around the city which shouldn't be here? Most of them are polite but puzzled. No, they haven't heard anything about a rogue beast. Once I get them talking, it's hard to get them to stop. They're glad of a sympathetic ear, all too ready to dive into an impassioned rant about their tragedy of choice. Plastic pollution. Cars. Pesticides.

River toxins. In other words: people. These are crusaders like me, I recognise, each fighting a private war. Unaided, unpaid, uncelebrated. Most of them, to be honest, somewhat unhinged. Yes, I do realise they likely think the same of me. I listen as patiently as I can while they talk themselves out, and finally, I strike something promising – Jack, a man from a wildlife project in the Lea Valley, just south of Walthamstow. I ask him about rogue mammals and his voice grows immediately defensive. 'Where did you hear about this?'

I reassure him that I'm not a police officer or a journalist, just investigating some unexplained sightings, which may be connected to animal deaths around north London. Sounding cagey, Jack says he won't say anything over the phone where he can't be sure I'm not recording the conversation. But if I meet him in the valley, he'll show me. He'll be there tomorrow, he says, all day, but best come around sunset.

It's probably not wise to meet a paranoid stranger near a river after dark. But, really, how can I say no?

In person, Jack turns out to be a sun-leathered bloke in his forties or fifties, wrapped in a coat which seems to be mostly made of mud. I've brought Deborah along as backup. After a half-hearted pat-down for recording devices, he leads us across Hackney Marshes. Now he's decided we're not here to expose his terrific secret, he's just as happy as the rest of them to jabber away about his life's mission, which turns out to be saving the Lea Valley's slow-worms. He shows us a photo on his phone of what looks exactly like a snake, but he assures us it's an entirely different type of animal. 'Legless lizards,' he insists, swiping through a dozen more shots. 'Marvellous creatures.'

He points out his wildlife group's projects as we traverse the fields. Wooden posts with holes drilled into them for solitary bee species. A tiny native wildflower meadow. A recently installed frog pond, fenced to keep the dogs out. Deborah asks if they get money from the council for any of this, which sends him into a furious rant about how the council's only interested in kickbacks from developers, and how they've already sold off some of the slow-worms' prime breeding grounds for an expansion of the leisure centre. Like me, Jack seems to be an engine that runs mostly on fury. Maybe furious people are the only ones who ever try to fix things, I muse.

We dodge the various groups of kids kicking footballs to each other and head for the treeline along the edge of the field, thick with the season's last brambles.

The Lea River shimmers in the twilight, stinking of mud and duck cack. I'm transported back in time seventy years, thinking of how my brothers and I would muck about along this riverbank all summer, fishing for tiddlers with little nets. When we got too hot, we'd jump into the icy water, until the boys would yell 'pike' to scare me out, laughing as I shrieked and splashed. Afterwards, we'd nurse steaming mugs of Bovril, bought for a penny.

I don't think you could stick a toe in this river now without picking up giardia. Strips of ragged plastic drape from the vegetation like flags.

'Sorry for the cloak-and-dagger,' Jack says, as we trudge into the mud, evading stinging nettles and dog crap. 'We don't want word to get out. A few months ago, one of them was run over by a car, and it made it into the local news. Last thing we want are nosy parkers trampling all over the riverbeds, ruining the habitat.' I start to remind him that he hasn't yet told us what this mystery beast is, but he's vanished into my void, and it takes me a moment to realise that he and Deborah are already halfway up the riverbed, their attention on the ground, eyes scanning for something. The bushes there are meagre, half-trampled, scraggly things. I try to picture a bear-sized creature crouching underneath, ready to pounce on us in the twilight. It seems unlikely.

Finally, with a happy cry, Jack squats next to a flat-topped rock. 'Spraint!' I follow them down, ignoring the creaks in my poor knees. On the rock, there's a half-dried turd, black, about the size of my forefinger. It smells faintly of jasmine. 'This is how they mark their territory,' Jack says. 'The otters,' he adds, to our bemused looks.

'Otters,' I echo, swallowing my disappointment. Deborah sighs beside me.

'We think the holt's just under the weir there. You won't see them. But they're here.' He crumbles the crap in his hand, revealing a red cable tie, small plastic pieces. Carefully, he picks them out and stows them in a pocket which is already bursting with rubbish.

'Not what you were after?' he says, noticing our expressions.

'No,' I say, pushing my tired body back into an upright position with an embarrassing amount of groans and creaking noises. I tell him about the cats, the impossible puncture wounds. 'Then there was a boy, a month later, attacked on Hampstead Heath.'

'We think it might have been the same animal,' Deborah adds. 'Like a rabid dog.'

'Hasn't been rabies in England for a hundred years,' Jack cuts in.

'Yes, thank you, we're not idiots,' I say. 'That's why we've been talking to wildlife charities. Trying to figure out what else might be running about.'

Jack looks thoughtful, picking a dried chunk of mud off his thumb. 'You know, we've got a few trail cameras dotted round the valley. There to track the *hedgehogs*.' He scoffs at the idea of people being interested in any animal which is not a slow-worm. 'People are so happy to donate if the animal's "cute". They're motion-activated, night-vision and all. I'm sure there are a couple in the Walthamstow Marshes.'

Pain fizzes up my spine as I twitch. 'Can you check if they picked up anything on the 31st of August? Or 29th of September?'

He shakes his head. 'They only went up a couple weeks ago. But I'll ask them to keep an eye out in case it goes by again.' He hesitates. 'But I'll be honest. An aggressive animal, the size you say, wandering round London? Someone would have seen it by now.'

He and Deborah start nattering about charity funding deadlines, meandering back up to the hedge line.

The last of the light drains from the sky as I think about crawling shadows, prowling voids.

Ignorant of my worries, waterthrush call in the evening, their soprano songs punctuated by the occasional boom of a bittern. Tampons and plastic bags float down the river. People think you can just toss things away and they'll vanish, but everything's got to end up somewhere. You can tell the health of a city by the health of its rivers.

Still, if there's enough life here for otters, it must be cleaner than it looks. I glance up at Jack, muttering about inconsiderate dog walkers as he adjusts some twine holding a baby tree against a stake. Is it only this, I wonder – the few earnest people on their little quests – holding the world together? Just us?

Headaches

Ellie

The text comes through from a number saved in my phone as 'Vaping Punk Lady'. *Hiya, it's Carol. We met at the menopause support group. Arse tusks, remember? I need some help running an errand. Up for it?*

I smile, tempted. But then I glance at the Bored Room wall covered in notes and ironic motivational slogans like 'Fail Faster' and 'Iterate to Infinity'. Demo Day's next week. No chance. *Sorry, another time!* I reply.

The Personalised Meditations team's been having daily meltdowns, begging me to please, for the love of God, not demo the feature live. They say it's getting weirder. That no one knows which build is running any more. *I have full faith in you!* I messaged them this morning, brightly, cruelly. They've been trying to pin me down for an in-person chat all week, but the Bored Room's blinds are down, the door is locked, and they'll never find me here.

Andreas has only seen the old version of the feature – the better one built on OpenMind. He's got no idea it's currently producing gibberish. I only have to get him onto that stage, then let karma have its way.

I'm keeping up the charade of testing the app, making sure I regularly tell it *what's on my mind*. I don't bother listening to the nonsense that comes out the other end. If anyone ever audits the records, I'll look like the world's most diligent team lead.

I scrub my tired eyes, returning my attention to the investor pack, the real one I plan to circulate once Andreas's gone. I've been noodling on it all morning. The numbers look great: the corporate module has us hitting break-even in under a year. It's the vision statement that goes with them that I can't get right.

Something is wrong in the world today. Tranquillity exists because people are suffering [add stats about anxiety disorders, burnout, teen mental health crisis blah blah]. But there's hope. In robust scientific studies, we've already proven the effectiveness of our meditation programme in addressing chronic pain: now we're extending our focus to everyday depression and anxiety. Tranquillity teaches people to master their own minds.

A dull pain throbs somewhere behind my eyes, the beginning of an insomnia headache. Isn't it a bit glib to suggest people should just meditate their way through an underfunded health care system? A broken economy? Aren't we just giving people a plaster to patch the crack snaking across the hull of the *Titanic*?

It gets worse.

Bad things happen to all of us, but they don't have to be traumatic. Some people crumble under pressure; others transform into diamonds. You can learn resilience and grit. Your boss yells at you? Your worth isn't defined by someone else. Your partner leaves? Well, everything ends eventually. Imagine a world where sadness never interferes with your goals. Imagine flourishing as much as you deserve to. With Tranquillity, you can learn not to turn your pain into suffering.

You can't always change your circumstances, but you can change yourself. Isn't it self-indulgent not to try?

I consider texting Don. He was always so good at this stuff. He could always make me believe. When he was around, the goodness of our mission felt so clear. But I can't bother him now. He sent me an update a few days ago saying Inez has decided to stop chemo, insisting they're both in good spirits about it – a lie.

I delete the last paragraph. Then the one before. I cut every word that doesn't feel true. Finally, I'm just staring at the words. *Something is wrong.*

My phone buzzes. Carol again. *Does it help if I say there are reward brownies?*

I stare at the banal vision statement, then reply, *You know what, Arse Tusks, my afternoon just opened up.*

Of all the places I might have expected Carol to suggest meeting, Chelsea is the very least likely. Yet here I am, waiting for her to pop out of Sloane Square. She's fifteen minutes late.

It's a warm October afternoon, bustling with shoppers making use of the last week of post-work sunlight before the clocks change. The Ralph Lauren store displays ripped tulle-layered skirts under navy blazers, in case you're going straight to a rave after the polo, I guess. Young couples holding hands peer into the windows at Tiffany & Co. Elegant blonde women with oat lattes push past them into a gym offering facial workouts. Next door, a boutique on-demand mental health cafe reassures customers that therapy is 'not just for the frazzled, but the self-improvers too'.

Finally, Carol emerges from the Underground, dodging through a swarm of tourists in a leopard-print jumper and violently clashing pink tartan skirt. A green rucksack bulges on her back. I'm struck by the ease of her, the way she seems out of scale with the rest of the world. She's delighted by my demure work outfit, saying it's just perfect, but ignores me when I ask for more information about this errand we're running.

She natters away as we walk, telling me about her former job as a drama teacher – *former* because, as she tells it, 'the cunty new headmistress thought politics doesn't belong in the classroom, the *drama* classroom, the wazzock'. Now, as far as I can gather, she lives on a houseboat ('barely a raft with a shack on it, honestly'), attends a lot of social justice protests, and eats vast quantities of home-grown magic mushrooms. Paige would love her.

She leads the way down a side street, past a French patisserie, into the handsome Georgian blocks of Chelsea proper. A black Audi roars past, a hand dropping a crumpled Pret bag to the ground as it goes. Before I know it, Carol is already half a block back, paper bag held high, running towards the car, which has been stopped at a red light.

'Oi, I think you dropped this, lad,' she shouts, shoving it back through the driver's window.

'You know he's just going to drop it out on the road again as soon as he turns the corner,' I say, when Carol wanders back to me.

'You underestimate the deep-rooted fear every Englishman has of disappointing their mam. It's a special kind of power, that.'

I should be wary, but I can't help liking her, this unkempt stranger with zero chill. After all of the confusion of the past few months, there's something reassuringly bossy about her. What a relief, to have someone else lead.

'Where exactly are you taking me?' I try again.

'Right here.'

The white wall of a massive house looms ahead of us, the single beady eye of a CCTV camera leering from above the gate. Carol ducks into a neighbour's driveway and unzips her backpack. To my horror, she pulls out two cans of spray paint, red and black, and hands me one.

'Ever committed an act of public vandalism before?' she asks.

'Sure...' I say, not adding that the last time was seven prime ministers ago, and the crime was defacing an RAF recruitment poster for the war in Afghanistan.

A feral grin rips over her face. 'Well, this is Lord Emersmith's house.' I recognise the name: it's been all over the news recently, some hereditary peer turned disaster capitalist, caught hiring mercenaries to incite a civil war over mining rights in the DRC.

'You can't be serious,' I say, eyeing the can she's shoved into my hands. She hands me a Covid mask from the bag.

'I'll take out the CCTV. We should have a couple minutes.'

'Aren't we asking for trouble?' Heat uncoils in my belly. Anxiety. And maybe something else.

'I bet he's not even *here*. Probably off shooting an animal at one of his other houses.' She slips on a floor-length hooded puffer coat, a baseball cap and pink plastic sunglasses, looking like the Unabomber on the way to Aldi.

'That's not answering the question.'

But Carol's already adjusting a Covid mask of her own. 'When I flash the signal, come quick.'

Then she's sauntering down the street. Casual as anything, she crouches down and places a small laser pointer on a little stand, raising it up to flash directly into the CCTV lens.

'Go!' she shouts.

There's no time to think. I pull the mask over my face and sprint to the wall, surprised by my own speed. I raise the can, fingers trembling, something baring its teeth from a dark pit inside of me, an urge to ruin, to piss on something.

Carol has the red can out and is spraying 'WE SEE YOU' right by the gate.

My skin buzzes, my nails sharp against the tin. I give my nozzle an experimental squeeze. It hisses like a snake. The spray is more violent than I expect, and splatters a black splodge onto the white wall. Well, I'm committed now.

I conjure Emersmith's face in my mind. Fury twists my belly like hunger. In jagged wild movements, I start writing, 'C... U... N...'

My brain interrupts with an internal clipboard-wielding *ahem*.

Ellie.

This is ridiculous.

What are you, sixteen?

I chicken out before I complete the word.

Shouts bellow from inside the building. Heavy footsteps.

Carol's already stuffed the bag, hat and glasses into the backpack. And now she's just any ordinary middle-aged woman standing about, looking politely baffled as two beefy men in uniforms burst out the front door.

I toss the spray paint in my handbag like it's bitten me. But the guards barely glance at us. They split up, each one running up a different side of the street.

Not seeing the culprit, the first guard jogs back to us. 'Sorry to bother, ladies,' he says, all politeness. 'Did you see who did this?'

Carol shrugs. 'Sorry, pet, they went past so quick.'

'I think they were wearing hoodies,' I add, noticing my fingertip is black and tucking it into a fist before he notices.

The guard gestures something to his partner, who's jogging back, similarly empty-handed. We stroll off, leaving them furiously discussing the laser pointer.

My eyes meet Carol's. She's got an animal grin on her face, laughter rippling out of her. 'Cur?' she whispers, through wheezes.

I'm about to sass her back. Tell her how unacceptable it is that she just threw me into that situation with no warning. How much trouble we could have been in. But then warmth prickles up my chest like a hot flush, only this time it bubbles out as a laugh, bright as barking.

Carol's houseboat is moored in the Paddington Basin, portholes glowing amber. Inside, it's a cosy, wood-panelled cabin crowded with plants growing out of bottles and alien-looking things fermenting in jars, so narrow you can stretch out your arms and touch both walls, like living in a gingerbread house. It smells of wood smoke from the cheery log burner in the corner, and Carol's vape, and brownies, and something else I can't place, something homey. Wet earth after rain.

I sink into the overstuffed sofa, feeling languid, sleepy, spent. Carol pours thick slugs of whisky into two tumblers and sets out a platter of dried venison and home-made brownies. The brownies are squidgy and bitter and delicious, the first non-meaty thing I've eaten in weeks that doesn't make my stomach squirm. Carol tells me the secret is an atrocious quantity of butter.

As I chew, the window creaks open, and a massive tomcat slinks in, a scrapper with a chipped ear and grizzled fur. I coax him onto my lap with a strip of venison and scratch his head while he settles, purring like a chainsaw. Carol watches this with a cocked head.

'You know, I thought you didn't like cats,' she says cryptically.

The walls are covered in framed documents, which, on closer inspection, are charge sheets. Breaking into a bank, supergluing herself to a motorway, public urination.

'Extinction Rebellion.' Carol smiles, answering my unasked question. 'Except that last one. That was personal.'

I find myself telling her about Paige, how she's doing PPE hoping to get a job in government working on environmental policy. That was the anxiety underneath all her other anxieties, the family therapist told us: that the world is ending and she's helpless to stop it. And it's hard to talk a child out of a fear you all secretly believe is probably entirely rational.

I swirl the glass, watching the amber glisten in the firelight. 'Sometimes I think her eating disorder was aimed at me.' I've never admitted that out loud before. 'Like she was punishing me for something. Is that the most narcissistic thing you've ever heard?'

Carol considers this, tapping at her glass with short fingernails. 'No, I get it. Isn't that just a rite of passage, teenage girls hating their mothers?'

'It's just your face on a punching bag representing the entire social role of adult womanhood. And you've got to let them believe it's your fault, *your* choices, to hang on to the hope that the world isn't going to fuck them over exactly like it fucked us.'

Carol smiles faintly. 'So then it's a gift you're giving her, letting her rage at you.'

'But it's not healthy. Haven't you heard that thing, about how holding on to anger is like grasping a hot coal intending to throw it at someone?'

'*You're the one who gets burned,*' Carol parrots back. 'Bollocks, I say. People could do with throwing some hot coals. Women especially. Most women aren't nearly as angry as they should be, in my experience.'

I long ago made peace with the fact that you can't have it all; no one can. I chose work, family and CrossFit. There was no space for friendship on the overflowing lists of my life. But sitting in this cosy barge with someone who *gets it*, for the first time in so long, I wonder if that was a mistake.

The barge grows hazy with her vape clouds and the wood smoke. My head lightens. The cat slinks off, and I get up to nose around Carol's clutter. On a bookshelf, a photo of four women catches my eye. Next to Carol, a tall woman in a wax-print headdress beams at the camera. I know her, but I can't place how.

The heat builds and Carol pulls off her jumper, revealing a green sports bra overflowing with abundant breasts. 'You know that full-moon retreat I mentioned? We're driving up next week. You should come.' There's a forced casualness about how she says this.

'I really can't. There's a big work thing next week. A make-or-break thing.' Hopefully a *break* thing, as in *break Andreas*.

Carol puffs on her vape. 'I admire what you do, you know. Helping people.'

I shrug, thinking of my awful attempt at a vision statement. 'Sometimes I wonder.'

'At least you're trying something. Most people just give up.'

She bustles over to the kitchenette to top up our glasses. I return to the sofa, watching her effortless movements. I have never met a woman so comfortable taking up space. Silver stretch marks catch the candlelight and glimmer across her shoulders. The skin of her bare back is pale as clotted cream, her flesh rippling in sumptuous rolls. Unbidden, my mind produces an image of my own fingers stroking gently into a fold, of my fingers lost in the landscape of her.

She puts on some music. I'm expecting something punky, but it's the ukulele cover of 'Somewhere Over the Rainbow' by Israel Kamakawiwo'ole. 'I always wanted to learn to play the ukulele,' I sigh. The words slur in my mouth. I'm more drunk than I realised.

She settles onto the sofa, closer to me than she strictly needs to be. 'Why don't you?'

'Christ, I'm far too old to learn an instrument.'

'We're really not that old, pet.' Carol nudges me with her cold glass. Her eyes flash amber in the firelight.

When I finally head home to Yusuf (unbathed) and Mo (miffed I'm home so late, again) and several thousand messages from work (frantic), I realise that over the past eight hours, I haven't thought about my List even once.

Inflammation

O

Brenda

The Walthamstow Central police station is a shiny glass-and-chrome building huddled under the railway bridge, ragged Union Jack hoisted above the doorway. It stinks of antiseptic and burnt coffee, with base notes of Sergeant Orten's BO. I've still heard nothing from Daniel, and I'm sick of waiting. I can't shake the feeling I'm running out of time. There was almost a full month between the first rampage and the second, and we're coming up to a month again. I know two doesn't make a pattern, but that's what I've got.

Constable Gardner's at the front desk again. She barely looks up from her paperwork as I march to the counter.

She raises a blonde eyebrow at my out-thrust phone. 'Oh yeah, Bigfoot. We all saw that one. You could probably get some money for that from one of those TV shows. The ones about the Loch Ness Monster and the like.'

I shove the mobile back into my bag. 'So you're still doing nothing.'

She thumbs through the thick sheaf of papers. 'See these? Friday night's reports. A stabbing outside the Rose. Burglary. Two domestic call-outs. This lady was punched so hard you could see her bottom tooth through her lip. So what you're saying to me is that you want us to take officers off the streets where they're dealing with all this, and get them to investigate some bloke in fancy dress you saw two months ago?'

I take a long breath, in and out. If she'd seen the faces of the cat owners. If she'd seen the bodies…

The surgery screw in my thumb needles the bone as my hands tremble.

'Can I talk to Daniel?' I manage finally.

'Who?'

'Pencil.'

'Oh. He's on lunch. Try the chippy.' She gestures vaguely across the road, nose already back in her forms.

It's bright outside, and it takes my pupils several minutes to adjust to the contrast. A child on a beeping Lime bicycle almost clips me when I step into the road. Shouldn't be allowed. Bloody absurd that they want to try to take away my right to drive when any ten-year-old can pilot an electric bicycle at 60 mph without so much as a learner's test. I yell after him, he swears back at me, before I trot the rest of the way, following the smell of grease and haddock because I still can't see a damn thing.

My vision returns in the dim light of the chippy. Daniel's at a table with a group of uniformed officers, laughing, drinking Cokes.

I come right up behind him. 'You haven't been answering my messages.'

He almost leaps out of his chair at the sight of me, mumbling something through a mouthful of chip.

'Leave him be, Brenda.' Sergeant Orten scowls. 'The boy's got real work to do.' They're leaning forward slightly, protective. They've claimed him as one of their own. My heart sinks. There's my most useful ally, gone.

'Let's talk outside,' Daniel says, wiping ketchup off his chin.

'Watch out for her claws, son!' someone says, chuckling, a bit of hake dangling off his moustache.

'You're avoiding me,' I chastise him, lighting up a fag as we re-enter the blinding sunlight.

He clears his throat at the sight of my lighter. 'Those'll kill you, you know.'

'Let's hope.' I take another drag, deeper this time, just to annoy him. The effect is somewhat ruined by a cough which rattles through my ribcage. 'Did you read the articles I sent you? The boy who was mauled on Hampstead Heath? The dead rabbits?'

'Sergeant Orten says it's not in our jurisdiction.'

'I just want to talk to them. The boy and the friend. Ask what they saw. You could just give me a phone number.'

Between the void and the piercing sunlight, I can't really make out the expression on his face.

'I tried, Auntie. I really did. Offered to interview the victims myself and everything. But they said I can't do it alone, and there are other priorities. You don't know how overworked everyone is here. And… you know, I've only got a few weeks left at this BCU. This job means a lot to me, yeah?'

I nod, curt. I should be used to this by now. People letting me down. 'So why'd you tell me not to post the video?'

'I just thought…' He lets the half-sentence hang in the air for a few seconds, before saying, 'I don't want people to get the wrong idea.'

'What idea?'

He clears his throat. 'I know it's real, yeah. But Facebook's full of fakes, and especially older people… I mean, people will think it's a hoax, and then they might start googling you, and…' I can hear him clicking his knuckles nervously, working up to say something. 'I think you should talk to somebody, Auntie. Like a counsellor or something.'

'Oh, piss off. I need a detective, not a shrink.' I take another drag.

The silence stretches, like he's hoping I'll fill it for him. More knuckle clicking. 'I looked up your file,' he says finally.

'My file.' Another drag. A spasm is starting in my chest again, but I hold the smoke in, willing it to poison my lung tissue into submission. Manage not to cough.

I'm sure my police file is as long as a novel. The feud with Harriet. The social worker who reported me for harassment, just because I dared ring her six, seven times a day trying to get Rayya onto universal credit. Banging my head against brick walls trying to make other people have some decency. But I know that's not what he means.

'Your husband had to file a non-molestation order.'

I flick the ash, maybe a little harder than I need to, hoping this covers how much my hands are shaking. 'My shithead *ex*-husband filed a non-molestation order to try to force me to talk to him again. I didn't give him the pleasure. The court granted it in my absence when I didn't show up at the hearing.'

'There were photos in the file. What you did to his face.'

I actually laugh at this. 'You didn't see the photos of *my* face.' Because I never laid a charge against him. Because I told the doctors that I'd fallen onto the open dishwasher by mistake, three surgeries to get my hand working again. Because I'd destroyed the other photographs by then, of the first and second time I tried to leave him. Because he begged me to. Because he said he needed help, and I've never met an injured animal I haven't needed to save. Even animals that sink their fists into me.

'I had a dachshund,' I say, exhaling smoke in his direction. It's hard to form the words in my dry mouth. 'Sausage Roll. Sweetest little thing. Desperately wanted to please. The Shithead loved teaching him tricks, except Sausage Roll could never do them good enough to please him. It wasn't really the dog he was training, see. One time I went to visit my brothers for a few days and I came back and the dog's collar was on so tight he could barely breathe. He was just lying there panting on the floor, his fur rubbed off all around his neck, and the Shithead said it was punishment for not following orders.' I hate dredging this up. No use in dwelling on the past. But I can feel how my words wound him, how he squirms at my side.

'See, shitheads always start with animals, but they don't stop there. That's not in your file, is it?'

Daniel begins to splutter out an apology, but I'm not interested. I throw the butt to the ground and stomp it out with my heel. Sharp grinding pleasure. 'I'll see you around, Pencil.'

'It's Daniel,' he says, hurt.

'Do they call you that yet?' I gesture to the two through the chippy window, already finished with their own meals, and stealing his fish.

'Auntie, please.'

I leave him there, marching off to my car.

'You didn't *drive*, did you?' he calls after me.

I ignore him, wiping the furious tears from my cheeks, thinking, this is what you get for hoping people will help you. I should have known better.

Forget Pencil. Forget the sodding police. I post the video on CATS, asking if other people agree it looks like it's walking upright.

The responses start immediately.

WTF

Is this a joke?

Hahaha keep your cats indoors, people! The Walthamstow Gorilla Man will scarf them up!

Make money from HOME zero risk £££ guaranteed CLICK HERE.

I sit in front of the screen, smoking down an entire pack of Chesterfields and posting furious replies, increasingly all in capital letters. I post a photograph of Melek and ask if they think I murdered my own cat. More people pile on.

After the first hour, I stop responding to the messages. Someone finds a local news clipping about the social worker harassment case, my photo staring gormlessly back out at me from the screen. I just sit and watch the mockery pile.

The fury blazes hot and white as ash on my lips. *Bugger you all*, I curse them. *I don't need any of you.* But I can't stop reading.

And then, hours later, my phone buzzes with a peace offering from Daniel: a phone number.

Loose Teeth

O

Ellie

Things I did not do today:

- Overthrow capitalism.
- Campaign for the humane treatment of migrants.
- Blow up an oil or gas pipeline.
- Build a hedgehog highway.
- Write a letter to my MP about the climate emergency/reparations for colonialism/modern slavery/voting reform/trans rights/genocide/the housing crisis/wealth inequality/tax havens/racial justice/NHS funding/animal welfare/the policing bill.
- End war.

Things I did do today:

- Put the finishing touches on tomorrow's Demo Day presentation for Andreas.
- Entertain an elaborate fantasy about pushing Andreas off the roof.
- Call Yusuf's doctor to discuss a new medication regimen.
- Tweeze dark hairs from my upper lip, chin and knuckles.
- Finally send Inez that care package.
- Rub Deep Heat on every inch of my aching body.

- Test the corporate module, which is reassuringly stable.
- Test the AI feature, which is reassuringly terrible.
- Replace my stupid Estragel patch, which seems to be doing exactly nothing.
- Make Paige a playlist called 'Bye Fuckboy' (it's 90 per cent Olivia Rodrigo).
- Buy Julia a sympathy bouquet.
- Message Mo another apology.
- Message Byron another apology.
- Wonder what any of this is fucking for.

The feeling of circling doom has returned. The building pressure, the prickling skin, the buzzing nerves, the simmering blood. Even my teeth feel loose, like there's a whole new, even more adult set pushing behind them. I keep thinking that the last time I felt like this, I lost a chunk of time and woke up to find a dead dog in the bathtub.

I've offered to pick up kebabs for Mash & Trash night, since Paige isn't joining us. She texted earlier to say she's got an essay due – that's the second missed dinner in a row. I'm trying not to read too much into this. She's probably still nursing her broken heart, and anyway, what nineteen-year-old wants to hang out with their parents and grandfather? Fine. Whatever.

Honestly, I needed to escape the house for a bit. Mo was driving me mad, talking me through the entire plotline of a new video game he's spent a hundred hours playing this week instead of, say, fixing the thermostat. I told him he can at least take his turn at giving his father a wash this week, since I've done it every other night this month.

Our old reliable kebab shop seems to have been taken over by new owners, who apparently felt that what the place really needed was fluorescent lights bright enough to banish seasonal depression. The air is full of hot grease and the rotating meat tower looks suspect. I'm about to slink out and get pizza instead, but the man behind the counter has already started dolloping hummus onto pitta and is asking me if I want falafel or meat.

I order the usual, then, on impulse, add a side order of plain doner meat. The kebab guy raises an eyebrow but doesn't argue, slicing off greasy strips of greying beef into a tin tray. I take it to one of the plastic-wrapped tables and pick at it while I wait for the rest of my order. It's fungal-tasting and chewy, like eating foot, but it takes the edge off the hunger that's been clawing at me since breakfast.

Everything's annoyed me today. Mo. Paige. The team's Demo Day jitters. The smell of Andreas's vile tea. And now the woman sitting alone in the corner of the kebab shop, wearing a puffer jacket over a nurse's uniform, and a furious expression. She's in her sixties, with a sharp chin and a thick skunk-stripe of grey roots growing into limp brown hair, and she keeps sneaking glances at me, then glancing away as I look up.

What's her problem? I pat my face with a napkin, wondering if I have meat grease on my chin, then flush realising she's probably just shocked that I've come out in public looking such a mess, my face puffed and sweaty, new dark hairs creeping down my sideburns. I didn't even bother putting on make-up today. What's the point, when I'd just sweat it off?

To take my mind off her, I take out my phone and whisper a new recording into the AI feature. I've been doing this several times a day. A dozen? More? I've lost track. Sometimes I wake in the morning and the app's still open, the voice-input icon blinking.

It's still producing meditations that are nothing more than profound-sounding gibberish. I never listen. That's not the point. It's the talking that helps. Unburdening into the cracked glass. Like extracting poison. It asks *What's on your mind?* and I tell it. Even the things I'd never admit to anyone else. The phone absorbs it all, unflinching. It's the only thing, right now, which feels like it's helping.

Better than the stupid menopause app, to be sure.

The kebab guy plonks the rest of my order on the table. I order another tray of plain doner meat for the walk home, since the first one's empty now.

I pinch beef into my mouth as I walk, more annoyances tugging at my attention. Discarded single-use vapes litter the pavement. A billboard advertises all-inclusive plastic surgery holidays in Turkey. An unhoused man under the awning of an organic deli burrows under his duvet against the light of the nearly full moon. I read there's been a 14 per cent increase in homelessness in London in just the past year, and no one's doing anything about it. The doner meat oozes down my gullet.

My recycling bags have been moved from the bins and passive-aggressively piled in the middle of my front path, thanks, Julia. I kick them aside, swearing at her under my breath.

'Oof!' I jump at the voice coming from the deep shadows next to my front door, where yet another light bulb needs to be replaced. I've kicked the recycling right into the belly of a boy, who steps into the light, doubled over in pain. *Young man*, I revise my assessment as he straightens. He's a little shorter than me, curly blond hair tumbling into his eyes. He's holding an enormous bunch of flowers. Yellow lilies, Paige's favourite. Is this the new Theo?

'Mrs Fourie?' he asks, nervously extending a hand.

'And you are?'

'It's Kyle,' he says, like I should know who that is. His hand is clammy in mine. 'Is Paige already here?'

'Ah, she forgot to tell you.' And that would be just like Paige, I think, overcommitting herself and then dropping balls because she was overwhelmed. It was like this before when the ED was bad. Still, quite a thing to invite a new boyfriend to meet your parents, then neglect to tell him you're not showing up. 'She's not coming tonight.'

Kyle turns a bright crimson. He's a handsome lad, under the nervousness. A bit skinny, a bit awkward, but tender, eyelashes so long they tangle. Reminds me a little of Mo at his age, actually. I'm pleased to notice that unlike Theo, who seemed to believe showering marked you out as a tool of the imperio-capitalist post-colonial hegemony, this one's made an effort with cologne. Too much effort, if we're honest. And he's wearing an oxford shirt and chinos still creased from the packaging.

'She's got a big assignment due,' he says, squirming in embarrassment, poor lamb. 'She must have just forgotten.'

Worry twists in my stomach, or perhaps merely the doner meat. 'Has Paige been forgetting a lot of stuff recently?'

He frowns. 'Like what?'

'It's just...' How do I say this without being indiscreet? I don't even know how long they've been seeing each other, since my daughter tells me nothing. 'When Paige's... when she's not healthy, sometimes she finds it difficult to focus.'

'Oh, you mean like the anorexia stuff? No, that's all fine now.'

The knot in my stomach untwists a bit. 'She's good at hiding it.'

'Don't worry, Mrs Fourie. I'm looking out for her.'

I size him up, Paige's wannabe-knight-in-chino-armour. I consider inviting him in for kebabs, but that would surely make things even worse. Feeling impulsive, I gesture for his phone. 'Look, take my number. If you're worried about anything and you're not sure what to do, you can call me any time, okay?'

'Of course, Mrs Fourie.'

'Ellie,' I say.

'Ellie,' he repeats, finally cracking a twitchy smile.

I wave him off, feeling a little lighter. At least now I've got eyes on the ground. Things can't be so bad if she's dating again. And seriously enough to invite him to Mash & Trash.

I text Paige as I step inside. *Kyle brought you flowers. He's cute.*

She's typing something.

Deletes it.

Typing again.

And eventually, all I get is a mouse emoji. Thanks, Paige.

'Dinner!' I shout for the boys, pushing aside the synthesiser box that still takes up half the dining table.

Mo's voice calls back from upstairs. 'Could I get your help up here, please?'

Grumbling, I grab the Please Take Me Upstairs pile and head up to find Yusuf on his bed with a pencil and yesterday's *Guardian*, unbathed, shirtless and still wearing his trousers.

'Tariq! Mistake in legend is annoying, eight,' he barks at Mo. My stomach twists. Tariq is his brother's name. Part of my argument to Mo about why Yusuf should move in with us was that it was so important we enjoy the little time we had left with him. I had a romantic notion about how we'd hear all of his stories, do crosswords together, bond. But the cruelty is that mostly he's already gone. We always think we have so much more time than we do.

'Annoying is you tonight, Abbu,' Mo says, fluffing his pillow. But the smile on his face is oddly stiff. He leans close to me and whispers, 'He won't let me take his shoe off.'

I sigh. 'Yusuf, how about we get you into your black tie for the evening?' Gently, I take hold of the sheepskin slipper on his right foot. Immediately, Yusuf tries to push me off, swearing at me in Urdu. 'Hold him down,' I instruct my husband, as Yusuf's left foot bicycle-pedals in the air trying to get purchase on my stomach. I twist my body away, struggling to keep the right foot firm in my hand.

The stiff smile falls off Mo's face. 'You're upsetting him.' He doesn't move to help.

'Mo, we have to check his feet.'

'Let's just leave it. We can try in the morning,' Mo pleads.

'And is that what you've been saying all week?' Fuck, has he not been washed *at all*? With everything else on my plate, I haven't double-checked. 'Yusuf, please!' I entreat him directly, barely dodging his open hand as he attempts to batter my face.

'I don't know you! I don't know you!' he screams, as he thrashes.

'It has to be done,' I shout. 'Mo, stop trying to be the fucking nice guy for a minute and actually help!'

Finally, Mo moves over to his father and presses his shoulders onto the bed, and I manage to peel the slipper off his foot.

It's clear immediately that something is wrong. The smell of sweet rot hits my face, making my mouth improbably fill with saliva. His ankle is sticky with blood. The stubs of his two already-amputated toes are swollen, skin shiny and taut. Glistening. The flesh of his foot is waxy and lifeless, necrotic.

'You're hurting me,' Yusuf screams, savage. 'Stop touching me. You hate me!' He wriggles away from Mo and punches me square on my nose. I reel back, momentarily blinded.

'Hey, Abbu, hey, that's not nice,' Mo says in a soothing voice. He settles Yusuf back against the bedcovers, redirecting his attention to the crossword. '*Mistake*, that's got to mean an anagram, right?'

Pinching my nose against the pain, I reach my hand into the slipper. It finds something metal. I pull out the aux jack from Mo's headphones. From the fancy new set he bought with his mid-life crisis DJ table. I hold it up to him, sharp and small.

I turn back to Yusuf's foot so I don't have to look at Mo's horrified face. The wound weeps blood, slow and steady, the flesh around it swollen and puckered. I don't bother saying 'this is why the nurse said we have to check his feet twice a day'. I don't bother saying 'you know the nerves in his feet are dead'. I don't bother saying 'you're supposed to have washed him this whole week, how did you not notice this in his shoe?' There's no point. We both know what a fuck-up it is. The smallest wound on Yusuf's necrotic feet will never heal. That's what happens, at some point, if you get old enough, sick enough. The small wounds never heal. The aux jack can kill you. They'll probably have to take his foot now. We both know that if they do, Yusuf's never going to learn to walk on a prosthesis. Mo's always going on about how I worry, worry, worry. But here, see: there are consequences to our actions. Someone has to worry.

All I say is, 'I'll call the podiatrist in the morning.' Silently, several awful new tasks slide onto the List.

Another sleepless night. Too hot again. Mo asked me to sleep in our bedroom tonight. He didn't want to be alone. We don't talk about it. Instead, I spoon him until his breath grows rhythmic, a little boy in my arms, before unpeeling myself to lie stiff and silent on the edge of the bed.

There's no breeze up here. My leg bones ache. My gums ache. The pain unpicks the fabric of my thoughts and pulls me through the seams into the dark place underneath, where thoughts twist and curdle in the silent hating hours of two and three and four.

I consider my husband, lying next to me in the dim light of the nearly-full moon, tracing the familiar outline of his body. It seemed like such wisdom, once, choosing a husband whose aspirations were modest, so there was more room for mine. But I hadn't counted on his passivity extending to so much.

I met Mo at a freshers' party at uni. He was trying to hit on my girlfriend, a closeted philosophy student I'd been covertly dating since sixth form. Laurette got a kick out of flirting with boys in front of me then waiting until I stormed off in a jealous fit and went to hide out – usually in the kitchen smoking cigarettes – where she'd come and find me and pull me into a dark corner to make out. It infuriated me and drove me wild in equal measure. Seduction by proxy. This must have been the fourth or fifth party we'd been to where Laurette pulled this trick. I looked across the room and saw her touching the elbow of a dorky-looking man with arms that clearly never lifted anything heavier than a gaming controller and a haircut which was trying too hard to compensate for it. I was sick of being Laurette's sexy little secret by that point, so instead of playing my usual part in the game, I strode right up to them and said, 'Excuse me, but you're hitting on my girlfriend.' Laurette tried to turn it into a joke – 'Ha ha, this is my friend Eleanor, she's obsessed with me' – then left the party when I refused to laugh, and sent me a message saying I'd just outed her in front of a bunch of strangers and she never wanted to speak to me again. I ended up spending the rest of the night sobbing on Mo's shoulder, drowning my guilt and my heartbreak in double vodka sodas and then, ultimately, in his saliva.

Mo loves to tell people that I was a lesbian when we met, but he talked me out of it. I laugh when he says this, even though it's a gut punch, a complete erasure of who I was. But what loyalty can I really feel to that feisty chain-smoking girl who wanted to be an avant-garde playwright, that total stranger?

And after years of confused secretive yearning for Laurette, being with Mo just felt so... simple. I could introduce him to my parents. I could have a conversation with him about my needs that didn't devolve into a fraught four-hour analysis of our deepest wounds and insecurities. I slipped into heterosexuality like a comfortable pair of slippers. We moved in together after a few months, and it was fun playing grown-ups, buying a casserole dish, starting an art collection and getting a cat. It was like being in a play, where someone else had written the lines, a whole life's worth of lines. Then Dad died and Mum was in hospital again, and somehow in this storm I found myself pregnant, and a baby felt *solid*, felt like a lifeboat, so I asked Mo if he'd marry me and start a new family to replace the one I'd just lost, even though we were far too young for it, but – hell – caring for other people had been the habit of my whole life, so why stop?

And that's where the script ran out. Where, suddenly, I turned to the next page and found something I couldn't back out of. Found an infant I didn't know what to do with, shitting and vomiting and screaming and cluster-feeding and screaming and jaundiced and screaming and screaming. Found 3 a.m. nights staring at Mo, wondering if he actually knew a single real thing about me. Found blankness. Found isolation. I kept wanting to say, *stop, this joke has got out of hand*, because how absurd, to find yourself suddenly someone's mother, suddenly someone's wife, like some 1950s sitcom.

I tug at the new sharp hairs growing under my chin, wincing at the pain, telling myself I should be more grateful. Mo's a better husband than most. People these days just want too much from marriage. One person to be your everything, to help you self-actualise, to regulate your moods, to continue delivering mind-blowing shags over fifty plus years, to be your career coach and playmate and domestic partner and co-parent *and* the person who evicts spiders from the bathroom? It's far too much. Mo's been a good collaborator on the project of our shared life. More employee than partner, no doubt, but his compliance suited me. I'm grateful, in a way, that I've never had to litigate any of my decisions. *I* wanted to move to London after uni, so we did. *I* wanted a child, and we had one. I wanted the house in Barnsbury we could barely afford. I chose the wallpaper. I chose his jumpers. He's been cheerful, content to go along with whatever I wanted. I've had full control. So how churlish of me now to feel annoyed at the dynamic *I've cultivated* throughout our relationship.

It's been twenty-five years. We've already made it through the place in the marriage where most people give up, when the veil is lifted, when you realise that the person you are married to is not the ideal you projected onto them. Reflecting now, I wonder if we made it through because Mo never projected any ideals onto me at all. He is as cheerful and self-contained as a seed. He needed nothing from me. He could be happy anywhere, with anyone.

On the morning after our tenth anniversary, we were lying in a hotel bed in Cornwall and I turned to Mo and asked him what it was that he liked about me. 'Not love,' I clarified. 'What do you like?' He laughed at the question, and began kissing my breasts, and I never asked again.

I imagine, for a moment, leaning over and covering his face with my pillow. He would thrust against me. He would writhe. I would feel his body thrashing hard beneath me, and the idea of it is exciting in a way that his thrashing body hasn't felt exciting in years.

This was all my choice, I chide myself. I turn away from him. Kick off the duvet. Wait for sleep, watching the gibbous moon, clutching my fury like a torch.

At least Paige is okay, I think.

The dread circles closer. Sniffing. Nipping.

Tachycardia
O
Paige

She lives one block away from the LSE campus, but it takes her forty minutes to get to her lecture. Today, her long, winding route has taken her past Farringdon, deliberately weaving through the throngs of tourists round St Paul's, onto a bus going the wrong direction, getting off after three stops and walking back along the riverside. She has huge headphones over her ears, with no music on, and her keys are gripped in her fist like a spike, tucked in her jacket pocket. She varies the route every day.

At the busy Strand intersection, she slows until the pedestrian crossing sign counts down to zero, waits until the traffic light turns green, squeezes her eyes shut and then sprints across the road, so no one would be able to follow. A van screeches behind her, missing her by a few inches. Paige has accepted the fact that the only way to survive this world is to balance some dangers against others.

She's developed a trick of keeping her eyes fixed straight ahead while sliding over faces, a quick scan that never makes eye contact. She has to check each face, looking for that curve of his chin, that shape of his eyes. He has blond hair but sometimes he wears a baseball cap. He's of average height but once got far too close wearing platform boots, which threw her off. That time she only managed to lose him by ducking into a McDonald's and pushing through the throng to the ladies, where she sat huddled for over an hour, heart hammering against her ribcage like a prisoner.

But did she scream? Did she call the police, or campus security? Did she even turn to him, and ask him politely to leave her the fuck alone? No. Because that would make this whole thing too real. That would remove him from the ambiguous space he currently occupies between 'maybe a dude with no social skills who really, really isn't getting the hint' and 'maybe a very dangerous man' and force him to be one thing or the other, and Paige isn't sure she wants to know which category he'll ultimately fall into. Mostly, Paige is furious with herself for overreacting. Kyle is harmless. *Probably* harmless.

She sees him everywhere, even when he isn't there. In GCSE French, they learned the phrase *entre chien et loup*, meaning dusk, meaning the in-between, meaning the moment when light fades into shadow and you can no longer tell if the figure in the distance is friend or predator. Paige has been living in the hour between dog and wolf for months now.

The problem is, if you point at a dog and call it a wolf, they're not always going to take the time to carefully identify the canine. They might just drag it to the river and drown it. What if she's wrong, and she ruins his life because she went into an anxiety spiral? *All cops are bastards*, something her white mother may frequently tout but will never feel. As they've discussed frequently in tutorials: power is intersectional. Points against her: brown, woman. Points against him: working class, possibly neurodivergent. He was bullied at school. He's got abandonment issues because of his dad. She knows all this, because of the long conversations they had back when they were still friends. Before she fucked him. Before she fucked everything up.

The fault lies in her body, she knows, pressing it up against the aluminium penguin statue in the sun-baked plaza, where she has a clear view of the door to the philosophy building. Her body's nothing but trouble. She's known this ever since she turned twelve and some creepy guy on the bus offered to pay her £100 if he could touch her breast. That set the value of her, just of her prepubescent left breast: £100. She wondered, if she tallied up all of the pieces of herself, what would she be worth?

It took her almost two weeks before she told her parents about Bus Creep. Her dad made a joke out of it, told it as a classic London weirdo story. And that made her feel better. His laughter defused the danger in the whole thing.

Mum, though. Mum was terrifying. She was on the phone with TFL in about five seconds, demanding CCTV footage she could take to the police. Paige had begged her not to. She wanted to never think about it again. But since when did her mother ever give a fuck about what Paige wanted?

Her keys are cold in her hand. She fingers the small round tracker key ring dangling there, the one Mum insists everyone in the family carry at all times, her electronic leash.

Finally, she spots Prof. Renkin hurrying across the plaza. She gives him an extra minute's head start before she follows him into the building and up the stairs, slipping into the back of the lecture hall just as class begins, squeezing into a seat between two of her classmates despite the entire empty row in front of them.

Kyle's already there, sitting in the front row, in his usual spot, laughing at one of Prof. Renkin's dad jokes like nothing's amiss. Her shoulders unknot at the sight of him. *See*, she admonishes herself. *He wasn't even following you. You are being a psycho.* She keeps her eyes fixed down, opens her laptop and ducks her head low. Kyle never looks back at her.

Prof. Renkin's eyes drift up to her every now and then, probably wondering why she never puts her hand up any more. She would have asked to take the rest of this class online, as she has for most of her other mandatory modules this term, but she couldn't bear to give up Prof. Renkin. She's already dropped most of her extramurals, her social life, and barely posts online. The only places she goes are the library – reliably crammed with people – her room, Mash & Trash, Theo's and this lecture hall.

A message notification pops into the corner of her laptop screen. Her heart jolts, but it's only Theo, whose name her best friend Jemma changed in her contacts to Emperor Fuckface.

Emperor Fuckface
hey beautiful
want to come watch that bulgarian orphanage documentary later
i hear it's super depressing
your favourite

Paige
in your room i'm guessing
weird foreplay
w/a farieda?

Emperor Fuckface
don't be like that
we can be cool about this
just because she's my gf doesn't mean we can't be friends

Paige counts down from ten, fingers hovering above the keyboard.

Emperor Fuckface
we don't have to stop hooking up

There it is. Ugh, he's the worst. If Paige was a good person, she'd tell Theo to fuck off. But she isn't, so she replies that she'll come over after dinner, which is just what she did after the last flimsy-pretext booty call.

Paige is not a good person at all. If she was a good person, none of this Kyle stuff would be happening. *She's* the one who came on to Kyle. She's the one who led him on, who drunkenly started grinding up against him at Tiger Tiger because stupid Theo had just broken off their stupid situationship because he wanted to get 'serious' with stupid Farieda and her stupid cool haircut, and she was heartbroken, and Kyle had been so obvious about how much he'd liked her for ages, and she needed the ego boost. So she used him: fucked him, then ghosted him. Left him on read. Just felt too embarrassed to respond to his increasingly confused messages asking if they could talk about what happened, so blocked him.

Then came the weeks of Big Gestures. Silly Wattpad romance stuff. The letter left at her hall's front desk, her name on the envelope underlined twice. Five long, lovesick pages in his juvenile handwriting asking if he did something wrong. The bouquet of yellow lilies delivered to the dining hall, greeted with mirthful 'woos' as the delivery guy asked her to sign for them. The link posted to his Insta stories of a playlist tagged with her username, before she remembered to block him there too.

And then the terrible horrible no good very bad day Jemma noticed Paige had been avoiding their group hangouts and asked her what was going on, and without thinking, Paige had said Kyle was 'stalking me or something'. It just slipped out. And once the word *stalking* left her mouth, there was no way to stuff it back in. Jemma told the others and they all sought her out, told her they believed her, this wasn't her fault, and parroted all the things you were supposed to say – told her they'd help her to stay away from him. Kyle was booted off the group chat, and she's sure someone told him unequivocally that he was no longer welcome to hang out with them.

Except Kyle wasn't prepared to go gentle into the social black hole. He started sending her DMs from fake accounts calling her an attention-seeking whore. Somehow, he managed to slip a note into her backpack saying EVERYONE SHOULD KNOW WHAT A LYING BITCH YOU ARE. That one freaked her out, the thought of how close he must have got to her without her knowing. He scrawled her phone number up in the men's loos in the politics building, under the message LIKE SMALL TITS? CALL PAIGE KHALID FOR A MEDIOCRE FUCK.

Well, *someone* did those things. She's got no proof it was Kyle.

All she knows is that she keeps seeing him. Everywhere she goes. Like her own Frankenstein's monster, the ugly twisted thing she made with one careless word. She called him a stalker, and turned him into one. Like she wished this into being.

She did this to *him*. She has to remember that. She's the worst thing men say about women: she regrets having sex with him and now she's making him out to be a monster.

After the lecture, she rushes out before Prof. Renkin's even done explaining the required reading for next week. Kyle cranes his head back, and it looks like he might come after her, but the jam of students blocks him just as she hoped it would. She ducks across the hallway to take the far stairs rather than the more obvious close ones or the lift, then sprints as fast as she can straight across Lincoln's Inn Fields, directly home.

She only exhales properly once she's back in her room, her heart a panicked bird. For the rest of her life, she knows, she will be at a higher risk of cardiac disorders because of a few stupid months of not eating when she was fourteen, of trying to wrestle control of her stupid dangerous teenage girl's body. Nineteen years old, and she's already done so much damage to herself, so much damage to others. She is a hand grenade. She is poison.

Flopping onto her bed, she opens Insta to post a bland 'loving that uni life' photo of a pile of her textbooks on the decoy profile she maintains purely for her mother's benefit (Mum hasn't clocked that account has three followers, thank God). Got to keep her from worrying. Her mother overreacts to everything. Like her eating disorder: she made it all more real than it needed to be. Turned it from a few weeks of out-of-control stupid teenage behaviour into a Disorder, into a Thing She Was, into a Thing She Will Have To Live With Forever.

No, that's not fair, Paige scolds herself. Mum didn't make up her wasted heart muscles. Her damaged brain. Her teeth that fell out. All the times she passed out at school, most of which her parents still don't know about. The fact that anorexia has the highest mortality rate of any mental illness. No. Mum reacted the right amount at the time. It's just that she was never able to *un*react once the crisis was over. Paige loves her mum, but she can be a bulldozer.

There's no way she could tell her about Kyle. She still has no idea how he figured out where her parents live. That's creepy, isn't it? Isn't that actual creep behaviour? But again, *he didn't actually do anything.*

He's never grabbed her, attacked her, like actually harmed her. What is she mad about, that he tried to bring her flowers?

Paige is not going to overreact. She's going to laugh this off, like her dad would do, and get on with her life. She's determined to be as different to her mother as possible.

She braces herself, tapping into her Snapchat inbox. Sure enough, there's a new message request. A throwaway account name, a profile pic of a cartoon snake. She goes still, prey clocking a rustle in the grass. She changed her number, how does he keep finding her?

g_03i62k_6
You can't avoid me forever.

They're all terse, like that. Correct punctuation, no spelling errors. Two to five words, like bullets, they ricochet around her brain for days and days.

Stop lying, bitch.
Everyone sees through you.

Sometimes there are photos, too.

She doesn't know whether to delete them or not. She could lock down her profile, refuse any follow requests. But one of the guides she found online said it's important to keep records of everything, screenshot each message. And you can't export your messages once you've blocked someone. Seems like a real fucking oversight from whoever designed the app, honestly. And this is the messed-up thing: the messages help. They make her feel just a little less crazy.

She exports them diligently each night and adds them to a file in her Dropbox. She prints the whole thing out once a week and keeps it in a folder under her bed, which has the label 'JUST IN CASE' on the front.

Still, this is nothing. Bits and bytes. Letters on a page. A dog-shaped shadow in the distance. He is harmless. *Probably* harmless. Nothing really has happened.

Her phone buzzes again. Another message. She can't deal with it now. It's not even 4 p.m. but she wants this day to be over. She's been sleeping so much recently. Sometimes ten, twelve hours a night. Maybe she can just take a nap until it's time to slink to Theo's, where she can shut off her brain for a few hours in the sweet oblivion of his wiry body. She pulls the curtains shut. Pushes in foam earplugs to block out the sounds of her peers playing music, laughing, living their lives.

She peels back her duvet.

Tucked in her bed is a single yellow lily. The petals are crushed, black pollen scattered across her sheet like insect shells.

Feeling nauseous, she opens the message on her phone.

g_03i62k_6
Sleep tight.

Vertigo

Ellie

Forty floors below me, the city stretches out like a diorama: Battersea Power Station huddling in the shadows of the Nine Elms skyscrapers, the Thames nosing through the buildings like a fat brown worm. A bird's-eye view across the capital from the vantage point of London's best-located tech conference: City MedTech Innovation Summit. Or, as everyone calls it, Demo Day.

An actual bird is eyeing me back. It's a peregrine falcon, I think, sleek machine-gun body perched on a vent outside. Dark wing feathers ripple like silk in the wind as it tears strips of flesh from the bright green parakeet pinned between its claws. Its black assassin eyes keep returning to mine through the glass, conspiratorial, like it knows what I'm planning.

I suppress a shudder and turn back to the room. Anxiety hums through the crowd, founders in barefoot shoes silently rehearsing their presentations to themselves, VCs in rumpled suits skulking around sad dry sandwich platters and hot-water urns. A few years ago, this would have been salmon and mimosas, back in the halcyon days when this conference was a more congratulatory affair, when we were all flush with money, when any monkey with a fitness app could secure a term sheet worth millions. But beneath the pizzazz, the tech industry's really just a financial instrument, and because the financial markets are limping, so are we. As much as we tell ourselves that we're curing cancer and treating anxiety and saving the world, our true product, all of us, is our share price. And without the easy money pumping in, the balloon's burst. The founder of what was the hot new surgery robot company just confessed to me over canapés that after his last down-round, he's had to retrench half of his engineers. Pay attention, and you'll notice the brave faces, the stink of desperation. Good thing, actually, that none of these windows open.

Is now the time to be sticking it to Andreas? My plan's a risk. To save Tranquillity, I need him to fail. Publicly. Humiliatingly. But I don't want to torpedo our whole company with him. I need there to be enough of a wreck left for me to put back together after the board fires him.

I sidestep a poster about a microdosing subscription box and make my way over to where he's set up in a quiet corner of the room, flicking through the presentation I put together for him. He looks like a human highlighter today in a canary-yellow suit with matching yellow Crocs.

'There you are,' he says, scrubbing a hand through his fuzz of hair.

It's been hard work to keep him away from a live demo of the AI feature, but I've managed it. Promising email updates that never arrived, telling him the engineers need privacy to do their best work. The last time he saw the feature, its brain was still OpenMind. He still thinks it is. He's got no idea how much the product has degraded since then.

'The new build's loaded on there.' I hand him the demo phone. 'Sorry for the delay – the team wanted it to be perfect.' My voice is chipper. 'It works just how you expect it to, don't worry.'

'You're a star, Ellie.'

He looks like he's about to test it, but I've timed it just right and the MC is asking everyone to take their seats. I wish him luck as he dashes for the AV guy to get miked up.

The AI devs pounce on me before I get to my seat. They've made an effort to dress up, i.e. they're wearing ill-fitting blazers over their hoodies. They've spent the past week begging me to cancel the live demo and show a video of the old model instead. They've sent me long updates explaining what's going wrong, which I haven't read.

They say it's got even worse. 'You don't understand,' says the one who looks like a giant mushroom, sweat stippling his long, pale forehead. 'We've tried clearing the vector store, rolling back to a previous version. We can't make it stop...'

'It's called Demo Day,' I say, shaking them off to head to my seat. 'Demonstration is kind of the point.'

I scratch at a patch of flaking skin on my arm with my talon fingernails, wishing I was in a better mood to appreciate my own scheming, but the perimenopause symptoms are bad today.

The audience around me is a mix of startup founders, representatives from the five major London VC firms who take large positions in MedTech, and a few students here for industry exposure. The conference is invite-only, mostly mature startups raising Series Bs and Cs, one disastrous telehealth business going for a D round because they're out of cash, a terrible sign. People are giving them a wide berth, as though the failure might be contagious.

Uri gives me a wink as I slide in behind our board. I return a polite nod; I've realised only he or Tom would have had enough sway to argue the rest of the board out of my promotion.

My heart swoops when I notice who's sitting next to him: Don. Inez is at his side. Her flesh seems to have evaporated, and her bright green shift dress hangs off her frame like an IV bag. Both of them perk up when they spot me, flashing warm smiles that make my stomach clench.

My gaze drifts back to the window as the first speaker introduces their product, a smart toilet that tracks the health of your gut biome. More birds have joined the falcon on the railings outside, I notice. Four pigeons, a starling, a gigantic seagull several times their size. I'd have thought it would be too high up here for anything except raptors. The birds are all staring straight in my direction. Bird eyes are a lot like fish eyes, I note. Glassy. Dead-looking.

After two more demonstrations of banal fitness apps, Andreas takes the stage. Anxiously, I fiddle with my phone, running the pad of my thumb up and down the crack in the screen (*Replace phone screen*, still sitting on the infinite List).

Andreas takes them through a presentation of our existing features, our impressive user numbers. My shoulders unknot – no matter how badly the final act goes, this should be enough to secure us investment, must be. Even though Andreas is ruining the careful script I wrote him, adding in some meaningless drivel about 'extended reality', 'multiplatform experiences' and 'hacking the human happiness algorithm', vom.

At last, he gets to the AI feature, now branded 'Tranquillity AI Opener', which is pronounced 'a eye opener', so I was wrong when I thought we couldn't come up with a stupider name than Tranquillity SMART.

'But all of that is the past,' he says grandly, dismissing the past five years of our work. 'Now, let me show you the future.'

He picks up the demo phone. The phone's screen is mirrored huge on the screen behind him, a calm green microphone icon button pulsing below the words *What's on your mind?*

Outside the window, two more pigeons have joined the avian audience.

Andreas holds the phone to his mouth and records. 'Well, I'm pretty nervous. I'm giving my first presentation at City MedTech.' He gives a self-effacing chuckle. 'It's a big deal for my team, and the audience is full of impressive and very attractive people!' The crowd responds with warm laughter, charmed, or pretending to be.

On screen, the loading icon whirls. *Generating your meditation.*

Maybe nothing will happen, I think.

Andreas's smile grows broader out of stress. A man in the front row clears his throat.

Then a voice booms out, too loud, setting the chairs vibrating. A smooth androgynous voice, low, even, that doesn't sound computer-generated at all.

rip them tear them the blood spurt the shadow the hate tear them destroy them no tear into the throat and the blood is sweet hot drink him lick the bare neck tendons bite in see his face freeze screaming haha eye burst slip out the eye slips out the eye pull at the optical nerve watch it unravel brain chunks stuck to the optic nerve

There's an uneasy laugh. Shocked whispering. A woman at the back of the room stands up and walks out.

Andreas is waving frantically at Mushroom Head, who's got his head buried in his laptop at the back of the room, typing quickly, trying to kill it.

The voice doesn't stop, speaking in a fast babble, emotionless.

push them off the balcony smug nothings see their faces splatter on the pavement they can't judge you then just fall forty floors cold blood splattered across the concrete push them take that one the tall one by the bar him first tip him over the edge let him look at the fall then push him push him make him cry make him bleed get a gun bring a gun and fire bullets into their smug faces hate him hate you destroy him fuck him take it

It cuts out.

A sound tech pops out from the booth holding the power cable for the whole AV set-up. Murmurs ripple through the room. A coffee cup clinks too loudly on the floor.

I glance at Don, but all I can see is the back of his head.

Andreas stands frozen, smile pinned into his cheeks like taxidermy. The MC steps in, defusing the tension with a joke about the thrills of live demos. Andreas vanishes backstage and the next CEO steps out to present a personalised vitamin subscription service.

I head for the loo, hoping to splash some cold water on my face and try to soothe my jangling nerves. This should feel like victory. But my mouth tastes of battery.

I thought the feature would be stupid, not frightening.

Mushroom Head follows me out the room. 'Ellie, I'm sorry, we tried to tell you. We tried everything. Wiped the codebase. Nuked the inputs and tried retraining the model, but it's like a toddler that learned a bad word, we can't make it forget. Most of the testers dropped out, they said it's too horrible.' His cheeks flush. 'We must have missed something. The versioning's a mess. We're not even sure which build we're running any more. It's like the model just stopped listening to us.' He pauses to wipe sweat from his forehead. 'Thing is, Ellie,' he says under his breath, 'most of the input data was logged by you...'

Before I can ask what he means, Andreas bursts through the door, the piece of Micropore tape that held his microphone still dangling off his cheek. His fingers dig into my upper arm as he drags me to the reception area, empty now, surfaces scattered with coffee mugs and pastry crumbs.

'What the *hell* was that?' he spits, Micropore fluttering for emphasis.

My mouth is dry. The room reels around me. Words I don't intend to say come out of my mouth. 'Well, Andreas, that was the feature I told you not to build.'

'I did not tell you to build a... that.' In a dark billow of wings behind him, the birds settle onto the railing, a dozen now, jostling together in malevolent scrutiny.

The apology prepares itself on my lips, the habit of a lifetime. *I'm sorry. I'll fix it.*

The birds' eyes glimmer in the afternoon sun, an array of dark pearls.

Reverberating with their avian daring, I tip back my head, feeling reckless. 'Maybe if you'd actually been involved in any of this, you'd have known what was happening. Instead of just *rolling in at the last minute to take the credit.*'

Rustling wings. Black eyes.

Andreas's cheeks grow ruddy. 'Go home, Ellie,' he says at last.

I scoff. 'You need me here,' I say, waving at the investors, the board, at Don.

'Go home and *calm down*. But I want to see you in my office tomorrow morning. Nine o'clock. We're going to have a talk, you and me.'

'I'm looking forward to it,' I say, hoping my eyes are communicating every ounce of contempt that I feel.

He marches back towards the room, leaving me alone with the birds.

So that's it. I've sacrificed five years of my life for this company and now I'm going to be fired by a man dressed like a banana.

I throw myself at the glass, hands up, roaring, startling the birds away in a flutter.

As I step into the lift, I think about what Mushroom Head said about all the testers dropping out. I knew that ever since the team pulled the OpenMind integration, the voice recordings were accidentally being fed back into the model, over and over, but I didn't think about what those inputs would contain. I balance my laptop on the handrail, open up the database and see who's been recording into the AI Opener. Mushroom Head was right. It's almost entirely me.

The glass-fronted lift whooshes down, leaving my stomach on the fortieth floor. The city rushes up to meet me and it feels, for a moment, like falling.

I don't remember the Tube. I don't remember the walk from the station. I'm just suddenly home, like I blinked and landed in my hallway, shoes already flying off my feet, bra hooks already unlatching, keys clattering into the bowl. I stare at an Ocado magazine lying on the hallway floor like it's going to explain what the fuck just happened.

He's going to fire me. That *clown* is going to fire me.

Blink again and find myself running a bath, the upstairs one – I can't bear the guest bathroom any more. I run the water cold, hoping it will cool the fury smouldering in my marrow. I tear off my careful outfit and crawl into the water. Goosebumps prickle my flesh, already so hairy again, Jesus. And I'm still too hot. Instead of it cooling me, I warm the water. Blink and find I'm sitting in a lukewarm Aesop-smelling stew.

Try to think through my options but I'm too angry. Could ask Don to talk to the board for me, surely five years of good karma counts for something – but *fuck* the board. Could use my savings and take my time finding a new job but I'll lose my shares, and that's most of what we have. Already increased the hours for Yusuf's nurse and he'll need more after the amputation. I could fight. Blame the team. But it's all in the logs. What if they listen to what I recorded? *I'm not even sure what I recorded…*

The company's probably dead now anyway.

My eyes keep drifting to the spiders. So many spiders in here. Tiny black-brown bodies twitching down the tiles, lowering themselves on gossamer threads towards my face. A clutch of eggs must have hatched in the air vent. Although – weird – they don't all look like the same species. Maybe a spider nursery in a wall somewhere. I use the lid of my Olaplex to flick them out the window, but they keep coming, so eventually I fold myself tight, making a moat of the water, and let them enjoy their arachnid congregation. Add to List: *Become spider god. First commandment: eat Andreas's eyes while he sleeps.*

I pass hours huddled in the water. Try vagus nerve breathing. Try visualisation. Try to recite my List. My muscles ache. My fingernails feel too tight. Eventually I hear Mo come home from work and bustle around downstairs, singing to himself. Should I tell him I'm probably going to get fired tomorrow? Would he worry? Would he figure out a way for us to pay our mortgage, or for Yusuf's nurse, or for Paige's uni fees?

Ha.

Finally, I pull myself out by puckered fingers. Flick spiders off my towel. Pull on my Buscemi pyjamas. Somehow I'm still hot.

'How'd it go?' Mo greets me with a sloppy kiss on my cheek. He doesn't wait for my answer, instead launching into an excited description of a new small-plates place he wants to try. 'Date night tonight, come on. It's been a while.'

'We can't leave your dad.' Artie weaves through my ankles, trilling for my attention. It's so fucking hot. Add to List: *Punch some holes in the wall, for ventilation.*

'I can cook here,' Mo offers. 'We could try that Ottolenghi thing.'

I picture Mo trying to initiate sex with me in the wreck of a kitchen I'm left with whenever he attempts an ambitious dish. My cunt shrivels at the thought.

I twist away. 'Sorry, love. Not in the mood.'

His face falls. Of course it does. But there's a fight brewing in me and this poor sweet man doesn't deserve it. The kindest thing I can do right now is take myself far away from him.

Artie, miffed that he's not the centre of attention, sinks his claws into my calf. I shake him off, grit my teeth and grab my keys and handbag, slip into my clogs. 'I need a walk.'

Mo says something I don't hear. The door bangs open and then I'm out. Cacophony of crow screams. Sky bruised purple. Last stains of red soaking the horizon. Round white moon whispering something to me. My blood hums a response.

Blink again. A long blink.

Hirsutism

○

Andreas

Andreas scowls at the small animated cars appearing and disappearing on the map. He's been trying to hail an Uber for ten minutes already. It's past midnight, and civilisation ends on the south bank of the river, apparently. He's a little tipsy from the cocktails. *Drunk*, if he's honest. But it was worth it. He's made up for the unhinged demo malfunction with several rounds of post-conference drinks with a group of VCs, one of whom has promised to call him in the morning. Turns out they summer in the same French village. And that's how business is really done, he thinks, smugly, drunkly. Shared *values*.

The temperature's dropping. The wind nips at the gap between his trousers and his Crocs, at his cheeks, his bare neck. He finally closes the app, decides he'll walk south, try to hail a cab again from the edge of Clapham.

His wife's probably worried. She's a darling woman, Alice, although it's unfortunate how she's let herself go since hitting thirty-five. Not her fault, he supposes, it's just biology. Women have a window, don't they? Peak fertility, peak fuckability, and once it closes, it's only natural men struggle to stay attracted. Fertility binds women to the animal economy. He still loves Alice, of course. Just wishes she'd nag less, and maybe try Ozempic.

He falls into step, enjoying the rhythm of his legs on the pavement, letting his mind unspool. The French call this *flânerie*, he thinks. The modern urban man enjoying the sights of the city. He read an essay, years ago, by Susan Sontag, where she called the *flâneur* a 'connoisseur of empathy'. This makes him think about a VR conference he attended a few months ago, where they experienced being in a migrant boat from South Sudan. It was terrifying, tragic, and also so thrilling – being able to expand one's experience. This is how Andreas's mind works, making connections, seeing the links no one else sees. It's his special gift, a responsibility he takes very seriously. He's often felt it's a burden, to owe so much to the future.

He wonders – once VR becomes fully sensorily immersive as it surely will – if there will be subjectivity restaurants, carefully curated experiences where you can slip into the mind of another for a few minutes. *Your hors d'oeuvre, sir, a Mongolian hawker calling back his falcon to his arm. For the entrée, here is a young woman who is swimming deep into the ocean trying to save her drowning brother. And dessert, the exquisite orgasm of a woman at the moment of childbirth.* This will probably be a special skill of the future, curating and assembling experiences like this. Empathy chefs. Andreas thinks this is something he'd be rather good at.

His mood lifts. Andreas is blessed with a naturally cheerful disposition. Anyway, he is pleased to have saved the day after the disastrous morning. There might be one good thing to come out of it, which is that he finally has a solid reason to fire Ellie, one the board cannot dispute. They all think she's the best thing since sliced bread; Don had to fight them so hard to hire him instead of promoting her. Bad enough that she's such a naggy fusspot, but clearly she's also clueless.

He's going to do a thorough pruning of the engineering team next, where she's had the most influence. Her small-minded thinking has taken root there like a mould he's determined to excise. People who only think in numbers, who are far more worried about maintaining the product they have than in helping him to build the future. Trained to think small, think short-term. No, they're better without them. He needs to make room for innovators, mavericks. Can't launch a rocket ship without offloading some dead weight. Andreas has already wasted too many years trying to convince small minds to think bigger. Brian, the co-founder of his old creative consultancy, turned the board against him after a small budget oversight and now runs the business solo up in Manchester, which is barely an overgrown market town if you think about it.

Rolling in at the last minute to take the credit. 'The captain's job is not to row the ship, but to keep his eyes on the horizon' – that's what he should have replied. He says it now out loud. Terrible how he always thinks of the perfect retort only much later. The French call this *l'esprit d'escalier*, literally, wit of the stairs. Andreas thinks he really should have been born European.

Somehow he's got turned around, and finds himself in Nine Elms. He's never been in a part of town so quiet. There's a single man drinking beer on a bench in the middle of a landscaped Chinese garden, no other person in sight. Even the pigeons seem unnerved by the quiet. They're gathered on the frosted grass, watching him warily as he walks by, glowing in the light of the full moon. Shouldn't they be in their roosts by now? Not that there are many available around here, all sharp edges and new builds.

He makes his way through the luxury high-rises, passing a row of sports cars with Qatari number plates and old fines flapping from under the wipers. The wind nibbles at the back of his neck. Goosebumps tingle up the top of his spine. But it's just the wind, he tells himself. Only the wind.

Then he hears footsteps, slightly out of time with his own. He stops, and they're gone, and he thinks – just an echo. He continues on, making his way down a side street next to a shuttered bubble tea shop, and he hears them again. He turns back and catches just the smallest blur of movement out the edge of his eye, as though someone has just dashed into the recessed doorway of the florist's. He realises he's being followed.

'Hello?' he calls back to the empty street. How strange, he thinks. What an oddball. He does not think of danger. He does not think of knives or teeth or rapists. He has never been followed before. He figures there is nothing to do but shrug and continue on, that this weird person will surely lose interest. He cannot imagine any other outcome.

To distract himself, he considers more plans for Tranquillity. The problem, really, is that Ellie and Don built the whole thing around illness. Deadly, for a brand – there's nothing inspiring about disease. We need to shift the narrative towards positivity, happiness, thriving, he thinks. Showcase pro athletes and business leaders who incorporate meditation into their routines. Make it aspirational. God, and the other day Ellie was suggesting they build a new menopause module. It's a complete dead end, chasing niche causes like that, appealing to old people and neurotic women, when they could be revolutionising human flourishing.

This is the real reason for the ad campaign; he needs them all to see that this is a fresh start. Ellie doesn't understand, he argues with himself; the ad was as much for the employees as for the consumers. Sure, the budget thing was an unfortunate oversight. But it's a small-picture problem. He's trying to take a step towards expanding all of human consciousness. And if Brian happens to see the ad, Johnny's music overlaid with *his* face, and sees the success he's made of himself, all the better.

But the distracting is no good. His thoughts keep returning to the person following him. He'd tell himself he is imagining it, were it not for the chuffing of someone breathing heavy behind him, getting closer, the hair standing erect on the back of his neck.

He turns back. Walks on. Whips round again. Walks. Looks. Trying to catch his shadow in the act, like a children's game. But he is not fast enough, or they are too fast. Each time, there is only a blur of motion, a soft rustle of movement.

His mouth is dry. He takes out his phone as he walks, opens Uber again. Now, the ride-request button is disabled, and an all-caps message at the top of the screen says 'NO CARS AVAILABLE'.

He puts the phone back in his pocket. Picks up the pace of his walking. If he can clear the empty broadways of Vauxhall, he can find a busy street, a safe place to wait for a bus.

But there are no busy streets in this part of London, at this time of the night. These apartments are real estate, not housing. He only passes a man in a pea coat, a little younger than himself, a little larger, a little stronger, and has to catch himself from running up to him and asking for protection. He scoffs at himself, at the embarrassing thought. He's being absurd. Just an eccentric, following him for no reason. A *hurluberlu*, as the French would say. He squeezes his hands into tight fists in his pockets to keep them from shaking.

He decides he will reassert the normal against the strange by being as normal as possible, even as his eyes scan for a better-lit street. He tries to make his walk more confident. Add some swagger. But his unease grows. And this is not a familiar sensation. He thinks of an old Italian proverb, *La fame caccia il lupo dal bosco*. Hunger drives the wolf from the woods.

As he steps past an alleyway, a voice calls out to him.

'Andreas?'

He can't help himself. He stops. Turns.

There's a dark shadow speaking to him from the alleyway.

'Andreas, come here. I want to show you something.'

It's a woman's voice. The realisation floods him with relief. Well, that's fine then. Harmless. Flattering, even. His jaw relaxes; he hadn't realised how tight it had been.

The voice is vaguely familiar. The glow of two pinpricks that might be eyes, but lower than they should be. Like perhaps this person is crouching down.

'Hello?' Andreas asks the darkness politely. Strange that the shadow knows his name.

It's no dark alleyway from a horror movie. No grimy cobblestones or convenient dumpster for a monster to hide behind. No, this is the Nine Elms regeneration district, one of the wealthiest square miles in one of the wealthiest cities in the world. The alleyway runs between the trendy glass-fronted reception area of a commercial architects firm and a small sculpture gallery. The floor is smooth porcelain tile, freshly re-grouted. Recessed LED spotlights march down the centre in a neat row. Only... they stop halfway in. And further, there is the shadow. Two flashing eyes.

'I need your help.' Definitely a woman's voice. And it's middle-aged, breathless. It's those facts that set him at ease, that tempt him closer.

The French call this *l'appel du vide*, the call of the void.

Then it steps forward, into the light, and Andreas wishes for the darkness back.

Because in the light, he can see each sharp blade of fur on its face.

He can see the ropes of saliva that dangle from its maw.

He can see the oil-slick sheen of black claws, dangling at its side.

He can see his own face reflected in its yellow eyes as it lunges for him, twisted in a scream.

But the scream doesn't matter. The district is deserted, and Andreas is alone with the beast.

Urinary Tract Infections

○

Brenda

My laptop grumbles on the laminate tray. I'm in bed, propped up in a nest of cushions, duvet covered in crumbs from the sausage rolls I bought for the CATS meeting. Only there was no CATS meeting. Deborah and Farah both sent cowardly excuses, so I told Reggie and Jin not to bother, either. I'll probably never hear from them again.

CATS's Facebook page is blanketed in aspersions about how I'm cooked, a mad old lady who was doing all this for attention. They say the video was doctored. They say the whole thing's a hoax. I don't read them any more.

I adjust the hot-water bottle under my knees and pull up the new Word file on my computer hopefully titled 'Witnesses', plural, although right now there are only notes on one. After a week's investigation, I've learned a number of facts about Oliver Ferrel, from his age (fourteen) to his ranking in the National English Olympiad last year (third) to his opinion about a specific bowling alley in Finsbury Park (scathing, they gave him pink-eye last year). Crucially, what I have *not* learned is anything more about what he saw on the night he and his friend were attacked on the Heath, because the silly twit refuses to talk to me.

He was awkward on the phone, stammering out that his parents told him not to speak to reporters. I told him I wasn't a reporter, I was a private investigator, and tried the cat killer angle, but his voice jiggled through a dozen excuses. He's got a lot of homework to do. He'd have to check with his parents. He can't remember much about that night anyway. He can't give me a description. No, he definitely doesn't think he can meet a strange adult somewhere (on that point: fair enough). His voice wibbled and creaked. At first, I dismissed it as puberty, but slowly realised it was something more. Whatever happened to him that night, the boy's scared out of his mind.

Finally, he shut me down with, 'I already told the police what it looked like, sorry,' then hung up. That was something useful, at least: *it*, not *he*. Still, it was twilight, when one thing can so easily be mistaken for another. When, perhaps, a weirdo dressed in animal skins might lunge with a knife at two confused children and be mistaken for a beast.

I managed to get hold of him once more, and, okay, I lost my temper a bit. Now my calls go straight to voicemail and I only get one tick on the messages I send, which I think means he's blocked me.

The moon mocks me through the open window, full and leering. One of the many mocking responses to the video on CATS pointed out it was a full moon that night, must be a werewolf, ha ha. But I once heard on a radio programme that crime rates really do rise when there's a full moon. Moon-madness. *Luna*-cy.

My phone rings and I almost knock my computer tray to the floor. I catch it on my foot just in time, sending a bolt of pain shooting up my knee. 'Jen?' I say, thinking no one else could possibly be calling me at this hour.

But it's a young man's voice, tense. 'You know the WhatsApp group I told you about? With all the Deliveroo drivers?'

'Yes?' It's Jin, I twig.

'Well, someone saw it.'

My breath catches, wondering if it was the same night as the attack on the Heath, or the night Melek was killed. 'Can you give me his number?'

'He's going to meet you there.'

'What?' The words aren't making sense in my brain.

'He's in Battersea and he says he saw an enormous creature climb out the ground. Moving just like in the video. Ten minutes ago.'

It takes me more than an hour to get to south London. It's too late for the Tube and too far to drive, so I brave the night bus, that travelling circus of the drunk and distressed. All the while trying to wring the pain out of my hand bones, hoping I'm not too late.

Finally, finally, the bus deposits me on a lonely paved street dwarfed by indifferent skyscrapers. I haven't been to this part of Vauxhall for years, and I can't believe how much it's changed. This used to be industry and council flats, duck ponds and gay cruising spots. Now it barely looks like London. The towers are so high, the spaces in between them sparse concrete deserts. There are no corner shops, no community posters, no lights on in the flats. A huge billboard stretching across the tower in front of me tells me that these 'investment-grade apartments' were built by an Emirati conglomerate and decorated by Versace. The only living thing I can see is a lone swimmer doing laps in a sky pool stretched between two buildings, glowing an eerie blue-green.

The location Jin told me is near the river. I make my way through the deserted streets, noting that my poxy battery's nearly dead again. I trot through a landscaped Chinese garden, the light of the full moon glinting off the koi pond. A group of pigeons huddle together in the grass, watching as I pass.

A shrill cry cuts through the night. I whirl around, but whatever it is is a few streets away. Foxes, no doubt, I reassure myself. Some vulpine drama that doesn't concern me now.

I pause for a couple of minutes, but there's no more noise, so I walk on. I dosed myself with my most powerful painkiller before leaving the house, but I suspect adrenaline is the main drug keeping me going right now.

I head towards Vauxhall Bridge. To my right, the squat fortress of the MI6 building; to my left, a deserted construction site. I lean over the bridge and check the shoreline, wondering if that's where I'm supposed to be. It seems deserted. I'm sure that I'm too late, that the Deliveroo driver is long gone, and whatever he saw is long gone too. Another dead end. Another waste of bloody time.

Then a voice from the shadows hails me. 'I almost left.'

He steps out from behind a tourist information board, swamped in a turquoise branded puffer jacket that looks like it's swallowing him alive. He eyes me sceptically. 'You're the one?'

I nod. 'What did you see?'

He hesitates for a moment before speaking. 'It came out there.' He gestures to the construction site.

'What was it?'

He chews on his lip. 'I have a picture.' He pulls out his phone and shows me. His hands are shaking, cold or fear, I can't tell.

I can't see a damn thing on the small screen, despite bringing my nose right up to it and moving it around the edges of my better peripheral vision. But I nod, trying to appear authoritative.

'I'll need you to send me that.'

'It climbed out the hole then crawled right up the wall to the roof.' He shudders. 'It moved weird. Nothing should move like that.'

I'm not sure what to make of any of this. The building isn't as high as some of its neighbours, but it's still ten or twelve storeys up, plate-glass windows, few handholds. A hotel or luxury flats, hard to say. No cameras I can see. I could come back in the morning and try to talk to the residents, see if anyone saw something, bring Reggie or Daniel for backup. It would be the sensible thing to do.

I dig out a small torch from my handbag and examine the fencing of the construction site. A sign tells me that this is something called the Thames Tideway, a new supersewer, and no other information apart from CONSTRUCTION SITE: KEEP OUT.

'Show me where it came from, there's a good lad.'

He nods and slips through a gap in the fence, turning to hold it open for me so that I can ease through. I follow as best I can as he picks his way down uneven brick steps to the riverside. 'What're you going to do?' he asks.

'See if I can find any proof,' I say, hoping I sound reassuring, hoping the boy hasn't noticed how I'm gripping the iron sheets of the temporary wall for support as I ease myself down.

'Hole' is an insufficient word for the gaping chasm that comes into view as we reach the riverside. Fifty feet wide, a concrete-ringed portal of deepest black. At least I have some experience with voids.

We peer over the edge. Impossible to tell how deep the shaft drops. The smell from below is rich, dank, animal. The walls, lit by a ring of tiny eye-lights a few feet down, seem to be smooth concrete.

I scour the area around it with my torch, searching for footprints, pawprints, blood trails. But dry concrete accepts no impressions.

'Here,' says the boy, waving me over to some scaffolding along the other edge. A zigzag of narrow steel steps plunges down into the dark.

'Not a chance,' I huff, thinking of my poor knees, and the difficulty of walking down stairs with my void.

But it's not the stairs he's showing me. Running up next to them are the tracks for what appears to be the world's flimsiest construction lift. Little more than a plank suspended between two rails, hanging over the hole. The remote control dangling from the rail has just two buttons, up and down.

The boy's eyes are huge, hollow in his underfed cheeks. 'I'm not going down there with you, missus. Sorry, but no way.'

I consider my options. CATS have all let me down. I could call Daniel and ask him to come down with me. It will take him ages to get here, if he even picks up the phone at this hour, by which time the city will be starting to shake itself awake and we'll risk being spotted. We could come back tomorrow night and hope that the dozens of construction workers haven't disrupted anything there might be to find. Or, I could do what I probably should do, which is go home, take another Nurofen, and try to get some sleep.

Before my brain has a chance to mount a logical defence, I step out onto the platform and hit the down button. The lift screeches to life, echoing through the column around me. I'm about to yell up to the boy and tell him that if I'm not back in five minutes to call Jin, but

I hear his footsteps already fading back up the steps in a frightened gallop.

The ring of lights closes in above me like an iris as the lift drops down and down. It grows colder, the air moist and thick and icy on my face. It doesn't smell like sewage, but like mud. I drop one hundred feet, one hundred and fifty, more. I must be well beneath the river now. My ma once told me there were hippopotamus fossils under the Thames. Relics from when this was a wild place, an untamed place. A tingle goes up my spine, thinking what other prehistoric bones they might have unearthed from their digging.

The lift bumps to a stop. With shaking hands, I click on my torch. At the base of the shaft, concrete glistens, machinery scattered around like dinosaur skeletons. I can't resist the impulse to check that there is nothing hiding behind them in the darkness as my torchlight makes enormous shadow puppets that stretch up the walls.

A tunnel runs east to west across the bottom of the shaft, maybe seven feet wide. Half a dozen bicycles lean against the wall. Just as I'm debating which direction to go, I spot footprints from the east. Too amorphous to decipher what made them, just wet splodges on the grey.

Slow-Worm Jack said he couldn't imagine how a huge creature was getting around London unseen. Here's the answer. Tunnels. Sewers. Water pipes. There's probably more tunnel than city, if you add it all up. *You can tell the health of a city by the health of its rivers.*

I get some photos of the footprints, but that's not enough. I press down my nervousness. I need something more solid. Spraint. A den. Proof.

I swallow my spit and head into the black. Wires and pipes tangle along the floor and ceiling, and each step must be slow and careful, feeling my way between torchlight and void to ensure I don't trip.

About five minutes in, my foot kicks something jangly. I grope around the pipes until I pull out a set of house keys. They probably belong to one of the workmen. Just in case, I stash them in my pocket for later inspection.

The wet footprints continue in a zigzag along the edge, vanishing into the darkness beyond. There's only a single trail, so whatever made them trod this route only once.

The tunnel starts to rumble. I gasp and throw myself against the cold wall, before realising it's a train rattling through the Underground, far above me.

Despite the painkillers, the ache in my knee is becoming unbearable. How far does this tunnel go? Could trace the river all the way to the sea, for all I know, and these footsteps with it. Those bicycles suggest it's further than you'd like to walk.

Chewing on disappointment, I turn and make my way back. This hasn't been a *complete* waste of time, I reassure myself. Now I know it's been using this sewer to get about, I've got plenty of new lines to research… in the morning, after a hot bath, an arnica rub, a few hours of sleep.

The lift is still right where I left it, waiting for me at the bottom of the wide central shaft.

Just as I'm about to climb on board, I hear something moving far above my head. A clattering, rattling sound.

It's the boy, I think dreamily. *He's climbing down the steps to fetch me. Or it's the first workmen arriving for their shift. It's the motor of a machine rumbling to life on the surface. It's a stone falling down the shaft. It's Daniel.*

But the noises are getting louder. Uneven. Like claws scrabbling on metal. Something so much bigger than an otter.

And then, a long, hoarse growl.

No time to think. I grab the closest bicycle. Panic throbs through me as I hoist my leg over the frame, my joints shrieking in protest. They say you never forget, but that turns out to be nonsense. My feet fumble for the pedals, the handlebars jerking wildly as I wobble into the side tunnel I've just come from.

Too late, I realise my mistake. I should have gone the other way.

A deep thud behind. It's reached the bottom, I'm sure. And whatever it is, I'm sure it can move faster than I can.

My wheels scrape against the curved walls, sending shocks up through my shoulders. Adrenaline keeps me moving, barely upright. The torch clamped in my teeth bounces erratically, flashing glimpses of walls, wires, the rushing void.

A sudden breeze on my face tells me I've come into another open space. I throw myself off the bicycle, sweeping the torch around, and make out a room the size of a chapel, filled with huge pumps. Large enough for me to hide behind, maybe.

Somewhere behind me, heavy footsteps, growling.

I glance above me into the black. This seems to be another shaft, as deep as the first one. Which must mean… yes! There's another lift.

I scramble on board and hit the up button. The lift rumbles to life, the sound echoing unbearably loudly. Slowly, achingly slowly, the ground falls away. I keep the torch beam trained on the tunnel below as I rise.

When I'm about twenty feet up, something passes through the halo of light, too fast for me to be sure what I've seen. It clangs in the darkness beneath me, far beneath me now. I exhale a shaky sigh of relief. There's not a second lift. No stairs. The tunnel grows lighter around me as I ascend back to the surface, back to sanity. Safety.

The lift platform jerks. I clutch the railing to keep from being thrown off.

Another jolt. A wild rattle – louder now, closer. *It's climbing up the lift tracks* – the thought comes numb and impossible and inarguable.

I crouch and see a dark shaggy shadow following me up the shaft, two sharp glinting eyes, a wide terrible grin.

A sob escapes me. I check above with my feeble torchlight. I've nearly reached the top. I might make it. Maybe.

But a few feet above me, to the side, there's a dark hole. A side tunnel, smaller, older.

No time to think. The lift jolts again, and I fling myself towards the hole. It's not a leap, more a desperate fall, arms flailing to catch the lip of the tunnel. My chest slams into the edge, winding me, but my body tumbles forward onto a solid surface.

The smell consumes me. A sour, festering stink that punches my nose, coats my tongue. I retch, bile burning my throat. I grope into the darkness, my torch lost. The smooth concrete is gone, replaced by weathered red brick. The walls are closer here, I can reach both sides if I stretch out my arms. Bracing myself against the wall to my right, I move as fast as I can away from the central shaft, from the echoing growls.

My footsteps turn to splashing as I get deeper. Wetness climbs around my loafers into my socks, up my ankles, fetid cold clinging to my shins.

The noises behind me have grown distant. I can't tell whether it's followed me into the sewer. Maybe the smell will hide me. Without the torch, I have to trust my fingertips, trailing along the slick brick, to show me the way.

Then I take a step and the floor is not there.

An endless fall.

Then: water.

In my eyes. In my mouth.

I try to suck in a breath and it's sewage, acrid on my tongue.

I break to the surface, gasping for air. I've fallen six feet into a torrent, swollen with rain and the combined effluence of nine million people. It's not so deep, hip height, but my feet can't get purchase on the slippery bottom.

Gasping, I allow the torrent to carry me along into the darkness, away from the creature. I can see nothing. The void has finally swallowed me whole.

Silly cow, I think. *Silly stupid cow. Could be in your bed right now enjoying the last few years of your miserable life.*

After a few minutes of drifting, I come to a stop, caught in a sticky mass.

My feet feel for the ground and try to push me upright, and it sends a bright bolt of pain up my spine, my femur grinding into the socket of my hip. Something inside me is broken.

I try to push at the mass which engulfs me. An oily sludge squishes through my fingers, only trapping me deeper. Fat. Grease. Wet wipes.

I am stuck in a web, and where is the spider? I think I can hear it sniffing for me, searching the labyrinth.

The cold seeps into my bones, my organs, my brain. The sightless world recedes further and further.

Push. Struggle. Stick.

Struggle. Push. Stick.

Pull. Stick. Stick.

Splash. Gasp. Stick.

Until there is no strength left in my body.

The only noise now is the slow burble of sludge through the sewer, and my own ragged breaths, echoing up the long tunnel into the nothing.

Yule Moon

Restless Legs

Ellie

I wake up on my feet. I wake up walking, eyes blinking in the glare of morning sunlight. I wake up with my feet bare on a chilled stone path, my legs taking one sleeping step after the other, without any instructions from me. I stay in this liminal place for a few more steps. Walking. Waking.

Still half dreaming, I stop and try to figure out where I am. The path runs along a rise between two large reservoirs. There are a few people around, bundled against the cold, clasping steaming Thermoses of tea. Ducks etch V-shapes across the water. V for vendetta, V for victory, V for vot the vuck is going on?

I'm not naked this time, small mercies. I seem to be wearing a shapeless dress I don't recognise, although something about it is vaguely familiar. A pink leopard-print pattern on cheap polyester that feels crunchy against my bare legs. And while we're critiquing the sartorial choices of sleep-me, could the bitch not have bothered to pull on some shoes?

My hair dripping cold onto my shoulders suggests I've taken a shower at some point in the past few hours, or gone for a swim. Remembering the last time I woke up near a bathtub, I check my hands nervously for any signs of blood, fur or dead dog, but I'm as clean as my kitchen worktop.

The remnants of the dream cling to the edges of my mind. A satisfying dream. Something about Andreas, I think. Which figures, after yesterday's Demo Day fiasco. I remember going home afterwards. Taking an angry bath. Telling Mo I needed a walk to cool off. That's the last thing I can recall – shutting the front door behind me and walking out into the cold; out into the dream.

I turn to take my bearings. A clutch of boujie new builds towers over the northern edge of the lake. Tottenham? That and the abundance of bird poo suggests these are the Walthamstow Wetlands, then. Christ, my sleepwalking self has the weirdest hobbies.

Once again I have no purse and no phone. I'm pretty sure I had both when I left the house last night, along with my Steve Buscemi-face pyjamas, which honestly I'd be even sadder to have lost. Thankfully the bus driver at Tottenham Hale doesn't comment when I board without tapping, casting a glance at my bare feet and wet hair and deciding I'm not worth the trouble.

Mo is frantic when I step through the door half an hour later. He's wearing his coat over pyjamas, on the phone with my brother. Yusuf is propped on the sofa making a list of other people to try calling. Mo lets out a sob at the sight of me. He sweeps me into a hug, burying kisses in my hair.

I let myself sink into the warmth and safety of him, the smell of our laundry detergent, the smell of home.

Yusuf reaches out and gives my hand a gentle squeeze, whispering a prayer of thanks.

'I woke up in Walthamstow,' I mumble into Mo's shoulder, numb. 'Did you call the police?'

He did not. It turns out he only noticed I never came home about an hour ago. He stayed up late composing and assumed I was already asleep in Paige's room. It wasn't until he came looking for me to help with Yusuf's breakfast that he found her bed empty and unrumpled.

'But where *were* you?' he asks, his voice creaking with the strain of worry.

'I don't remember,' is all I can say. I say it over and over, until frost crystallises in his eyes.

I can't bear to say more. I can't bear to tell him this has happened before. Mo has always seen me as capable, as strong, as the person who keeps everything together. Right now he's looking at me with bafflement and hurt, and maybe even the first shadows of distrust. I can live with that. What I couldn't bear is for him to see me as broken, as vile, to catch a glimpse of the ugly dream-things that still cling to the edges of my mind.

I force something like a smile onto my face. I tell him I'm fine, this is normal perimenopause stuff, it's stress, I've got to get to work.

Finally he gives up. 'Let's talk about it later,' he says, a muscle pulsing in his jaw, before retreating back up to the study, to dissociate with dubstep.

After a (another?) shower and pulling on a cashmere knit dress from Reiss, I'm feeling like myself again. I check my laptop. The location tracker on my keys is offline, but *Find My Phone* tells me I dropped it near Sadler's Wells, a quick walk away. I decide to swing past before heading to the office, although it seems unlikely it will still be there. Provisionally add to List: *Block bank cards; Order new phone; Change passwords (ugh)*.

As I walk, I queue up one of my favourite anxiety meditations on my backup phone: James McAvoy guiding me across the Scottish Highlands through my earbuds. 'You are a droplet of water bubbling up through a spring,' he says in his own rich Scottish accent, rolling the r's extra hard so they shiver down my spine. 'If thoughts arise, observe them, then let them go.'

Thoughts arising. *I dreamed of Andreas.*

'You tumble over smooth stones in a rushing brook.'

I dreamed a creature peeled his face off his skull.

'You are carried along by the river, flowing free and effortless.'

I dreamed that something wrapped its fingers around one of his ribs, wet and blood-slicked.

'You are the river.'

Even James McAvoy's Scottish trill can't calm me today. Curious, I switch to the AI feature instead. A stream of filth fills my ears, and that – finally – soothes my nerves.

My phone is right where *Find My Phone* said it would be, nestled deep beneath a hedge lining a quiet mansion block, along with my bag and my pyjamas, all mud-soaked and wet. The pyjamas are ripped, a jagged seam running all the way up the back, bisecting several Buscemis. My house keys, sadly, are nowhere to be seen.

I cram all of it into my reusable shopping bag. It hangs heavy at my side, dripping like carrion.

Lanying finds me at one of the desks in the UX department an hour later, nine thirty, obsessively refreshing Slack, waiting for Andreas to summon me into his office for the guillotine. I've seen neither hide nor hair of the Personalised Meditations team this morning. Word about what happened doesn't seem to have got round yet, but everyone will know soon enough. *Five years*, I keep thinking. *Five years of work gone to shit because I was reckless, because I was stupid enough to believe there was any point trying to fight back.* And I'm going to lose my shares. The company's going to fail. All these people are going to lose their jobs, too.

'Why aren't you checking your emails?' Lanying asks, flopping into the empty chair beside me.

'Drowning in work, sorry.'

'Are you going to handle Town Hall this afternoon? We've got to say something about Demo Day.'

I frown at her. Town Hall is about the only thing around here that is *not* in my job description, and she knows it. 'Where's Andreas?'

She blinks at me. 'You didn't hear? In hospital.'

The saliva evaporates from my mouth, instantly. *I dreamed his bones cracked like porcelain.* 'What – what happened?'

Lanying leans in, dropping her voice. 'It's crazy. He was attacked by a stray dog in Vauxhall. It nearly ripped him to pieces.'

The typing noises in the room distinctly drop in volume as every designer around us tunes into our conversation. Lanying cocks her head for me to follow her to the corridor away from listening ears. 'They thought he was dead,' she continues in a whisper, once we reach a quiet corner. 'But the paramedics were able to stabilise him, and Uri says he woke up a couple hours ago. He's going to need a ton of plastic surgery by the sound of it. Apparently, the animal just about tore his face off.'

'Jesus,' I say, which doesn't begin to cover it. 'Did they catch it?'

'What?'

'The dog.'

Lanying shrugs. 'So, are you going to run Town Hall?'

I tell her to postpone it and wander back to my desk in a daze. The designers are staring at me openly now.

'Will he be all right, Ellie?' one asks.

I don't know how to respond. I open my inbox and find the blast from Uri on behalf of the board. It's vague: '... Terrible accident in the early hours of this morning... critical but stable... if any reporters contact you, direct them to the PR team... Ellie, Meredith and Zayn are there if you need anything... our thoughts are with him and his family during this difficult time.'

I dreamed I dragged long claws through the skin of his face and peeled it away from his skull like an orange peel.

Hands shaking, I log into my menopause app on my laptop. There's a cheerful graph of all my symptoms. Hot flushes. Fits of rage. Night sweats. Insomnia. All reduced to colourful bubbles on a chart. I scroll up the calendar and notice, for the first time, a pattern. They follow a perfect twenty-eight-day cycle. A lunar cycle.

Which, another google confirms for me, perfectly matches up with the actual moon.

A crazy thought bubbles up within me. A thought so absurd I can't even form the word in my mind. A cheesy horror movie trope. An unlikely love object for teenagers. A myth. A leftover from the days when humans lived in small villages terrorised by beasts prowling the wild woods.

I fire off a message to Lanying, carefully avoiding the broken A key on my old MacBook. *Feeling very shook up by the news. Stepping out for ten minutes.*

I trudge up High Holborn, making my way towards St Paul's, trying to walk off my panic. It's a crisp October morning. Two out of every three people I pass have relented and donned the black puffers that will be their uniforms for the next few months. But every now and then a holdout passes, still stubbornly wearing shorts. Some of the shops have already strung up Christmas lights, and others have yet to take down the faded back-to-school posters. It's the in-between time. The cusp. The membrane between light and dark growing thin.

The buildings grow taller around me as I approach Bank, old Georgian facades framing well-lit takeaway spots at street level. Itsu. Pret. Costa. Wasabi. Pret. Costa. I count out the familiar names in a frenzied beat. You could follow them from one end of the city to the other, block by block, a breadcrumb trail through the wild woods.

I woke up in Walthamstow, I reassure myself. *I was nowhere near Vauxhall.*

But I keep feeling his bare rib in the palm of my hand, remembering how it cracked in the strength of my grip.

And weren't there other things in the dream? Concrete tunnels and – oh God – so many small animals.

I collapse onto the edge of a fountain and watch the water ebb in and out, like breathing. A plaque tells me this is Cristina Iglesias's homage to the lost Walbrook River, paved over by the Victorians. A jagged reproduction of the riverbed rendered in bronze, layers of matted mud and half-rotted logs and fishbones. Water fills it slowly then filters out again to a reservoir underneath in a mechanical tide. A monument to the ancient city, the wild city, still buried somewhere underneath the concrete and the glossy high-rises.

I dreamed I stalked the night on four legs.

I dreamed I let the fury tear through me, twist me into another shape.

I dreamed I ripped through flesh and bones and delighted in the ripping.

I run my hands up my shins, trying to calm my breathing. Already, I can feel the stubble prickling through my thick tights. New fur growing in.

Of course.

Because I'm a fucking werewolf.

Vaginal Atrophy

◯

Ellie

To-do List for lycanthropy:

- Obtain wolfsbane (try Holland & Barrett; failing that, dark web).
- Call broker to ask whether disability insurance covers werewolfism.
- Buy more stretchable clothing.
- Download lunar calendar app and set up notifications.
- Review key werewolf texts as research: *Ginger Snaps, An American Werewolf in London, The Bloody Chamber, Werewolves Within, Wolf, Dog Soldiers, Wolfish, The Howling, The Wolf Gift, Werewolf of London.*
- Find place to secure self for evening of next full moon (27 November).
- Buy manacles and cable ties (Amazon).
- Silver bullets as backup?
- ??
- ????
- ??????????

And there I run out of ideas.

I'm back at my desk after my long walk, scribbling the strangest List of my life, hunched over my notebook so that passers-by don't see that I've apparently gone mad. *Have* I gone mad? I've probably gone mad.

I glance up to see Uri and Tom deep in conversation, huddled near the Chillax Zone ball pit. Uri looks relieved to see me and waves me into Andreas's office, née my office. There are few signs of him among the Nothing decor: his tea set on the floating Perspex shelf next to a stack of business books, a 3D-printed bust of himself, a framed NFT chimp print. Somehow these personal items make the room more bland, not less.

'It's bad,' Uri says. 'I was just on the phone with his wife. They're still not sure if he's going to make it. Even if he does, they're looking at months of rehab. So we've got a leadership gap, regardless of the outcome.'

I don't comment on the appropriateness of the board calling this poor woman while she's at her husband's maybe-deathbed to talk about succession planning.

'We're hoping you'll step in,' Tom says. 'A steady hand at the wheel, that's what we need now. It's such a sensitive time. We've got meetings lined up with investors all next week. After yesterday, we need to convince them that the core product is sound.'

'Explain that the AI feature was Andreas's thing,' Uri continues.

Their voices feel very far away. Steady, that's what they think I am. *His screams started to gurgle in his throat as it filled with blood.*

'We're all in shock too,' Uri says, misinterpreting my expression.

'Terrible, terrible thing,' adds Tom. 'And of course Don's available if you need someone to bounce ideas with. I know you two are close.'

I blink up at them, struggling to understand what they're saying.

'I think we'll stick to Acting CEO, for now. We can make it official as soon as we've landed an investor. Don't want to alarm anyone,' says Uri. 'Between us, Ellie, some of Andreas's decisions have been… questionable.'

'Yesterday's Demo Day fiasco.' Tom shakes his head. 'Regrettable.'

'And the snafu with the ad campaign. This might be a blessing in disguise.' Tom blanches, realising what he's just said. 'Speaking purely from a business perspective, obviously.'

'Terrible thing.'

'Terrible thing. We're all just torn up about it.'

'We're sending flowers.'

'So, if you're happy, we'll send out the announcement this afternoon, yeah?' Tom says. 'Important that we settle any nerves. People like to know who's in charge.'

Uri grasps my elbow. 'There will be a pay increase, of course. We can discuss all of that once we've got term sheets signed.'

'Whatever you need, Ellie. We know how lucky we are to have you.'

'Thank you,' I manage finally. I'll say anything to get out of this room, away from the lingering smell of Andreas's tea.

A few months ago, this was everything I wanted.

I head back to my desk, and my pathetic List. Where is *Be CEO* supposed to fit around lunar schedules and devastating violence? I was barely managing work-life balance as it was, before I had to think about work-life-wolf balance. Yup. *Definitely* gone mad.

Maybe it's fine. Uri goes on an ayahuasca retreat once a month. This will be like that, only manacling myself in a shed somewhere deep in the countryside so I can't hurt anyone.

This thought snags on something in my mind. Moon cults, lunar retreats, cherry vapour. *Sometimes you just need to let all the anger out.*

It takes me ages to craft a message to Carol that doesn't sound utterly insane. I eventually settle on *Sorry to message out the blue, but something strange happened to me last night and I need to talk to someone about it. Would you be up for a coffee? So sorry to impose.*

If I'm wrong, this poor woman is going to think I'm loony. But I literally have no idea what else to do right now.

I'm just about to start on a second message with more advance apologies for how batshit this is, when my phone buzzes in my hand. Her voice sounds hoarse, like she's just woken up, even though it's past noon. 'I've been waiting for you to call,' she says. 'Were you safe last night? Did you hurt anyone?'

I clutch the phone like a mother's hand against my face. She *knows*. How does she already know? 'I can't remember.'

'Where were you?' Carol's voice is matter-of-fact.

Walthamstow, I tell her. But I might have been in Vauxhall too. I'm not certain.

Carol says she'll be back in town tomorrow. She tells me to hold tight in the meantime. 'Tonight should be fine,' she says. 'Just don't get agitated.'

Don't get agitated. Fat chance of that. I break my usual Protestant aversion to medication and down three strong antihistamines, enough to allow me to drift through the rest of the day. I go home early. Mo's at the pub with some colleagues, I think avoiding me, so Yusuf and I rewatch last week's *Love Island* together. He pretends to find it ridiculous but then monologues at length about the fitness of all the pairings. Tonight, he doesn't seem to notice that I'm less responsive to his chirps than usual.

I'm in bed by eight, pulling the curtains tight and slipping quickly into a dreamless sleep. Better than I've slept in weeks.

Carol meets me the next afternoon at a bus stop in North Finchley. It's a mizzly day, the high street leached of colour. With her unapologetic slime-green trousers and bright red curls, Carol is the brightest thing for miles.

'Glad you came.' She smiles at me as I clamber off the 263. 'We're meeting the others just round the corner.'

'What others?'

'Others like us,' she says, leading the way down a street of shabby terraced houses. 'If you pay attention, you can smell them out, you know.'

'Like you smelled me out?'

She grimaces. 'Sorry, pet. You're right. I wasn't at that pointless support group for my health.'

The casual confession tightens my chest. I leave some distance as she strides ahead.

My phone is buzzing in my pocket. It's been going all morning: meeting requests, budget sign-offs for the investor pack, the shiny new business of CEOship. Not enough to distract me from the gnawing sense of betrayal. Here I was thinking I'd made a spontaneous connection, that most precious of things after the age of forty: a new friend.

'You've been watching me,' I say.

Carol glances back at me, and doesn't deny it.

I follow her at a distance, torn between anger and curiosity. Our destination turns out to be a scraggly allotment. The corkboard near the entrance is wallpapered in notices about updates to bylaws, contestations to those updates, updates to the contestations, signs of the sort of fierce internecine battles that can only be fought by people with not enough to do. I wonder whether any of these committee positions were won by savaging the incumbent in an alleyway.

A few old people are rambling around, completing the last jobs of the season: plucking out wonky carrots, raking rotting leaves into piles, tucking rows of young pear trees into fleece for the winter. The annuals are clinging to their final weeks of life, leaves wrinkled and frost-glittering. The air smells of decay.

Carol leads us to a group of four working a well-tended plot near the back. 'Fresh meat,' she says, sing-song voice, nudging me forward like an offering.

My stomach flips.

I know them all.

The tall woman in a wax-print headwrap and splattered dungarees saved me from the Ladies Pond.

The scowling woman with silver roots slicing dyed-brown hair stared at me in the kebab shop.

The smooth-skinned woman with long hair that shines like mahogany goes to my CrossFit gym.

And the last one, the oldest one, short and stoop-shouldered in a rumpled man's suit, crouching over a bunch of purple cabbages, her wild, wiry hair revealing the translucent architecture of her skull – I know her too, but I can't place from where.

'You've all been following me,' I say, standing numb as they introduce themselves. Grace (pond), Alex (kebab shop), Payal (CrossFit) and Martine (?).

'We've been trying to *help* you,' says Grace, handing Carol and me each a mug of steaming tea. Carol tops them up with something from a hip flask in her coat pocket. 'You haven't made it easy.'

My hands are shaking too much to hold the mug, which splashes warm tea all over my hands. 'What is happening to me?' I ask.

Payal rescues the mug from me. 'You already know, I think. Once a month, the wild part takes over.'

'But it's impossible,' I say.

'Of course it is, pet.' Carol toasts me sardonically with her chintzy mug. 'Yet, here we are.'

Appearing to lose interest in this conversation, Martine drifts back to her brassicas.

'But...' I swallow, my mouth gone dry. 'How?'

'We don't really know what it is, where it comes from,' Payal says. 'Except it's old. Every culture has stories about shapeshifters. Hyena-women, jackal-brides. People have a way of turning the truth into fairy tales.'

I take them in: Carol cackling as Martine hands her a gnarled carrot which she waves like a sceptre before tossing it into a crate. Grace play-swatting Alex with a marigold stem. Payal topping up everyone's tea. Their movements are effortless, interlocking, like they've done this a hundred times before.

I feel like a raw wound among them, ugly and exposed. 'It's not just us?'

Grace shakes her head. 'Got to be nearing a hundred in the UK. A couple dozen just in the city, we think.'

'How are *dozens of werewolves* running around London attacking people once a month and no one's noticed?'

'They're not,' says Alex darkly, crumbling dead petals in her hand.

'The five of us have a place up in Yorkshire, remote as you like,' Carol says, leaving a smear of dirt across her forehead as she pushes her sweaty mane off her face. 'The locals don't bother us, they're used to strange noises up there. If you let it out, run wild for a bit, it's not so bad.'

'Do you have any idea how much of your mess we've already had to clean up?' Alex's voice is full of spikes. 'There was CCTV of you last night, scaling a building near Battersea,' she says to me. 'Don't worry, it's been conveniently deleted,' she adds, to my expression of horror. 'We've got friends in useful places. But this is getting completely out of hand.'

'And I had a chat with the boy from the Heath last month,' says Grace. 'He's not going to be a problem. Lucky you just scratched him. He won't turn.'

I blink back at her. 'What boy?'

'You've been quite a handful, pet,' says Carol, who's now pushing garlic cloves into a fresh-churned patch of soil. This plot is twice as verdant as the neighbour's, I notice, still thick with amaranth, rainbow chard, sprawling pumpkin vines.

'You really don't remember anything?' Grace narrows her eyes at me shrewdly.

Images from my terrible dreams these past few months. Ribs. Tunnels. Fur. Julia's dog. Andreas. Shame burns through me like fever, hotter than the tea. Is it safe to tell them? I shake my head. 'Nothing.'

Grace looks disappointed at this. 'Well, I'm afraid someone's noticed your *nothing*.' She hands me her phone. It's loaded to a Facebook group, some neighbourhood-watch type thing about missing cats in Walthamstow. *Walthamstow*, where I've woken up after a blackout, twice. Fuck.

'The woman who runs it hasn't posted anything for the last couple of days, thank you, Jesus,' Grace says. 'But she's tracking you. Even managed to get a video, luckily not a good one.'

My stomach heaves as I scroll through the posts. Missing cat after missing cat. Sweet feline faces, heartbroken owners. 'Stop it,' I say, pushing the phone back. 'This isn't me. I love cats.'

'But have you attacked any other people? Is that why you called Carol? It's very important that you don't leave any loose ends,' Alex says, tossing cabbages into a crate with the skill of a professional cricketer. 'Especially men. Historically, they've not proven themselves to be reliable... stewards of violence.'

Payal idly calls Alex sexist for saying this, Alex calls Payal naive, and the two of them descend into an affectionate well-rehearsed argument, before Carol calls them back to the matter at hand, in what must be her Teacher Voice. 'Ellie, *is* there anything else we need to know about? Because if you've passed it on… that could get bad. We'd need to contain it.'

I recoil at this. Andreas is in *hospital*, is that what they mean by loose ends? What does 'contain it' mean? What would these madwomen do to him? He's horrid, but human. For one paranoid moment, I imagine them mulching this fertile soil with bones and meat, the earth reeking of rot, and have to step off the plot back onto the solid grass.

'We can't help you if you don't talk to us.' Carol gives me a look like she's coaxing a stubborn seedling.

'Lone wolves do not survive,' Grace adds.

'Just tell me how to stop it,' I plead.

'Oh, sweetheart, you don't,' Payal says. 'You can't. We all tried, at first. It just makes it worse, trust me.'

'Seriously?' Alex shakes her head at the others. 'Cowards. Tell her the truth. None of us were as bad as this.' She locks eyes with me. 'Something's wrong with you.'

'Alex, don't be rude,' Martine says. Her voice sets off a chime in my memory. I definitely know her. 'She has a point though, luvvie. Usually, it starts much slower. The first few transformations are barely anything. We've got more time to help people adjust, make a plan for their safety. I've never seen it come on so intensely, so fast.' The tone in her voice is curiosity, rather than horror. It's still bugging me that I can't place where I've seen her before.

'I have,' Alex spits. 'Back in '81. The American boy who turned me. He was out of control, too. Very first month, he went full beast-mode, killed a dozen people over two days.'

'What happened to him?'

'Shot by police,' Alex says. 'Which is what's going to happen to you if you keep going on like this. Unless one of the other packs gets to you first.'

'An uncontrolled beast risks the safety of us all,' Grace adds, impassive.

'Whatever's making you so angry, pet, you've got to deal with it.' Carol's eyes glisten pale blue in the setting sun. 'Or it will tear through you.'

A snuffling at my feet announces the arrival of a small white dog, his twists of belly fur encased in mud. A little Maltese poodle. After deciding he likes my smell, he trots over to Martine and flops at her feet.

I'm bewildered by all of this information. Trying to marshal my thoughts, I return to my list of questions. 'Alex, you said you were attacked, is that how it's transmitted?' I've been thinking back to the night at the Emirates Stadium, the catcallers, the feeling of being chased, the missing chunk of night.

'I didn't get it from a bite,' Alex corrects me. 'We slept together, although it usually doesn't transmit that way. Unlucky me. Payal got hers from a blood transfusion.'

'An aunt gave it to me,' Grace says. 'Back in Uganda. When I asked her for help with a bad husband.'

'And I got it the same place you did.' Carol cocks her head at Martine. 'Agent of chaos, that one.'

That's when it clicks. Martine. The woman from my bike accident. The woman I've seen staring at me in the streets around Islington. The woman who, I suddenly remember, *dragged her wet thumb across my open wound*. The words catch in my throat. 'You did this to me.'

Martine shrugs. 'Sorry, luvvie. You seemed like you needed it.'

'What the actual *living fuck*.' Shards of mug explode on the ground at my feet.

Payal stretches her hand towards me, like she's trying to calm an angry dog. 'It's going to be okay. You just have to let us help you.'

These unhinged *hags*, covered in mud and bonemeal, accusing *me* of being out of control. 'You're insane,' I say finally. 'That's what this is. You're insane.' I spin on my heel and march back to the road. These women have followed me, *infected* me, implied that the problem here is that I have some unprocessed rage, which is fucking nonsense. I'm a sane person. I am a rational person. I'm not *violent*.

I just happen to have a beast living inside of me.

And, as usual, I'll find a way to deal with it. Myself.

Discharge

Ellie

Paige's room at home still smells faintly of her organic shampoo. I pull her duvet tighter around me, staring at the bare patch of wall where her *Totoro* poster used to hang. Now it's just blank space, a slightly darker patch of wall. Her Penguin Classics stand neatly to attention on the bookshelf, flanked by academic trophies and the little crochet animals she churned out during lockdown. I wish that Paige had acted out more. That she'd picked up smoking, or bunked off school occasionally, or shoplifted, or done some graffiti, or punched someone. But she only ever acted *in* – her pain was always self-directed. Starving herself. Destroying herself. My sweet serious good girl. Where did she learn this? Sometimes I think about the fact that the eggs which became Paige grew in my mother.

I open the family location sharing app and check Paige's dot, safely in her student room. I try to imagine it's the pulse of her beating heart. It's not stalking when it's your own daughter.

I don't want to annoy Paige with my overbearing mum-worry, so I text Kyle instead. *How did the big assignment go?*

He replies within minutes. *She smashed it. Still recovering lmao.* He follows this with a close-up photo of Paige fast asleep, head down on a desk in the library.

I reply with a heart and return my attention to my laptop, where I've been puzzling how a beast got from Islington to Vauxhall to Walthamstow without anyone seeing it. The location tracker on my house keys is still offline, so I can't trace the route. It's twice now I've woken up in the north-east – why? Are there more shredded bodies scattered around London I don't know about? There's nothing on the CATS group about any attacks, not even Andreas's. In fact, the old lady who runs the group, Brenda Martins, hasn't posted anything in two days.

Some of the beast's night-time troll emails, I'm ashamed to say, seem to have been sent to her, but I assume the amount of swearing in them means they were caught by the spam filters.

I slam my laptop closed as a floorboard creaks. Mo appears in the doorway carrying two mugs of camomile tea.

'Peace offering,' he says. His hair is damp from the shower, curling slightly at the nape. He's wearing the cream Guernsey jumper I bought him on holiday in Cornwall six years ago. Possibly the last holiday we took, now that I think about it.

He climbs into bed beside me, his weight pulling me towards him. I nuzzle into the woolly softness of his shoulder.

The tea is revoltingly sweet. He always forgets I don't take sugar any more. But I sip it anyway. It's warm, and he was kind to make it. His father's amputation is scheduled for the morning. I should be the one making *him* tea.

'I'm sorry,' I mumble into his arm, meaning much more by the word than he can realise.

He shifts closer, his shoulder reassuringly solid against my cheek. 'Love,' he begins carefully, slowly. Rehearsed. 'I think you should speak to someone.'

'I tried,' I scoff. 'The GP wouldn't even—'

'That's not what I mean.' He presses his lips into my hair. His fingers linger on the edge of my arm where the sleeve has ridden up. I feel him hesitate, then lightly trace his thumb along the inside of my forearm. His touch catches on the rope of a muscle that wasn't there a month ago. He doesn't say anything, but I see his throat bob as he swallows.

'I was looking for my old PlayStation controller,' he says eventually. 'I thought it might be in the hallway cupboard.'

Yikes. The hallway cupboard's where I've been hiding my menopause hoard. All the fixes I bought and never got round to returning. The wrong fixes, it turns out. Being the place we keep the deep-cleaning chemicals and emergency gifts, I fairly assumed Mo would never open it.

He clears his throat. 'Maybe you need antidepressants, just until this work stress settles down. I've read that there are some mental health things that can manifest in middle age. You know your mum—'

'No.' I pull away, placing my tea on the bedside table with a sharp chink. My nails, longer and harder than they've ever been, clink against the porcelain. Inhale. Hold. Exhale. *I'm not the fucking problem here*, I think, but can't say. *My inconvenient feelings are not the problem.*

Mo is looking at me with those huge brown eyes of his, kind eyes, pleading. *Pathetic*, whispers the thing inside me.

I haven't even told him they've made me acting CEO, I realise. The stack of unsaid things between us is piled so high, it's hard to know where to begin.

'Fine. I'll speak to someone, okay?' I say, softening the growl in my voice. 'Promise.' Easier to lie than to try to explain.

He melts immediately. He is always so quick to forgive, so eager for things to be fine. He pulls me close and kisses my forehead, my lips. He keeps going, leading one thing into another. And this is right, I tell myself, ordering my tense muscles pliant. This is how we make up. This is what a good repentant wife offers her kind patient husband. I remember Alex saying, *We slept together, although it doesn't usually transmit that way.* I picture Mo's startled face if I handed him a condom now. How could I possibly explain?

My gaze locks onto the mug of tea cooling on the bedside table. An image forms in my mind of my hand gripping the handle and smashing it hard into Mo's head, shards of porcelain ripping apart the soft skin of his beautiful face.

I push the image away, lie back and think of houseboats. I let him make love to me, there in our daughter's bed, while my mind hovers three feet above my body.

* * *

Something's happened – the message wakes me early the next morning.

My brain flashes through a flipbook of potential disasters. *I killed someone in my sleep. Yusuf died. I ate a cat. Brenda Martins has tracked me down. Paige was in an accident.* All possibilities in the spiralling disaster of my life.

But no, Lanying clarifies in a second message: *Someone released the faulty AI feature. It's all over the blogs.*

Unsure whether this is a relief, considering the alternatives, or a shock, I tell her I'll be in as soon as I can.

The glow of my phone has woken Mo, who blinks at me blearily in the dark. 'Dad's got to be in by nine,' he mutters, voice sleep-softened and thick with anxiety.

Yusuf's fractious bed-creaking answers from upstairs. We have to shepherd him through nil-by-mouth this morning, emergency pills on hand in case his blood sugar drops too low, and get him to St Thomas' Hospital. The doctor said to expect intake at nine, theatre at eleven, out by eleven thirty. Half an hour: that's all it takes to remove a foot, to disassemble a person.

Lanying's already sent five additional messages. There's no way I can leave them waiting until noon. After all, I'm the goddamn CEO. This is what the monster has bought me.

'I just need a couple hours, love, I'm so sorry. I'll meet you at the hospital.'

Mo replies by rolling his back to me, all the goodwill I earned last night evaporating into the air.

The guilt gnaws in my belly like hunger. I dress quickly in the dark, pulling on yesterday's clothes and hurrying out the door before my resolve crumbles and I prostrate myself at Mo's feet. Today's going to be a hard day for him.

Most of the core team are already gathered in the box-fort by the time I arrive, still long before sunrise. Lanying, Zayn, our account manager from the PR agency. Even Mushroom Head is huddled in the corner, sipping a popcorn-tub-sized macchiato. *He knows I'm the one who turned the AI feature feral*, I remember. I might have to find an excuse to fire another junior, this month.

I plonk into the chair they've left for me at the head of the table. 'Tell me.'

'We dug through the logs,' Zayn begins, his face etched with deep grooves of worry. 'We think it was Millie. That DevOps girl you fired.' Audible accent on the *you*, heavy with accusation.

I frown, pinning him with my gaze. 'And how did she still have prod deployment permissions?' There's not a hint of tremor in my voice, I'm pleased to note.

Zayn looks away, mumbling something about forgotten GitHub permissions and stale deploy tokens, which I take as an admission of fault. He also tells me we can't just roll back to the old version, because of some data migration issue.

The woman from the PR agency, a minuscule twenty-something who's managed to slap on a full face of make-up despite the hour, brings a live social media feed onto the screen. 'Unfortunately, we hit West Coast US users at peak sleep meditation time, so we're trending.'

A stream of text rolls up the screen, too fast to read. My stomach knots, realising these are real-time comments, firing into the internet at machine-gun rate.

'Hang on,' Micro-Vamp says, switching to a view which shows the top posts over the past twenty-four hours.

Horrified users, demands for subscription refunds. Links to breathless thinkpieces speculating on how this happened and what it says about the awfulness of AI and the inevitable collapse of all civilisation.

But, to my surprise, among them are other posts which seem... jubilant?

So I told this meditation app I was mad with my math teacher and it suggested I rip out his throat. OKAY THEN, MEDITATION APP, BRB!

lololol tranquility got based

Me: Hey tranquility, late capitalism is making me sad.
Tranquility: Have you considered running a knife through a senator?

The knot in my stomach loosens, just a little.

'All the major tech sites have reached out for comment,' PR girl says. 'We're working on a draft statement – disgruntled ex-employee, not in line with our values, committed to regaining the community's trust… standard stuff. Regret without admitting legal fault. We can have it out within the hour.'

I'm distracted by the gloss of her skin, so shiny it looks like she's covered in a layer of glycerine. Is that the look now? When I was growing up, it was blue eyeshadow that gave you away as being old. I touch my face, wondering what I'm doing that gives me away. My hands brush a brittle thatch of beard growing under my chin. I remember my mother used to carry a pair of tweezers on her at all times, neurotically checking for errant moustache hairs every time she passed a mirror. Lady Macbeth frantic at the invisible stain. *Come you spirits, unsex me here.* Time queers us all.

'Ellie?' Lanying interrupts my reverie. 'What should we do?'

They're all looking at me. Waiting for my decision. Mine.

'Nothing,' I say. 'Draft the statement, but don't release it yet. Let's watch and listen a little longer, make sure we know what we're dealing with before we act. We've got to think about how this impacts the investor meetings.' This is the opposite of every instinct I usually have: do all the things! Try all the solutions! But after this week of tragic action, I am wary of rashness. (*And also*, says that deep-inside voice, the voice that sounds a bit like the AI feature, *aren't you a little curious?*)

'Want us to take the service down while we work on a patch?' Zayn asks.

'Not yet. Get everything ready to go but don't release until I say so. I want an update every hour.' I gather my things. 'I have an appointment, but my phone's on if you need me.' And I stride out the room, just like that, hoping that my confidence implies that I'm going somewhere desperately important. I don't tell them that my appointment is with my father-in-law's surgeon. I don't try to make excuses, or apologise for leaving them to deal with this crisis while I manage a different one. And you know what? No one seems to care! They thank me. They leap into action. They are happy to please.

There's no one's ego to manage any more except my own.
Maybe this was the trick all along.
Maybe all effective CEOs are monsters.

The hospital is a maze of sterile rooms, linoleum, the sharp tang of sickness and starch. Yusuf is in the last bed of a shared ward, holding Mo's hand and eyeing the leftover porridge on his neighbour's breakfast tray with longing.

'Everything all right at the office?' Mo asks, his voice stiff.

I squeeze my husband's shoulder and bury a kiss in his soft, sweet-smelling hair. An insufficient apology. 'They can cope without me for a few hours.'

Yusuf's already in a hospital gown. He has also, in the twenty minutes since they've been here, managed to completely charm the nurses, who keep popping by to fluff his pillow and offer him extra blankets. Add to List: *Get thank-you biscuits for the nurses. Check in on the social media shitstorm. Ask whether we need to source our own wheelchair. Buy emotional-support whisky for Mo. Install handrails in the bath. Find out whether Andreas is still alive.*

The surgeon stops by just after nine, a cheerful full-bodied woman who must have to stand on a box to reach the operating table. She and Yusuf quickly fall into a comedy routine as she works through her checklist ('Ah, you must be the twenty-two-year-old I'm seeing this morning', 'Yes, miss, I'm here for the nose job, I want to look like Colin Farrell', 'Oh! I had you down for radical weight loss', etc.).

She turns to me and Mo. 'Did his GP explain what's going to happen afterwards?'

'Yes,' I confirm. All this has been explained over endless medical appointments these last few weeks, only half of which Mo made it to. Yusuf will recover in the ward for a few days, then move to a step-down centre where they'll fit him for a prosthesis and teach him how to walk again. If all goes well, he'll be home before Christmas. I took careful notes of all this, but now it's jumbled up in my notebook among research into mythological cures for animal shapeshifting. Some of it's hard to distinguish. 'Tie living eel to the forehead when walking under the moonlight' is probably for lycanthropy; 'tea of boiled garlic' could be for menopause or for Yusuf; 'rub crushed snails into skin' might well be something Reddit suggested for wrinkles.

'Right. Let's take a quick look then,' she says, carefully peeling back the bandage from Yusuf's leg.

The stink of it wallops me in the nose. Pus and rot. The gangrene has turned his toes black and eaten a hole in the arch of the foot, muscles gaping open. On cue, my mouth fills with saliva.

The doctor's smile doesn't budge a millimetre, pro that she is. She re-bandages the leg and draws a large Sharpie arrow just below the knee. 'Just to make sure we take the right one!'

'Take them both, all the trouble they give me,' Yusuf says.

'Last question. Have you made a living will?' the doctor asks.

'He has,' I answer, pulling the document from my carefully organised medical binder. Mo's eyes widen at the sight of it, but I give his hand a quick squeeze, marriage code for we'll talk about this later.

They wheel him out an hour later, Yusuf apologising to the anaesthetist for causing him so much inconvenience.

Mo and I retreat to the coffee shop downstairs to distract ourselves with oily Chelsea buns and weak tea. Families wander past with corner-shop bouquets and gift bags, hurrying in small groups of twos and threes, living their own private dramas. A father shepherds two young boys ahead of him, his arms full of a stuffed elephant half as big as an actual elephant. I should have bought Yusuf something, I think.

A laminated poster brags that this is the top-rated hospital in central London, four years in a row! Could this be the hospital Andreas is in too? I haven't worked out yet what cleaning up loose ends could look like. Right now, I just want to make sure he's going to live. Thankfully, there's still nothing on that Facebook group about his attack, just some post about foxes, which I haven't had the guts to read properly yet.

Down the corridor, the door to the Family Room is shut, the blinds down. There must be someone in there. They took me to a room like that when I was twenty-two, to tell me my mother had fallen onto the Hammersmith & City tracks and she was in a coma, and they weren't sure if she was going to wake up. *Fallen* – I remember thinking that was such a casual word. Like you fall in love. Fall pregnant. Fall apart. 'She didn't fall,' I remember repeating, over and over to the kindly doctor. I wasn't there but I knew. 'She wanted to die.' He had the saddest eyes. He said it was okay if I needed a minute to absorb the information. I said I didn't need a minute, I needed to know what had to be done. Did they need her NHS number? Should I check her will for an advance directive? I was familiar with the process; my father had died just a few months earlier. The doctor seemed uncomfortable. He offered me tissues I had no need for. He said, 'A lot of people in your situation might feel some anger—' and I cut him off. What would be the point of that? Mum was ill. How could I blame her for her own illness?

'Why didn't you tell me about the living will?' Mo asks me over his untouched tea, bringing me back to the coffee shop.

'I didn't think to, love. I'm sorry. There's been a lot on.' Understatement. *Help Yusuf put together living will* was item 292 on this week's List. *Tell Mo about Yusuf's living will* did not make it on, so sue me.

'What does it say?'

'Yes to CPR, but he doesn't want to go on a machine.' I reach across the table to take his hand, which is warm from the undrunk tea. 'The doctor says his heart's still in good shape. He'll be back home making shark-attack jokes in no time.'

'Part of me thinks it might be better if he dies.' Mo says this to the full teacup.

'Well, of course. If he's dead, you don't have to do the work of looking after him.'

That slipped out. Mo's face crumples like tissue paper, his beautiful long lashes blinking rapidly as though trying to clear the words away. A deep flush rises up his neck, spreading across his full cheeks. His dark eyes flicker over mine, wounded, like he's trying to locate the person he thought I was beneath the awful words that just came out.

'Sorry, I didn't mean...' I squeeze his hand harder, trying to assemble enough new words around the terrible words that might hide them from view. 'I'm just saying that I understand it might be a relief... You're going through so much... He's your father and I know how much you love him...'

'I'm getting another tea,' Mo says, ripping away his hand and returning to the counter. His warmth lingers in my palm like an accusation.

I drop my head into my arms, wondering whether the surgeon could squeeze in a tongue amputation while she's at it.

My phone buzzes with updates from the team. Zayn says the patch is almost ready to go, we should be able to disable the AI feature by this afternoon. The data analyst says engagement is through the roof, no such thing as bad publicity. Customer support reports a mixed bag, but a surprising number of people say they love it. The PR team have sent through a list of links. It's hit one of the major tech blogs, with the headline: MOVE OVER, POSITIVE THINKING: USERS OF THIS POPULAR MEDITATION APP SAY RAGE IS ALL THE RAGE.

Anger is a hideous emotion, I've always said. It keeps you focused on your pain, which just reinforces its impact on you. One of those early Tranquillity meditations I recorded said that every thought you have is like water dripped onto a rock. The water flows down the rock, finding the easiest path it can down the rock's surface. If you keep dripping water onto the same place on the rock, eventually the water starts to carve a groove into it, until the path of the water is etched onto the rock. Thoughts are like this. Every time they go into a negative spiral, you're firing neurotransmitters along a specific set of negative neurons, and the connections between those neurons are reinforced, until the neurons themselves start to look different. You have to be so careful to protect your brain from negative thoughts, or you end up like my mother. Wedded to your victimhood, your weakness. You have to work to be happy. I can't believe these rage meditations are actually good for our customers. Isn't this all the beast's work, its corruption?

And yet. And yet. Look at all these people loving it.

I post a company-wide update saying we're going to leave the feature up for now. Just until we know more.

Lanying replies in a DM. *You're brilliant, Ellie.*

At least someone thinks so. I look up to see that my husband has now vanished from the cafe completely. My head flops back onto my arms, filling with guilty half-memories. Rib bones. Tunnels. Cats. Slippery words.

What else has the beast been up to?

Itching

Ellie

Things settle into a rhythm. Mo and I trade off the first and second visiting hours of the day, and both join Yusuf for the third. The old man's in good spirits, albeit one leg lighter, lopsided under the thin hospital blanket. He isn't always sure who we are, or where he is, but they're pumping him full of enough meds that the confusion does not seem to concern him. The surgeon is pleased with his healing. And against all expectations, Mo and I are pleased with each other. The awful thing I said unlodged something in him, and Mo has been stepping up. *He* even took notes at one of the follow-up meetings with the geriatric specialist! A tiny list of his own! He got the names of two medications wrong, but points for trying.

In fact, it turns out that channelling the constant unbridled fury of an apex predator has a number of benefits.

What it turns out you can accomplish if you stop trying to please everyone every moment of every day:

- You can dazzle every VC firm in town and receive *four* term-sheet offers containing more zeros than the alphabet in binary, enough to fund Tranquillity for the next three years.
- You can announce this to the whole company, to thunderous applause, and then leave early to go to the first

yoga class you've had time for in years, practising your downward-facing wolf.
- You can order a brand-new top-of-the-range MacBook Pro, which, *yes*, you are only going to use for email and Microsoft Office, and typing A-filled sentences with gleeful abandon.
- You can send your daughter an expensive florist gift card with the note containing lyrics to that Miley Cyrus song about buying yourself flowers.
- You can fire Andreas's 'imagination division' and use the savings to give Lanying a long-overdue pay rise.
- You can dig out your dusty vibrator and spend an afternoon luxuriating in yourself, stretched across the bed and imagining bright red hair cascading over your face while your husband visits his hospitalised father, and it's even *medicinal* because the internet says orgasms are the best way to fight the creeping incontinence.
- You can roast a brisket and eat the entire thing yourself, directly out of the pan, while watching the season finale of *Love Island*.
- You can rebrand 'Tranquillity AI Opener' as the 'Virtual Rage Room' and find it's soon your app's most popular feature.
- You can spend £28 on a ticket to an experimental one-man show in a basement in Dalston involving a surprisingly moving twenty-minute monologue about milk, and feel more like yourself than you've felt in years.

Even more luck from the universe: an email from Uri saying that Andreas's recovery has been almost miraculous. He's responded well to the skin grafts and they think he might be home by as soon as the end of the month. Uri follows this up with a private email to me saying that this alters nothing, I'm the CEO Tranquillity needs – they'll manage it gracefully with Andreas when the time's right. I wonder when Uri's attitude to me changed so much. Wasn't it just a few months ago that this man argued that I didn't have any *vision*?

But best not look at this gift horse's teeth too closely. I have what I wanted. I didn't even have to murder anyone to get it.

I still have two weeks to figure out what I'm going to do during my next transformation. But now that I'm aware of it, it feels like maybe the voice of the beast is always there, whispering at me just below the level of consciousness. A foreign body. A parasite inside me. It sounds a bit like the AI.

'Natural smile, darling, just a natural smile,' says the photographer from the *Financial Times*, failing to hide his annoyance behind a demonstration grin. He's been making the same request in increasingly exasperated words for most of the past hour.

I force an acceptable expression through the thick strata of foundation the make-up artist deemed necessary to cover my forty-something skin. My cheeks still sting from her earlier plucking spree. I doubt that the male CEOs being interviewed for 'Five Disrupters Reinventing Health Care' have been subjected to such torture.

Sitting across from me in one of the lido reception deckchairs, Hallie, a baby journalist trying to look older in an oversized blazer, nervously glances at her phone, where I suspect she's downloaded '101 Interview Questions for Dummies'.

'Just a few more,' she says, her voice wobbling with nerves. 'Um… Ellie. Where do you get your drive?'

'Anxiety,' I reply flatly, trying to expose all thirty-two teeth as the photographer takes another snap.

He exhales through his nose. 'Natural, easy smile, please, darling. Try smiling with your eyes.'

Hallie clears her throat, checking her list for the next pre-scripted question. 'And… uh, how do you balance it all?'

I try allowing my eyes to pull up the corners of my face, feeling the caked foundation crack around my nose. I should really just cave and get Botox. 'Do you want to try asking another question?'

Her cheeks flush. 'Right. Yes. Um. Let's talk about your Rage Room feature. It's been getting a lot of attention this week. What do you say to critics who accuse you of celebrating violence?'

At last, a slightly interesting question. I lean back, the deckchair creaking beneath me, and catch the photographer fiddling with his lens and muttering about shadows. 'It's just fantasy. Nobody bats an eyelid about teenage boys blowing things up in video games. They're only clutching pearls because our primary demographic is women over thirty.'

'Oh.' Hallie hesitates, finally looking at me instead of at the list of questions she's been doggedly working her way through over the past hour. 'But… obviously, like… violence is bad, right?'

'Of course. This isn't about violence. It's about power.'

The photographer blots sweat off my face with a tissue. I fight the urge to swat his hand away, the beast in me bristling at the contact. Instead, I take the tissue from him and use it to wipe off as much of the foundation as possible.

'We teach women to be agreeable,' I continue, once he's retreated. 'To comply. To play by the rules. And it works great… when they're at school. They're the top achievers, the obedient strivers. Then they get out into the world and they get screwed over, because in the real world, it's still the law of the jungle.'

I think of Paige as a toddler, her furious biting phase. All children start out as the same beastly violent little savages. I taught Paige empathy, and now she's so empathetic she can never get angry at anyone.

Hallie is frowning. 'So you're saying violence is empowering?'

'No, not violence.' I pause, choosing my words carefully, struggling to untangle my own thoughts from the muttering under-whisper of the beast. 'Maybe just permission to be angry. There's this proverb: "The sheep spends its whole life fearing the wolf, only to be eaten by the shepherd." Women are trained to fear some strange man in an alley, but what really gets us? The homemaking. The care work. The emotional labour. Martyring ourselves until we're too tired to think about what we want. What kills us isn't the man in the alley, it's the slow, psychic death of trying to make ourselves small enough to be good.'

Hallie cocks her head. 'Sometimes it really is a man in the alley, though.'

That draws the first real smile to my face. The photographer pounces on the moment, muttering 'Thank fuck', and snapping four shots in quick succession.

I'm saved from more questions by my ringing phone. Unknown number. Normally, I'd ignore it, but I'm happy for an excuse to end this diatribe before the beast smuggles any other words into my mouth.

'I'm sure you have enough,' I say, waving the PR girl to wrap things up as I answer the phone.

'Is this Ms Fourie? Paige's mother?'

My stomach tightens. 'Speaking.' I hold my hand up to stop Lanying, who's following me with a list of whatever today's latest crises are.

'This is the warden from High Holborn. Is Paige with you?'

My mouth goes dry as my grip tightens on the phone. 'Has something happened?' I ask, but the beast in me, uncurling, already knows. A line from *The Bacchae* runs through my head. *Harsh truth, how you come to light at the wrong moment.*

The warden asks me to come over, immediately, because she'd rather talk in person.

I tell her I'm on my way. Then I'm holding a black rectangle, still cracked. I flinch briefly at the reflection of a stranger standing behind me, self-assured and handsomely middle-aged with just a hint of five o'clock shadow, before I realise it's me.

I arrive at High Holborn first, nearly tumbling out the Uber in my hurry. Mo's still on his way from Stratford. Paige's phone is going straight to voicemail, her cheery recorded voice mocking me, 'Uh, send a text, weirdo, I'm never going to listen to a voicemail, byeeeee.' Her location tracker claims she's in her room, which can't be true.

A police car squats in the loading zone in front of Paige's residence building, chequered neon yellow and blue. My ribcage is wired too tight.

Inside the lobby, I find the warden pale-faced, flanked by Paige's friend – the one who showed me to her room a few weeks ago – and a uniformed police officer with a notepad. The officer's boots are planted firm, her pen scratching as she listens.

On a sagging sofa nearby, another officer sits beside a young man in a hi-vis workman's uniform, wrists cuffed and resting on his lap.

He looks up at me and I recognise the soft brown eyes, the floppy blond hair. Kyle.

The officer at the warden's side checks my name and asks if I've been able to get in touch with Paige. I shake my head, panic thrashing in my stomach. 'Please tell me what's happening.'

The warden's obviously tried to clear the space of onlookers, but a few beady eyes peer through the glass pane of the inner doorway. Other students craning for a glimpse of the drama.

The officer nods towards the sofa. 'Do you recognise this man?'

'Kyle,' I say, my throat tight. 'He's... I thought he was... Paige's boyfriend.' I riffle through my memories. Fuck. Did she ever actually mention him? Did I just assume?

'That uniform's not his. He posed as a workman to get into the building and was caught trying to pick the lock on your daughter's door. Luckily, Paige wasn't there. Her friend came back from dinner and found him. She claims this man has made several attempts to contact Paige against her will.'

'I *said* he's been *stalking* her,' Paige's friend Mia/Olivia/Ava says.

Kyle stares at his cuffed hands, hiding his face behind his blond mop. But I can smell him, cheap cologne and the sharp stink of fear. My nails dig into my palms. When I messaged Paige to say he'd been round, she replied with a mouse emoji, I think, numb. Tiny. Hunted. I gave him my number. I've been *messaging him*. How long has this been going on? Why has Paige not told me? And the more pressing question, which I ask out loud: 'Where is Paige?'

The officer shifts. 'We've been asking the other students on her floor. No one seems to know.'

My brain tries to assemble a list, but nothing comes, just the repeated pounding thought: *Where is Paige? Where is Paige? Where is Paige?*

Then the front doors swing open, and Paige answers the question herself, strolling in with a breezy laugh, arm in arm with Theo.

The smile slides off her face as she takes in the scene: me, the police, the warden, her fuming friend. Her eyebrows shoot up. Then she spots Kyle, and her expression goes blank. Her feelings vanish behind shutters.

I swallow her in my arms, relief flooding my body like a hot flush. 'Thank God. Thank God. Where were you? Why weren't you answering your phone?'

'We were watching a movie.' Paige untangles herself from my grasp. Her eyes are still locked on Kyle.

Theo mutters something, casting eyes around under fringe, and slinks away, spineless rat.

The officer steps forward. 'Miss Khalid, we need to ask you a few questions. What's your relationship with this man?'

She's quiet for a moment, but when she speaks, there's not a tremor in her voice. 'He's a friend.'

Sophia/Grace/Rosie shrieks so loudly it echoes through the lobby. '*Friend?* Are you joking? Paige, he—'

'Jemma.' Paige's voice slices her into silence.

'What did he do? Paige? Jemma?' I turn between them.

'Nothing.' Paige's tone is even. She hasn't looked at me.

The officer watches this exchange, pen hovering over her notebook. 'Do you have any reason to believe he might want to harm you?'

Paige's eyes haven't moved off Kyle. Her expression remains blank, but knowing her as well as I do, I can read the minute tightening of her jaw as she hesitates.

My nails dig tighter into my palms, drawing half-moons into my flesh. The beast inside me would like to grab the officer's baton, throw Kyle into the cop car myself, and make sure he's locked up somewhere Paige never has to look at him again.

Then Paige's voice pipes up, small but unwavering. 'He's harmless. Please let him go.'

The officer glances at her partner before turning back to Paige. 'We're going to take him into the station and ask a few more questions. Attempted burglary, trespassing, those are serious charges. Would you like to come in and make a statement? If you can explain what happened, we can reassess.'

I hoist my bag onto my shoulder. 'We'll come.'

'*I'll* come.' Paige's eyes track Kyle as he's guided out the front door, his head ducked, disappearing into the back seat of the police car.

'Don't be silly, Paige. I'm coming with you.' I reach for her hand. Paige's palm is limp and wet in mine.

'I'm nineteen,' Paige says to the constable. 'Does my mum have to be there?'

The police officer shakes her head. 'Not unless you want her to be.'

Paige squeezes my hand. 'Let me handle it, okay? I'll call you later. Mum, really, I'm fine.' Her voice is chipper. Far too chipper. So chipper I can hear the chips in it. 'Don't be mad.'

'I'm not mad,' I say. *Never mad.* 'I love you.'

Paige follows the officer out without replying. Jemma trails them, urgently whispering.

And just like that, she's gone.

The warden and security guard retreat to the office to review CCTV footage. The gawkers have dispersed now that the show's over.

I should go. I should meet Mo at home and we should wait for Paige's call. That's what she wants.

The air is hot in my lungs. A thin stream of blood drips from my right palm from where my nails have dug through the skin.

The lobby's empty.

Fuck it.

I slam through the inner glass doors and storm up the stairs towards Paige's room, thinking, how did I miss this? *How did I miss this?*

A student watches me march past her on the stairs. She makes a half-hearted attempt to stop me, before cringing at the sight of my expression and running back down to the lobby.

The photograph, I think, bile rising in my throat. *He sent a photograph of her sleeping.*

There are scratch marks around the lock on Paige's door. Fresh gouges in the wood. The door is shut tight.

I don't hesitate. I slam my shoulder into it. The wood buckles easily as I sprawl onto Paige's floor in a shower of splinters.

This is a step too far. I *know* this is a step too far. A violation of her trust and her privacy. A grave betrayal of a person who, according to all the laws of the country, is now a legal adult.

But I'm not snooping. I'm just checking that she's okay; it's entirely different. Especially if she won't even talk to me, her own mother.

A stalker.

Her laptop is open on her desk. Her location tracker lies next to it, useless. I pound bloody fingers on the keys to wake it. Password-protected, of course.

'Fuck!' I yell, smashing the laptop onto the floor, as though I could smash right into Paige's brain, find the answers. The screen cracks. Keys scatter across the floor.

There's a commotion out in the corridor. The girl I passed on the stairs is there, the warden and security guard following close behind her.

'Ms Fourie,' the warden says kindly through the broken door, 'I know you're upset, but you're going to have to come downstairs with me now.'

'Sorry. I'm so sorry.' I kneel to gather the laptop pieces. I'll get it fixed for her. I can fix this.

The security guard steps through the hole in the door cautiously. 'Just come with me now, nice and easy, please.' He holds out his hand but seems reluctant to grab me.

My face is flushed. Some of the keys have scattered under Paige's bedspread, the one I bought her from John Lewis when she moved in a few months ago. I scoop my hand under her bed to gather up the final few keys, thinking I'll fix it, I'll get it all fixed and Paige won't even have to know. My fingers brush a pile of paper. I pull it out. It's a blue A4 folder from the stash I keep under the stairs. A bold Sharpie heading across the front reads 'JUST IN CASE'.

'Come now, please. Put that down, and let's leave your daughter's room,' the security guard says again, creeping closer.

I flip open the folder. Inside are screenshot printouts of texts. Awful, ugly texts. And written in Paige's neat block letters across the inner front cover is his full name: Kyle Michael Law.

'Miss,' the guard says again, his hand firm on my shoulder.

I growl at him, tucking the folder under my arm and pushing past them both.

There are a million things I think about doing as I run down the staircase. *Call the university. Get a lawyer. Head to the police station and scream at Paige asking her why why why she didn't tell me.*

And a new idea, bubbling up from somewhere deep inside me in the beast's voice.

Find Kyle Michael Law and rip him to fucking shreds.

Chills

●

Brenda

Death is the void. Death is darkness. Death is cloying cold, the gurgle of running water. Death is bobbing deep down in the black, caught in an eddy of the river of time. Death is an hour that is maybe three days that is maybe a minute. Death is forever, and never, and now. Death is the smell of shit.

In death, I have been dreaming of my mother. I see her in the draughty house where we grew up, where the wind was always setting the crockery rattling like the whole house was alive, no double glazing back then. Ma, wrapped in that yellow shawl she loved. Ma, pulling a date loaf from the gas oven. Ma, always begging us to put on another jumper because the sight of our bare limbs was making her cold. But we never felt the cold, my brothers and I. We were too full of blood, full of youth, full of fight. We'd tear through that house looking for anything to wallop, anything to eat, anything that could be turned into a game (everything). Ma, older, hacking hacking hacking as the cancer spread through her lungs. Ma never smoked, but the Walthamstow factories smoked for her.

Long dead now, my mother. Both my brothers dead; one ate a bullet, one ploughed his Volkswagen drunk into a road barrier. Ex-husband dead, heart attack, good riddance. Melek dead. Sausage Roll dead. And now I've joined them, drowned in piss. I thought maybe I'd find them all here in the dark, waiting for me. But no. Death is loneliness. Death is only yourself, your own terrible self.

Death is cold.

Death is the feeling of matted hair tickling your frozen ears. Death is a sharp pain stabbing up your thigh bone into your hip, a bright flash of *ow* in the fog of cold gasping nothing. And this disturbs me, because there should be no pain in death.

In death, I think of a story I once read about in the papers, of a group of rugby players whose plane crashed in the Andes and then was buried by an avalanche. Trapped for weeks in the cold and the ice. Debating, for weeks, whether to hike out or to wait for rescue. They had to eat their dead to survive, those lost men, but the Pope forgave them. Anything you have to do to survive death is acceptable, he said.

I dream the question: could you eat your own foot if you were hungry enough?

Death is an avalanche in the mountains. Death is waiting for rescue, and knowing there is no rescue coming.

Death is voices, cheery, talking about overtime pay. Death is splashing sounds, a gloved hand gripping my face. Death is the baffled cry, 'Fuck! Jim, I think there's a body.'

Death is to be a body, cold and limp in the claws of the darkness. Death is a thick film of oil over decomposing skin. Death is feet lost in a tangle of rot and fat.

Death is slipping back underwater as hands move and jostle you. Each movement is pain. Death is begging them, *no, please, do not displace me, leave me here in this cold comfort of death*, but death is knowing that you cannot move your jaw, you are slack-jawed, you are a wide maw. Other voices do the screaming for you, 'She's alive! She's alive!'

Death is nosing back into the void, to Ma's voice singing Bing Crosby in August, where it's warm. Dreaming of how the laundry would bake in the sun, how I'd hide under the bed when she'd call to ask me for help because of the injustice of the fact that she never asked my brothers. Dreaming that I should have just helped her, I should have taken every second with her that I was offered.

Death is time skipping, and it suddenly being sometime later.

Death is a rhythmic beeping, the smell of disinfectant. Death is rough hands sliding underneath aching shoulder blade and aching hip to tip you up far enough to pull out the sheet below you, twice a day. Death is the smell of your own faeces, liquid, soaking into thick pads the nurses have wrapped around you. Death is still the smell of shit, only now it is your own.

Finally, Death blinks down at me, in the shape of a bright smile over turquoise scrubs, an angel filling my vision. 'There you are!' Death says, in a cheerful Eastern European accent. 'I will get the doctor.'

The curtains around my hospital bed are patterned pink and green. No windows in the ward. It could be any time of the day or night, on any day or night. A drip is plugged into my wrist, but whatever sweet oblivion they've been pumping into my blood is ebbing away now, and my whole body screams with pain.

So, not dead.

Shit.

Everyone just wants to tell me how lucky I am. Most of those sewers aren't serviced for months at a time. It was pure fluke that Thames Water had their lads down there, armed with hand tools and high-pressure washers to clear out the enormous fatberg that was blocking that conduit, just in time for tests to begin on the grand new supersewer being built below. I was down there for just over three days, they tell me. A few more hours and I wouldn't have made it.

They found me dehydrated, fighting a raging E. coli infection, ankle buggered, skin scraped up like someone had a go with a cheese grater. My right hip is fractured in two places, but they can't operate until I'm stronger. My cheekbone is also smashed and now held in place with a small metal plate. I'm very lucky there was no bleeding into the socket, or I might have lost my eyesight, they tell me, entirely unaware of the irony. Lucky, lucky, lucky, they say.

I don't feel lucky. I feel stiff, and sore, and furious. My body is a pincushion run through with a dozen nails and pins and scalpels, touched and probed and prodded. Hands change my sweat-sodden sheets. Hands wipe crusted sweat from my armpits. Hands wipe my arse, like an infant. The indignity of it is too much to bear. I scream at the nurses that I can do it myself, but I might as well *be* a pincushion for all they listen.

A policewoman comes to take a statement from me. Tall, young, no one I know. I tell her the truth. I say I was chasing leads on the Walthamstow Cat Killer. A witness said he saw something strange climb out of a hole in the ground and I went down to investigate. Something chased me in the dark, enormous, it didn't move like a human being. I ended up in the old sewer system and I got trapped there.

I use these formal words – witness, leads – the words they use in procedurals on the telly. Words I hope they'll take seriously.

The officer nods, writes down everything I say. She says, 'Well, the good news is that the CPS is not going to press charges. Trespassing,' she adds, seeing my confusion. 'I think everyone is just glad you're okay.'

'Yes,' I say, 'I am so *lucky*.'

She leans closer and lowers her voice. 'Between you and me, you might want to talk to a lawyer about bringing private action against the construction company. The security on that site didn't seem very robust.' She touches the side of her nose. 'Of course, I can't give you legal advice.'

I ask if they're going to look for the creature that was down there with me. The officer pats my arm, just above the place where the IV tubes snake into my bloodstream. 'It must have been horrible, being down there in the dark. You focus on healing now.' Gentle, kind, condescending.

No one can tell me what happened to the clothes I was wearing. Probably binned, so I must suffer the additional indignity of a papery hospital-issued nightdress. They never found my phone, probably floated out to sea by now. The only object that survived my ordeal is the set of keys I found down there, which seem to be ordinary house keys with a small disc key ring, nothing to identify them, but in any case, I seriously doubt the nightmare creature that chased me has a front door. Must have belonged to a workman, after all. It's stashed in the cupboard next to my bed, the only thing in there. A pointless talisman.

In the time I was dead and dreaming, my void seems to have eaten away a little more from the centre of my vision. Darkness fed by darkness. I struggle to tell the nurses apart. I can see just enough to catch them throwing meaningful glances at each other when I mistake one for the other. They think I'm simple. Demented.

I grab the wrists of one of them when they pass my bed. One of the blond ones, Darius or Mylo, I can't tell, face twisted in the abyss. 'You have to let me go home,' I beg him. 'I have work to do.'

'We can phone your boss for you?' Darius says.

There's no boss, I say. But my work is important.

He pats my shoulder. 'Maybe there's someone else we can call. Any family…'

No, no, I thrash away from him. No family. No one who wants me.

The nurse sighs, adjusts my IV tube, continues on his rounds.

I'm not the only one alone. Most of the people in the high dependency unit are my age or older. Most of them have been visited once or twice, if at all. There was one twenty-something who came in after a motorcycle accident, his parents refused to leave his side, visiting hours be damned, but he was discharged soon after I woke up. The only other youngster is a woman in her thirties or forties; her family is in here three times a day, a red-eyed husband who smooths her hair back and repeats over and over how much he loves her, children clasping her hands and telling long-winded stories, curling up on the bed with her to show her things on their iPads. They brought her a stuffed elephant the day I arrived, so huge the nurses had to tie it to the railings around her bed curtains. Every evening they bring a new member of the entourage – friends, a sister, a mother. It's an affront to the rest of us, flaunting these riches. Unjust that one person has such an excess of love when all the rest of us have is endless Channel 4 reruns of *Gogglebox* on the TVs bolted to the ceilings, on mute, interspersed with the same dozen advertisements for food delivery apps and sports betting apps and dating apps playing over and over again. Secretly, watching the woman and her abundance of visitors.

It's a relief for all of us when she dies.

The man in the bed next to me tells me his son lives in Liverpool, he'll be down by tomorrow, he's just trying to figure things out with work. He says that every day for three days before I stop believing him. Either no son exists, or no son cares. Still, his eyes stay fixed on the doors to the ward every visiting hour. Three hours a day he watches that door. No one ever comes.

'That's what you get for relying on other people,' I inform him.

This is where they send us, we old unlovables. We who have outlived being wanted. This is where most of us will die. What's wrong with this country, that it produces so much loneliness?

I lie on my mattress and will my anger to knit my bones back together, to poison the bacteria inside me, to keep my heart beating just a little longer.

'I cannot die,' I mutter to myself. '*I cannot die.*' Because there is a monster out there and I have to kill it. It's the last thing I'll do.

Breast Tenderness

◯

Ellie

27 November. Full moon tomorrow. I myself am gibbous, swollen. All the meat I've been gobbling has packed itself around my belly, my body clutching every precious last oestrogen molecule and wrapping it safely in fat, like a bear might ready herself for a long winter. I can feel the change beginning. My senses are heightened. My emotions simmer right beneath the surface of my skin. The beast is waking.

I have decided that the safest thing for everyone is for me to get far away from London, far from anyone who can get hurt, far from a boy named *Kyle Michael Law*, who is currently the subject of a full university disciplinary investigation, and of every violent daydream I have had for the past two weeks.

The city is a smear of lights and smog behind us as we crawl up the M1. In the driver's seat, Carol's wearing oversized white-rimmed sunglasses and a ratty pink fake-fur-trimmed coat which clashes violently with her red hair. Her car seems to be powered mostly by optimism; the fuel gauge already on *E* when I climb in, moving junk off the passenger seat to make space for myself. Carol shrugged and said it's been broken for years. I'm about to ask when she last filled up the tank, but Carol is too busy singing along loudly with David Bowie about turning to face the strange.

I lean against the window, remembering to do my vagus nerve breathing. I am trying very hard to keep my mind off anything that might make me agitated. This means *not* thinking about how many murdered women were stalked before they were killed. This means *not* thinking about the vile printouts in the A4 folder, which included dozens of copies of the photo of Paige sleeping. Kyle didn't only send it to me, it seems; he also posted it on a 4chan board asking other men to print it out and masturbate on it, and sent the resulting cum-stained images back to Paige in a series of anonymous DMs. It means *not* thinking about how the police decided not to press charges once Paige made it clear she wouldn't be giving any evidence against him – making this case just like the 94 per cent of reported stalking incidents in England where no one is ever charged. It means *not* thinking about how Paige is furious with me for breaking into her room, furious with me for forwarding the contents of the folder to the police and the university without asking her, furious because it's easier to believe (along with Mo) that I'm 'blowing this all out of proportion' than to acknowledge what he's done to her. My sweet daughter. My endlessly empathetic girl. My misguided fool.

Most of all, I can *not not not* allow the beast to think about what it wants to do to Kyle Michael Law, whose home address Paige had diligently recorded in her evidence folder.

My breathing deepens as the car crawls further north, putting more distance between me and my problems. I don't believe in the death penalty. I don't believe violence can be a simple solution to injustice. The fantasy is one thing; but *actually* unleashing the beast? It would rip my life apart.

Liberated from traffic, Carol's driving speeds up until she's well over the limit. Even over the exhaust fumes, I can smell her. *If you pay attention, you can smell them out, you know,* she'd said, *others like us.* I get it now, with my moon-heightened senses. It's not one distinct smell, but every smell. I am hyper-aware of the musk of her armpits. The earthiness of her bare feet. Eucalyptus shampoo. The sweet tang of her crotch. Cherry vapour clinging to her eyebrows. A chocolate smear in the valley between her second and third fingers.

Christ, get a grip on yourself. To start lusting after some manic pixie dream woman when there are so many more important things going on? Preposterous.

We careen past Coventry and stop for pasties at a service station outside Sheffield. I suggest we fill up with petrol, just to be safe, but Carol is too busy arguing with a fellow motorist about his Britain First bumper sticker.

I fall asleep as soon as we get back on the road, partly from the stress of Carol's crazed driving. When I wake, it's almost eleven, and the car is winding through a country lane somewhere in the Yorkshire Dales. It's like driving through a maze, huge hedgerows hemming us in, barely enough space for the car.

We wind up to a stone cottage at the edge of a village, the lights glowing through small windows. The others are already there, crowded into the cosy living room. Alex is nursing a fire to life in a wood stove, housed in a hearth as tall as she is. Empty bottles of wine crowd a solid oak coffee table. Exposed beams thick as railway sleepers run parallel across the ceiling. Payal and Martine are halfway through a game of Bananagrams, which Payal is losing badly. Grace watches from a rocking chair, resplendent in a green headwrap and oversized gold hoop earrings, heckling them between sips of wine.

Carol presents a box of brownies from her luggage. 'They've got skunk in them, but it's just CBD. Keep you mellow. But I do have the vape pen, if anyone wants the spacey stuff.'

I perch in the corner, feeling like the new kid at school – but of course it's nothing like school. These women have already lived entire lives, and I start to relax as they tell me about them. Martine moved to communist Poland in the seventies to live out her revolutionary fantasies in a rural commune. Grace is a retired energy engineer from Uganda, who moved to London to live with her adult daughter after she was arrested for performing rude poems about Museveni's testicles. Payal, who I could believe was thirty but insists she's fifty-two, says she's a high court judge with three teenage boys. She laughs when I ask what face cream she uses. 'Oh, darling, it's Botox and fillers. Don't let the skincare companies lie to you.'

Only Alex still seems distrustful of me, and refuses to tell me much more than that she used to be a nurse, and she has a daughter named Serafine.

I give them a brief biography in turn. Tranquillity. Mo, Paige, Yusuf. And, wanting to seem cooler than I am, I mention that I used to direct plays.

'You never told me that,' Carol says, twirling a red curl around her finger. 'Were you any good?'

'I was young, so probably not.' I haven't thought about this in ages. 'It was all very self-important. But I was happy, I think.'

'Happy, in your twenties!' Payal exclaims. 'Goodness. I was a mess. Couldn't pay me enough to go back and be twenty again.' Easy for her to say, with her glass skin.

'So much angst,' Martine agrees. 'Your whole life stretching out ahead of you in infinite branching possibilities, what a nightmare. My forties, though. Those were fun. I felt like I just rediscovered everything I loved as a teenager, only this time without giving a toss what anyone else thought of me.'

'I am so far finding them quite stressful,' I say.

Carol laughs at this. 'That's because you've made your life too complicated, pet. You could try just feeling your feelings sometime, instead of covering it all up in hyperfunctioning.'

To hide my awkwardness, I grab one of Carol's brownies. It's perfectly gooey and salty and sweet, and I immediately want to wolf down another. Maybe instead of turning feral I could just eat myself into a brownie coma once a month, I think.

'You know, all this time I thought it was the menopause,' I say.

'Well... it's not *not* the menopause.' Carol stretches out one of her feet, tendons rippling luxuriously through her socks. 'Everyone takes the change differently, you know. Most men, I'm generalising here obviously, almost immediately do something stupid and get themselves killed, so there aren't many of them around. The infection often doesn't take in young women at all; their emotional immune system just represses it. But women our age...' She smiles. 'You ever read Caitlin Moran on the menopause? She says it's like coming off Ecstasy. All the fertility hormones that kick in around puberty, their job is to make us soft and pliable and loving so we're able to tolerate men and babies, she says, so we spend half our lives rolling our faces off on love drugs. And then one day it wears off and we realise we spent the best years of our lives slaving for people who don't even like us very much. It's like waking up and realising you spent thirty years being roofied. She says the menopause doesn't *make* us angry. The menopause is finally getting sober, and seeing how badly we've been fucked.'

'Do you think Caitlin Moran is a werewolf?' I ask, scarfing my second brownie.

'Dunno.' Carol shrugs.

'Nigella is,' Payal says. 'I bumped into her in Soho once and she had an unmistakably wolfy whiff about her.'

Martine nods. 'Makes sense. I don't think anyone can be so consistently elegant without going on a rampage once a month.'

They start riffing on other people who must be werewolves. Olivia Colman. Richard Ayoade. The late Queen. It's been so long since I've done this, I realise, just shoot the shit with other women. Amazing how lonely it's been, truthfully, since Paige left. I've got Mo and Yusuf, sure, but Yusuf's only really present for a few hours a day. And now, lying here on this overstuffed sofa, I have to admit to myself that being around Mo hasn't felt nourishing in a long, long time. But I can't blame him. If I have anyone to be angry with, it's that twenty-something idiot I used to be, who thought that working so hard to manage a hundred people's lives would get her power or love, who thought that pouring a million hours into making her home beautiful would make up for the lack of money in her pension, who thought that investing in carefully planned date nights with Mo to keep the spark alive would make up for her total lack of female buddies, her bone-deep loneliness. Maybe this is what I've been missing all this time. Friends. A pack.

My eyes drift back to Carol. Under the coat, she's wearing a band tee emblazoned with the words DAISY CHAINSAW, stretched tight across her monumental tits. She lounges easily on the sofa, her limbs loose and pliable.

Come now, whispers the beast inside me. *Friendship isn't what you want from this woman.*

As the night ages, they peel off to bed one by one. Martine and I are the last two awake, watching the embers crackle in the log burner. We sit in silence for a while, until I gather the courage to ask the question I've been trying to form all night.

'Why did you do this to me?'

'I told you, luvvie. Seemed like you needed it. That day with the bicycle. There you were, bleeding out, worried about everyone else. Couldn't even take one minute to look after yourself. I thought, now there's someone who should be introduced to her shadow.'

'Bet you were sorry when you found out how ugly my shadow is.'

'I didn't put anything in you. I just unlocked the cage. Now you've just got to find something worth fighting for.'

I join the others upstairs, where a row of single beds crowd in one huge room under the eaves, dormitory-style. I lie in the dark, listening to the rich harmonious octaves of Grace's snoring a few feet away. Payal is wrapped up like a burrito, Carol sprawled starfish. I haven't slept like this, tucked among almost-strangers, since teenage sleepovers. There's a comfort to the rich farty smells of their bodies, the intimacy of sleep.

I compose a goodnight message to Mo, but there are no bars on my phone. He thinks I'm in Cambridge with Meredith preparing for a series of meetings with our new investors. I should say that I miss him. But he doesn't deserve to be lied to, on top of everything else I've done to him, that I've imagined doing.

None of Paige's anger about Kyle is directed at Mo, for the record. Mo has been infuriatingly calm about the whole situation, convinced, along with Paige, that we should let the university investigation take its course. Just like several years ago when I noted that Yusuf seemed scattier than usual and he accused me of being a fusspot. Like at fourteen when I said Paige looked skinny and he told me I was being paranoid.

Somewhere in these angry ruminations I slip into sleep, soothed by the snoring.

I wake to find myself standing next to Carol's bed.

You freak, I scold myself. Carol's hair is spilled across the pillow, luxurious, thick – there's so much of it. So much of her. Her mouth is a little open O of darkness in the dawn grey. A light sheen glistens on her cheeks. Carol, too, gets the night sweats, clearly.

Her eyes flicker open, sensing me there.

'Sorry,' I whisper, mortified, turning to go back to my own bed.

Her fingers wrap around my wrists. And I swear I can smell it, the blood pumping faster beneath her skin. I'm sure she can smell mine in return, the dilating blood vessels so close to the surface, skin growing full, nerves whistling, fine hairs standing on end like a static charge.

Silently, she shifts aside and unpeels the duvet, making room for me to join her. Her body is a sprawl of soft skin and luscious mounds, bare but for her knickers. She smiles up at me in a way I can only describe as *wolfish*.

'Sorry,' I whisper again, yanking my wrist from her grasp and fleeing the room.

It's dawn anyway, so I might as well get up, and I don't trust myself to try going back to sleep just a few feet away from her. Flushing in embarrassment, I hurry downstairs and occupy myself with tidying the living room.

God, what a ridiculous stereotype, to have some menopausal mid-life crisis and run off to Yorkshire for some Sapphic reawakening. I'm not going to cheat on my husband of twenty years because the beast's horny. Martine said she 'unlocked the cage', but some urges aren't meant to be freed. Some doors I bricked up and caulked shut long ago. Far too painful to reopen them now. I will not let this creature inside me make a mockery of everything I've spent my whole life building.

This isn't me, I reassure myself. *This is the creature inside me. And it's only in charge one night a month.*

By the time I've scrubbed the coffee table to within an inch of its life, the others are up, bustling around the kitchen, producing an extravagant breakfast.

'You'll need your strength tonight,' Martine says.

Carol's eyes meet mine. Feeling awkward, I look away, tell them I'm going out for a walk. Unprepared for the weather, I borrow Grace's coat. The zip's stuck halfway up, the wind whipping around my body. It's at least a season later up here. Cold forces the air out my lungs. Unhappy sheep are lined up along the low stone wall, taking shelter from the biting wind, snow gathered in clumps in their wool. They bleat and run towards me, smelling the beast stirring inside.

Neat little fields of England. We killed all the real wolves on this island long ago, five shillings per tongue the reward. We killed the wolf because we fear death. We killed the wolf because of the myth of infinite growth, infinite productivity, because if we couldn't master the fields for our economy, what value did they have to us?

My hypersensitive nose follows a trail of iron into the woods. Everything feels so much more real here. I can't believe I was so insensitive to forest before, all the layers of rot and murder, the small skittering things moving through the underbrush. The bark is scratched off a tree, eight feet up.

I find the lamb ripped wide open in a clearing, organs glistening purple and blue, dark crystals of blood scattered across the snow. A crow unburies its black beak from the soft parts of the stomach and meets my eyes.

Was it one of the pack, out on a little ramble last night? Was it *me*?

The tears are cold on my cheeks, like blades. I deserve them.

I remind myself it wasn't full moon last night. Sheep die all the time, chased down by dogs, by boys, little lambs taken by eagles or badgers. Better than dying in an abattoir, perhaps. That's the whole reason the pack come out here, so their carnage won't be commented on. So they can do as they please.

The lamb's eyes are closed, poor sleeping creature. For a moment, it morphs into Paige's face. I think again of Kyle Michael Law. Of all the murdered women who were stalked before they were killed.

What am I doing here, halfway across the country, roaming the dales with a bunch of middle aged hippies? I shouldn't be here. So far from the people who need me. Putting the beast so close to Carol.

I leave the sad carcass in the snow and climb a hillock, holding my phone in the air. Finally, near the top, I locate a single bar of signal. My phone goes into an electronic tantrum in my hand. Yusuf's going to be discharged on Friday and Mo wants to know if I can pick him up. The term sheets are signed and the board wants me to organise a big celebration party with the whole team. Byron wants to know if I can give him an advance on Mum's house sale, although he still hasn't contributed any effort to finding an estate agent. And Paige wants me to call her back.

Only seven hours until nightfall. But I cannot be here for a minute longer.

I trudge back to the cottage and ask Grace to drive me to the station.

'It's not safe for you to be in London tonight,' she says.

My eyes meet Carol's, watching me over a mug of steaming tea, her expression unreadable.

It's not safe for me to be here, I think.

Dizzy Spells

O

Brenda

'Isn't that nice, Brenda? You've got a visitor!' Nurse Mylo this time, I think. They all talk to me like I'm a toddler. Because I can't tell them apart, they've mistaken me for soft in the head. When really, my brain has never felt so clear, honed sharp by fury.

He's mistaken, anyway. Haven't had a single visitor in the three weeks I've been here, doubt I have one now. They've moved me from the HDU to a regular ward, where I'm recovering from my hip replacement, enduring twice-daily torture marketed as 'physiotherapy' and adjusting to life as a creature made partially of metal and cement. I'm giving it my all, doing their poxy exercises, enduring the pain and the embarrassment and the tasteless food and the slow shuffles to the toilet in the name of revenge. I have a mission. They say I might be able to go home as soon as next week. Let's be honest: they can't wait to get rid of me.

But a lanky shape does, in fact, materialise next to my bed, heralded by a thick fog of Lynx body spray.

'Hey, Auntie B,' says Daniel, dragging up a plastic chair. I struggle to see him in the bright morning light streaming in from the window.

'How did you know I was here?' I ask. I've found out that the ambulance took me to the hospital closest to where I was found.

'It was all over the news! Famous, you are. The woman who survived seventy-six hours stuck in a sewer. They're calling you the Fatberg Grandma.'

'Just what I always wanted on my tombstone.' I punch at the remote control trying to get my bed to sitting position. It elevates my feet up instead. 'Blasted thing!'

Daniel takes the remote from me and the headrest pushes me upright. 'I'm sorry for what happened.'

'Are they even looking into it? Whoever did this to me?'

'Not... specifically. They did look into the cats, though. That Facebook group of yours really put the heat on. People calling the station every day asking what we were doing about it. We even got a call from the mayor saying his office was being flooded with queries. So eventually Sarge sent one of the bodies for proper genetic testing. CSI treatment and all.'

'Which body?'

'One of the first ones, from back in August? A local vet said he had a body on ice that no one had claimed. Paul Demopoulos – that ring a bell?'

Mr Bojangles. The cat belonging to Jin and the other two in the house share. I never did call Paul back and arrange for the body to be collected after the necropsy. Once I'd got the information I needed, it didn't seem important.

'He's my vet. Was my vet.'

'Well, they swabbed the fur and sent it to a university lab to look for DNA. They... ah. They found fox saliva. There was human DNA too; probably the owners, nothing that showed up on a criminal database. Nothing else, no dogs or anything. But there was definitely fox saliva.'

I try to recall the details of my conversations with Paul – it all feels so long ago now. 'He said that foxes are opportunistic scavengers. They might have a nibble of a body if it's already dead, but foxes almost never kill cats. Especially not cats as big as mine.'

'Yeah.' I can't tell for certain, but he seems to be staring at the linoleum floor, shuffling something around between his feet. 'Thing is, once they had an answer they liked, they didn't really need to keep looking, did they?'

I run my finger along the stitches holding my surgical wound together, using the pain to focus my mind amid the swirling anger.

Tiny things: a cut barely three inches across my skin; a few tissue samples of cat. That's all they need these days. To replace a foundation of your body; to unravel a crime. The marvels of science.

'What about the thing we saw on CCTV? The thing that chased me through the sewers?' Daniel doesn't respond directly to this. He's not in his uniform, I notice, but wearing a colourful hoodie emblazoned with a Japanese cartoon character. Not official business, then. He ducks down and places something heavy on the mattress next to me.

'I thought you might want some of this.'

I bring it close enough to see around the void and realise it's my carpet bag, crammed full of my own things. Two sets of pyjamas, my slippers, a house dress, a dog-eared romance novel which I confess might have been on one of my bookshelves, a badge saying FRIEND OF THE CATS, and right at the bottom, the thing responsible for the weight of the bag: my laptop.

'You broke into my house?'

Daniel's hands wrap around mine, long-fingered and warm. 'Auntie, I have to tell you something. Your landlord got a possession order from the court.'

'But I was here,' I splutter.

'He didn't know that. He felt bad when he found out afterwards, I think. But the movers had already been and gone by then. Your things are all packed up in a storage unit in Edmonton. He let me pop in and get some things for you.' Daniel pulls his hands away from mine and lays something small and metal on the trolley next to me. The key to a storage locker. The key to all I have left in the world. 'He's paid up three months. Says that's the best he can do.'

'Wanker,' I say, twisting the thin blanket in my hand. 'He can't do this to me. I have rights. I'll take him to court, see what they think of him turfing out an old woman when she's in hospital.'

'It's too late, Auntie. Someone else is already living there. It's Walthamstow, yeah? I don't think it even took a week for him to get new tenants in. He said he was very sorry, your landlord.'

'Fuck him. Fuck his sorrys.'

Daniel smiles. 'I said the same thing.'

Nurse Mylo is back, clanging a brass bell, heralding the end of visiting hours. He stops at my bed. 'Ooh, I don't like that blood oxygen reading, Brenda. We've got to try to stay calm and take deep breaths, remember! How long has it been this low?' He's gesturing at the monitor next to my bed, which I obviously cannot see.

'My friend is blind,' Daniel corrects him. 'Visually impaired,' he corrects himself.

I swat his arm away. Judas. 'I'm not *mute*,' I hiss. 'I can talk for myself, thank you very much.'

I hate the way Nurse Mylo pauses at this news, a number of things clicking into place for him. Yet more evidence of my incapacity. My weakness.

'Guess I'd better get going,' Daniel says. 'I'll come and visit again soon, yeah?'

I tell the boy he should do whatever he bloody wants, it's nothing to me, and then pretend to be very interested in the bed's remote control again until he leaves.

At least I have a computer again. I bark at Nurse Mylo, who has since morphed into Nurse Darius, to plug it in for me, and it whirrs to life, heavy on my lap. Three weeks of messages to catch up on.

The most promising emails are from Slow-Worm Jack. The field cameras picked up an unidentified large animal, heading north through the Lea Valley in the early hours of 27 October. Vaguely canid, he says, but far too big. Leading theory is a fallow deer that wandered down from Epping Forest, but it didn't look anything like a deer, and a deer doesn't explain the string of dead rats and voles they found scattered around. He's attached a photo still, no clearer than the black-and-white footage we got from the launderette CCTV, which has already proved insufficient to convince anybody I'm not mad. Still, it's interesting to know that after the thing nearly killed me, it apparently ambled up the marshes for a celebratory romp.

The CATS group is a mess. Someone posted an article from the local news titled WALTHAMSTOW CAT KILLER HOAX: FOXES RESPONSIBLE, STUDY FINDS. So testing one single cat is a 'study' now, is it? But the comments are livid. People feel betrayed. They say they dedicated so much time to this, all for nothing.

Wonder what the CATS people have to say about this?

HAHAHAHA this is why old women shouldn't be allowed on the internet.

Explain to me how a fox opens a locked guinea pig cage?

Disgusting!! This is all about money!!! I gave £1,000 to those grifters and you'd better believe I'm going to get it back!!!!

Hello my family and I are travelling to London in April and excited to see our first West End show!! How do we buy tickets?

Will foxes kill my cat? There is one that lives near my house and my cat goes out to do his business. Should I put out poison???

Brenda Martins is a scumbag.

A fox killed my sister's cat! If you're letting them roam, you might as well be strangling them directly! Responsible owners are #indoorsonly

Duck you liberal aunt try to take my OUTDOOR cat from me and I will show you strangling

Jin, I see, has been commenting below the most unhinged posts. *She's just a lonely old lady,* he says. *I don't think she meant for it to go this far. Be kind.*

I slam the laptop shut, my hands shaking from anger. I think of all my worldly possessions sitting in a storage unit somewhere. I think of my life, grown so small, shrunk to the size of this hospital bed, my busted hip and my vengeance.

Night Sweats

○

Ellie

I lean my forehead against the Uber's window, watching my breath melt the lace of frost. An indifferent sun races to its early rendezvous with the horizon, the day already growing dark even though it's barely past three.

'Sure you gave me the right address, miss?' The driver's eyes catch mine in the rear-view mirror. We're weaving through the outskirts of Enfield, where the city finally crumbles into the greenbelt. It's all industry and garden centres out here. And quiet. On the train back from Yorkshire, I found an abandoned warehouse on an online list of 'Most Hidden Spots in London' where I'm planning to secure myself tonight. Not a well-considered plan. But the best I could pull together in a hurry.

'Just keep driving, please.' Add to List: *Tip extra; he's unlikely to find someone for the return trip.*

Paige calls just as we make the final turn past an artificial grass depot.

'Kyle's been suspended,' she spits down the phone.

'This isn't a great time, love. Can I call you later?'

'This could ruin his life.' Her voice is thick with tears. Rage, not sadness, because she is my daughter.

'And what about your life? Tell me the truth: were you so afraid of him you were barely leaving your room?'

'Mum, I have an anxiety problem. You know that. Kyle never actually *did* anything.'

'Except that vile photograph. Except the harassing messages. Those are crimes.'

'He says the messages weren't him. And he apologised for the photo.'

'Why do you think he tried to *break into your room?*'

'It was a stupid thing. He was going to paint something on my floor, like a prank. He had the paintbrush and everything in his bag. He was just trying to get my attention because I ghosted him…'

Christ, and this is how it goes. Young women contorting themselves into knots to make everything their fault. Kidding themselves that they're the ones who secretly have all the power, rather than actually fighting to get any of that power. Maybe Carol was right. Maybe this rage is a gift. *What if I went over there right now?* the thought flashes into my mind. *What if I gave it to her?* What if I could break the cycle and one woman in our family could spend her life being angry instead of being so fucking sorry all the time?

I flinch, physically, at the ugliness of this thought. Infecting my own daughter.

The driver glances at me in the rear-view again, expression kind and concerned, steering into a car park at the edge of a shabby industrial park. Another sedan follows us in and parks in front of the synthetic grass supplier opposite.

Paige's voice has become clipped, reading something she pre-wrote. 'Mum, I love you. But I have decided that for the sake of my own wellbeing, I need to not talk to you for a while. I will not be able to accept your phone calls or messages. Please respect my boundaries.'

'Paige, come on. This is ridiculous. I'll stop by tomorrow and we can talk properly.'

But she's gone, and I'm listening to my own ragged breathing, and the sound of the creature in my head roaring at me to *go there now, fucking make her listen.*

There's no time to deal with Paige. Shove those worries onto the List. I thank the driver and stumble into the icy air, heaving my backpack over my shoulder. The car park is almost empty, save for a few men loading bags of dog food onto a truck, and the odd car. The online write-up said most of this industrial park has been abandoned for decades, a popular destination for urban explorers and addicts.

Not wanting to draw attention to myself, I slink between two warehouses and head for the darker cluster of buildings at the rear. The cold air stinks of diesel and piss.

I wrap my arms around myself, but my tremors have nothing to do with the cold. The change is coming. I recognise it now, this twisting unease, this unmoored terror. Raised hairs on the back of my neck. Prickling skin. The feeling that someone is stalking me. But this time I know the truth: the thing I fear is already inside.

Flies find my face as I weave through the squat buildings, drawn to my pheromones. The moon is already high. Time is running out.

I stumble into a cacophony of rough voices, shrieking laughter. A missile smashes into the corrugated iron next to my face, missing me by inches.

'Oi!' I yell, rounding on the group of yobs filling the space between two empty buildings. Teenagers, I clock, three girls and four boys, one of them wearing a pink plastic top hat, all of them holding bottles. They're smashing windows, I realise. There is broken glass scattered on the ground between us. Broken glass in their voices, too, which have begun laughing again, high-pitched and mocking.

'Watch yourself, lady!' The tallest of the girls picks up another brick, faking like she's about to throw it at my head, before smashing it into a pane behind me, sending the others doubling up in erratic laughter at my glowering expression.

And the script now is that I should nervously clutch my bag and scurry along so they can continue their youthful boisterous play. And they are seven and I am one, and they are young and I am old, and some of them are male and it has been my fate to spend my life trammelled into the mask marked female, marked Mum, marked whingy white lady, marked prey.

Instead, I take a step towards them. And I bare my teeth. And I growl.

My teeth are larger than I expect them to be, hard against my lower lip. And the growl grows rich in my throat, deep, thunderous, boiling with murder. And my hands have found their way out of my pockets, and my fingers are longer than they were, perhaps, and I am a few inches taller, and I take a step towards them, and they drop silent.

They cower.

'*Little pig, little pig…*' The beast speaks this using my mouth. A broken brick crunches beneath my heavy foot.

The toughest-looking boy takes a step backwards, grabbing his friend's hand, trying to pull her away. 'Sorry, miss,' he's muttering. 'Didn't mean it.'

The boy in the top hat has already vanished, running as fast as he can into the night.

But their leader, the tall girl, stands her ground, eyes huge, refusing to accept that the script has changed. She puffs out her chest, draws herself bigger.

My heart pounds in my chest and the creature is rearing in me now, and I am hyper-aware of the flutter in her throat which is her carotid artery, so close to the surface where the littlest scratch might let it flood out, this little *shit*, and my nails feel like they might even be sharp enough, they really might…

'Fallon,' the friend hisses, before dropping the girl's hand, shrinking.

I take another step towards the girl, who is trembling, but still standing straight. '*My, Granny, what big teeth you have.*'

The beast's lips peel back. There are knives in its mouth, shining knives glistening with spit, sharp white razors, neat rows of little deaths.

And the girl spins, finally, and she runs, leaving me alone in the twilight. Their footsteps echo into the distance.

It takes everything in me not to chase them. I conjure James McAvoy's voice in my mind. *You are a droplet of water bubbling up from a spring.* A lifetime's worth of mindfulness meditation training kicks into play. Resting my awareness on my own breath, tickling in through my nostrils.

And out.

And in.

And out.

I really do not have any more time to fuck around.

I stagger towards the next doorway I see, my backpack cutting heavy into my shoulders. The door of the warehouse (*werehouse?*) is chained and padlocked, but the broken windows gape open like mouths, so I swing myself into the gloom.

The space inside is cavernous, a single huge room the size of a cathedral, a mausoleum to inter my creature inside. Graffiti snakes across a wall, the human version of peeing on it to say I was here. My nose wrinkles at the stew of rust, damp, and the acrid remnants of whatever was once manufactured here, a long time ago, when Britain still manufactured things. And something else, which seems out of place among the rest: a smell at once fishy and floral. Familiar.

A thick steel support beam will serve as an anchor. I am a fool to have left it so late. I'll do better next time. Hands shaking, I dig my supplies out of my backpack, carefully obtained over the past few weeks, and arrange them around me like a salt circle in the moon glow:

- Bioidentical oestrogen cream.
- Break-glass-in-case-of-emergency tranquilliser pills, prescribed by my GP to stop the panic attacks, when my mother was dying but it was the pandemic so I couldn't visit her. I've never taken them, but just knowing they're an option has been a powerful talisman.
- Handcuffs, obtained from a specialist BDSM shop in Camden.
- Iron chain, obtained from B&Q.
- Backup cable ties.
- Backup-backup bungee rope.
- An Aesop candle.

Everything I might need to girlboss my way through this breakdown.

My hands tremble as I thread the chain around the beam and click the manacles tight around my wrists and ankles. I stash the key behind a nearby girder, out of sight but still within stretching reach. The beast's mind is not my mind. I can only trust that it won't know where I've hidden it, and that it won't have the patience or dexterity to use it if it does.

Finally, I place my phone at a careful angle on the beam where the steel will amplify its sound, and press play on our most popular new meditation.

Scurrying sounds in the shadows. A fat cockroach crawls over my foot. Another. A small grey rat noses at my hand. Far away, corncrakes sing the evening in. I've lost track of whether they're part of the soundtrack, or really singing outside. The sounds telescope shut. The world closes in.

Heat simmers inside of me, my muscles melting, my limbs growing longer. A diffuse, burning pain. I stretch my foot to relieve the cramp, and it keeps stretching out, longer, longer, until my heel is twenty inches from my toes. Viscous bones pulled like toffee. Tickling on my scalp as cockroaches climb into my hair. Hair on my bare arms growing thicker. Evolution in reverse. Boiling fever. Moon-madness.

More dark tiny shapes boil from the shadows, drawn to the frenzy of me. Rodents and silverfish.

My fingers grip the ground. My teeth grind to keep from screaming.

Fight it. Focus on the meditation.

A heavy thud rattles the window frames. Footsteps in the ruin, coming closer.

My eyes snap open and take in a tall silhouette framed in the last of the light.

'Don't come closer!' I shout. 'It's not safe.'

But it advances. Shoulders hunched, forearms lengthening towards the floor. And I recognise him, finally, from his smells. Hospital disinfectant. The pus of healing wounds. That awful fucking tea he likes.

I lick my tongue across lips which are already pulling into an unfamiliar shape. 'Andreas. I'm so sorry.'

He steps into the glow of my candle and I see what a monster I have made of him, what miserable daemon I have sent abroad into the world.

My loose end.

His Garfunkel fuzz is now shaved short. His face is a quilt of scars, fresh-grafted skin stretched between shining keloid tissue. He frowns, but the lines don't stop at his forehead, they run down his face, deep cracks right into the black heart of him. His whole face is shifting as I watch, like bugs moving under his skin, like his skin is just a flesh-mask hiding a roiling, hideous mass of something terrible. A thick rope of saliva drips from his jaw.

He's been stalking my scent.

Panic bubbles like acid in my throat. I am suddenly extremely aware of the fact that I am immobilised. Handcuffed. Completely at his mercy.

He paces, tracking me, his eyes flashing yellow in his ruined face. He moves with a lupine grace. 'What did you do to me?'

I twist my hand in the manacles, wondering if I can somehow grab the key without Andreas noticing, and free myself before he has a chance to lunge at me. 'I wasn't myself,' I say, trying to buy time. But the beast is growling in me, *I gave you what you deserved.*

He continues pacing, nostrils flaring, reading my panic, sizing me up. He is larger than me. He is stronger.

Maybe I could take him.

Maybe he will kill me.

Maybe we could feast on his intestines, says the beast, unhelpfully. *I hope they don't taste like his tea.*

'Andreas, listen to me.' I try to keep my mind focused on the shrinking part of me that can still think. 'There are cable ties in that bag. You need to secure yourself to something.'

'Why?' His face is lengthening, a snout pushing out of his face, a mouth designed not for speech but for rending flesh. Agony in my jaw tells me that mine is doing the same.

Hands shaking, I reach for the key. Slowly. Keeping my eyes fixed on his. Moonlight stirring in us. Wildness stirring. Bones cracking. The click of the lock.

The handcuffs clatter to the floor. All my careful plans for nothing. My heels leave the ground, and I am eye to eye with him, our heads stretching towards the ceiling. My arms are longer too, sharp searing pain as claws push through the skin of my fingers.

Ripping sounds as my dress tears up the seam. It's so short now that it barely covers my stomach, let alone the white pants reaching their limit across my broadening hips. But my skin prickles as thick hairs sprout from me, and I no longer care about my nakedness, and I hook what is now a two-inch fingernail into the band of my bra and rip it away.

Andreas does the same to the shreds of his shirt and trousers. He is more beautiful without his clothing. His body beneath is middle-aged, like mine. Ragged and scarred and life-worn and strong. He is well dressed in his skin, adorned in rippling flesh, alive. *It is such an ordinary thing to be alive; such a miraculous thing.*

Freed, now, I am no longer afraid of him. We are evenly matched. It occurs to me that I have just as much ability to hurt him as he has to hurt me. There's a curious frisson in the thought. I might pin him down. I might test my strength against his strength.

The smells of him are overpowering. The laundry powder he used on the tearing clothes, the upholstery of the car he sat in to trail you here, the toast he ate for breakfast – the beast can read the whole day on him. And underneath it all, the blood and sweat and the damp fur of him. Pheromones suggesting a dare, speaking of pack. Like Carol, yesterday, like her hair and her creamy full body and her small red tongue. Carol who you cannot have.

My human thoughts slip away.

The beasts fall on all fours, sizing the other up.

They circle, eyes fixed on each other's necks.

Unclothed, feral.

The beast leaps. Heavy and strong.

I have him pinned beneath me, his eyes yellow and wild.

I could kill him, now.

Instead, I find myself reaching down to grasp his cock. It is smooth, warm, thickening in my clawed hand. I fucking hate this man. But – it occurs to me now – hate and desire are not opposites.

He wraps a hand around my waist. Squeezing flesh.

I pull him into me. I am slick, hungry.

The beast pants as a wave of pleasure throbs through her belly. She grinds herself wet and hungry on her enemy. Wanting.

It all falls away from me.

Bye, Ellie.

The beasts begin to howl.

Wolf Moon

Mood Swings

◯

Ellie

I jolt awake, the tang of violence still coating my tongue, lying on something velvety. The smallest mercy is that I am still in the warehouse. Everything else is bad. Bad.

Bad.

Empty cockroach carapaces crunch under my fingers as I sit up. The soft thing I was lying on turns out to be the body of a dead rat squashed flat beneath my cheek. More dead vermin carpet the floor between me and the most bad thing among all the bad things: Andreas's naked body, curled a few feet away.

His body is a lattice of fresh scratches and old scars. My beast's handiwork, both times. He got a few of his own in last night, I see, wincing as I explore the deep gouges across my torso, along my shoulder blades. Already healing.

Beneath the scratches, Andreas's pale body is covered in fine blond hairs, all over his small paunch, his testicles purple and drooping like rotting fruit. Poor pitiful mangled creature. All I can smell on him now is myself, everywhere.

I think of Mo.

Andreas's eyelids flutter open as I pull on the spare jeans from the bottom of my backpack. There's still a glint of something yellow in his eyes behind the blue, yellow and feral. My vulva is throbbing and tender.

'I'm sorry,' I mumble. 'I'm so sorry.'

A laugh erupts from his throat, rich and wild. 'Sorry? Ellie, look at me.' He sprawls on the floor, a king among ruins. 'I've never felt better.'

I pause, jeans half buttoned, to look at him. Really look at him. The beast has only added to his appetites. There's a vitality to his madness, an edge of lunacy sharpened by power. Untamed. Unrepentant. Fuck, isn't he married?

I'm married.

'You can have your job back,' I say. Thinking, *undo it. Undo it all.*

Another bark of laughter. 'My *job?*' He rolls onto his side, propped up on one elbow, looks at me as though I've just suggested we train the dead rats to tap dance. 'I don't give a shit about the job any more, Ellie. How can you? *Qui n'avance pas, recule...*' He stretches, languid and unhurried as a cat basking in the sun, except the sun here is meagre winter morning light filtering through grime-crusted windows. 'You really are a small-minded, stuck-up bitch, aren't you?'

'Fuck *you*, Andreas.'

'Yes, you just did,' he smirks.

I leave him there, luxuriating in his vermin-strewn den. An Uber drives me home. I stink beneath my coat, blood and sweat and Andreas. It would be so much better to not remember.

Mo is still asleep when I get back, a puff of dark hair over our duvet. Our bed creaks as I climb in, echoing right through my hollow heart. The mattress is a Naturalmat premium pocket-sprung natural fibre super-king. The upgrade we treated ourselves to when Mo got his lectureship. Carefully chosen. So many careful choices that made our home. This precious life we built together.

I wrap myself around him. His body is warm. Solid. So familiar.

He grasps my hands in his and pulls me closer, before he feels me shaking against him.

'Hey,' he murmurs, turning to me and seeing the tears streaming down my face. 'Hey, what happened?' His voice is soft and thick. He presses an undeserved kiss into my hair. He cups my face in his hand, noticing one of the deep scratches down my collarbone. 'Whoa! Hey.'

He leads me to the bathroom and unwraps my coat, eyes full of concern as he takes in the damage.

Sobs wrack my body. The tiles are cold against the soles of my feet, and his hands are warm as they lift my shirt, follow the wounds down my belly, trace the contours of my shame.

'Do you need a doctor? Do you need the police?'

His body puffs up like he's ready to protect me now from whatever attacked me. But I am the monster in the house. I am the bad thing.

'Love, talk to me...' he says.

'I slept with someone, Mo.' The words fall out of my mouth, traitors, heavy as dead rats. 'I slept with someone last night.'

His hands freeze, still holding my hips, his eyes fixed on my naval.

We stand there in the moment, in the fracturing. Two decades to build it. One sentence to shatter it.

The silence stretches.

Far away, a barking dog, the sound of cars, the neighbour's Vitamix.

'Mo...' I begin, but I don't know what to say next.

He withdraws his hands. Collapses on the toilet lid, eyes still fixed somewhere around my middle.

'I thought you were,' he says finally. 'All those nights you never came home.' His voice is cracked, a ruin. He just stares at my body. My destructive body.

'No, that was...' I fall to my knees in front of him and reach out my hands for his, but he folds them away from me. 'It was just last night.'

His brows pull together, his eyes finally meeting mine. 'Congratulations?'

For a long moment, he hides his head in his hands, breathing heavily. I prepare myself for all the questions he must have. He must have so many questions. *I have to tell him about the beast*, I think. *It's finally time that I tell him.*

But there are no questions. He takes a deep breath, and mumbles through his fingers with surprising calm, 'We can fix this.'

'Fix this?' I echo.

'Counselling.' His voice gains steadiness as he lowers his hands from his face. 'We'll go to counselling. Everyone makes mistakes. You regret it.'

'Of course,' I say, my knees cold on the tiles.

He nods, satisfied at his own virtue. He stands, towering above me. 'Then I can forgive you, if you're willing to put in the work to make this right.'

A wave of relief washes over me, but catches on something, eddies. 'If I can put in the work,' I repeat.

He places a hand gently on my head. Saintly.

And this is how it will be from now on, I realise. I will apologise, and apologise, and spend the rest of my life prostrating myself.

I'll be the one who hit menopause and had a breakdown.

He'll never ask himself if there was a reason.

It must be the remnants of the beast in me that take over my limbs, because I find myself pushing past Mo back to the bedroom, reaching up to pull an overnight bag from the top of the cupboard.

'What... what are you doing?' Mo blinks at me as I toss in clothes.

'Don't you even want to know who?' I ask, voice hardening.

He physically cringes, unable to hide his disgust. 'Don't put those images in my head. I don't deserve that. I've been nothing but patient with you.'

'So you're not curious. At all. About me. About what I've been going through.'

'Hang on. You're saying you cheated on me because you were miffed you didn't get a promotion?'

I bark a laugh.

His voice cracks for the first time, a tremor almost human, as I stuff knickers into the bag. 'Ellie, please. We can work this out.'

'*You* work it out, Mo. You go and sit in counselling and moan about how your bitch wife ruined your perfect life. Be my guest.' I zip the bag and sling my coat over my arm.

I'm trembling now, and not only from sorrow, thinking how unfair it is that I'm the one who has to leave this house, when it's my job that's paid off most of the mortgage, when I'm the one who chose every piece of furniture, who painted every wall, Lists on Lists on Lists to make this home, to make this marriage. Mo teasing me all the while for overthinking, Mo whose sole piece of decor when I met him was a Klimt poster an ex-girlfriend had given him, Mo who said he didn't really care if we had kids or not but he'd go along with whatever I wanted, Mo who shrugged when I said his father should move in with us so we can spend the last good years with him, Mo who replied when I asked if we should get married that he was easy, Mo who thought it was absurd when I suggested we do an annual 'marriage review' like Esther Perel suggests, Mo who has never read a single book about healthy relationships, Mo who – *I see it so clearly now* – picked me up twenty-five years ago like a burr on his sock that was never quite worth the hassle of picking off.

He follows me as I walk down the stairs. I take a moment at the Please Take Me Upstairs pile, and kick it across the hallway.

'Ellie.' Mo stands in the doorway, blocking my exit, disbelieving. 'This isn't you.'

'How would you know?' I say, brushing past him.

And then I'm gone.

Don even pretends he's pleased to see me, God bless him, when I show up on his doorstep trailing my sad wheelie bag.

'I know it's the worst time,' I say. 'Can I stay for a few days?' I couldn't handle the thought of a hotel, being alone. I need someone who knows me, who can look at me and not only see the worst things I have done. 'Sorry to tell you this, but you might be the last friend I have in the world.'

'Of course, silly goose,' he says, ushering me into the warmth. 'You've come at the perfect moment, actually. I was just about to make the most virtuosic mah-jong meld. It deserves an audience.'

'He lies!' Inez calls out. 'He hasn't won a game in two days.'

It's a shock how much Inez has withered in the few weeks since I last saw her. She's propped up in a hospital bed in the middle of the open-plan living-dining room, cheeks hollow, oxygen tube snaking beneath her nose. An outline of the woman she was. Her shirt is lopsided where her left breast isn't. I can smell perfume struggling to assert itself against the sterility of sickness, various chemical tangs, the port in her armpit, the stink of a wound that hasn't quite healed, that won't ever heal.

I look around, thinking with a pang of all the cheerful dinners Mo and I ate here, in better times. Surfaces are cluttered with the detritus of dying: mah-jong tiles, empty Lucozade bottles, pill packets, lotion, endless bouquets of flowers and framed family photos. They've managed to put up a Christmas tree, real pine, life's last stand against the darkness.

Inez grips my hand warmly, her fingers papery in mine. 'I'm so sorry,' I say. 'I shouldn't be here. Mo and I…' I can't say it.

'Shh, honey,' Inez says. 'We're glad you're here.' She asks me to make her some tea, letting me feel useful. Letting me imagine for a moment that I am not the biggest piece of shit in the universe.

We fall into an easy routine over the next few days, a choreography of pillow-fluffing, water-glass refilling, medicine-redosing. I tell the team I'm going to work from home for a while. I take over the cooking and the cleaning so Don can spend most of the day at her bedside. It's good to have something to do, a way to feel helpful. It feels like penance.

There are no Lists for this type of care. Inez's moods change like the winter weather, minute to minute. She spends her most lucid hours writing long letters to everyone she's ever met. School friends she hasn't spoken to in years, old colleagues, distant family members. She is often frustrated and furious. It turns out no one is their best self while dying. She tells me dying peacefully is overrated, and says that the Virtual Rage Room is the best thing we've ever made. 'See, Don, you should have handed her the reins sooner,' she tells him. He winces at this, keeping his eyes averted from mine. *Inez is only ten years older than me*, I keep thinking. When exactly was I planning on getting to all those things at the bottom of the List, the things that were just for me?

Inez says it's the itching that's going to end her. Don spends long hours each day rubbing lotion into her skin, head to toe, toe to head.

In the end, this is what love is, I think. Not self-actualisation or sex, not economics or child-rearing or companionship. It's someone who will rub the itchy parts of your back that you cannot reach, with perfect patience. Even though it soon won't matter. Even though you will shortly be dead.

They teach me mah-jong. I'm terrible at it, but somehow better than Don, who loses every game and makes a big show of it, dredging up vulgar curses in his thickest Scots to make us laugh.

When she sleeps, which she does a lot, Don and I retreat to the dining table where we can keep half an ear on her laboured breathing. He reads psychology journals while I send emails. It feels right, to be driving Tranquillity from the virtual control deck of this 16-inch screen, while Tranquillity's first customer stubbornly clings to life a few feet away from us in the meatspace.

The Virtual Rage Room's been removed from the App Store for legal reasons, but you can still download it directly from our website. It's by far the most successful thing we've ever made.

My precious corporate module, on the other hand, doesn't yet have a single customer.

Don tells me about a piece of research he read showing that men are seven times more likely to leave their wives if they are diagnosed with cancer than the other way round. 'It's all I can think about sometimes,' he confesses. 'Just feeling furious at men I've never met before. My therapist would probably tell me it's displacement.'

'Or maybe it just means you've got a heart, Don.' I tell him Inez's theory, about how maybe we should all be much angrier than we are.

'Aye. Tranquillity was always for her.' His gaze drifts over to the bed, where Inez sleeps, small and broken as a doll. 'I think that's why I didn't like what you kept trying to turn it into.'

'What did I try to turn it into?'

'Another tool for repressing your feelings,' he says, with a gentle smile. 'You're very repressed, you know.'

I scoff. 'Less and less these days.'

'Don't take this the wrong way, but I think Tranquillity was always your fantasy of being able to fix your mother.'

'Thanks, Doctor Freud.' I flick some of my tea at him.

Don bats me with his journal in response, then takes my hand. 'Ellie, I'm proud of what we made. And I'm sorry.'

I rest my head on his shoulder. 'None of that matters now, does it?'

We sit together in the silence, watching Inez sleep. All of us are only temporarily healthy, I think. Only temporarily sane. All of us able-bodied twenty-, thirty-, forty-somethings with fitness trackers and podcasts and science-based supplements and anti-ageing creams and bioidentical hormones fooling ourselves into believing we can body-hack our way to lifelong independence. Don's right: I've been as guilty of the fantasy as any of them.

Lying in their spare bed that night, I find myself staring at the dots on the family location sharing app, wondering whether Mo would care for me if I found out I was dying of cancer. *Of course he would*, I chide myself, disgusted by this urge in myself to recast the story with me as victim not villain. This is my fault. I kept things bottled up for too long. I let my needs curdle into resentment because I felt my emotions were so dangerous no one else could ever see them. Where'd I learn that?

If I am going to fix this, I have to begin by taking responsibility. An honest accounting of my sins.

I stay up late writing a long List about how I am going to fix my life.

- Write Paige an apology email. She is not answering my calls.
- Write Mo an apology email. He *is* answering my calls, but only to tell me not to call him without my divorce lawyer present. Yusuf's back home, but Mo refuses to let me visit him. I'd never have imagined he was capable of such cruelty; never say a spouse can't surprise you.
- Restart CrossFit for its mood-stabilising effects, and also to undo the effects of all these late-night rat binges.
- Find an iron-clad once-a-month solution to locking the beast away from all potential to cause harm, far away from

Andreas, or from Kyle Michael Law, or from a certain red-haired someone who keeps intruding on my thoughts, when what I need to be focused on is saving my marriage.

The next full moon is just after Christmas. I have plenty of time.
    I silently say goodnight to their little pixelated dots. Yusuf and Mo at our home in Barnsbury. Paige in her residence hall in Holborn. Then I notice that an extra dot has reappeared, right in the middle of the hospital Yusuf was at: my missing house keys.

Electric Shocks

Brenda

I've been ready to go home for days now. But there's no home for me to go back to, so here I am, still occupying a bed in Ward C of St Thomas' Hospital, a pointless drain on the British taxpayer. No one's sure what to do with me. My overworked social worker says they're waiting for a spot to open up at one of the care centres nearby (read: waiting for someone to peg it). I've begged her to get me a council flat instead, but she says there are no council flats. In any case, she is not confident that I can cope with the 'activities of daily living' on my own. She always uses those words exactly, not specifying exactly what 'activities of daily living', in the eyes of the council, are required for a meaningful life. I don't bother to explain that there's only one 'activity of daily living' I'm interested in now, which is finding the thing that did this to me and proving that it's real.

Those double-crossing nurses told the doctors what Daniel said about me being blind, and next thing I knew I was being summoned to an eye-testing room in the bowels of the hospital, where a doctor blew air into my face and made me stare at grids and injected dye into my veins and photographed my pupils. Then he started lecturing me about something called Charles Bonnet syndrome, which apparently makes you hallucinate after you lose your eyesight. 'Explains what you think you saw in the sewers,' he said, smug, until I asked him if my ears were blind too, then, because I bloody heard the thing growling.

The telly flickers hypersaturated colours across the dreary hospital walls. Nurses shuffle by in squeaky shoes, clearing away the breakfast trolleys, served at the ungodly hour of five a.m. I return my attention to my laptop, whirring and whining away on my lap like a flatulent cat.

No new leads. It's been just over a month since the last attack (my attack). So much for my full-moon theory, unless I've missed something. Nothing new on the CATS group either. Everyone's swallowed the story about foxes. Although I find it somewhat suspicious that all the articles were written by the same person, Martine Gilbert.

Someone's been sending me private messages from a fake Facebook account, too. Horrible missives with no coherent grammar, all sent between 2 and 4 a.m. – *don't fuck with me you don't know who I am I'm going to find you and tear out your eyes and snap off your fingers old woman old OLD woman you don't know who I am...* On and on it goes. The nom de plume is 'Electric Fury'. I think of the Norwich Cat Killer, who used to follow his victims on Facebook and like their missing cat posts. But the creature I'm hunting isn't human, so this is just some unrelated arsehole. World's full of them.

Forget Facebook. Instead, I'm working on a new spreadsheet, this one a database of every animal larger than a cat existing in the British Isles. It must have two-inch-wide canines. It must be able to climb. Ideally, it must also be capable of opening the fiddly lock on a guinea pig hutch, but that one's a stretch. It must be shaggy and dark, almost as large as a bear.

I have considered *bears*, obviously. You'd think England's free of them, but you'd be dead wrong, according to a woman who runs a wildlife-in-captivity advocacy group based in Sussex. By her estimate, there are at least thirty-seven within an hour or two of London. Brown bears at Whipsnade. Polar bears in Ipswich. Black bears in Bedford, roaming freely on some nutter duke's estate.

Other options I've considered and ruled out: large wolves (they don't climb), leopards or lions (fur not dark enough), some kind of cow or buffalo (if the punctures are horns instead of teeth, but again, they don't climb).

Today, I'm considering the primates. Google tells me London Zoo has western lowland gorillas, which can grow to six feet tall. Chimpanzees are clever and dextrous, and could definitely have figured out how to open a guinea pig hutch. The teeth of chacma baboon males can grow to the length of your forefinger.

I dig up a report suggesting that nearly seven thousand primates were imported into the UK last year alone, but they were all tiny macaques, bred in Vietnam and Mauritius for lab experiments. I find a video showing rows of them pinned against metal frames, heads held still with steel collars while their bodies thrash and writhe, and need to slam the laptop shut. There is nothing so beastly in this world as humanity.

The motor of my laptop slowly whirrs into silence. It's been getting louder and louder recently, and it's taken to switching off at random moments. What will I do when it's gone?

A knock on the door and a waft of expensive perfume heralds a strange woman. 'Excuse me, sorry. Have any of you seen a set of keys?' What I can see of her around my void is smooth blonde hair, a posh camel coat. She's tall. Not a nurse.

My ward-mates shake their heads and mumble 'no's.

'Why in sod's name would we have your keys?' I grumble.

'My father-in-law was here recently. Well, actually he was on the other side of the hospital, but the AirTag's saying the keys are nearby,' she says. 'Guess I must have dropped them.'

I don't know what an AirTag is. But the back of my neck tingles, remembering the set of keys currently sitting in my bedside table. The keys I picked up on the floor of the supersewer.

'Do you work in construction?' I ask.

'Sorry?' There's something about this woman I don't like, now snapping her fingers to try to wake the girl sleeping in the bed opposite me.

'Are you an engineer? Something to do with the sewer system?'

'No, I make apps. Computer programs for your phone.' Even from here, I can see her dazzling bleached smile, too many teeth crammed into her small mouth.

'I know what bloody apps are, thank you.' My heart monitor gives a warning beep. 'Are you sure you lost them here at the hospital?' Could this woman have been attacked by the creature before it dived into the sewers with her keys? Could this, finally, be another witness?

But there's not a scratch on her I can see. Not a shred of fear in her voice, only impatience. 'Have you seen them?'

'I don't have your keys,' I say, as my heart monitor beeps again.

She thanks me curtly and asks me to tell the nurses if I spot them. I wait until I hear her footsteps clip neatly to the next room, the soft rumble of her voice repeating the question to our neighbours, before I pull the keys from my bedside drawer. Dangling among the house keys is a smooth disc I took for a key ring. It must be a location tracker.

'Oi!' I toss a pillow at my sleeping neighbour, who's the only one in here of understand-technology age. She wakes with a startled yelp. 'Is there any way to find out who this belongs to?' I ask, jangling the keys at her.

'Just tap it to the back of your phone,' she says.

'I don't have a phone. You do it.'

The girl gives a long-suffering sigh as she scrabbles languidly for her mobile among the mess next to her bed.

'Get a move on,' I hiss. The posh woman will have to pass our room on the way back.

Finally, she finds her phone. She's just touching the keys to the back when they start to vibrate in her hand, emitting a screechy electronic jingle. The girl drops them in surprise, and they clatter along the floor.

'Bollocks.' I fall to my knees and feel for them underneath her hospital bed.

Clipped footsteps come up behind me.

I turn to see the woman towering over me, a six-foot void in a camel coat.

'We found them,' I say. The tag buzzes between my thumb and forefinger like a furious insect.

'You're a hero,' the woman says, reaching down to help me up. Her grip almost crushes the bones in my hand.

Standing close, I can now see her face properly, even though she's a full two feet taller than me. Complicated make-up. Green eyes with an edge of amber.

A puzzled furrow appears between her brows as we lock eyes. Like she knows me from somewhere she can't place. I'm certain I've never met her before.

'When did you say you lost them?' I make one last attempt.

But she's busy tucking them into her glossy leather handbag, hurrying out, every gesture communicating that she's far too busy and important to chat.

My ward-mate is staring at me with a baffled expression. She holds up her phone. 'So, I can delete this number?'

I chew my bottom lip, wishing for a fag to help me think this through. This woman's keys end up in a newly constructed sewer on the same night a beast runs through it? It's too much of a coincidence.

On the other hand, can I really believe that blonde lady is the kind of person who'd keep a *pet bear*?

Maybe those people on the CATS group saying I'm just a crazy old woman are right. This is what happens when you spend too long bored and alone. Like the Charles Bonnet syndrome the eye doctor was talking about. When you've got nothing and nothing and nothing, your mind starts to make things up.

I tell my roommate to do what she likes, and climb back into my prison bed.

Hollowing Bones

●

Ellie

It's a Saturday, the second week of December, but I'm spending it in the office. Inez stopped eating yesterday. I'm giving them some privacy.

I love the quiet of the office on the weekends. It's the last place I don't feel like a fuck-up. Out of one window of Don's treehouse, I can watch Christmas shoppers bustling around Mayfair in the afternoon grey. Out the other, I can see the whole office, empty desks and adult toys. Deserted, apart from the two customer support reps who drew the short straws and are working the weekend shift. They seem to be keeping merry enough down there, blasting bad Christmas pop and working their way through a box of mince pies.

On the desk are the divorce papers that were hand-delivered to me this morning. I haven't had the courage to read them yet, but it's on the List. I always wanted Mo to take more initiative, and the one time he does is to file for divorce. Good job, Mo.

Another alarming new acquisition: the .38 bolt gun hidden in the bottom of my handbag, the kind used in abattoirs. It's heavy, unlovely, functional. A thick steel tube with a blunt nose, designed to drive a metal bolt through the skull of a cow. Ordered online; no licence required. No luck yet finding someone who can replace the bolt with silver for me, but I'm working on it. Maybe it's not even necessary, if police managed to shoot Alex's boyfriend. But I have to be ready if Andreas finds me again, or if any of my other unremembered crimes come back to haunt me. Uri says no one's seen Andreas for weeks. He's been reported to the police as a missing person, and his poor wife is beside herself.

Luckily, the next full moon is still a few weeks away. For now, I'm trying to focus on Tranquillity. I threw away the old vision statement I wrote, and it didn't even matter. In the end, the investors were happy enough to see the words 'AI' and 'mental health app'. The tech industry has no room for complexity, for the wild depths of the full human experience. Our app isn't therapy. It isn't even, truly, mindfulness.

Nonetheless, I've been seeing the true potential of the business more clearly than I have in years. I've had some *vision*, you might say.

Tranquillity always felt like such a powerful tool to solve the mental health crisis, because your phone is already an extension of your mind. Your phone already knows about the gap between your ideal self and your real self. The phone knows you stop at KFC and then spend the night on your sofa googling healthy recipes. Your phone knows that you go to a climate protest and then order trendy new polyester blouses from Shein. Your phone knows about all your Lists. Your phone knows you think you'll be happy if you put together a capsule wardrobe, if you exercise more, if you eat more beans, if you buy that cast-iron pan that will be the last pan you ever need, if you raise chickens, if you implement an AI diary planner, if you build your social media brand, if you start a Substack, if you buy a set of Japanese knives and a whetstone, if you learn to sharpen them yourself, if you keep up with your friends, if you let this app help you keep up with your friends, if you respond to the email your school friend sent you three weeks ago, if you donate to Ukraine, if you pay your water bill. Your phone knows you haven't got around to doing any of these things, but that instead you spent four hours yesterday watching tiny house videos on TikTok. And anyway, who is all of this productivity for?

Your phone knows what you think the solutions are. But can it also tell us about the *problems*?

It occurred to me recently that the most interesting thing about the Virtual Rage Room isn't the meditations it produces, but the audio recordings people input. A treasure trove of information about what's *wrong*. I'm working on a brief for our research team, asking them to think about how we can anonymise this data and make it available to mental health researchers. All the studies say rates of depression and anxiety are through the roof, higher every year, so that's what I expected people to talk about. Their depression. Their anxiety.

But what most of our users seem to talk about are their problems. They're stressed about money, they're sick, they're alone, they're worried about their kids, they've been left or abused or raped or used or discarded or exploited. People are in pain, and instead of helping them, we tell them their brain is broken. The mental health crisis isn't a mental health crisis, it's a symptom of the broken world, the polycrisis, the omnishambles. Affirmations can't replace a broken social contract. Positive thinking won't save you from a flood, or a drone bomb, or a knife, or cancer.

And all this medicalising of our pain, it circumvents our *rage*. It turns our pain into a set of symptoms to be managed. Instead, could it be energy that could get us to change the world?

What if our anger forces us to notice what's wrong?

What if a little rage is great, actually?

I pull out my phone, wanting to share this revelation. Hover for a moment over Mo's contact. Then Paige. Then Yusuf. None of them want to talk to me. I just stare at their names like I'm looking through a cracked window into a house I no longer live in.

'Ellie!' a voice hails me. I peer over and see one of the customer support staff waving up at the treehouse, worried look on her face. 'Someone's making a fuss in reception,' she says.

I head down to the lido, my head still buzzing with these thoughts. Wondering, for perhaps the first time: is this business I've devoted so much of my life to even *what I believe in*?

And if it isn't, does that mean all these sacrifices were for *fucking nothing*?

Standing in reception is a woman, around my age. Bobbled jumper over thin leggings. Hair pulling out of a bun. Face blotched red. Leaning on the security turnstiles, yelling, 'Come down here.

Someone come down here and talk to me.' There's a funky stink on her, someone who hasn't showered or slept in a few days. *Unhinged*, I can't help thinking. *Menopausal.*

I want to laugh at her. It's so pathetic, it's incontinent, a middle-aged woman so undone by her impotent anger.

I'm embarrassed for her.

Two teenagers have stopped on the street, peering through the glass doors, filming on their cameras. Another #karenfreakout.

'Who are you? Do you work here?' Tears are streaming down her face. Fury, not sadness, I recognise.

'I'm the CEO,' I say calmly. 'Can I help you?'

'You made this. You're *sick*.' She hits play on the Virtual Rage Room. The voice fills reception. *Run a knife through him run a knife through him run a knife through him.* Stuck on a loop. *Interesting*, my mind thinks in a detached way. The engineers explained this to me: if the AI model isn't tuned correctly, it will keep deciding that the 'best next sentence' is the same one, every time. We control this with a randomness variable, which injects enough chaos to keep the AI trying new things. Add to List: *Review the analytics and see if we need to retune the model.*

The woman interrupts this reverie by throwing the phone at me. It smashes on the corner of the mosaic reception desk, glass scattering across the floor.

'Lady, I'd love to help you, but I need you to calm the fuck down.' My nostrils flare. 'I'm sorry, but if this offends you, you can just turn it off. No one's forcing you to use the app.'

'That's my son's phone! He's twelve. And he stabbed another boy at his school!'

I have to push down the inevitable question that bubbles in me: 'Well, did the other boy deserve it?' *Plenty of reasons you might need to stab someone*, the beast inside me growls. *They bully you. They threaten you. They hurt someone you care about. They disrespect you.*

The woman lunges, nails clawing at my face. Instinctively, I bat them away, my arms so much stronger than hers.

'They arrested him. You destroyed my family,' she screams. 'You crazy bitch! You took my *family*!'

It's the word *family* that does it.

That puts Paige and Mo and Yusuf into my mind.

That makes me think, what if I'd let myself be angry sooner?

What if I'd been honest instead of nice?

Would any of them still love me?

The thought opens a hole in my chest *and the beast crawls through it.*

It stirs. *Fast. Faster than it's ever taken over before.*

Horrified, I realise the woman is shrinking beneath me, because *the beast is growing taller.*

My mouth can no longer form words as *the beast's teeth push through bleeding gums.*

People are watching through the glass windows. People with mobile phones.

It's the middle of the afternoon.

The 9th of December.

A waning moon.

And the beast doesn't give a shit about the rules.

The beast rears tall, cackling.

Do you know what's fun? Ripping cables from the walls. Pulling on them hard enough that they come right out through the Rhino Board. Tug on the other end and you can tumble a whole bank of expensive monitors off the desks; they smash merrily to the ground, SMASH SMASH. The customer service reps are huddling in the private call booth. Smell them there, the stink of terror, but the beast has no interest in them. The beast's pleasure is in smashing. They have called 999 but who cares. Who cares about the security cameras. Who cares about anything these tiny people can do.

Smash the Nothing room. The box-fort. The servers. Fuck this place. A stinking rotten exercise, all of it.

The beast surveys the wreckage. She has smashed everything smashable and it's not enough. Fury pulses through her blood.

The beast thinks: I should find out where Suella Braverman lives. I should eat the head of BP. Hunt Prince Andrew. Pay a visit to my GP. So many choices.

She races to the streets, out into the city. Dark now. Christmas lights are strung across buildings, glittering like moonlight on pond water. Crowds throng the pavement, tourists snapping photos in front of Paddington Bear souvenir shops, innocent families out buying a present for granny.

Gasps and screams, laughter, people thinking this must be some kind of prank, right until the moment the beast barrels into them and throws *their bodies into the road, cars screeching to a stop just in time, too late for one boy who the beast tosses in front of a bicycle. They will need stitches later, cyclist and boy both.*

Ha! Send a rickshaw skidding, the driver shouting obscenities. She veers towards the smell of alcopops and perfume, scattering a group of women who've come into town for a hen night. The beast half raises herself, staggering forward on her huge hind legs. The women scream, running, SNAP SNAP SNAP after them as they go.

Videos and photos go streaming onto the cloud. Some of them wind up on a Facebook group called CATS. Isn't this just like that video that was posted here a while ago?

Pathetic people. Sharp nails leave deep gouges in the pavement. Sirens and frantic dog-barking. She races across Waterloo Bridge.

The Thames is a stew of smells. There are seals living in there now, fish species that haven't been seen there in years, wild things returning. All their stomachs are full of plastic.

On the south bank, the beast veers onto a quieter side street behind King's College, where she can smell water flowing into a drainpipe. Easy work to tug up the manhole cover and slip beneath the city, the secret ways. The place where all unwanted things go.

Kyle

Twenty fucking years old and grounded, can you believe it? Skint. Stuck in his mum's living room in Raynes Park, playing *Counter-Strike* with online strangers because none of his real-world friends will talk to him, his so-called friends.

His mum's at his aunt's, drinking wine and crying probably, pretty much all she's done these past two weeks. Mum locked the door, took his keys, said she couldn't trust him not to do 'something stupid'. Not like he has anywhere to go anyway.

He's already spent most of his life on this sagging settee, sipping Ribena on schooldays as a sickly kid, playing *League of Legends* as an awkward teen, trying to do lessons on his brother's busted laptop while the pandemic stole the years when he was supposed to learn social skills, and never gave them back.

He's banned from campus while LSE completes its investigation. All he can do until then is shoot pixels. Wait to hear whether his life's over.

As he told his mum, the student counsellor, the dean, the two impatient police officers who interviewed him at length: he is working hard to turn his life around. And it's true. You can see the evidence of how hard he's trying in the tottering stack of library books on his bedside table: Ryan Holiday, James Clear, Gary John Bishop. No Andrew Tate or Jordan Peterson, Kyle's not like that. He's gone monk mode. Making his bed every morning. Doing a thirty-day NoFap challenge. He's bought a set of kettlebells and a pull-up bar. Installed a parental control app on his own browser to keep himself off Pornhub and 4chan. Off Snapchat too, where he could be tempted to message Paige. Ask her again, *why?*

There's no acceptable script for guys like him. He tried PUA when he was younger – kino escalation, push-and-pull – got laughed at, called an incel. But no one told him what to do instead. He daydreams about having a girlfriend so much it's hard to think about anything else. Not even sex, that's the really pathetic truth. Small things: going for walks. Soft arms around him. Sitting on a park bench, her hand on his knee, her eyes crinkling as she smiles at him, saying *I love you*. The fantasies feel so real, and the pain when he crashes back to reality, to his mother's sagging fucking settee and his own BO, and remembers no one will ever look at him like that... it's too much to bear.

There was a stretch when it felt like uni might be the time things finally clicked together for him. He had a group of friends who got him out of his room. People who wanted to talk about philosophy and films, who didn't tease him for being scrawny and unfunny and pale. And Paige, brilliant beautiful liar Paige, who actually seemed to like him. She was so far out of his league it hadn't even crossed his mind to hope for more.

She came on to *him*, that's what no one seems to believe. *She*, out the blue, started grinding on him at that party. Kissing him and climbing onto his lap and whispering in his ear, 'I want you.' She came back to his room that night. For just a moment, he tasted paradise. He thought this was the beginning of his life.

Surprise! All a lie. She was just using him to cuck that low-IQ Neanderthal Theo. And afterwards she tossed Kyle away like the condom. He didn't understand. He'd always been taught that if you care about something, work for it. He tried to win her back. Wrote her long letters. Made her playlists. Offered his pathetic heart up on a plate.

Then she said that word. *Stalker.* She came on to *him* and then said he was a stalker! No one even asked for his side of the story.

One word from her and they closed ranks, turfed him out, left him out in the cold like always. No more friends. No more Paige. No reason why.

He lost it a bit after that, he knows. He followed her just to prove she couldn't erase him. He only wanted her to feel how she'd made him feel. Just settling the score.

He shifts in-game, picks up an AK. His thoughts circle. *Paige. Paige. Paige.* It's so unfair. If anything, didn't his actions *prove* how stupid she was being acting like he was some crazed creep? He broke into her room to demonstrate how easy it was. *See? Don't I deserve some credit for not taking this further? For not hurting you 1 per cent as much as you've hurt me?*

Thump.

Something hits the roof. Hard. Scrabbles on the tiles.

He flinches. In-game, his character takes a bullet to the leg.

The rats around here are monsters, he thinks. One day he'll get his mum out of here. A saint, that woman. She was so proud of him when he got into LSE, scholarship and all. God, the look on her face when she found out about Paige. 'I didn't bring you up like this,' was all she said after the meeting with Student Services, tears in her eyes. It's Paige's fault she looked at him like that, like he's garbage.

He wipes sweat from his upper lip. His fingers twitch, halfway to his phone before he remembers – it's upstairs. He has to break the habit. There's a real chance this might be it for him. *Stalker* is the kind of stink that follows a man around forever. *Stalker* might mean he's alone his entire life. Unloved and untouched. Might as well kill himself now. Or maybe kill her. Better to be labelled a *killer* than a *stalker*.

He squeezes his eyes shut. *No.* He still has a chance. The solicitor that drained all of Mum's savings said the police are unlikely to prosecute – Paige won't give evidence. Maybe, deep down, she still cares.

If he survives this, he swears he'll fix things. He'll try again. If LSE lets him stay, he'll work harder than anyone. Dating's nothing but a humiliation ritual, but maybe he can just channel his energy into getting rich. No one cares you're a social autist if you've got a Bugatti.

He reloads. Breathes.

BANG.

Something crashes down inside the wall cavity. He flinches so hard he drops the controller. A furious, thudding scrabble, down from roof to floor. Too big to be a rat. Too loud and too heavy.

A moment's silence, then a scratching sound begins on the other side of the room. Claws scratching the plasterboard.

His brother sealed up the fireplace with drywall years ago to keep out draughts. Maybe a bird flew in. A crow. One of those massive greasy ones that looks like it's crawled out of hell. If it dies in there, it's going to stink like shit.

On screen, an enemy pumps bullets into him. The screen drenches red. At least on Counter-Strike, if you fuck up you can just start a new life, try again.

'Hang on,' he says into the headset. 'Something's fallen in my chimney.'

'Bro got a Santa stuck,' someone snorts. Laughter.

He drops the headset and shuffles over to investigate, hand rubbing at a cramp in his lower back. Ugh, he needs to start stretching more. Do five press-ups between every new match, to begin with. No one will ever love him unless he's jacked. Girls have made that abundantly clear. Girls are so fucking shallow.

As he watches, a fleck of plaster falls from the Rhino Board. Something is pushing through. Not an accidental talon brushing from scrabbling bird legs. Something working at it, slow, deliberate.

Scratch scratch scratch scratch scratch.

It pierces through. Long as his middle finger. Curved. Black. Sharp enough to open his throat. A talon the length of a dagger.

No bird has a talon that big.

He staggers back, his calves bumping the coffee table, scattering empty Fanta cans onto the floor.

It must be a burglar, he thinks, reaching for his phone to dial 999. But it's in his bedroom upstairs.

He glances at the front door. Locked.

Should he break a window? Run?

But why the fuck is a burglar coming through the chimney?

His legs won't move. His brain glitches. He tries to toggle through the loadout in his mind – flashbang, Molotov, pistol – but this is happening for real. Here. In the room.

A muffled giggle echoes from the wall, feminine.

A flash of anger pulses through him. What kind of sicko prank is this?

What would the self-help books tell him to do? They'd tell him to confront his problems. To be a man.

He grabs his headset, fumbling the mike into place with clammy fingers. 'Call 999,' he whispers. 'Someone's in my house.' He tells them his address.

A cacophony of laughter from the headset. Ha ha ha, all a big joke. 'Yeah, fucker!'

'Whack him!'

'Not a joke, help me.' But these aren't friends. Just randos on Discord. Voices in the void. Could be on the other side of the world for all he knows. Because he's unloved, unlovable. A stalking creep.

Now a growling is coming from the hole in the wall. Wet. Deep. Rattling through his bones.

Sweat is dripping from him. He freezes.

'Come out,' he says to the black hole. He hopes he sounds braver than he feels.

Obediently, hands appear in the hole. It crumbles open like an egg, birthing a creature from his nightmares.

Kyle is cowering now, back against the settee. Cans clatter. His hands brush one of his new kettlebells. Cold iron. Heavy.

A monster steps out of the shattering plasterboard.

Roughly human in shape, but so big, too big. Saliva drips from its gaping jaws in thick, slimy strings. The limbs are bent at unnatural angles, joints popping and cracking as it slinks towards him, slow. Yellow eyes are sunken into deep hollows, nothing human left in there. No compassion. Only rage. It opens its maw wide, and he can see that the inside of its mouth is lined with two rows of teeth. The outer ring, jagged, razor-sharp, cradling white human squares. A new face grown over the old one.

A mad thought in his mind: that it looks a bit like Paige.

She blows her hot breath on his face as she leans closer. Kyle can smell the putrid stench of her, rotting meat and stomach acids.

He needs his phone.

As the beast raises her paw, claws glint in the dim light of the TV.

Kyle feints left and throws his body the other way, an instinct honed through years of childhood wrestling games with his brother Marcus. The brush of fur against his arm, but the creature misses him.

Just enough time for him to scramble up and away, heading for the staircase, his brain a white light of panic telling him to *run*.

She smashes into him just as his foot meets the second step, a heaviness into his torso, too fast for pain.

His whole body vibrates as she tears into him. Digging into the back of his thigh. It burns, the pain moving deeper and deeper as she gnaws into his muscle, right to the soft insides.

He twists, grabbing her fur and tries to push her off him. Might as well try to push off a hurricane. She shakes her head, tearing his muscle out. A whole chunk of him pulled away.

There are screams. They might be his own. She pulls him back down to the ground floor, stepping her weight onto his chest, jaws clamping around his waist. His flesh pulses as she chews at him.

His brain keeps saying the least helpful things. *How strange. A monster climbed in through my chimney and now she's eating my stomach. What an odd way to die.* He grasps weakly at her fur, trying to get enough purchase to push her away. Bright hot pain. The snapping of teeth. *Why is this happening?* says his brain, numb, stupid. He should know by now not to expect the world to tell him why. The creature's fur is wet. *Why is her fur wet? There is no water in here.*

He pulls up his right hand, meaning to push her away, but it's trapped in the handle of a heavy iron object. The kettlebell.

Gripping it with all the strength his masturbation-and-PlayStation-trained arms can muster, he swings it hard across the creature's face.

There's a yelp, a hard crash onto the ground below.

He drags himself up the stairs, panic blotting out the pain, only set on reaching his phone. He wants his phone. He wants his mum. He is crying now and he is ashamed and he is afraid.

Low growling again, below him, wary now. Heavy breathing.

He makes it as far as the landing. There is a plate-glass window up here, floor-to-ceiling. He drags his body towards it, pushes his face up against the glass. Through the trees, he can see the street, lights glowing in neighbours' windows. A car cruises down the road. 'Help me,' he whispers to it, as its headlights vanish round the corner. 'Help me,' he whispers again to the empty night, the uncaring, lonely night.

There's a dark shape moving on the landing with him, heavy footsteps. But his eyes aren't working properly and it's darker than it should be. 'I'm sleeping, Marcus,' he says to the silhouette. 'Leave me alone.'

And he must have wet his bed, because the lower half of him is sopping. It's pooling all around him. Sorry, Mum. He needs to get up and clean it before she sees. He's a big boy. He's far too old to be wetting the bed. Or is it cum? But he's supposed to be doing NoFap. He's confused. He's sorry. He tried his best but it's so hard sometimes, being a person. Don't look, Mum, he wants to say, but his mouth is curiously slack. He just needs to change the sheets before she sees. He wants to get his phone. He just needs to send a message to his mum. He just needs to say it's not what she thinks. He just needs to say he's sorry.

There is a hole in the side of the boy and his eyes have fluttered shut. But his chest is still moving up and down. It's possible that he might survive. Andreas did.

The beast considers her options. She could let him live. He would become another creature like her, released into the world. Another monster. Another howling beast, roaring its pain into soft bodies.

Can't let that happen. Not someone like this.

The beast lifts the kettlebell in her hand, and drops it hard onto the boy's head.

Brain and bone explode across the carpet. A glimpse of the bright white of his skull, a fine mesh of bone like lattice lace. Beautiful.

She leaves his body there, beast-mauled and broken.

Kyle Michael Law.

She totters to the room the boy was dragging himself towards, the floor slipping closer to her now, her long heels retreating back into the pads of her feet.

Schoolbooks on the shelf. Some of the same textbooks Paige owns, the beast recognises.

A Dune *poster. A bass guitar. A pile of self-help books on the bedside table. Not a bad selection. I've read most of them myself.*

A reeking pile of laundry, a bin full of empty Fantas.

Scratchy black cotton sheets, in dire need of debobbling. Instinctively, I add to List: *Debobble this poor boy's sheets.*

A boy's room. A child's room.

I turn back and look at the steaming puddle of Kyle that the beast has left on the landing.

Honest, now: that I have left on the landing.

Incontinence

Brenda

Moving day. On the one hand, I'm thrilled to finally be free of this nightmare hospital ward, though I'm not convinced it's going to be any better where I'm going: Peartree Manor, a care home out in Colchester. I'm almost certain that the grandness of the name implies the opposite level of actual grandness. Mostly, I'm worried about how regularly I'll be able to get to London to continue the hunt.

Despite how much it's changed, I feel a real pang to be leaving Walthamstow. It's where my whole life's happened. Can't be upending your whole life at my age. And with my eyes going, I'll never see this new place. I'll have no mental image of it. It won't even be a place I can imagine.

My confidence is further eroded by the arrival of the care home aide who's going to drive me up there.

'Brrendaaaaa!' She greets me like a long-lost relative, in a voice sweet enough to rot teeth. 'I'm Sue. Are you ready for a brand-new *adventure*?'

I decline to respond to this. Even through my void, Sue's looks are as unsubtle as a slap. Beneath her blue uniform, she's wearing rainbow-striped tights, a matching pompom beanie on her head, like a knock-off *Blue Peter* presenter.

The nurses have come to see me off, thrilled to see the back of me, no doubt. Nurse Darius, or maybe Nurse Mylo, is holding my possessions: my carpet bag, and the new white stick the doctor insisted on, along with instructions to attend weekly mobility classes once I've settled into my 'new home'. He said the stick will allow me to help myself, but it will also signal to others that I need extra help. Ha! Might as well just wear a sign saying 'Frail old lady, please rob and/or mock'.

'Your throne, your majesty,' Saccharine Sue says, producing a wheelchair with a flourish.

'Absolutely not. I can walk. That was the entire point of having the new hip put in, you know.'

'Of course, of course,' she replies, like she's humouring a child denying bedtime. 'But let's not tire those legs out just yet, hmm? There'll be plenty of time for strolls in the garden soon!'

We stare at each other, unmoving. Her plastered smile doesn't falter. I suspect in a battle of stubbornness, I might have met my match.

Joy.

I lower myself into the chair with a huff.

'Off we go!' Saccharine Sue squeals, pushing me through the corridors, while I consider that if this is how it's going to be for the rest of my life, I rather wish I'd died in that sewer.

We stop off at the pharmacy to collect the prescription for the party pack of pills that the doctors want me to take every day. The pharmacist, moving with about as much urgency as a sponge, informs us that there will be a bit of a wait.

'Mind if I grab a coffee?' Sue chirps in her sunshine-spun voice. Her question is rhetorical; she's halfway out the door before my brain even processes the request.

I'm not the only one waiting. There's a businessman speaking loudly into a phone, and a young family opposite, two mothers and their young daughter, huddled together playing a hand-held bubble game.

Figuring I've got some time to kill, I dig my laptop out of my bag. It whirrs to life, rattling like a chainsaw, eliciting an annoyed glare from the businessman. He paces to the counter to check on the pharmacist, who now seems to have vanished, before returning to his seat defeated.

Blimey, dozens of notifications. There's been some stir on the CATS group, a video posted earlier this afternoon. I turn the volume off and hit play.

It's shaky mobile phone footage of two women in what looks like the reception of a fancy lido, shot from outside. One of them seems to be yelling at the other, face growing bright red. She throws her phone, barely missing the other person, who looks vaguely familiar. Why has some posh-lady brawl ended up in my CATS group?

My pulse quickens as I realise what's happening.

The other woman, the taller one, the beautiful blonde, starts to lose her temper. She snarls, and her face begins to twist and change. The camera zooms in disbelief as she grows taller. As hair begins to sprout from her body. Like Hollywood special effects.

Until, moments later: there it is. My creature. Rearing on huge hind legs in the middle of – according to the comments – Mayfair, just a couple of hours ago.

My heart thumps as I read. Apparently, there are several more videos. CCTV. Ample eyewitnesses. The beast went on a rampage all the way through central London, before someone saw it vanish down a sewer.

This is it.

This is *her*.

This whole time, I could never be sure if I was tracking man or beast or a man *with* a beast. The frustrating in-betweenness of it: this was why.

I scroll back up to the video, and play it from the beginning again. My pulse hammers in my neck, beating out their names. Mr Bojangles and Lady Whiskers and Luna and Buttons and Dog and Oscar and Chairman Meow and Loki and Frieda Cahtlo and Mew Paul and Tomcat Wambsgans and Duchess and Gizmo and Katy Purry and Kittgenstein and Melek.

Finally, I recognise her. The woman with the missing keys. Did I ever learn her name?

I no longer own a phone, or a purse, or any clothes that are not pyjamas. But I manage to find Daniel's phone number in my computer thanks to some wizardry Jen's eldest set up for me last Christmas. I read it over twice, enough to commit it to memory. Nothing like years of bookkeeping to hone your short-term memory for numbers.

Despite all of my diligent physiotherapy exercises, my shuffle is slow and careful. Saccharine Sue is in the cafeteria, working her way through an enormous sandwich. I duck behind a plastic Christmas tree and wait until she's mid-bite before slipping past unnoticed.

Nurse Darius's face falls at the sight of me. Bet he'd already popped the champagne at the thought of never seeing me again.

'Need to do my ablutions,' I say, gesturing to the tiny toilet in my old room. He sighs but waves me through. I shuffle past, really playing up how dishevelled and doddery and old I am.

The girl with the headphones is sitting in her bed, picking morosely at a wilted salad.

'The phone number from the tag thingy. Did you delete it?' I ask.

She shakes her head. 'Want me to dial it for you?'

My hands are trembling. 'No, but there's someone else I need to call.'

There's a minor manhunt for me by the time Daniel arrives. Saccharine Sue doing increasingly frantic circuits of the hospital grounds in the twilight, along with several security guards, probing the bushes like I'm a lost cat.

I watch this all from the coffee shop across the road, where I've cunningly disguised myself as a person buying coffee. This is the true superpower of old age: invisibility.

I'm expecting a police car, so it takes me a minute to realise that the mobile dog-grooming parlour that pulls up outside is his.

'It's my sister's,' Daniel says, ushering me into the passenger seat. I didn't know he had a sister. I have to remember that we're still strangers to each other. Just because the boy came to visit me in hospital doesn't mean he gives a toss about me really.

'Shouldn't you be in uniform?' I ask him, turning the heater up to full. It's Baltic in here.

'I'm not sure yet that this is official business,' he says.

'So you didn't bring a gun?'

'Rah! Mental if you think I have access to a gun. Pepper spray, a radio and an HB pencil, that's what I've got.' He's not moving the van.

'Did you find out who the phone number belongs to?' I ask.

'You know I only just passed my exams. I could lose my job.'

'Did you watch that video? Are you telling me that's not the same thing we saw on the CCTV?'

He scratches his head, hesitating, then: 'The number's registered to someone named Eleanor Fourie. Two addresses for her. Barnsbury and Chingford.'

Barnsbury's closer. But Slow-Worm Jack photographed her in the Lea Valley. If she's using the sewers to get around, it makes sense that she would have popped up near the Coppermills pumping station, and made her way through Walthamstow on her way north.

'Let's start in Chingford.'

Daniel taps his thumbs on the steering wheel, still not driving. 'And do what?'

'Arrest her!'

Daniel scoffs, dropping his head into his hands. 'That's not how it works. What happened in the city this afternoon, that's a major incident. There's a whole team on this, yeah? The right thing is to contact the lead investigator and say there's a witness to a potentially linked offence.'

'So let's do that,' I huff. 'Take me there right now and I'll tell them.'

He turns to look at me properly. 'Auntie B, you know I'm your friend, so please don't take this the wrong way. But you don't come across as a very believable witness.'

My brain sticks on *your friend*. Eight decades on this earth and literally no one's ever said that to me. 'But you believe me?'

'I do.'

'Okay,' I say. 'So then we need proof.' Thinking, I fiddle with the carpet bag on my lap, the white stick. People only believe what they see.

'Daniel,' I say, 'let's go and put that HB pencil to good use.'

Depression

Ellie

If anything on earth is likely to set a person off on a murder spree, it's the fucking Victoria Line in rush hour.

I'm crammed into a corner seat as the train rocks and screams. The carriage is sardine-tin full, and yet everyone is giving me a wide berth, holding their coats because it's three degrees outside but forty down here. I catch a woman's eye standing next to me. Her gaze flinches away. She whispers something to her companion and they squeeze into the crowd huddled by the door. Londoners know all too well to avoid crazies on the Tube.

I must be quite a sight. Sweating bullets, wearing one of Kyle's oversized T-shirts like a dress. I rinsed my hair in the sink of the office loo when I went back there to fetch my handbag, but I think there's still blood in it. I can feel parts of him swishing around my stomach, gristle caught in my teeth.

The train lurches, bodies sway. A man stumbles, catching himself before he falls too close. His eyes are wide, apologetic. 'Sorry,' he mutters, scuttling away.

'Sorry,' I echo, my voice cracking. Sorry for the boy, the blood, sorry for all of it. But some things are beyond apologies, aren't they?

I killed the boy, but I can still feel the beast, sitting right behind my eyes telling me to *kill him kill him kill him*. Violence only fed its hunger. Violence doesn't extinguish rage, it only traps you in its consequences. *Mine*, now. What Kyle did was terrible, and a crime, and the harm was real. And maybe if he'd lived he'd have done worse to Paige. Or he might have reformed and lived a normal life afterwards. No one will ever know. I'm the one who will carry the weight of all those extinguished possibilities. *Extinguished possibilities*... I clutch that idea like a life raft.

There must be videos of me by now. I wonder how many of these people have seen them. It's just matter of time until someone recognises me. A few hundred years ago, they'd have come with pitchforks, burning torches. Now it will be flashing lights and handcuffs.

I have no intention of letting that happen. All I need is a quiet spot I won't be disturbed, and I have the ideal place in mind. My fingers drift into my handbag, brushing the cool steel hidden at the bottom. It's not silver bullets. But it should be enough for my human skull.

Look: all werewolf stories end the same way.

End of the line, Walthamstow Central. I swap onto the Overground. It's cooler here, easier to breathe. I watch the reservoirs speed past, glistening in the lights from the new builds as my wet hair drips cold onto my shoulders.

It's funny, I woke up here after the full moon a few weeks ago, I remember.

And in September, I found myself in Leyton, just a few miles south.

And after the terrible GP visit, I brought myself out here, awake.

Oh God.

This is where the beast has been coming.

Repressing. Bloody Don and his bloody insightfulness. He was right all along. He said that's why he didn't like what I kept trying to turn Tranquillity into.

And then it suddenly clicks into place.

Don's the one who told the board you weren't ready to be CEO. It was never Uri or Tom. Don's the one who wanted to hire Andreas instead.

I thump my head against the cold window. The beast whispers inside of me. *Don, who you trusted. He lied to you. You gave the best years of your working life to him. Confront him. Go there now and...*

I beat my forehead on the glass until the thought knocks away. More violence. More fury. More revenge. And who next, Mo? Paige? You cannot hate anyone as much as the people you love.

No. It would never stop. Unless I stop it.

The final walk through Chingford is automatic, a route etched into my earliest memories. My breath catches at the sight of the pebble-dash exterior. The paint peeling from the window frames. The bumblebee knocker on the front door which I came home to every day of my miserable childhood. My mother's house.

I avoided this place my whole adult life. Said it made me too sad, watching Mum slowly burying herself alive. Or more truthfully, it made me too sad that I was unable to pull her out.

Angry that she wanted you to pull her out, whispers the beast.

It's the oldest and ugliest thing on my List. *Sell Mum's house.*

Mum died of a broken heart. Literally: a heart so clogged up it eventually stopped beating. They realised after she died that she'd been having heart attacks for months. Pain in her jaw, tightness in her chest, a sudden rush of panic. Everyone chalked it up to her anxiety. No one recognises a heart attack in a middle-aged woman.

I push open the front door. It's already ajar, wood splintered up the lock. The beast's doing.

As I step into the darkness, I remember a line from an Anne Sexton poem, 'Some women marry houses.' This house my mother married is a corpse. I can smell the million creatures feeding on its rot. Termites nibbling through the floorboards, silverfish working their way through the books, moths dining on jumpers, house spiders sipping moths, earwigs feeding on spider eggs, dust mites chewing skin flakes, flapping pigeons pecking larvae out the eaves... each finding their place in the feast. A flourishing ecosystem. Maybe this is how we rewild Britain, I think – we all die.

No point even trying to find a light switch in all this. I probe my way through the passage, careful not to topple the piles of clothes, the towers of yellowing *Hello!* magazines. There's barely enough room to squeeze through, like crawling through a rabbit warren.

A honeycomb city beneath the hedges, the wolf agrees, *snippety snap, little rabbits, hot blood spurt, yum yum.*

The living room is little better. This mostly seems to be boxes, Tetrissed floor-to-ceiling, most still sealed. The last time Byron and I tried to forcibly part my mother from her hoard, we found seventeen full dinner sets, unused. She said she was saving them for Paige, who, at the time, was three. I can't help but admire this about my mother, how she externalised her anxiety. Here it is, a solid mass, enormous, undeniable. *Look at it*, it insists. *Look how big my pain is.*

I pop my head into the kitchen, where there's a little room in front of the sink, at least. I suspect the boiler packed up years ago, but Mum was too embarrassed to let tradesmen into the house. I picture her here, washing her tired body in freezing water from the kitchen sink, given that the shower was dedicated to a collection of broken computer monitors from the 1990s.

There's a door which leads to a damp crawl space under the stairs. Byron's favourite hide-and-seek spot, because he knew I found it too creepy to look inside. Something's rotting in there. I don't bother checking what.

I squeeze through the piles on the staircase, the grown-up versions of my Please-Take-Me-Upstairs piles, only there's nowhere left to take them. I can definitely smell pee upstairs. Cats or me, I'm not sure. A lot of what's piled up here are the stuffed animals and sympathy cards Mum brought home after people died in her hospital. What strange noble work she chose, nursing the dying. She was better than me at sitting with people in pain.

The door doesn't even open fully to my old room, blocked by what seems to be – as far as I can tell in the meagre light filtering through the grimy windows – a mountain of empty ice-cream tubs.

I try Mum's room instead. This is better. There's a little nest on the floor, a depression in a pile of quilts. The wolf-smell is strong here.

The beast turns over within me. *Home.*

So many times Mum hid in here and I'd be the one who'd come in and wrap myself around her, hold her till she stopped crying. Where was my father? *She used to hold you and call you her good girl, her perfect precious girl.*

Mum was so full of pain. Too much for one person. So much it can't all have belonged to her. It must have been her mother's, too. And her mother's mother's. A terrible inheritance. I didn't want it, any more than I wanted this house.

Where do you put them, the feelings you have no place for? Do you chunk them down, alphabetise the pieces? Do you slug them glass by glass, promising yourself you'll cut back for Lent, do a dry-month challenge? Do you slam the feelings onto the keyboard and email them to HR? Do you tell a cop the feelings were walking suspiciously down your street in the form of a Black man? Do you eat the feelings late at night in the glow of the fridge, just so you can hate your body in the morning? Do you push the feelings into the spaces between cells, the membranes, the hidden emotional lymphatic systems; do they drain into your breasts and metastasise and kill you slow? Do you collect the feelings, erect a tower of grief around yourself? Do you tell yourself, 'Oh no, I don't get angry. Sometimes I just get a bit down, but never angry, no.' Do you cage the feelings? Do you *make a list*?

And if you ignore the feelings for long enough, what might they curdle into?

I curl up on the quilts, dig out my phone and start typing an email.

> *Love, on my desktop, there's a file titled 'In the event…' It's a list of everything you need to do. How to get into my password manager, all the assets and insurance policies, where you can find my will. Everything is in order. At least I can do that for you.*
>
> *Paige, I am so sorry. But believe me when I say that it's the only way. You are not safe as long as I'm in the world.*
>
> *I love you. More than I ever knew I could love anything.*

I tap send, safe in the knowledge that she's blocked me, and she won't find it until it's done.

The metal is cold in my hand. It came with an instruction leaflet, thank God. I don't think I could bear watching a how-to video right now.

I never wanted Paige to feel responsible for fixing me, like I felt responsible for fixing Mum. I never forgave my mother for throwing herself onto train tracks. But isn't that every woman's tragedy? We all turn into our mothers eventually. How do you kill a monster when the monster is you?

The steel barrel is heavier than I expect. Clumsy. Ugly. No elegant pistol. You have to press it flush against the skull and pull the release with a savage snap, the leaflet says.

'Goodbye, beast,' I say out loud, before lifting the muzzle to my temple.

A growl rumbles deep in my chest.

The bolt gun slips through my fingers.

Annoyed, I grab it again, more firmly. I press the barrel back to my head, harder now.

Nope.

My hand drops back to my lap. Knuckles popping, engorging. Hair prickling through. Nails click-clacking against the lever, twisting it to safety.

'Fuck you,' I hiss, fighting to maintain control.

Not happening, the beast says, tossing the gun through the doorway. It clangs down the stairs, taking what sounds like an avalanche of books down with it.

I chase after it, my own body resisting me. I'm thrown onto the floor of the landing, held there as my limbs twist, fingers turning to claws as I try to push myself back up. The bolt gun has vanished, lost in a collapsed pile of sympathy cards at the bottom of the stairs. And I'm losing my grip on things. My joints crack and pop, my muscles pulling over lengthening bones.

From my mother's room, I can hear my phone ringing. High-pitched, urgent. No time for that now.

Oven. The idea plumes in me like poison. I stumble down the stairs towards the kitchen, sending more piles flying as I go, trying to ignore the stink of decay from the crawl space. I twist all the knobs to full and wrench open the oven door, grateful that *Get someone in to turn off the gas in Mum's house* is still sitting somewhere on my List. I push my head into the hollow, waiting for the hissing dizziness to claim me.

No. No. The beast clicks the knobs back into place. Then, for emphasis, pulls off a cupboard door and snaps it in half. Heat rushes through my body.

Frantic, I run through my options. Pills, too uncertain. A rope, the beast wouldn't let me tie it. Fire, it could spread to the neighbours. Christ, I'm a Dorothy Parker poem.

But the beast is almost all of me now, proceeding to tear off a second cupboard door, snarling. *Rip it. Destroy it.*

We both freeze at the sound of a car engine outside. Lights sweeping across the room.

Someone's here.

Oh good, says the beast. *A distraction.*

Blurred Vision

●

Brenda

'Promise me you're not going to do anything stupid,' Daniel says, tucking his bodycam into the breast pocket of my blazer.

'I'm not actually as daft as you think I am,' I grumble. He's made me repeat the plan to him three times already. If she is home, we're not going to engage her. Just pretend we're canvassers, and ask her to add her name to the registration book we found in the back of the van. We're going to hope that she doesn't notice that the other names on the list include 'Empress Tzu Tzu' and 'Colonel Tailwags'.

'We just need her to confirm her name,' Daniel says. 'If the footage from the bodycam matches the footage from town, that's enough to make her a suspect. Then we hand that over to the lead investigator and let them take it from there. That's the best we can do.' He presses something hard and circular into my hand. A can of pepper spray. 'I'm not giving you this, yeah?'

'Got it.' I slip it into my pocket. 'Wait—' I grab his wrist before he can climb out the car. 'What are we canvassing for?'

'Ah. Well, she's posh... What do posh people like?'

'Waitrose?' I suggest. 'Tax breaks? ULEZ?'

'Right. We're getting signatures for ULEZ.' He tries to pull away again.

'Daniel.' I keep my hand on his wrist.

'Auntie B.'

'Thank you for believing me.'

He flashes me a smile, crooked and so bright it shines through my void. 'Let's go get her.'

I hesitate before following him, then decide to bring my despised white stick. Just to really sell it.

The neighbours all have their Christmas trees up, fairy lights twinkling through the windows. But her house is dark, cold, dead. The desiccated remains of whatever used to grow in hanging pots suggest that no one's lived here for a long time. Silly of me, to think I'd be so lucky that she'd just happen to be home, when a lifetime's worth of unluckiness really should have taught me better.

I'm just about to tell Daniel that he'd better take me back to the hospital, so that Saccharine Sue can bundle me up into a cartoon straitjacket and drown me in condescension, when we hear the sounds coming from the house. Crashing. Groaning.

The front door is gaping open. A portal into darkness.

The smell spilling out of it is familiar to me, rank and terrible. The smell of the sewers. Danger.

'Daniel,' I start to warn him, but the heroic git has already rushed into the void, pulling his radio from his hip and holding it to his mouth at the ready, following the woman's voice calling for help from the depths.

'Wait!' I yell after him, but he's enveloped by the shadows. I inch forward, gripping my stick, fear clawing at my throat.

A gasp cuts through the house. Daniel's gasp.

The unmistakable thud of something heavy hitting the ground. Ripping, growling.

'Help!' I cry out through the doorway, hoping that someone from this suburban street will come to our rescue. But when has anyone ever come to help?

I gather my courage, and plunge inside. This thing has taken enough from me already. It can't take Daniel.

Thump. I walk straight into what feels like a tower of magazines.

I probe the darkness with my hands. They fall into something soft – fabric, grown brittle. It sends a cloud of dust into my nose. It's a maze in here.

'Daniel!' I hiss. My voice echoes into the silence.

Somewhere upstairs, a phone rings. Sharp, insistent.

My elbow brushes a pile of trinkets, which clatters around me.

I will myself forward, step by step, until my foot squelches into something wet.

I drop to my knees, feeling along linoleum, following the stink of Lynx and iron until I find the smooth soft mass of his puffer jacket. I find his face, still warm, grazing the boy-stubble of his chin. Run my hands down to his chest. It's moving, thank God, a ragged gurgle telling me he's still breathing, for now. I run my hands down the arms of his jacket, hunting for the radio. His right arm ends too soon, in a viscous puddle.

A crunch and a rich slurp from the darkness suggest the creature is enjoying her snack.

The radio. I can't find the radio. It was in his hand. He must have dropped it when she tackled him. I grope around the floor, my hands slick with Daniel's blood.

The phone upstairs stops ringing, the silence more piercing than the sound.

A thud behind me. I whirl round to see that the dim light from the street has vanished; the front door has swung closed. A heavy clatter as the beast knocks something over.

The ringtone starts again. I grab my pepper spray, aiming it at the void, grateful that it's dim in here.

Two yellow points flash in the darkness of the passage. High, almost at the ceiling, almost as though the creature is crawling along the ceiling like a spider, barrelling fast towards us.

Breath hitching in my throat, I press my thumb hard into the nozzle.

An explosion of mist, then the beast roars, thwacking hard against the floorboards, and my face is on fire: fire in my eyes and my nose and my throat. I can hear it in the front room, pawing at its face, mewling and furious.

I have bought precious seconds.

I stagger to my feet, tears streaming from my eyes. But I don't need my eyes. I need to move. But where? A back door. There has to be a back door.

My hands explore the darkness. All these old Victorian houses are basically the same layout. I grew up in one just like it. There must be a back door.

My hand finds a handle, cold and chrome. Relief floods me, short-lived as I step not into open air but a confined, stinking space. Something has died in here recently. I gag on the smell of rot. But there is no time to be precious. I throw myself into the space, a wall of damp boxes catching my fall. The door clicks behind me.

Outside, the creature is growling, incensed, pulling itself together.

I find the dead thing with my foot. It's small, feathered, probably a pigeon. It's cold in here, uninsulated, walls dripping with condensation, sticky with mould. It's an old coal store, I realise. Most of them have been waterproofed and turned into precious storage space, these days. But this house is long unloved, long unremembered.

Through the door, the beast prowls, hunting me. I can hear its deep searching sniffs.

I slow my breath, drawing in the cold, damp air until my lungs protest. *Be still. Be quiet. Be like dead.* Hoping the stink will be my saviour.

Far away, on the upper floor, the shrill cry of the phone again. Someone really wants to discuss whether this woman is happy with her current mobile plan.

The phone. If I can just get up to the phone.

My fingers grasp the handle. I can't hear the creature. But how quietly can it move?

The door yields without a sound. I ease out into the kitchen like a spectre, sweeping the stick ahead of me in a silent arc.

It finds Daniel. Still unmoving. Then taps onto the foot of the stairs.

There's a pile of papers down here, books, assorted junk. I find my way across it, silent, careful.

The second stair creaks. I pause, nerves on high alert. I can hear it, breathing heavy, but it feels like it's coming from everywhere. A growl that thunders deep into the bones of the house. I can't tell if it's upstairs or down.

But Daniel needs me. The phone is upstairs, ringing again.

Slow. Careful. I proceed.

The beast is downstairs, I'm sure of it. I hear it sniffing around Daniel, going in for seconds. He doesn't have long.

I make it to the top step when I step on something soft.

'I wuv you! I wuv you!' A talking teddy bear, voice distorted from a drained battery.

The creature roars in answer. A guttural howl. Ground floor.

Heavy footsteps thumping up the stairs, fast and implacable as a bear.

I throw myself through the first door I find, hoping hoping hoping it's the room with the phone. I land hard on a mountain of plastic tubs, feeling my recently replaced hip cracking all over again in a bolt of agony. I can't hold in the scream.

The beast is at the door, enormous, raking a claw towards me. But it can't come closer.

The door's stuck on the trash inside, I realise, opened just wide enough for a Brenda to slip through, but not a monster.

Emboldened, I jab at it with my stick. It goes straight into the soft palate of the creature's mouth. It roars in rage.

'I'm not afraid of you,' I hiss. Whatever it's taken from me, life has taken more.

The phone starts to ring again. This time, I'm sure it's from the next room.

We're at an impasse, the beast and I. Its yellow eyes flash at me through the doorway, a rope of saliva dripping slow from long teeth.

It begins to push on the door. Slowly, the wood cracks and splinters. A chunk falls to the ground with a *knock knock knock knock*.

I elbow-crawl backwards. *Knock knock knock knock*. Again.

Not here. Downstairs.

'Mum!'

I hoist my aching body upright, legs screaming, to peer through the grimy window.

A girl is downstairs, bashing her shoulder against the front door. 'Mum!' she calls again, desperate. I can hear the tears in her voice. She thwacks the front door with everything she has in her, but it's blocked by the hoard.

In the dimness of the doorway, the creature's eyes flash from amber to green, back to amber.

'Help me.' A soft growl, from inside the beast.

It slumps against the crack of the door, snout suddenly blunter. It's clearer, now, that somewhere beneath fur and fangs there is a person.

It could be a trap. I fumble around, searching for anything I could use as a weapon. But the clutter in this room makes no sense. A mountain of broken furniture. A stack of framed photographs. Infinite empty plastic tubs. No weapons.

Until one literally lands in my lap: heavy, cold steel.

Ellie

The old woman's got fight. Good. Good. Maybe she can do what I can't.

Downstairs, Paige screams, thin and breaking. 'Mum, please, I need you.' How long before she breaks in? *Teeth in her sweet soft neck.*

'Please,' I beg, voice slurred and blood-gurgling. 'The beast won't let me die. I have to die.'

Clattering sounds from my bedroom as the old woman fumbles with the bolt gun. I try to explain how to use it, but it's hard to form words. Tongue too big. Teeth too many. Mouth full of shame.

The house groans around us. Piss-stink and mildew and mould spores fat as moths. Forgotten things left too long and fermented.

Paige's voice bright with panic below. The smell of her shampoo.

No. Not her. Anyone but her.

Keep her out. Keep her safe.

'*Hurry!*' I splutter, foam flecking the floorboards.

'The lever's stuck!' Brenda snaps back, still crouching out of reach of my fangs.

Loud crashing sounds from below. Paige has found something to bash in the door with. I can smell her panic.

'On the side. The lever. On the side!'

'I can't see it,' The old woman says, staring right at the fucking thing.

'The side! Right there on the side.'

'I'm fucking *blind*!'

And I crumple. Legs gone. Muscles unravelling. Knees on the decaying carpet. Forehead on the doorjamb, cold against my hot skull. 'I've ruined everything.'

It leaks out of me, the whole long story in a confused confession. The rabbits. The cats. Mo. Don. Andreas. Kyle. Paige. Paige. Paige. Right there downstairs. Too close. I can't save her from me. From all my ugliness.

Thunk.

The bolt gun hits my skull. Not enough to hurt me, but it stings.

It shuts me up.

'Christ, woman,' The old woman mutters, 'you think you've got problems.'

She frowns. Stern. 'Listen. Downstairs, there's someone who loves you. I'm homeless, and I'm old, I can't drive any more, my body's falling to pieces, and my only friend is bleeding out on the floor.' She throws something else at me. An ice-cream tub. 'Also, you killed my bloody cat.'

I stare at her, mouth agape, shocked back into its final human shape. My skin prickles as fur retracts. My bones crack back into place with soft wet clicks.

'The girl downstairs,' The old woman says. 'If you die, she's going to live with that. Don't you love her enough to deal with your nonsense? Don't you love her enough to *try*?'

Inhale. Choke. Nod.

'I do,' I gasp. 'Yes.'

Egg Moon

○

Darling Paige,

I hope this letter reaches you. I don't know whether the last one did. The people helping me say that old-fashioned physical letters posted via a few extra people are safer than email. Even with encryption and VPNs and all of that, a sufficiently motivated law-enforcement agency could hypothetically trace an email back to our location, and there are many of us here who can't risk that.

Anyway, I find pen and paper quite therapeutic. I'm trying to wean myself off writing lists, but I'm getting into anger journaling. It's basically like gratitude journaling except you write down everything that infuriates you. The other women here say it's important to train yourself to recognise the bad feelings, to let yourself actually feel them. Rage isn't the problem, they say, repression is. Repression is rage turned inwards, and that the beast is the part of us that will no longer allow us to do that. Honestly, half of my anger journal every day is just about how much these fucking platitudes drive me nuts. I think that's progress.

There are more people like us than you'd believe. They've helped me manage the fallout from my rampage: I believe the official story on the beast sightings in Mayfair was that an actor on a film shoot had a psychotic episode, in full make-up. There was only one video of my actual transformation, which has been pretty thoroughly scrubbed off the internet (you wouldn't believe the services you can find on the dark web).

It doesn't undo what I did. A boy is dead, and sometimes it feels like the guilt could swallow me whole. I don't think I'm ever going to be able to come home. That, I'm not so sad about. I'm not sure what home even means any more. I heard about your dad's new girlfriend. Sincerely, I'm happy for him. More than anything, what your father wants is an easy life, and he deserves one. He's a good man. But I don't miss him.

After the stabbing scandal, Tranquillity was sold to one of our competitors, who were really only interested in buying the content library. A nice payday for everyone except me, I'm sure. You can still find open-sourced versions of the Virtual Rage Room online, though. Parts of my ugliness still haunting the internet.

It could have been worse for me. I heard Andreas's body was found in a peat bog near Manchester, so mangled they had to identify him from his dental records. Carol thinks a pack up there must have taken him out. That's what usually happens, when someone can't control the change.

Carol's a friend, by the way. She's just visiting briefly before she leaves on a very top-secret ecoterrorism mission she won't even tell me about. I hope one day you can meet her. I think you'll love her.

Of course, I can't tell you where I am. But I'm safe. It's sort of a commune for people like me, those of us who didn't adjust well to the change, who tried to deny it, and repress it, instead of letting it become a part of them. I can tell you that it's achingly beautiful. We're on the edge of a forest, near a crystal-blue lake, far from anyone we could hurt. Thirty of us live together in a sprawling compound, bunk beds and a communal kitchen, like a summer camp. We're learning how to manage it. It's a lot of deep breathing, and attuning to our bodies, and letting ourselves feel our feelings so they don't go rancid inside us. Like meditation, but deeper than what I realised that could mean. Don was always trying to tell me, but I wasn't ready to listen. Don't laugh, but I've even taken up pottery. It's quite relaxing, mostly when you mess up, because then you get to smash stuff.

It's warmer here, already full-blown springtime, bright flowers stirring in the soil, the tips of trees bursting into bud, birds I don't know the names of chattering in the trees. I've been thinking about T. S. Eliot, 'April is the cruellest month'. How awful it is to be disturbed from a long slumber. How odd to be forty-five and learning entirely new things about yourself. To have to start again. But that also feels like a miracle: to *get* to start again. Life is long, Paige. It's short, but it's also so much longer than I'd let myself believe. And there are still so many things I want to do. Simone de Beauvoir once wrote that the menopause was far less sombre than she'd foreseen, at the end of the day.

I feel everything more intensely now. Joy and sorrow, desire and grief. Heartbreak for the world. Fury too, sometimes. I'm trying to learn to be okay with that. The more I accept the beast, the less violent she becomes. She only loves me, and wants to protect me, and the less I hate myself, the less need she feels to displace that hate elsewhere.

The transformations are getting easier. Some nights we run wild in the woods and let it all out, which helps. Honestly, I think what's made the biggest difference is just living in a community with other people. People who get it. We don't even speak the same languages, but it doesn't matter. Humans are pack animals, we forget that sometimes.

You won't believe it, but Brenda writes to me sometimes, via our mutual friends. She's a battleaxe, that one, but she grows on you. Our friends back in London have taken Daniel under their wing. They were sceptical at first, about a boy being able to handle it, but he's won them over and now he's got to be the most doted-on twenty-something in the UK, grannies coming out his ears. He's still a cop. It seems losing his hand means they've fast-tracked him to the financial crimes unit, which is where he always wanted to be, so there's a small upside. And at least no one's going to tell Daniel his weird monthly symptoms are the menopause.

Brenda's moved in with him and his grandmother and is apparently running to be a local ward counsellor. They've adopted a little dog named Dodo. She sent me a photo; it's the most hideous creature I've ever seen.

I've suggested to Brenda she should let Daniel give her a lick sometime. I think she'd do productive things with the power. Aggression can be used for domination, but it can also be used for justice, for protection, for change. It all depends what you're doing with it, I guess. You've got to fight for something. Rich women mostly fight for ourselves; I've been trying to imagine what it could look like if I channelled my energy into something more interesting.

Brenda told me you went to visit her, and that you were looking better. She said you're planning to go back to LSE next term, and in the meantime, you've been keeping yourself busy with XR. She said you told her you're angry with me, but you're trying not to be.

That's why I'm really writing, I suppose. Not to say sorry – I can never begin to apologise for what I put you through. No daughter should ever feel like it's her job to save her mother's life. All I can say is that I'm working to earn your forgiveness. I'm trying to be better. It's pretty embarrassing to reach the age when you're just starting to feel like you've got it all figured out and then realise that you don't know a bloody thing. 'If we don't keep changing, we die' – that's another one of the platitudes the women say. But it's true.

What I wanted to say to you is: please be angry with me. Be furious. Don't try to be understanding, or sympathetic, or forgiving. Don't turn it inwards. Don't let yourself believe that if you were better or kinder or tried harder it wouldn't have happened. Don't believe for one second that I'm your responsibility. Don't be good. Don't be nice. I want you to have your biggest, boldest, most beautiful life. What I'm starting to understand is that it's my job to make sure that I have one, too.

Write back to me, when you're ready to. If you're ever ready. Give it to Brenda. She knows how to reach me.

Paige, I love you always, more than anything.

Your mother,
Ellie

AUTHOR'S NOTE

Midway through the journey of my life, I found myself within a dark forest, for the straightforward path had been lost. Until that point I had been a chronic overfunctioner, hyperactively taking care of everyone and everything around me. It had been an effective lifelong strategy: when I was a child, adults complimented me by saying I was 'three going on thirty-three'. I was very good, very productive, very nice, very competent. I truly believed that I did not ever feel angry.

One day, as I approached forty, all these carefully cultivated coping mechanisms failed. I had a quite exciting breakdown. I finally understood that underneath all my spreadsheets and my smiles and my lists lay something old, and festering, and *furious*.

This novel came roaring out of that place.

The process of writing it took me through some fascinating conversations and many twisty research rabbit holes, which is my favourite thing about being a writer. I'd particularly like to thank Dr Maya Jaffer, a dear friend and psychiatrist, and my psychologist Linda Brash, who helped me to puzzle out my own beliefs about emotion, repression and the psyche. I would also like to remind the reader that Ellie is a character in a novel, and her views on mental health and mindfulness are not my own, nor those of any mental health professional I spoke to. I have many points of disagreement with Ellie. This is probably why she pisses me off so much. *Definitely* not because of how much she reminds me of myself.

The core joke of this novel is that the medical industry knows as much about perimenopause as it knows about lycanthropy. This is changing, but far too slowly, and there's a lot of catching up to do. In the United States, the National Institutes of Health didn't require research trials to include women until 1993. Even now, menopausal women are often excluded from clinical trials because researchers worry that our hormones make things too complicated. Men, of course, do not have hormones.

Thankfully, the past decade has seen an avalanche of superb books, films and podcasts come out, bringing conversations about menopause and perimenopause closer to the centre of our culture. I'm particularly indebted to the work of Karen Arthur, Sam Baker, Jancee Dunn, Mariella Frostrup, Miranda July, Caitlin Moran, Alice Smellie and Phoebe Waller-Bridge for their nuanced thoughts about the radical power of the mid-life shift. Myisha Cherry's and Josh Cohen's books helped me to understand the positive potentials of rage. Tania Glyde and Kelsey Elizabeth Henry offered insight into queer menopause and the queerness of menopause. We've come a long way since David Reuben's 1969 comment that 'Having outlived their ovaries, [women] may have outlived their usefulness as human beings'.

CATS was inspired by the South London Animal Investigation Network (SLAIN). Thank you to Boudicca Rising and Rob, my courageous guides through the dark (sadly all too real) underworld of London's cat killers. The stories they shared with me are far wilder and more horrifying than anything in this book.

Dr Alan Underwood of the Stalking Threat Assessment Centre and Louise from the Paladin National Stalking Advocacy Service helped me to understand the motivations and tragic impacts of stalking. If you suspect that you or someone you love is being stalked, please don't hesitate in taking action. In the UK, **Paladin** and the **Suzy Lamplugh Trust** websites are excellent starting points.

For understanding werewolf mythology, the most helpful resources were *The Book of Werewolves* by Sabine Baring-Gould, *Wolfish* by Erica Berry, *Hunt for the Shadow Wolf* by Derek Gow, Grady Hendrix's *Super Scary Haunted Homeschool* podcast, *Shapeshifters: A History* by John B. Kachuba and *She-Wolf: A Cultural History of Female Werewolves* edited by Hannah Priest. I also had far too much fun watching and reading every werewolf story I could get my paws on (including some of the smutty stuff, purely for research, you understand). Ellie mentions my favourites in the 'Vaginal Atrophy' chapter, but the most essential were *Ginger Snaps*, *An American Werewolf in*

London (which observant readers might spot some subtle nods to) and Alan Moore's foundational comic 'The Curse' (*Swamp Thing*, vol. 2, no. 40). I'm so grateful to London's many wonderful librarians, specifically those at the Wellcome Trust and the British Library, who helped me to track down the most obscure sources.

The line Ellie thinks of as she steps into her mother's house is from the poem 'Housewife' by Anne Sexton, and the Caitlin Moran piece Carol quotes is 'Me, Drugs and the Perimenopause'. They're both well worth a read.

This book is set in the tech industry, and explores the hype-train around AI, as well as how few values the tech industry has – and how sceptical we should be that this technology can solve the same problems it is largely guilty of creating.

Because this is a book specifically mocking how banal and unhelpful AI Large Language Models are in the context of mental health, I thought it would be useful and interesting (as well as funny) to have ChatGPT itself generate the nonsense meditation that appears in the chapter titled 'Generalised Anxiety' ('Close your eyes and find comfort in your breath…'). The gibberish meditation in the chapter 'Brain Fog' ('Let your thoughts be your guide and the path to destiny is and you are not afraid…'), was generated using Apple iOS 17's predictive text. Both texts were then heavily edited by me to make sure they worked for the story. All other AI meditations that appear in this novel are my original creations, as is every other part of the novel.

This is, alongside many of the subjects in this book, a sensitive point, and I understand that some readers would have preferred I didn't use ChatGPT at all, but I just couldn't resist using the thing itself in this small instance to demonstrate its own ridiculousness. If this is an issue you care about as much as I do, I recommend engaging with your local representatives to insist that they push for better regulation of this industry, as I have.

This is a work of fiction, and despite all the experts I spoke to, I'm certain there are still many factual errors, which are my fault completely.

Lastly, this book is a love letter to all the brilliant women in my life I've watched get passed over, get dismissed, get talked over, get misbelieved, get burnt out by the mental load, get attacked, get abused, and then get treated like they should be fucking grateful for it. It's a howl in solidarity for those of us who've held it together for too long.

All you angry menopausal bitches out there, this book is for you.

ACKNOWLEDGEMENTS

In addition to the people mentioned already, I would like to thank:

- My editors Nidhi Pugalia and Vicky Leech Mateos, who saw right into the gruesome bloody heart of this book from the beginning.
- Rachel Mazower, who was this book's first reader, and who convinced me to add more lists.
- Laura Del Col Brown, who bought the rights to name the most hateable character in the novel, in support of trans rights.
- My hero Stella Nyanzi, who inspired Grace's story.
- Taylor Geall from Tideway London, my guide through London's sewers.
- Dr Imraan Coovadia, who helped me figure out what this novel was actually about.
- My beloved literary agent Oli Munson, who keeps me focused on what matters, and handles the parts of my job I hate doing.
- Katherine Fry, who patiently weeded out my South Africanisms and tightened my prose.
- The teams at Viking Penguin and Bloomsbury Archer, who have been my wolf pack.
- My film and TV agent Sean Taylor, who loves gore as much as I do.
- Early readers and dear friends Meghan Finn, Dashe Roberts, Beatriz Costa, Peter Cardwell-Gardner, Maya Jaffer, Charne Lavery and Jade Alexander. Conversations with you inspired the best parts of this book.

- Angela Cheng Caplan, who offered me invaluable advice about building a career beyond a single book.
- My therapist Linda Brash, who once banned me from making to-do lists.
- London, the city of my heart, which never ceases to present me with new interesting corners to get lost in.
- My students and colleagues at Bath Spa University, who have been an inspiration and a joy beyond what I could have imagined.
- Linda Mackay Pettersen, the best boss I ever had.
- The booksellers, bloggers and press who have been so supportive, especially in South Africa. You've made it possible for me to do my dream job.
- My team at Jonathan Ball, who've always had my back.
- Melanie Smuts, my soulmate, who was with me when I got the news, and has been with me all my life.
- Lauren Beukes, my favourite favourite, who allowed me to capture her infuriating GP experience almost word for word, and whose support has been my sunlight and air.
- Digby, to whom I must apologise for the number of dead cats in this book.
- Matthew Proxenos, who makes me decoy loaves and washes his face with body wash, who goes on long walks with me to help me talk through plot holes, and who loves even the ugliest parts of me.

I'm so fucking grateful.

A NOTE ON THE AUTHOR

SAM BECKBESSINGER is a bestselling South African author who teaches creative writing, pens horror stories and kids' TV shows, and once wrote for Marvel. She survived working in the tech industry but insists that any references to murdered co-workers are entirely fictional. She lives in London.

Sign up for updates on sambeckbessinger.com